WEDDING THRASHERS

A Bird Lover's Mystery

J.R. Ripley

Beachfront Entertainment

Wedding Thrashers

1

"Guess who's getting married!"

That was Kim Christy, my best friend, bursting through the front door of Birds & Bees, my little home-based downtown shop for bird lovers here in the equally little and historic Town of Ruby Lake, North Carolina.

Kim panted excitedly. Her face lit up like she'd just won a million bucks in the North Carolina state lottery.

I wish. Maybe then she would pay me back the bajillion or so dollars I estimated she had borrowed from me over the years.

"You?" I slowly lowered the pair of binoculars pressing against my eyes. I'd been studying an energetic brown thrasher rooting around in the flowerbeds bordering the front porch. Thrashers love to, well, thrash around, looking for insects lurking under the leaves and debris to snack on.

The binoculars dangled over my chest on a black nylon strap.

On the subject of snacking, Kim is a long-legged, blue-eyed blonde who could eat practically anything and not gain so much as an ounce of fat.

I've got blue eyes too and she and I are about the same height but there the similarities end. My wavy and mostly unruly hair is the shade of a chestnut-colored woodpecker. If I so much as look at a bar of chocolate, let alone an onion ring, I put on five pounds. And I've never been known to stop at simply looking.

I could have hated her for being too pretty, too thin and far too unreasonable in all matters that I believed required a certain level-headed pragmatism but I didn't. Kim and I go way back. Practically to the womb.

Kim's vivacious smile turned into a dispirited frown. Oops.

I had hit a nerve there with that crack about her getting married. Kim has big, maybe too big, hopes of marrying her beau, Dan Sutton, one of our local police officers. One of the better ones, I might add.

Kim's hints regarding matrimony had been getting a little heavy-handed lately. She'd recently coerced poor Dan into binge watching a reality series about an L.A. wedding planner when he would have rather been watching the latest NASCAR race.

She had even resorted to taking subscriptions to a couple of bridal magazines, monthly copies of which she placed strategically around her house, mostly on the coffee table and nightstand.

Adding fuel to the matrimonial fires, one of Dan's old police academy buddies, the gorgeous and vivacious Paula D'Abbo, had taken up temporary residence in Kim's house. At the moment, however, she was in Arizona assisting her mother.

To be fair to Paula, the entire living situation thing was Kim's fault. Both Dan and Paula thought they were doing Kim a favor by having Paula stay with her. Long story short, rather than admit to even the teensiest bit of jealousy, my best friend had gone the I'm-not-jealous-I'm-a-lunatic route. That led to Dan and Paula worrying about the state of her mental health and coming up with the idea that she could use a roommate.

Paula, a young brunette with eyes the hue of a golden brown kestrel's wings and a perfect bottom, had chosen to continue her leave of absence from the Scottsdale PD and nurse Kim back to good mental health.

I wished Paula all the luck in the world with that.

She was going to need it.

"No," said Kim, in answer to my question as to who was marrying. "Amy Harlan." She tossed her black leather jacket over a hook on the coatrack inside the front door and squeezed my arm. The jacket merely grazed the brass hook and fell to the floor to the accompanying slap of leather on wood.

Kim ignored the fallen jacket, knowing I would pick after her. I always did. I sometimes thought Kim's mother had retired to Florida so she wouldn't have to keep picking up after her daughter.

"Isn't that great, Amy?"

"Amy-the-ex is getting married?" The binoculars flopped against my chest as I snatched her jacket off the ground. I hung it properly on an empty hook.

Amy-the-ex is not me. That is, she shares my first name.

We share little, very little, else.

I am Amy-the-present, in a manner of speaking.

Amy-the-ex and I did have one thing in common: the same man. That is to say, she was once married to Derek Harlan, my current boyfriend. Amy-the-ex had long carried a torch for the guy even though the marriage has been over for a number of years. To which I say tough noogies because he is mine.

Now she was getting married?

"Are you sure?"

"Yep. Absolutely positive. I heard it from Rhonda who heard it from Sally May when I was getting my hair done."

Sally May is a manicurist. Rhonda is my cousin Rhonda. She and her twin brother Riley are two of my nearest and dearest relatives. Not that they were without their challenges. Who wasn't?

"Are you sure?" I couldn't help repeating myself. "How did this happen?" I crossed to the sales counter, threw off my binoculars and tucked them safely away in their softshell case under the counter.

"*When* did this happen?" I pressed my hands against the countertop and leaned into Kim standing on the opposite side. "Does Derek know about this?"

I glanced up the staircase in the middle of the store.

Birds & Bees is located in the charming three-story Queen Anne Victorian house that also serves as my residence. It further serves as the residence of one of my employees, Esther Pilaster, and Paul Anderson, one of the owner-operators of Brewer's Biergarten, which sits on Lake Shore Drive adjacent to my place.

"Don't ask me. He is your boyfriend." Kim's eyes followed mine up the stairs. "He hasn't said anything?"

I shook my head. "Not a word."

"Not a word about what?"

I jumped out of my jeans. "Stop doing that!"

It was the septuagenarian she-devil herself, Esther Pilaster, or Esther the Pester as I frequently thought of her. In a manner of speaking, I had inherited her. She had been renting a second floor apartment in the home when I bought it from the previous owner—a difficult woman named Gertie Hammer.

What I did not know was that the two were sisters. As a stipulation of the purchase agreement, I had been forced to agree to let Esther remain in her apartment.

Ever since Gertie joined us on her very first weekend birding expedition, she had become quite the pest too. It must run in the sisters' genes. Gertie was always popping into the store with that big camera of hers. It had a lens so long it would have been right at home at the end of some bushy bearded, one-legged pirate's kneecap.

Gertie takes hundreds of photos of wild birds to post on her blog and in her scrapbook.

As for Esther, it had begun to dawn on me that she was never going to leave. In fact, she was now part of my business. A ten percent part to be exact, according to the papers Derek had drawn up and I had signed. Derek was a lawyer and a good one. So I knew there was no way I was breaking that contract.

If I ever really wanted Esther out, I'd have to buy her out. My finances being what they were—and me selling cheap bird seed at low margins, not pricey rubies with a fat markup, my finances were unlikely to change dramatically—therefore, buying her out was out of the question.

Esther's recent investment in Birds & Bees made her a member of an ever-expanding group of partners that now included my mom, my aunt Betty and Kim.

Some days I had more partners than I had customers. Something was going to have to change. At the rate I was going, soon everybody in Ruby Lake would be my partner. Then who would I sell my goods to? Birds don't have credit cards.

"Apparently, Derek hasn't told Amy, *this* Amy," Kim poked me in the chest as she addressed Esther, "that his ex is getting married."

Esther cackled. Esther worked part-time hours, those being pretty much whenever it suited her. Not me, her. She's also given herself the title *Assistant Manager* and has the badge to prove it.

Esther is a small woman with narrow shoulders, sagging eyelids and a hawkish nose. She keeps her silvery hair in a tight knot at the back of her head most times. She keeps her gray-blue eyes trained on me more often that I would like. She has a mysterious past that may or may not include a string of broken hearts and international spy rings.

I am pretty sure she keeps a cat in her apartment, against house rules. Regarding said cat, Esther and I have a sort of Schrödinger's cat mind game going. That is, if I never actually see her cat with my own eyes, does it really exist?

Sometimes I lie in bed at night pondering that very question. These are not things a sane woman does. Is it any wonder I have nicknamed her Esther the Pester?

"So Derek's breaking up with you and remarrying his ex, eh? I'm not surprised." Esther grabbed an apron from the hook behind the cash register and tied it snugly around her waist.

"Hey!" I folded my arms over my chest. "She's getting married, not *re*married," I snapped.

I swiveled my head towards my best friend. "That is it, isn't it? She is getting married not remarried? To Derek, I mean." The celebrity rags were full of such stories. Didn't Elizabeth Taylor marry Richard Burton twice?

"Um, I guess so."

"You guess so?" I drilled her so hard with my eyes

that a yellow-bellied sapsucker couldn't have done a better job pounding a string of holes up and down the trunk of a thirty foot maple tree.

"Easy there, Amy. I'm only teasing. Rhonda says Amy Harlan's fiancé is some hotshot real estate developer. His investment firm has bought the Rivercrest Country Club. The scuttlebutt is that they are planning to remodel the whole shebang and expand its size."

Kim had recently quit the real estate business as a result of some messiness involving her former boss. She still kept her ear to the ground when it came to the Town of Ruby Lake's real estate doings, however.

"You are evil." I swung my finger from one woman to the other. "Both of you." I pushed past Esther and took the central stairs upward two at a time.

"Where are you going?" demanded Esther.

"I left something burning on the stove."

"Ha! Derek's up there. I know," said Kim, "because I called your apartment phone before I left for work and he answered. Spend the night, did he?"

"You shouldn't gossip, Kim." Esther shook her head side to side. "Now, pull up a stool while I tell you who Mrs. Early told me she saw making out like two school children behind the farmers market yesterday morning."

2

I found Derek right where I had left him earlier that morning—sprawled out on the sofa, gray socked feet on the coffee table, watching golf tournament being broadcast from Scotland on the flat-screen hanging on the exterior wall of my third-floor apartment.

The sweet scent of maple syrup and toasted pecans hung in the air, a reminder of our pancake breakfast that morning.

The brown leather sofa and not-so-matching dark green easy chair taking up the bulk of my living room floor space had been fixtures in my parents' house for as long as I could remember. Now they'd come to rest here in the top-floor apartment along with my mother and me.

That suited me just fine.

"Hey, Amy." Derek greeted me lazily, cradling a beer can in his lap. "What's up? Taking a break?"

"Sort of. Scoot over." I shoved his legs to one side and sat.

"Sure. Can I get you a beer?"

"No, thanks. This will do." I grabbed the open can from his hands and tipped its contents down my throat. "So," I cleared my throat. "I hear your ex is getting married again?"

A red flush rose along the side of Derek's neck. His hands fiddled with the remote control. "You heard about that, huh?"

"I heard about that." I pressed my finger against his chin and forced his head around so that his eyes were on me rather than some guy in a hundred-dollar polo shirt taking a swing at a little white ball.

The pro swung, a clod of wet grass flew further than his pricey golf ball. The golfer cursed and banged his iron into the sod.

"What a waste of space," I said. "They could use all that green space to go bird walking. Why, with a decent pair of binoculars and a cheap digital camera, I could teach that guy to have a lot more fun communing with nature than he seems to be having now. I'll bet there's some great birding over there."

"That's Patrick O'Brian. If he looks frustrated, it's because he's bogeyed the last two holes and dropped out of the lead. A few more and he'll be out of contention. Why don't you suggest that to him?" Derek said on the wave of a chuckle. "Did you know that the Royal Course at—"

"Oh, no, you don't." I chopped the air with my hand. "You are not changing the subject."

Derek raised a brow. "I thought the subject was golf?"

"The subject," I stressed, "is your ex-wife and marriage. Care to address either or both?"

Derek forced a small smile. A dimple appeared almost magically on his cheek. I felt my resolve softening. His dimples have that effect on me. He's tall—when he isn't loafing on the sofa in a horizontal position—dark and ruggedly handsome, with a touch of gray at the temples. A combination that I find very sexy.

"I'd been meaning to talk to you about that. In fact

—" The remote control slipped out of his hand and slid down the back of the sofa, promptly disappearing under the seat cushion. "Oops." He thrust a hand in after it.

"No you don't." I grabbed his hand and squeezed his fingers. "Never mind that. I'll fish it out later."

"Okay. Sure."

And who knew what else I'd find when I did go sofa cushion fishing? Esther had a way of breezing in and out of my apartment as if it were her own. She's been known to squirrel away all sorts of things under the cushions, including a slender bottle of bourbon and some knitting-in-progress that looked suspiciously like a leisure outfit for a cat.

Once, I found a pair of tiny booties and what looked like a tail warmer, all fashioned out of gray yarn. When I asked Esther about the items, because who else could they have belonged to, she insisted they were for the stray cats at the animal shelter. I wasn't sure I believed her, but I let it go.

A male robin appeared at the bird feeder outside the living room window and grabbed an unshelled black oil sunflower seed, distracting me momentarily from my thoughts. A second and then a third robin joined it. The American Robin is a gregarious bird.

I patted Derek on the knee. "Back to your ex."

"Amy met this guy, Tom Visconti, two, three months ago. Two weeks ago, he asked her to marry him and she said yes."

"Wow," I whistled. "The guy moves fast."

"What is that supposed to mean?"

"Nothing," I said hurriedly. "What do you know about him?"

"Not much. We've never met. When I drop Maeve off

at her mom's house, from the car I can sometimes see him inside through the windows but he's never come out and introduced himself."

"Don't you think that's strange?"

Derek shrugged. "Maybe he feels awkward, what with me being the ex."

"He's going to have to get used to having you around sometime. Like it or not, you are going to be a part of his life, if only because of your daughter."

"True."

"Amy?" Derek wrapped his hands around mine.

"Yes?" I watched the robins hop from perch to perch as they pecked for more seed.

"Will you marry me?"

"Huh? Those robins are so cute. Did you see the way that little one—" I froze. "Wait. What?" I twisted quickly, banging my knees against his.

Derek grinned. "I asked if you would be my wife."

I swallowed so hard I figured I'd be looking for my tongue for a week. "I-I mean, that is...YES!"

I leapt from the sofa. What was left of Derek's beer spilled down my blouse and over his khaki trousers.

Frightened by the commotion, the robins went flying up into the blue sky. If I squinted hard enough, I was pretty sure I'd see my heart fluttering around up there too.

I grabbed a beige cotton sweater from the hall closet and dabbed wildly at my damp blouse. I threw open the front door of the apartment as my mom was reaching for the knob from the opposite side.

"Whoa!" She moved aside in the nick of time. "What's going on, Amy? Where are you off to in such a tizzy?"

"Sorry, Mom. Getting married!" I smacked my lips

against her cool cheek and kept moving.

"What?" Mom flattened herself against the wall to keep from getting steamrolled. She moved pretty good for a woman in her sixties who is also burdened with adult onset muscular dystrophy. It must be those water aerobics classes she's started taking at the community center.

"Where are you going?" shouted Derek, still attached to the sofa.

I ran slash fell down the stairs faster than I ever had —and that included the time I had found a dead body on the second floor.

Esther and Kim were right where I'd left them earlier.

"Where's the fire?" demanded Esther, hands on hips.

"Yeah, or in your case, dead body," teased Kim.

What can I say? Dead bodies have a way of popping up all around me. It's a curse.

I scooted to a stop at the edge of the sales counter. "Derek," I panted, struggling for breath. Bird watching doesn't exactly require Olympics-level training.

"What about Derek?" Kim handed me a glass of water from the cooler.

Esther leaned toward me and sniffed. "Have you been drinking?"

I sucked the cold water down in one big, noisy gulp. "He asked me to marry him!"

"That's wonderful!" Kim raced forward. She slammed into me and wrapped me in a bear hug.

"Too hard!" I banged my fists against her shoulder blades until she let go.

"Sure, that's swell," agreed Esther. She held a cup of tea in her right hand. "The fact is, I was sure you'd end up an old maid. I mean, once a woman gets to be your age—"

"Esther!" snapped Kim. My best friend and I share the same age, give or take, both being in our mid-thirties. So she was as sensitive to the whole ticking clock thing as I was.

Esther, on the other hand, is older than dirt—her words, not mine.

"That's okay," I laughed. "Tease me all you want. I'm getting married."

Kim hugged me anew. "This calls for a celebration!"

"When?" Esther demanded.

"When what?" asked Kim.

"When is the wedding date? When are you getting married, Amy?"

"I...it's...I'll be right back!"

I dashed up the stairs to the third floor, taking them three or four at a time. Who's counting?

Derek and Mom were seated on the couch chatting. Mom had a big grin on her face.

"Hey, Amy. I was just telling Barbara how—"

I held up a hand and cut him off. "When?"

Derek furrowed his brow. "When what?"

"When are we getting married?"

"Oh, uh...I don't know." Derek looked helplessly from me to my mother. "Next year?"

"A whole year?"

Mom threw up her hands. "Don't look at me. This is between the two of you. Of course, I am more than happy to help in any way that I can."

"The fifteenth," I blurted out.

"The fifteenth?" echoed Derek, clearly confused.

"Yes, June fifteenth. *This* year. That's the date Mom and Dad got married. Right, Mom?"

"Yes, but—"

"That will give us plenty of time to prepare." A couple of months anyway.

Derek nodded. "I suppose that might—"

"Great." I clapped my hands and flew out the open door. How I got downstairs after that, I do not remember. Maybe I flew. Maybe I took some secret passage or a portal through another dimension. It didn't matter.

What mattered was that I was getting married. To Derek Harlan. On June the fifteenth.

3

I could picture the wedding invitations already. *Please join us in celebrating the marriage between Amy Hester Simms and Derek Benjamin Harlan to be wed on this fair day...*

"June fifteenth," I blurted to Esther and Kim, bursting in as they helped a pair of well-dressed women choose a brown and green nesting and roosting box made of recycled plastics. All four women looked at me like I was crazy, the two customers more so than Kim and Esther. Those two knew me.

"Would you mind ringing these things up, Esther?" Kim handed Esther a small nesting box that was perfect for wrens.

The small birds aren't picky when it comes to nesting but prefer boxes with openings no more than about an inch and an eighth. Being cavity nesting birds, they will also make themselves at home in jars, old leather shoes, woodpecker-created holes and just about anything else that strikes their fancy.

"I guess not." Esther grudgingly carried the nesting box to the sales counter. One of the customers carried a matching one for herself.

"You are going to need a fifty-pound sack of birdseed," I heard Esther say. "I'll add that to your orders.

One sack each. And you'll both need mounting posts for the birdhouses. And mounting brackets and screws."

The cash register went ka-ching!

"And baffles."

Ka-ching!

"What are baffles?" one of the women made the mistake of asking. She was clearly baffled herself.

Esther explained. "They're made of metal, aluminum, I think. You wrap them around your mounting poles. You're gonna need the baffles to keep the nasty snakes and squirrels from climbing up into your nesting boxes."

The two women clutched their purses and looked uneasily at one another. "Snakes?" echoed the first woman with an accompanying shudder. "I don't like the idea of snakes in the yard. It was bad enough seeing them loose in that plane in that movie. Couldn't fly for months. You remember that movie, Janet?"

"I do," answered Janet of the red hat. "Is all this really necessary?"

"You don't want the nasty snakes and squirrels eating your baby birdies, do you?" Esther rattled her fingers along the countertop.

"Of course not," answered red hat lady.

"I didn't think so. I'll grab you a couple of our best baffles from the storeroom."

I sighed. Watching Esther in action could be painful. Then again, it could also be quite profitable. The woman was all about the up sell.

"Amy?"

I felt a tug at my sleeve. "What is it, Kim?"

"First, congratulations and everything."

"Thank you." I plucked at my shirt. "I'm going to

clean myself up." With a smile that I couldn't have scraped off my face if I tried, I walked to the rear of the store with Kim at my heels.

Birds & Bees offers a cozy kitchenette and lounge area for employees and customers alike. Every day we laid out coffee, tea and other beverages along with a sweet treat or two to nibble on. Anything to keep our customers happy and coming back for more.

A small bookshelf purchased at a church thrift sale held our modest lending library of bird-, bee- and nature-related reading material.

I plopped the beer splattered sweater in the sink and opened the spigot. All the while, my heart was racing like a racehorse sprinting around the track. I was getting married. To the most wonderful man in the whole world.

Kim snatched a sugar cookie and nibbled at the edges.

"What's wrong?" I asked. "You don't look so happy."

Kim glanced at her feet. Always a bad sign.

"Hey, what is it?" I bit my lip in thought. Suddenly, I understood. "I get it. I'm getting married and you're still waiting for Dan to ask you."

I wrapped an arm over her shoulder. "You know Dan loves you, Kim. He moves slowly. That's all. I'll bet he asks you any day now."

"No." Kim shook her head. "That's not it."

"It's not?" I folded my arms across my chest. "Then what's up?"

"You did say the fifteenth?"

"Yeah…"

"June fifteenth?"

"That's it." I beamed. "Mark that date in your calendar, baby. *You* are my maid of honor."

"Thanks. There is just one little thing." She held up one finger.

"What's that? And why am I getting a feeling that I am not going to like it?"

Kim took a deep breath then said, "June fifteenth is the date that Amy Harlan is getting married."

For a minute, all time and sound stopped. It was a real freak of nature. And physics.

I barely understood nature. And I have never understood physics.

"She stole my wedding date?"

"Technically, I'm not sure that you could say she stole —"

"That bi—" I noticed more customers in the store and they were within hearing distance. "That *woman* stole my wedding date?" I hissed.

"Calm down, Amy." Kim reached for me. "I'm not sure you could really say she stole your wedding date. And is it really that important?"

"It's my wedding date. It was Mom and Dad's wedding date. Why didn't Derek tell me?"

"Did you give him a chance? It seems to me you were running up and down those stairs like you're training for the Empire State Building Run-up."

"This is so unfair!"

"Shh. Keep your voice down."

"Don't mind her, folks," Esther barked from across the sales floor. "Amy gets that way when she hasn't had her cookie. Have a cookie, Amy!"

"I don't want a cookie. I want to get married. On June the fifteenth." I folded my arms and pouted.

Derek and I had agreed to meet up later for dinner at Brewer's Biergarten. With the brewpub only steps from my place, I arrived first. I sidled up to the bar while I waited.

I ordered a glass of Chablis and spilled my troubles and woes to the bartender on duty, Connie.

"Look at the bright side," Connie said, holding a stemmed glass up to the light while rubbing it with a bar towel. "You're getting married." She slotted the glass on the hanging rack and reached for another off the tray on the back bar. "Derek is a great guy. You couldn't do better."

"I know." I planted my elbows on the polished wood bar top and stared into my wine glass. A shadow appeared on my right followed by the intense and overpowering scent of spicy cologne.

"You look like you just lost your best friend," said the stranger.

I turned a glum eye to him. The middle-aged man towering over me and extending far too close for comfort into my personal space was a tall, rail-thin man with a cream-colored ten-gallon cowboy hat stuck to a long, rectangular head.

His suit was beige, almost yellow. His eyes were dark brown like those of a barred owl.

Like the barred owl, I immediately got the vibe that this guy liked to do his hunting at night.

"Do you mind?" Without waiting for my reply, he slid onto the stool beside me. "Scotch and soda," he said to Connie.

"Sorry, no hard alcohol. Beer and wine only."

"Okay." He slapped his right hand on the bar top. "Whatever you've got on tap. The darker the better."

"Yes, sir." Connie rolled her eyes for my benefit and wandered off to the taps where she was waylaid by a couple waiting for their appetizers.

"My name's Tim." He extended a tanned hand adorned with a black onyx fraternity ring.

"Amy," I replied, taking a small sip of my wine. I heard the front door open and glanced toward it hoping to see Derek. No such luck.

"Amy? Huh. How about that." He touched the brim of his hat and ran his finger along the edge. "I hate to be forward but seeing as I am only in town for a few days and I don't know a darn soul, how about you and me having a little dinner?"

He gave me what I expected he considered his sexiest, come-hither smile. "This place doesn't look like the food could kill you. What do you say, Amy?"

Connie settled a tall, perspiring frothy mug of beer down in front of him with an extra hard bang before moving away.

"I say I am engaged to be married. But thanks, anyway." I jumped off my barstool and ran to the front of the restaurant to greet Derek as he entered. In my hurry to escape, I left my Chablis at the bar.

Derek and I smooched and, despite the chill in the air, I insisted on being seated at a table outdoors in the courtyard. I wanted to be as far away from Tim with his ten-gallon hat and twenty-gallon ego as I could.

"It's so not fair," I griped over drinks and wood-fired pizza.

"I know." Derek waved to our waiter for another pitcher of IPA.

"That woman is always ruining my life." I knew I wasn't being completely rational. Amy Harlan had moved to Ruby Lake with Maeve, which had prompted Derek to move to town as well—that and the fact that his father, Ben Harlan, had recently semiretired here. If she hadn't moved to Ruby Lake from Charlotte, Derek and I would likely never have met.

As everyone in Ruby Lake knew, Derek and I had met when Chief Kennedy had locked me up on suspicion of murder soon after I had moved back to town. Mom called Ben Harlan for legal assistance and one thing led to another.

Funny thing was, when I had first laid eyes on Derek, I could immediately see how handsome he was. And I got the feeling he was flirting with me.

But—and it was a big one—I also thought he was married at the time. That had made him a cad in my book and since my book was already filled with a cad of the first order, Craig Bigelow, I had valiantly resisted Derek's charms.

Things were different now. And, rational or not, I considered myself wholly within my rights to claiming Amy-the-ex was the source of many, if not all, of my current woes.

Plus, she'd had the audacity to open her shop, Dream Gowns, right next door to the law offices of Harlan & Harlan.

If that wasn't an act of war, I didn't know what was.

"Sorry about that," Derek said in response to my grousing about his ex. He refilled my glass and pushed it gently my way. Next, he dumped a third slice of mushroom and artichoke pizza onto my plate.

I took a half-hearted bite. "There is something else that I forgot to ask you."

"What's that?"

21

"Is Maeve okay with us getting married?"

"Of course, she is."

"Are you sure?"

Derek reached across the table and squeezed my hand. "She adores you."

"Me, too." I brushed back a tear. "I mean, I adore her."

"I know. And I love you for it." Derek dropped a kiss on my forehead. "I only hope she gets along half as well with Tom."

"Are there problems?"

"Not that I've heard. But still..."

"I'm sure everything will work out fine. Does Tom have children of his own?"

"Possibly. He's a bit older." Derek shrugged, sipped his brew, looking troubled. Maeve was his baby girl. I got that completely.

Then Derek took my hands and hit me with a lightning bolt.

"Let's get married now."

4

"What?" The world collapsed down to a small point. Me, Derek and a table. I couldn't see or hear anything else.

"I said, let's get married. We could elope. Fly to Vegas."

I forced myself to breathe. "Yes, I mean, no. I can't. It would kill Mom. You know I'm her only child. She's been dreaming about my wedding since the day I was born. I can't disappoint her. She's done so much for me."

I sucked a half inch of foam from my beer mug. "So if you insist on us flying to Vegas to get hitched by some tacky Elvis impersonator, you'd better buy a pair of one-way tickets. Because there won't be any coming back, mister."

"Yeah, I get that. It was just a thought."

"And a sweet one."

"Let's get out of here." Derek signalled our waitress for the check. "Come back to my place?" Derek's place was a cozy little apartment upstairs of his law offices. Convenient for getting to work but also far too convenient for Amy-the-ex to come wandering over from Dream Gowns whenever she liked. Once we got married, Derek could move in with me. My place was the bigger of the two.

"Love to."

Paul Anderson intercepted the young woman and sent her away. "Dinner is on me, lovebirds." He shook Derek's hand and kissed me on the cheek. The restaurateur was about my age with a shock of wavy brown hair and wicked brown eyes. He preferred tight black jeans and tight black tee shirts bearing the Brewer's Biergarten name and logo.

"Thanks," said Derek. He pulled some cash out of his wallet and left a big tip for our server. "Awfully generous of you. What's the occasion?"

"Your wedding, of course," replied Paul.

"You heard already?" I said.

"Are you kidding? That's life in a small town, Amy. You ought to know that."

Paul was right. I ought to. I had grown up here. He was a newbie.

"Wait until I tell Craig," Paul went on. "He doesn't know yet, does he?"

"Nope. Not unless the small town grapevine runs all the way to Raleigh."

"Great." Paul rubbed his hands gleefully. "I can't wait to be the one to break the news to him."

"Go for it," I said. I would have loved to have seen Craig's face when he broke the news. Craig Bigelow is my ex-boyfriend. He and I had dated longer than I had ever dated anyone previously. Because I had often boasted about the Town of Ruby Lake while dating Craig, he had decided to open the biergarten here with his partner, Paul, managing the place. Much to my displeasure.

Fortunately, Craig himself was a rare visitor.

At one point, I thought Craig and I might marry. What a fool I had been.

Craig is tall, dark and handsome, with an MBA degree that I helped pay for. Unfortunately, he is also a jerk. A two-timing jerk. Breaking up with him and moving home to Ruby Lake was the best thing that I had ever done.

Up till meeting Derek, that is.

Last I heard, and I tried my best not to hear anything about him, Craig was dating a woman way too young for him practically a child really. Her name is Cindy Pym. I'd met her and had the misfortune of spending the weekend with the two of them. It had not been fun.

Not that there was anything wrong with Cindi. I liked Cindi. She was blond and beautiful. And smart. The woman's got a master's degree in psychology. But if she really thought Craig was ever going to marry her, she was going to be in for a surprise.

"When is the big day?" Paul wanted to know.

"June fifteenth," I said.

"June fifteenth? Isn't that the same day that—"

"Don't even say it," begged Derek.

"Right." Paul smiled awkwardly. "I'll be looking forward to it. Who's catering?" His eyes lit up with hope.

"Jessamine's Kitchen," I said, improvising quickly. Derek hid his surprise. "No offense, Paul. You know I adore you and the food you serve here. We wanted something a bit more upscale than beer and pizza at our wedding reception. Jessamine was Mom's idea." Now I just had to remind myself to tell Mom that.

"Good choice," Paul answered, trying and failing to hide his disappoint at losing the gig—not that we had much money to spend on the food and refreshments anyway.

"Tell me, did everybody in Ruby Lake know about

Amy-the-ex's upcoming nuptials before me?"

"Liz told me," explained Paul. "We've been out a couple of times.

"You're dating Liz Ertigun? I'd watch out for frost-bite, if I were you." Liz Ertigun was Amy Harlan's plat-inum-haired, bony-shouldered partner. They ran the gown shop together. Her cold blue eyes give me freezer burns.

Paul shifted uneasily. "Actually, I'm invited to the wedding. Liz is Amy Harlan's maid of honor. Hey, maybe you could make it a double wedding?"

I raked my eyes over him. "Not on your life."

"Yeah, that could end up more a double murder than a wedding," joked Derek.

"Yeah, right," agreed Paul. "Dumb idea."

"I'm sure it won't be your last," I said, ponying up a fake smile.

"Speaking of maids of honor," Paul clamped his hand down on Derek's shoulder. "Have you given any thought to who your best man is going to be?"

"Actually—"

"Keep in mind, I throw a mean bachelor party." Squeeze squeeze went Paul's hand.

"How mean?" I screwed up my eyes at Paul.

Paul threw up his hands. "Strictly PG, I promise."

"The truth is, I sort of promised Dan Sutton."

"Oh, sure. Right. I get that. Dan's a good guy." He folded his arms. "How about two best men?"

"Two best men?" considered Derek.

"Boy, you must really want this," I said.

"How about if you be best man in charge of the bach-elor party and Dan stands up with me as best man at the ceremony? Would that work?"

Paul nodded slowly. "I can handle that."

"Amy?" Derek asked. "What do you think?"

"Sounds like a win-win," I replied. Paul and Dan would see to it that Derek had a perfect end-of-bachelorhood send-off. Unlike my own pending bachelorette party that Esther and Kim had put themselves in charge of. I had visions of hard liquor, fizzy pink drinks, over-sugared, carb-loaded desserts, fuzzy pink slippers and lots of drunken knitting, all under the watchful eyes of my mother.

After squeezing out our promise to invite him to our wedding and let him host Derek's bachelor party, Paul got back to work. This work, from what I'd seen since the brew pub's opening, consisted mostly of chatting up the single ladies.

Robert LaChance tumbled off a stool at the bar and oozed over to our table. He's a divorced local businessman with his fingers in lots of pies. Among other enterprises, he owns the biggest car lot in town, LaChance Motors. His son, Jimmy, is a friend of Maeve. Robert's ex, Tiffany, is one of my best friends.

"Let me be the first to congratulate the lucky couple," he said. His wavy dark hair was beginning to gray at the temples. He'd be going to the salon for a touchup soon.

"Too late," I said snarkily. Robert has a way of getting under my skin.

With good reason. He had unceremoniously dumped Tiffany for a much younger woman and once tried to practically steal my house from under me.

He's fond of pinstripe suits and his fake tan follows him from season to season. Tiffany told me he bought his custom-made suits at O'Neill's Men's Clothing here in Ruby Lake. I wasn't sure where he bought his tan.

"Thanks, Robert," said Derek. He followed his words with a look at me that said *play nice*. "Is it true you and Tom Visconti have had some business dealings?"

"You bet," Robert replied. "In fact, you just missed him. We're cooking up some things together now."

"He's here?" I swiveled my head around, although I had no idea what the man looked like.

"He was. Like I said, you just missed him but you must have seen him. Wearing a cowboy hat and one of those funny bolo ties." Robert chuckled. "We don't get too many of those around these parts."

"Cowboy hat?" I gulped.

"Uh-huh. Mind if I sit?" He pulled out an empty chair at our table and sat without waiting for a reply or even a nod.

Neither of which he would have gotten from me.

Not to mention I was still hung up on Tom Visconti and the cowboy hat. That had to have been the man who had come on to me at the bar. Had I heard him wrong? Hadn't the guy told me his name was Tim?

And, oh yeah, he had failed to mention that he had a fiancée. If I wasn't mistaken, and I wasn't, it seemed Ruby Lake had yet another cad on its hands.

"What can you tell me about him?" inquired Derek.

I suddenly had a thing or two I could tell Derek but thought it best to wait for another time.

Robert smirked. "Checking up on the guy? Why? Because he's engaged to your ex? Remember, she's not your Amy anymore. This is your Amy."

He poked a rude, fat finger in my direction. I resisted the urge to bite it off.

"I'm a concerned father."

"Yeah, I get that."

I wondered if he really did.

Robert helped himself to the last slice of pizza while he explained that Tom Visconti was some hotshot developer operating out of Nashville, Tennessee. "You heard that he is planning on expanding Rivercrest Country Club?"

Derek nodded. "That's where Amy and Maeve live."

In fact, Derek had told me his ex was on every Rivercrest Country Club board from architectural to zoning and each committee—making sure the fine denizens of Rivercrest Country Club toed the line.

"The ex? Right." Robert LaChance stroked his chin. "I've seen her around." The businessman also resided in the exclusive country club. "Tom is a helluva savvy business man. One of the best."

"That's pretty high praise coming from you," I quipped. Robert LaChance always considered him the best at everything.

"Tom is really going to take the place to the next level. He's thinking million dollar condos and estate homes. Another eighteen holes of championship golf."

"Great, just what we need in this town," I said, hoping my sarcasm came through loud and clear.

"I had no idea the guy had that kind of money behind him," replied Derek.

"Oh, yeah, Tom's got some serious money. His corporation has already bought up just shy of two hundred acres in the area surrounding the country club."

"Sounds disgusting." I lamented the development of all that pristine land even more than I lamented watching the last bit of our pizza go down Robert LaChance's gullet.

Robert ignored me. "It's all on the hush-hush, mind

you, but he is looking to purchase another fifty acres. Minimum."

"That's pretty much what I heard," said Derek. "I know little about the guy. My ex has been a bit close-lipped."

Robert chuckled. "Like I said, he is in town now. I'm playing golf with him tomorrow. Why don't you join us?"

"Are you sure he won't mind?"

"Nah. One of our foursome had to back out. Tom will be thrilled."

"Okay, I will."

"Is that really a good idea?" I asked Derek.

"What's the harm, Amy? Besides, once he and Amy are married, Maeve is going to be around him a lot. I've got a right, as her father, to know as much as I can about this guy's background."

"It's your duty, man," agreed Robert. He scooted back his chair. "We tee off at nine. See you then." He gave Derek a final slap on the back. He tried to kiss me but I ducked out of harm's way.

Little did I know that there was still plenty of harm coming my way.

"What's wrong?" Derek asked, leaning back, studying my face. "You look troubled?"

"It's nothing. Really."

"Amy?"

I chewed my lower lip a moment, wrestling over whether I should mention to Derek that Tom Visconti, alias Tim the hound dog, had tried to pick me up earlier at the bar.

No good could come of it.

"Don't hold out on me. Whatever is on your mind,

spill it. You usually do. Besides, we are going to be married soon. No secrets, right?"

"Right," I agreed, blowing out a breath. "First, promise me you won't get angry."

"Why would I get angry?" Derek replied, already sounding a bit annoyed.

"See what I mean?"

"Okay, sorry." He splayed his hands on either side of his empty plate. "Go ahead. I'm all ears and as calm as the Buddha."

I frowned skeptically but knew there was no holding back now. "It's about Tim."

"Who?"

"Tom Visconti."

"But you just said—" Derek looked totally confused.

"I know, I said Tim. That's what he was calling himself an hour ago. At the bar."

"I don't get it."

"When he tried to hit on me."

Derek tilted his head. I could see the wheels in his head turning. "I'm not sure I understand, Amy. Give it to me in layman's terms."

I did. "I was waiting for you at the bar, chatting with Connie. Tom Visconti came in and sat down beside me. Only I didn't know he was Tom Visconti. He told me his name was Tim, that he was alone, and that he was passing through town."

"And?"

"He asked me out."

"Out?"

"He asked me to join him for dinner."

"That son of a..." The fork Derek had been fiddling with bent between his fingers. "What did you say?"

"What do you think I said? I told him no thanks."

"Then what happened?"

"You came through the door and I left. As fast as my feet could carry me."

Derek puffed out his chest, exhaled. "Are you sure you didn't misunderstand?"

"Maybe," I allowed. "But I don't think so."

Derek's eyes took on a distant look.

"Derek?" I tapped his wrist. "Maybe you should cancel this golf match tomorrow. I don't think it's a good idea. Telephone Robert. Tell him you can't make it."

"Oh, no. Not a chance," growled Derek. "I wouldn't miss it for all the world."

5

Against the advice of Kim, Esther and Mom, I drove to Dream Gowns the following day to have it out with Amy-the-ex.

"What's the harm?" I had said to Mom one last time over coffee and toast slathered in grape jelly. I bought the big, economy-size jars of jelly up the street at Lakeside Market. I loved it and the birds, notably the woodpeckers, tanagers, catbirds and the occasional oriole, loved it just as much. I kept a wild bird jelly feeder hanging from the branch of an oak in the front yard.

Between myself and the birds, the stuff went fast.

Mom was toying with the idea of canning jams and jellies herself with the idea of selling jars of it in Birds & Bees. We were already doing a fair trade with her Barbara's Bird Bars, so I was all for it. Any additional source of income would be a welcome and much needed addition to the store's bottom line.

Mom already had a name for the product picked out: *Barbara's Bird Jam*. She had even doodled up a label for the jars using a program on her laptop, a trio of birds playing horn, guitar and harmonica.

Mom's got quite the imagination. Maybe retirement does that to a person.

"It's not like I'm going to scratch her eyes out," I said,

getting back to Amy-the-ex. "I only want to see if we can come to some sort of reasonable accord."

"Promise me that you will be civil," Mom implored. "Soon she'll be married to Tom Visconti and you'll be married to Derek. That makes you practically related."

"On what planet?"

"Amy."

I mumbled what may or may not have been a yes and cleared the table. Accompanying me downstairs, Mom planted a kiss on my forehead as I climbed in my van parked behind Birds & Bees.

"Remember what I said, Amy."

I promised I would but the closer I got to my destination, the more steamed I was becoming. I was like Icarus, all flappy, waxy, glued-on wings. And Amy Harlan was like a red giant star threatening to burn me up if I dared to get too close.

Parking in the public lot within walking distance of the farmer's market, I waved to Susan Terwilliger, owner of the Coffee and Tea House on the street corner. She was married to another Tom, this one a dentist.

As was wiping down one of the outside tables, I detoured over to say hello and to give myself time to compose myself before facing my nemesis.

"You look frazzled," noted Susan. "What's wrong? You should be the happiest woman on the planet."

"You heard too?"

"Is there anyone in town who hasn't?" replied Susan.

"I am. I'm happy. It's just wedding stuff." Like telling Amy-the-ex to get stuffed.

"I understand. Sit." She pulled out a chair at the table closest to the door. "Enjoy the sun. I'll bring you a nice cup of soothing herbal tea. And an orange scone," she added with a wink.

"You read my mind," I said. "Make it a big one. The biggest you've got." I tilted my head to the sun, shut my eyes and waited.

It hadn't taken long. I drank my tea, ate my scone and scooped up every last sugary crumb with a finger. "Thanks," I said to Susan, joining me at the little table. "I needed that. Have you met Amy Harlan's fiancé?"

"The two of them have been in a couple of times."

"Nice?"

"He's a generous tipper. Prefers coffee to tea." She smiled.

"What?"

"I was just recalling how he always adds a shot of cognac to his coffee."

"You serve alcohol now?"

"No. He's got one of those fancy little flasks."

"Oh, brother."

I debated asking her if Tom Visconti had ever come into her café, calling himself Tim and hitting on her. In the end, I decided not to.

"Why the concern, Amy? You should like him," Susan said. "After all, he is marrying your mortal enemy. You used to worry that she was angling to get Derek back."

"True." I laid some money on the table. "You know, you're right. Mom pretty much told me the same thing."

"Smart lady." Susan waved goodbye to a departing customer.

"I should like him. And I should like her. After all, soon we will be one big happy family," I said, thinking of my mom's recent words. "I *will* like her," I vowed. "If only for Maeve's sake."

"That's my girl," said Susan, tucking my money in

the pouch of her apron. "You make sure I get a wedding invitation."

I promised. "It's time to resume my self-appointed task." And fulfill my promise to my mother that I would be civil, and to myself that I would make every effort to like Amy Harlan and her soon-to-be husband.

Walking past the plate glass window of Harlan & Harlan, I caught sight of Mrs. Edmunds sitting primly at the reception desk. The redoubtable receptionist/secretary was in her forties and dressed conservatively, favoring modest calf-length skirt suits.

Today was no exception, this one being dark blue, a sharp contrast to her deathly pale complexion. I had a theory that she only went outdoors after dark. The possibility that there was some vampire blood in her DNA was not out of the question.

Kim thought I was crazy to suggest such a thing, but it would explain why Mrs. Edmunds always arrived at the office quite early and left quite late.

Derek's father, Ben, was in his front office, talking on the telephone. He's a distinguished looking man in his early sixties. His black hair is streaked with silver. He has a Roman nose and unflappable brown eyes. I've rarely seen him lose his composure.

He waved hello through the window and I waved back.

Right about now, Derek would be out on the links slapping a little white ball around, so there was no reason to go inside. I would find out soon enough how his meeting and golf outing with Tom Visconti had gone.

I told myself I had nothing to worry about. Derek was calm, rational and sensible. The most civil and civilized man I knew.

And, if he could do it, so could I. Girding myself, I grabbed the door handle, closed my eyes, and counted slowly to ten before entering enemy territory—Amy-the-ex's shop.

Stepping into *Dream Gowns* was a bit like stepping into fairyland. Every little princess's dream. The salon's walls had been plaster-coated a light gray. Future brides and grooms were encouraged to trace tiny hearts onto the plaster walls and scratch their initials inside. One such couple was doing so now. Having scraped out a lopsided heart replete with compulsory arrow, and having added their initials, they now posed with a cellphone next to their creation and snapped a few pictures for all their friends and the social media world to see.

I had to give Amy-the-ex credit for that. It was a very sweet idea. The closest thing we had to it at Birds & Bees was a bulletin board where customers could post pictures of the birds they had seen locally. So far, we were anything but a social media sensation.

Billowy, silver curtains hung from the corners of the main luxe salon, suspended on thick brass rods. Fashionable, pricey gowns dangled enticingly from long, chrome dress rods along the walls. *Touch me, feel me, buy me,* they seemed to whisper.

Low glass-topped display tables, placed strategically about the salon, offered an overpriced assortment of accessories, including veils, belts, and crystal-studded shoes. Perfectly spaced chandeliers hanging from the tin tile ceiling created a soft, intimate ambience.

I'd heard that Dreams Gowns had, in its short existence, already gleaned quite the reputation, with buyers coming from as far away as the Outer Banks.

Detecting the subtle scent of gardenias, no doubt being piped through the store's ventilation system to lull customers to relax and hand over their credit cards without argument, I took a deep whiff. The fragrant aroma carried me back to my childhood days and my mother's beautiful backyard garden.

Wandering toward the consultation area with its overabundance of full-length mirrors—that suspiciously made me look thinner than I had since I was fifteen years old—I caught sight of Amy-the-ex installed on an armless raspberry leather sofa with a quilted back. She posed regally, like a queen on her mighty throne, legs crossed, cool eyes passing judgment on everything and everyone that dared cross her path.

Her platinum-dyed locks were pulled back in a loose ponytail held in place with a diamond clip. Her expensive deep blue dress showed a little too much cleavage and a whole lot of tanned leg.

She slid off the sofa like a snake sensing that its prey was nearby. "Ms. Simms, this is a surprise. Then again, I did hear that you are finally getting married. And to *my* Derek. My, my."

"Good news travels fast." I kicked myself mentally for starting out our conversation so cattily. But I would have had to be a robot not to have let that *my Derek* remark get under *my* skin.

"Yes, Maeve told me. *She* is quite excited for you."

"And you?"

Amy-the-ex tugged at her ponytail. "What about me?"

"You must be awfully excited to be getting married again. Congratulations."

"Very excited," she answered with a smile. "Thank

you."

I helped myself to a spot on the edge of her sofa. "We do have one little problem."

"What's that?"

"It seems your wedding and mine are scheduled for the same day."

A throaty sound escaped from her lips, like the sound a frog might make regurgitating a harmonica. Her version of a laugh, I supposed. "That's not my problem. It's yours."

"Don't you think that two weddings on the same day is going to create complications? I mean, Ruby Lake is a small town. There are only a limited number of venues and caterers. Plus, there is a lot of overlap here. Guests may be forced to choose which wedding to attend."

"I cannot imagine that being a hard choice to make." Amy-the-ex could cat it up with the best of them. "You only now decided to get married, Ms. Simms. That is hardly my fault." Her hand fluttered to her breast. "Our invitations have already gone out. RSVPs have already begun flooding in."

Funny, I hadn't received one.

"It seems to me," she went on breathily, "that you're the one creating the problem. You're copying me." She leaned closer. "I know. Why don't you get married next year? I'm sure Derek won't mind waiting."

There was a dig behind those words and that vacuous grin.

I ignored it and tried again. "My mother and father got married on June fifteenth. Mom is all alone now, you know. Dad passed some years ago. Before his time."

"I'm sorry to hear that." Amy-the-ex's response came out mechanical and emotionless.

"I thought, that is, I was hoping, under the circumstances, that you might consider moving your wedding date."

"Not on your life. I've waited a long time for this. I'm not about to let your little to-do interfere with my perfect wedding."

A long time? She and Tom Visconti had only been dating a couple of months or so.

I stood. "Fine. Be that way. But it doesn't have to be this difficult, you know. You're getting what you want. I'm getting what I want. Why can't we all just be happy?" I asked, trying valiantly to soften the hard edge creeping into my voice. "Bury the hatchet?"

"I have an appointment." She twirled a diamond-studded watch round on her impossibly skinny wrist. "My bride-to-be should be arriving any moment now for her fitting. I'm sure you understand."

Amy-the-ex laid her icy fingers on my shoulder and pushed me to the door. I felt my core temperature drop twenty degrees.

"Wait," I begged. "Have you considered Vegas?"

"Goodbye, Ms. Simms."

"Wait," I said once more. Liz Ertigun was hanging a dress in the window. "That's a beautiful gown." In fact, it was the gown of my dreams. "How much is that dress?"

"Thirteen-five." Liz twisted the front of the gown around for me to admire all the more.

"As in thirteen thousand five hundred dollars?"

"That's right, Ms. Simms," Amy-the-ex said sharply. "It is a Donatelli original."

"A what?"

"She is an immensely popular Italian designer," Liz

explained.

"I don't suppose you can afford it," Amy Harlan drawled with a distinctly haughty overtone.

"No," I said, crestfallen. "I don't suppose I can. Have you got anything in the thousand-dollar range?"

I knew she was the enemy and that I shouldn't have been doing business with her but I couldn't help myself. We were about to be related. Sort of. "Maybe I could get some sort of family discount?"

Both women snickered but it was Amy Harlan who said, "True fashion does not come at a discount."

"We do have some shoes in the thousand-dollar range," suggested Liz.

Seriously, was she trying to be helpful or was she mocking me? And Paul Anderson was dating this woman? What did he see in her? Beyond the obvious runway model good looks, there seemed to be little worth bothering over.

"I'll keep that in mind," I snapped. I wouldn't pay a thousand dollars for a pair of shoes unless it was attached to a decent used car.

"Try the Bridal Barn down in Charlotte," quipped Amy Harlan. "I'm sure they will have something suitable for you." Her eyes raked over me, judging every inch of my flesh, divining the depth of my purse.

"Money can't buy happiness, you know."

"No." Amy Harlan gave her ponytail a regal flip. "But it can buy a beautiful wedding for one hundred and fifty guests and live music by MC and the Moonlighters."

Wow. Tom Visconti's pockets ran very deep. I didn't know what the going rate was for an R&B band whose biggest hits came in the seventies but I knew it was far out of my league.

"May I ask where you are getting married?" I had one more question.

"Magnolia Manor, of course."

"That figures." Magnolia Manor was the region's premiere wedding event space. I was setting my sights on it for my wedding.

I had some major thinking and planning to do.

More than that, I needed a Plan B.

6

I called a war and wedding planning party up in my apartment for seven o'clock that evening. All my top lieutenants were in attendance: Kim, Mom and Esther. The Major, the General and the Pester.

We had lots to talk about.

To grease our mental wheels, Kim brought over a batch of her homemade apple pie shooters—a delicious, if mind-bending, mixture of bourbon, apples, sugar, cinnamon, ginger and nutmeg—served up in diminutive Mason jars that she bought at the farmer's market.

I was on my third shooter.

Mom was seated in Dad's favorite old chair. I still miss him dearly. I'd miss him even more on my wedding day.

The rest of us were on the rug, arranged around the coffee table. We were riffling through the stack of bridal magazines that Kim had insisted on bringing too.

"The magazines were a good idea," I admitted. "I never realized how many options and choices went into a wedding, not to mention such add-ons like bachelor parties, bridal showers and rehearsal dinners."

"Where are you going to register for gifts?" Kim needed to know.

"Good question. I really hadn't given it any thought."

"I've got some ideas," Kim said.

"I can imagine." My best friend had been dreaming about her wedding since as long as I had known her.

"You could go with one of those online wedding registry sites," Esther surprised us all by saying. "Then you don't have to pick any particular store."

"Given it some thought, have you, Esther?" Kim nudged Esther. "You and Floyd thinking of getting hitched?"

"Don't be silly." Esther blushed.

"Silly?" Kim swilled her bourbon. "I've seen the way Floyd looks at you."

"That's his myopia," Esther insisted. "And *you* are tipsy." She reached for Kim's glass but Kim dodged out of her reach.

"That online registry idea is a thought," agreed Mom. "Although it does sound a little impersonal. What happened to the good old days when people actually went shopping for gifts, wrapped them up prettily and brought them to the reception?"

"Gone with the dinosaurs, Mom."

"And the twenty-five cents a gallon gas," added Esther. "You've gotta get with the times, Barbara."

"I suppose," sighed Mom. "Who is going to officiate?"

I had already given this some thought. "I was thinking Steve Sharpe."

"Who?" Kim snatched a magazine out of my hands and deftly tore out a photo. "Sorry. I love this gown." She stuffed the torn sheet in her jeans for future reference.

"Steve Sharpe. He's that guy from L.A. who used to be a heavy metal musician." He was a regular at Birds & Bees.

"Hmm." Mom tapped her jawline. "I believe I've seen his advertising flyers."

"From rock and roller to preacher?" Esther shuffled off in her slippers to the bathroom.

"Yep. To be precise, Steve is an ordained non-denominational wedding officiant. He calls his business A Beautiful Ceremony. When he lived in L.A., the music was his main occupation and the officiating was a side gig. Now that he's living here, the two jobs have reversed."

"I don't blame him," said Kim. "There certainly can't be many jobs for heavy metal musicians around here."

"Exactly. Derek and I will go to town hall and pick up the license. Steve will perform the actual ceremony."

"Instead of an organist, he's going to play heavy metal guitar?" Mom looked a bit worried.

"That wasn't the plan but now that you mention it, Mom..."

"Very funny."

Kim nudged me. "Call him."

"I will."

"No, I mean now. Before Amy-the-ex snatches him up."

I leapt for my cellphone on the table by the door. "Good idea." Fortunately, I had caught Steve at home and free to talk. We chatted a few minutes then said goodbye. "Unfortunately, he told me he's already booked for that day. With you-know-who."

"Cheer up, Amy," said cheerleader Mom. "We'll find someone perfect. How about Reverend Anderson? He married me and your dad."

"You'll have to dig him up first," replied Esther, returning with a plastic pumpkin head filled with leftover Halloween candy. "He died ten years back."

"Right." Mom swirled her shooter. "I had forgotten."

I cast my accusing eyes on Esther. "I had that pumpkin stashed in the nightstand drawer." Always keep chocolate nearby in case of emergencies. That was my motto.

"I know. Dumb place to keep it." Esther passed my bucket around.

Kim grabbed a handful. Mom deferred. I took two bite-size Snickers.

"Didn't you notice Esther dipping into your stash?" Kim's lips were smeared with chocolate.

"All these months, the candy had been dwindling more quickly than I would have imagined." I leaned against the couch. "I thought I'd been sleep eating." Now, I didn't feel so bad.

"Sleep eating?"

"Like sleep walking but with benefits." That elicited a few chuckles.

The planning party went downhill from there.

By the third hour, I was beginning to consider that Derek's idea of eloping to Las Vegas might not be such a terrible idea after all.

Although Esther's wild suggestion of running Amy-the-ex out of town was also not without its merits.

Only the unstopping look of joy on my mother's face, despite all the obstacles, kept me from throwing up my hands and surrendering completely.

"Let's focus on the positive things," Kim suggested. "We should go down to Charlotte and shop for your wedding gown. You've got to allow plenty of time and it is already very short notice. How does Saturday work for you?" Kim passed me a fresh Mason jar.

"No more shooters for me, thanks. I couldn't possibly drink another." I could but I wouldn't be able to get out of bed and open the store the next morning. "Shopping for my dress in Charlotte is what Amy-the-ex suggested."

Esther hiccoughed. "Shouldn't you be calling her Amy-the-next?"

"There's lots of things I'd like to call her. She recommended I shop for my dress at the Bridal Barn."

Kim scrunched up her nose. "Is that for cows or people?"

"Very funny. I can't believe that woman wouldn't budge on the date. It's Mom's wedding date. Everything would be so easy if she would just move her wedding date up or down a little. That date means nothing to Amy Harlan. She probably picked it out of a hat."

"A witch's hat," added Kim.

They had heard me say all this before and were probably tired of hearing it. I, on the other hand, hadn't yet gotten tired of expressing my frustration. I banged my fist into a pillow.

"Really, Amy," Mom reached out and tousled my hair. "I think you're making too much out of this. Yes, it was your father and my wedding date. So what? Pick another date. Make it your and Derek's special day."

"You don't mind?" I blinked back tears.

"Of course, not. Not in the least. Why not postpone your wedding by a week? Nothing is set in stone."

"True," Kim replied. "It's not like you or Derek have shelled out any money. No deposits to forfeit."

"Good idea, Barbara." Esther grabbed her yarn and knitting needles from under the sofa cushion.

"I suppose we could do that. It would give me more time to plan. And with as little time as there is, an extra week is big."

"I'm certain Derek won't mind," Mom said.

"Your mom's got a point, Amy," agreed Kim. "Let Amy Harlan have her wedding first."

"Save the best for last. That's what I always say." Esther started whistling the melody of Wagner's *Wedding March*. She wasn't in tune but she was lively.

"What about a venue?" I stood and wobbled to the kitchen looking for something to eat to sop up all the alcohol floating around in my stomach. The Snickers weren't helping. "Anybody want anything?"

"I already checked," Mom said. "And there's leftover bagels in the breadbox." Mom had to be the last person left in America who owned and operated a breadbox.

"As for a venue, Magnolia Manor has the date available. In fact," Mom winked at Esther and Kim, "I've already reserved it for you."

"Aw, Mom." I sniffled for real this time, wiping my sudden tears on the tea towel draped over the edge of the faucet. "Thanks."

"No thanks necessary. As for the gown...Kim, would you mind?" Mom bobbed her head in the direction of her bedroom.

"Sure, Barbara." Kim jumped to her feet, spilling bridal magazines to the rug. She returned moments later bearing a large white box.

I gaped. "Is that—"

Kim laid the box reverently on the coffee table and lifted the lid.

"My old wedding dress."

"It's beautiful," whispered Kim, gently lifting the voluminous dress from the box. The vintage dress had long, delicate sleeves, a scoop neck and lovely lace and pearl detail running vertically up the right side.

"Gorgeous." I gave my mother a kiss. "It looks every bit as beautiful as I remember seeing in all your old wedding photographs."

Mom wiped a tear from her eye. "Your father loved it. I hope you will too. I won't be offended if you'd rather buy something yourself. I could pitch in—"

"No," I interrupted her. "It's perfect!"

"I'm not sure you'll fit in it," remarked Esther, looking me over.

"I'll diet," I vowed. "Take more bird watching walks."

"All well and good but why don't you get it altered?" suggested my mother. "After seeing all the gowns in these magazines of Kim's, I can see that mine is quite old-fashioned by today's standards. You should take it to a bridal shop and see what they can do to make it yours."

I blew out a breath. "I love you, Mom."

"You too, dear, though I think you've had enough to drink for one night." She looked meaningfully at my hand. I hadn't even realized I'd picked up another full Mason jar.

I reluctantly set it down on the coffee table. "Okay. But I am not taking your wedding dress to those wicked witches at Dream Gowns. We'll take the gown over to that dress shop in Swan Ridge."

That was the nearest town of any size. "If they can't help, we'll try Asheville or Charlotte."

"Who's going to walk you down the aisle?" Esther wanted to know.

"That's a good question. Mom's already turned me down." I winked at her.

"What?" Kim gaped.

"I plan to sit in the front row and enjoy the show,"

Mom explained.

"I guess I get that," Kim replied.

"Kim, you're my maid of honor. Maeve will be my flower girl..."

"What about me?" demanded Esther.

"You want to walk me down the aisle?"

"No, Simms. Don't be a nincompoop. I want to know what my role is going to be."

Role? I looked at my mother for help. Mom mouthed the word *bridesmaid*. I mouthed the reply *thank you*. "Didn't I tell you? You're one of my bridesmaids, You, Rhonda and Tiffany."

"Fine. Only don't ask me to wear some hideous purple bridesmaid dress with gaudy silk flowers plastered all over it.

"Amy, you wouldn't!" gasped Kim, fearing she'd be forced to dress in matching attire.

I promised I wouldn't, although that wouldn't have been the ugliest thing I had ever seen Esther wearing.

"How about Floyd?" Esther asked. She counted stitches while waiting for my answer.

"What about him? He's invited, of course."

"No, I mean Floyd could walk you down the aisle."

"I think that's a wonderful idea," Mom was the first to say.

"I agree." Floyd had been one of my first customers when I opened Birds & Bees. He was a wonderful older gentleman. Like a favorite grandpa, really. He had lost his wife a couple of years back. He and Esther had something going.

"Great. That's one thing we can cross off the list." Kim made an imaginary check mark in the air. "I already know that Dan's going to be Derek's best man. He asked him today. Dan and Paul are co-chairing his bachelor party."

"Dan spoke with Derek today? That's funny. I've been trying to reach him all day myself. His phone keeps going to voicemail. I assumed he was tied up with work."

"Oh?" Kim pushed off the floor and strolled to the kitchen.

"He was playing golf with Robert LaChance and Tom Visconti this morning. I haven't heard from him since."

"Huh." Kim's face was buried in the open refrigerator and her reply came out half-smothered.

"You may as well tell her, Kim," Esther said out one side of her mouth. A six-inch long flamingo-pink knitting needle dangled from the other corner.

"Tell me what?" I looked at Mom but she had no clue and merely shrugged.

"Fine." Kim reappeared with a plate of leftover meatloaf wrapped in plastic. "Derek's probably down at the police station." She focused on peeling away the plastic wrap.

"At the police station? What is he doing there? Does he have a client who's in trouble?"

Esther cackled. "*In* the police station, you mean. And it depends on how you mean *client*."

"In the police station?" Mom was leaning so far over in her chair that I feared she would plant her face in the coffee table.

"Yeah, what do you mean *in* the police station? And what's with all the innuendo about *client*?"

"Relax, Amy. It's nothing." Eyes on the meatloaf, Kim pulled a fork from the utensil drawer and dug in.

"Sure," agreed Esther. "He might be out by now."

"Out of what? Somebody please tell me what is going on!" I demanded.

"Nothing," Kim chewed and swallowed. "I'm sure it is all a big misunderstanding. Got any ketchup?"

"There is a big misunderstanding here, ladies. Somebody needs to clear it up." I snapped my fingers. "Pronto."

"Your fiancé got himself arrested," Esther announced.

7

"Arrested?" Mom and I chorused.

"For what?" I demanded.

"Disturbing the peace."

"Disturbing the peace?" I hollered. I felt a thump beneath my feet. It came from the floor, which also served as Paul Anderson's ceiling.

"Are you really trying to get me to believe that Derek, *my* Derek, has been arrested?" Thump-thump. "And for disturbing the peace?" I added more softly. It's a sad world when a tenant has to admonish a landlord to keep the noise down.

"Cheer up, Amy," said Esther. "It could have been worse."

"I don't see how."

"From what Karl told me, Derek could have been charged with battery."

"Don't forget assaulting a police officer," Kim said to my horror, waving a slab of meatloaf in the air.

Karl was Karl Vogel, Ruby Lake's former chief of police. Although retired, the man still knew what was going on in the world of local law enforcement. Far more, certainly, than our current excuse for a chief of police did. Karl was also Floyd's best friend.

I raced to the door, grabbed a light jacket and my car

keys.

"Where are you going?" asked Mom.

"To find out what's going on."

"You can't drive. You've been drinking." My mother motioned for Kim to help her to her feet. "I'll take you."

"If this is you two's idea of a joke, you had better both be gone when I get back!"

Mom rarely drives so it took us forever to get to the police station.

"Thanks for bringing me, Mom," I said as she deftly slid my van neatly up to the front curb outside the police station. "I didn't realize you still had your driver's license."

"License?"

"You mean you don't—"

Mom waved her fingers at me. "Go see about Derek. I'll keep the getaway car engine running."

Oh, brother.

In a daze, I stepped out of the van—which might make a reasonable getaway vehicle if the police chose to chase us in a one-man horse and buggy—and grabbed the front door handle. *Remain calm,* I told myself, *remain calm.*

I threw the door wide open with a resounding bang and stepped inside.

"Why didn't somebody tell me?" My voice boomed across the small room.

Officers Dan Sutton and Larry Reynolds, seated at their respective desks, leapt to attention. There was no sign of the town's newest officer, Albert Pratt.

Chief Jerry Kennedy stepped out of the john. "Keep your voice down, Simms." Jerry was smirking and buckling his belt. "I've got a prisoner in back."

"Where is he, Jerry?" I crossed the floor in long strides until I was face to face with the man in charge of keeping us citizens of Ruby Lake safe in our beds at night. "I want to see him."

Jerry was making his happy pumpkin face. I hated that face. Blond crew cut hair. Fleshy, squat nose, freckles and dark jade eyes. He had the face of a perpetual middle schooler. The maturity of one too.

"He's snoozing in a cell." Jerry drew himself taller, at least tried to. Jerry's gut gets a little bigger and rounder every year. If you cut him open in cross-section, I had a hunch you could calculate his age by counting the growth rings as accurately as that of any sugar maple— emphasis on the sugar.

I smothered Jerry with my most bilious look. Even more bilious than I had given him the one time we had gone out on a date in high school and he had tried to touch me.

Ick.

Since my return to Ruby Lake, the two of us have had our share of ups and downs. Mostly downs. "Wake him up. I want to see him."

"One of us is the chief of police, Simms, and it ain't you." He adjusted the shiny badge on his shirt meaningfully.

There he stood in his spotless brown uniform, me in my rumpled, lazing-around-the-house blue tracksuit that had never seen the surface of a track, let alone made the circuit of one.

"Want me to handle this, Chief?" Dan said, laying a calming hand on my shoulder.

"There is nothing to handle, Sutton. Go home, Amy.

You can see your boyfriend in the morning."

"He is my fiancé, in case you haven't heard, Jerry. That makes him practically family."

"I heard." Jerry grabbed a mug of coffee from the refreshment center in the corner. He plopped himself down at his desk near the back of the station. "I suppose that means I'll have to buy you a wedding gift." He didn't look happy at the thought.

Jerry is one of the cheapest men I've ever met. He does half his snacking for free out of the seed bins down at Birds & Bees. No matter how often I scold him not to.

"Huh. You'll be lucky to get a wedding invitation."

Jerry pressed his palms into his desk. "You wouldn't dare."

"In a heartbeat." Not getting an invitation to a wedding in this town was akin to being ostracized. It was considered one of the biggest social embarrassments one could suffer.

Well, that and being related to Jerry Kennedy.

We stared one another down from opposite sides of the desk, neither wanting to be the first to avert our eyes. I fired another shot. "How is Sandra going to feel about being left off the invitation list, Jerry?" Sandra was Jerry's long-suffering wife.

"I am putting my foot down. Sandra is gonna have to learn to live with it," he vowed through gritted teeth.

"Why don't you take your foot out of your—"

"What's going on out there?" We heard Derek's voice from the back of the station where the cells were located. "Amy? Is that you?"

"Derek! Yes, it's me. And I am not leaving without you." The words were intended for Derek but my eyes and intent were locked on the chief of police.

"What would you like to do, Chief?" Dan was doing his best to control a stubborn smirk.

"I'd like to get some peace and quiet. But I can see that isn't going to happen." Jerry relented with a sigh. "Go get him, Sutton."

Dan cast me a quick grin, followed by a wink, and disappeared down the narrow corridor that led to the solitary cell. A moment later, he reappeared with Derek in the lead.

"Derek!" I threw myself into his arms.

"Hi, Amy."

I peppered Derek's blushing face with kisses. Gripping his hands, I took a step back. "What's happening? What is going on? Is everybody punking me? Is that what this is? Punk the bride-to-be? And why on earth are you dressed for golf?"

My boyfriend, no, fiancé, was dressed absurdly in a pair of cuffed pink trousers and a pink-striped polo shirt. White Oxford golf cleats covered his feet.

"These?" Derek tugged at the open button on his collar. "I played golf this morning. Remember?"

"Yes. I do remember." I made a show of crossing my arms across my chest. "With Robert LaChance and Tom Visconti."

"And the mayor," Jerry added.

"Okay." Our mayor is Mac MacDonald. He, too, is in real estate. Was something fishy going on? I made a mental note to ask Derek about that. "What I did not know was that the Rivercrest Country Club required all its players to dress up like flamingos."

Jerry snorted hot coffee out his nose. Cursing, he snapped his fingers and ordered Dan to fetch him some paper towels.

"So what happened? The fashion police here arrest you?"

Jerry and Dan were laughing even as Dan tried to wipe his boss's shirt clean. He was doing a fine job of making it worse.

"Don't blame them, Amy." Derek leaned his hand against the back of a stiff chair angled across from Chief Kennedy's desk. "I wanted to keep you out of it."

Gently grabbing Derek's chin in my hand and raising it up until he was looking me in the eyes, I said, "Out of what exactly?"

Derek's jaw worked but no sound escaped.

"Go on, counselor," urged Jerry. "Tell her."

Heaving a sigh, Derek spilled it. "Tom Visconti and I got into a small shouting match."

"A small shouting match?" huffed Jerry. He shooed Dan away with a slap of the hand. "Stop it, already," he muttered to Dan while reclaiming his chair. "You call that a small shouting match, Harlan? You busted that flag pole on the fifteenth hole."

"That was an accident," Derek frowned in reply. "I was taking a practice swing. I accidentally hit the flag."

"You broke it in two. The groundskeeper says he saw you. He says you did it on purpose."

"He's mistaken, Chief. I already told you that." Derek stuffed his hands in his front pockets.

"He also says you took a poke at Mr. Visconti."

"Derek!" I stared at my fiancé. My soft, gentle, non-violent fiancé. Or was he? "You didn't!"

"It was an accident, Amy. My shoe was untied. I tripped and threw out my arm and *accidentally* connected with Visconti's jaw."

"Oh, brother," I groaned.

"That's when the course superintendent called us," put in Dan.

"Yeah," said Jerry. "To come break up the fight."

"There was a fight?" My eyes flew from one man to the other and finally alit on Derek.

"It wasn't a fight. Visconti thought I hit him on purpose. Words were exchanged—"

"And fists," Jerry was quick to point out.

Derek shrugged. "It was all a big misunderstanding. We could have settled it like gentlemen and none of this would have happened if Jerry hadn't thrown gasoline on the fire, so to speak."

"All I did was enforce the law, Harlan. You of all people ought to know that. You are a lawyer."

"You see, Amy?" Derek was looking at me. "Stubborn as a mule."

Jerry's cheeks puffed up like a red balloon. "You struck a police officer!"

"I accidentally rolled over your foot with the golf cart *after* you jumped in front of it."

"You were fleeing from the police!"

"I was driving five miles an hour back to the clubhouse to put my golf clubs away."

"Yeah, well, anyway it still hurts." Jerry rubbed the top of his foot against his opposite calf.

"Oh, Derek." I ran my hand along his stubbled cheek. "Did you do all this because Tom Visconti hit on me at the bar last night?"

"He what?" growled Jerry, half rising from his seat.

Derek snatched my hand. "You're not helping, Amy."

"Well, well," Jerry was smiling like he had just struck gold at the bottom of a mine shaft. And I had helped him get there. "Isn't this interesting. Visconti hit on

Simms here. Personally, I can't understand why."

"Hey!" I said.

"But I can understand why you would be mad," Jerry said to Derek. "Mad enough to take a swing at the fella."

"The only thing I was swinging was my golf club, Chief."

I leaned all my weight, both literal and otherwise, against Jerry's desk. "Did Tom Visconti file charges, Jerry?"

After a beat, Jerry said, "No."

"Then let Derek go, Jerry. And I mean now."

"He struck a police officer. The chief of police, I might point out."

"It sounds to me like your foot got in his way, Jerry."

"I did say I was sorry," Derek added in a tone heavily-laced with sincerity, real or not.

"See? Derek is sorry. Let him go. I'll take full custody."

"Why should I? His twenty-four hours ain't up."

"You've locked him up for twenty-four hours? That's ridiculous, Jerry."

"It was his idea."

I swung around. "Your idea?"

Derek colored. "I suggested I spend the night in jail. In exchange, Chief Kennedy drops the entire matter."

"That's absurd," I replied. "Have you all lost your minds?"

Not one of the men dared reply. Maybe they weren't all as dumb as they looked.

"In my position, in my job," Derek clarified, "it wouldn't do to have a police record. You can under-stand, Amy."

"Good grief." I flopped my butt down on Jerry's desk-top, sending official documents scattering like nervous pigeons. He complained but my ears were not hearing.

"Like Derek said, his twenty-four hours are nearly half up," Dan stated, trying to placate everyone involved. That was the sort of guy he was. "Maybe we could let Derek out now. I'm sure we'd all like to get home and sleep in our own beds."

Dan knew Chief Kennedy hated late nights. Keeping Derek locked up overnight was proving to be a headache for all involved.

"Fine. You can collect your things but I expect you to stay out of trouble," he said to Derek. "And you," the chief said while kicking me in the rear with his right foot to remove my butt from his desktop, "I expect a wedding invitation from."

"Absolutely. Cross my heart." I waved my hand haphazardly around my chest.

"Front row, center."

"Done," I pledged.

"And my Cassie gets to be flower girl." Cassie was Jerry and his wife's lovely young daughter.

Wiping Jerry's footprint off my butt, I said, "But Maeve is flower girl."

Jerry Kennedy narrowed his eyes at me.

"That's okay," Derek called as he collected a set of golf clubs from a rack near the back door of the station. "You can have two flower girls, can't you, Amy?" He hefted his big green golf bag over one shoulder and headed for the front door.

"Fine. Anything to get out of here." I had almost caught up with him at the door when Jerry's voice brought me to a halt.

"Hey, Simms, what's on the menu for the wedding dinner? Not birdseed and suet cakes, I hope!"

Jerry laughed uproariously as I slammed the door on our way out.

8

"The joke is going to be on him." I climbed into the van. Derek stashed his golf clubs in back. "Jerry wants birdseed and suet cakes? I'll give him birdseed and suet cakes."

I envisioned Jerry munching down on beefy suet cake while the rest of our wedding guests feasted on grilled steak and fried chicken.

"Thanks for coming down to the station, Amy," Derek said from the second row of seats. "You too, Barbara."

I filled Mom in on what had happened inside the police station. Derek remained unnaturally quiet in the rear seat, embarrassed, I suspected, by what had transpired.

As I unfolded my tale, Mom, to my surprise, appeared amused rather than mortified.

"It sounds to me like Jerry is blowing everything out of proportion," Mom declared. She swerved, narrowly missing two large plastic trash bins on wheels that someone had left out in the street. "Typical of the man." Mom clicked her tongue.

She hit the curb rounding the corner onto Lake Shore Drive. We, and a handful of golf balls, bounced noisily around in the van a bit until Mom managed to get the vehicle under control.

"Want me to take over, Mom?" *Please, please, please,* I prayed.

"We're nearly there, dear." Mom tuned the radio in to AM Ruby, the town's one and only local radio station. Violet Wilcox, the owner, generally runs oldies music this time of night.

Derek asked to be dropped off at his apartment. We obliged. Outside the van, he grabbed his golf clubs and kissed me goodnight. We promised to meet up the next morning.

I still wasn't sure I had heard the whole truth and nothing but the truth. Once we'd both had a good night's sleep, I'd resume my questioning.

Getting back to our apartment, we found that Kim and Esther had disappeared. The empty Mason jars and the rest of the mess, however, they left for us.

There was only one thing to do—ignore it and go to bed.

The next morning, Derek and I settled down at a table inside C is for Cupcakes with our coffees and baked goods. The bakery is located a couple of shops upwind of Derek's law offices. Its walls are pastel blue and pink and all the employees wear pink aprons and ball caps. A rustic wooden sign above the door reads: We Believe In Sugar.

That was a motto I could get behind.

Derek opted for a mocha cupcake with toasted coconut flake frosting. I went for the raisin and walnut muffin. It wouldn't have been my first choice but, since I was now getting married and had a wedding to look forward to and a dress to fit into, I needed to be good.

I wisely waited until Derek had a sufficient amount of sugar and caffeine working its way through his system before beginning the questioning.

"Let's have it. What really happened yesterday?"

"What do you mean? You heard it all last night."

I looked down my nose at him. The cupcake shop was crowded, as it always was this time of morning, so I kept my voice low. "I got the PG version. Now, I want to hear the adult version."

"Oh?" Derek wriggled his brow.

"Very funny. Let's start with Tom Visconti. What happened? Why did you slug him?" Derek opened his mouth quickly. I threw up a hand. "Before you say anything, please, do not tell me that you tripped and *your* fist accidentally hit *his* jaw."

"No, huh? Have I told you how beautiful you look this morning?"

"Please. Nice try. My hair is damp. I'm wearing mud-crusted hiking boots and I've had far too little sleep. Which is your fault, I might add."

I stuck my finger in his coconut frosting, scooping up a glob of sugary heaven and stuck said finger in my mouth. "Stop trying to give me a snow job, counselor."

I was a wreck, physically and mentally. The weather had turned from sunny blue skies to cold and damp, as was frequently the case in western Carolina. For a jailbird, Derek looked great. He'd wrapped himself in his black knee-length raincoat. He'd also had the foresight to bring along an umbrella.

I had trotted over from Birds & Bees in a decade-old pair of blue jeans, a store polo shirt and the leather jacket that Kim had left hanging near the entrance the day before. For her sake, I hoped the jacket was waterproof.

"Have you given any thought to where you would like to go for our honeymoon?"

"Seriously?" I took a sip of coffee giving myself time to compose myself. "Okay, since you seem loath to start, I will. Cousin Riley says he saw you and Tom Visconti fighting on the golf course yesterday."

"Riley was there?" Derek sounded surprised.

"Yes. He was." My cousin is sort of Ruby Lake's jack-of-all-trades. "He was scooping up balls on the driving range. He says he saw you clearly."

Derek dunked his cupcake in his coffee.

"I don't know, Amy. You've said it yourself, sometimes golfers all look alike. You said it was the clothes."

I had said costumes—because they frequently looked so clownish—but his words were close enough to the truth.

"Besides," Derek continued, "how could Riley see much of anything with all those golf balls flying around and bouncing off the tractor cage while he was working?"

"He saw enough to know that it was you and Tom Visconti."

"How would Riley even know what Visconti looks like?"

"Wow, you are really going to be argumentative, aren't you? Okay, Riley knows who Tom Visconti is because the guy is buying the Rivercrest Country Club. That means he's been hanging around, inspecting, poking his nose into things, checking out the operations. Talking to the manager and employees."

"Hence, counselor, Riley has seen him around." I folded my arms over my chest. "Any other objections?"

Derek shook his head sullenly. "No objections."

"Fine." I took Derek's hand to show him there were no hard feelings. "Riley says Tom hit you first and pushed you. Then there was a scuffle. He said Robert just stood there."

Derek nodded. "Yeah, clutching his putter. I think he was too stunned to do anything. Eventually, he did start yelling for us to stop. By then, a couple of the grounds-keepers were zipping over in their carts." He chuckled.

"I don't see what is funny."

"Sorry."

"Okay." I rubbed my hands together. "Now we are getting somewhere." I leaned in for the kill. "*Why* did Tom Visconti attack you?"

"Like I said, we had a small...disagreement."

"Oh, brother," I groaned. "Here we go again."

"Tom Visconti is not a nice man, Amy. He said some things I didn't like." Derek's face colored in anger. "And that's all I am going to say about the matter."

"No-no-no. What kind of things?"

"I don't like this guy, Amy. Not just because he hit on you. I don't think he's good for my ex or my child. He said some nasty things about her."

"Your daughter?"

"No, my ex-wife." He bit down on his lower lip, then added, "He also said some unkind things about you."

"Me? He doesn't even know me!" I was starting to think that if I had been there, I might have socked this guy in the jaw myself.

"Yeah, well, he had some bad things to say anyway." Derek pushed the remainder of his cupcake at me.

I picked off a corner and dropped it on my tongue. "I'm sorry," I said finally.

Derek reached into the inner pocket of his raincoat. "That's not the worst of it, said Derek, extracting a folded document from his coat pocket. It looked official. "There's this."

"What is it?"

Derek handed it over. "Read it yourself."

I scanned the typed and stamped document quickly. "A restraining order?"

Derek nodded. "I'm not allowed to go near Tom Visconti, my ex or my daughter."

"Maeve?"

"Only court-monitored visits."

"This is ridiculous. How dare he do this?"

"He didn't do it." Derek tapped the bottom of the page. "That's Amy's signature there."

I looked. Sure enough, Amy-the-ex had requested the restraining order. "We've got to do something about this. She can't keep you from your daughter. You didn't do anything wrong. Tom Visconti started it. We'll go to court. Cousin Riley will testify to your innocence."

Even if I had to twist his arm to do so. "Don't you worry."

"No, I don't want to make too big a deal about this. Dad is working on Amy. She likes him."

I dropped the document on the table. "Your ex-wife works fast, doesn't she?" My head was spinning. These were supposed to be good times. Marriage was in the air.

"Yeah, she got some hotshot attorney from Nashville. This order was waiting for me in the office when I got in this morning."

"Wow, I don't know what to say." I felt tears welling up and kissed his fingertips. "Don't worry. We'll get through this. And if I ever get my hands on Tom Visconti..."

"You stay away from the man. There's something else I didn't tell you."

I felt queasy, like my stomach was performing somersaults. I wasn't sure I could stand any more bad news but I asked anyway. "What is it?"

"Visconti bragged that after he and my ex were married, they were going to take Maeve and go live in Nashville.

"Oh, no..." Derek adored his daughter. A move like that would break his heart.

"If he thinks he's going to get away with that," growled Derek, "he's got another thing coming." He twisted and tugged his paper napkin with both hands. "I'll strangle the guy first."

The couple at the next table gave us a hard look, grabbed their things and left.

"Why didn't you tell Jerry all this?" I said softly.

"I didn't want to cause any more trouble than necessary. But then, I didn't know about this."

He picked up the restraining order and thrust it roughly inside his coat pocket. "I didn't want to mess up Amy's wedding. More importantly, I didn't want to make life miserable or uncomfortable for Maeve. Kids are sensitive, you know."

I nodded and Derek continued. "So I made it sound like it was all a big misunderstanding that got blown out of proportion."

"I hope you know what you're doing, Derek."

"Don't worry. Like I said, Dad is going to work on my ex. He's going to try to convince her to drop the restraining order. This will all blow over before you know it."

"I wish there was something I could do."

"There is. First, take a bite." He presented his largely uneaten cupcake to my lips. "You know you're dying to." I opened wide. How could I refuse? Leaving behind even a smidgen of a cupcake should be a crime, let alone leaving nearly two-thirds of one.

"Second," he said, wiping away the cool frosting on my lips with his warm lips, "plan the wedding of your life. Because I love you and can't wait to spend the rest of my life with you."

Tears of joy blurred my vision.

That was an offer I couldn't refuse.

9

Time flew by faster than a flock of eider ducks in a strong tailwind. It was June fifteenth, Mom's wedding anniversary, the day of Amy-the-ex's marriage to Tom Visconti and only seven days until I was going to be married to the wonderful man sitting beside me.

And I had lost nearly seven pounds in a matter of weeks!

Derek and I were two bodies in a sea of white folding chairs set out on the immaculate lawn of Magnolia Manor. Cousin Riley had carefully mown it himself that very morning. He promised to do the same for me next weekend.

Situated off a dirt road in the green foothills above Ruby Lake, Magnolia Manor, a white Southern mansion incorporating Greek revival and Georgian styles, was the perfect place for a wedding. The home and gardens were a postcard come to life.

I was glad we had decided to wait for a chance to use the venue rather than settle for something less.

Mom and Ben sat beside us. Dan and Kim had found two open seats further back. Kim looked adorable in a knee-length pink dress and strappy heels. Rhonda had given Kim an up-do. It took some getting used to, but it was a good style for her.

Derek told me over and over how beautiful I looked in my blue floral dress. He had insisted on buying it for me for the occasion.

Many town dignitaries were there, including Mayor MacDonald, who sat squeezed between some man I didn't know and a woman I had met briefly before the ceremony, Gloria Bolan, dressed in a plain white shift dress and white gloves. She said she worked as Mr. Visconti's executive assistant.

Robert LaChance sat next to them with a redhead half his age whom he had been parading around on his arm before we'd been told to begin taking our seats. Her name was Monica and she was employed at LaChance Motors. I had a feeling most of her work was done after-hours.

Wearing a navy suit with wide lapels, Steve Sharpe, the wedding officiant, stood towards the rear of the gazebo, mopping his bald head with a towel. He had an infectious smile and piercing dark eyes. Speaking of piercing, each of his ears was studded with a tiny silver cross. At the moment, he was speaking with an elegant older couple I didn't know.

I glanced at my watch. In a matter of minutes, Amy Harlan would become Amy Visconti. If only I could convince her to change her first name—perhaps after a couple of bottles of celebratory champagne—to something other than Amy, such as Gamy, life would be perfect.

"You look nice," I whispered into Derek's ear. "Smell nice too." I pressed my nose into the shoulder of his dark blue suit. Next week, he would be attired in the black wool suit that we had picked out together in Charlotte. It fit him perfectly.

"Thanks. I'm not so sure I even want to be here." Derek squirmed on his folding chair.

"Remember, you are doing this for Maeve."

"Yeah." He beamed at his daughter pacing nervously up and down off to one side of the chairs. She bore a white ribbon-tied bunch of yellow tulips in her clenched hands. She was waiting for her scheduled walk up the aisle preceding her mother.

"Is it hot or is it just me?" Derek ran his finger under his snug collar and tugged at the knot of his necktie.

"It's you." I opened my purse, pulled out a tissue and dabbed his perspiring forehead. "Not nervous, are you? You're not the one getting married."

"No, of course not. I wish they'd get on with this."

"Relax. It will be over before you know it." The ceremony was taking place out-of-doors in the luxuriant Magnolia Manor west gardens. The sun was shining and the temperature was in the mid-sixties. Near perfect. "Hopefully, the weather next week will be just as nice for our wedding."

Derek grunted.

Vows would be exchanged under the lovely white gazebo with the Greco-Roman columns. Pink and white roses decorated practically every inch of space. A beautiful Celtic walnut harp stood in front of the gazebo. Hand-carved inlay of a floral and dove motif shone in the dappled sunlight. The flaxen-haired harpist smiled and flexed her long fingers.

Amy Harlan didn't do anything in a small way.

Violet Wilcox, from AM Ruby, would be DJ'ing our wedding. She owed me a few favors. Plus, Birds & Bees was an occasional advertiser on her station.

I was grateful that I had ordered wildflowers for our

upcoming nuptials rather than roses. I would have been horrified to have Amy Harlan's wedding and my wedding contain very many similarities. Similarities led to comparisons and I wanted there to be none.

The low portable stage across the shallow glen was all set up. Dozens of white folding chairs and tables filled the area with a large space left open for dancing. The reception would be held there once the ceremony was concluded.

MC and the Moonlighters waited to perform. Walking to our seats towards the front, I noticed the band seated in the last row. Each member wore a shiny neon blue tux, white shirt and skinny pink necktie. The star himself had squeezed himself into a pair of black leather pants, white shirt with frills and a bold black and white striped jacket with a skinny tie designed to mimic a piano keyboard.

Amy-the-ex, soon to be Visconti, was nowhere to be seen at the moment. I had spied her earlier having her photos snapped by a professional photographer out in the gardens. She was showing off her figure and her goods in a form-fitting mermaid gown with enough sequins to cover three counties. Her half-exposed boobs stuck out for all of Ruby Lake to see.

I'd be settling for Gertie Hammer as my wedding photographer. The only real wedding photographer in town wanted something I didn't have—real money.

Derek had offered to cover all the related costs but he was already spending way too much on the wedding and the honeymoon. Gertie was providing us with her services for free. Well, that and giving her blog a mention in the next Birds & Bees newsletter and a twenty percent discount on everything in the store for the next twelve months.

"I can't wait until this day is over," Derek said. "You know I never wanted to come."

"I know." I patted his knee. He'd said that a hundred times already. And that was just on the drive out to Magnolia Manor this afternoon.

"I'm only doing it for Maeve."

"Yes, dear."

"Can you believe it?" he went on. "She insisted on keeping that restraining order on me for almost two whole months. Two whole months!"

"Shh. Not so loud." Curious faces peered at us.

"It was humiliating," he groused.

"It's all over now. Let's put it past us. Focus on the future. Our future."

"I'm trying," he said. "Being here just brings it all up again."

"We're getting married in a week, Derek. It's time to bury the hatchet. Let's all try to get along and be friends. Okay?"

"You're right, Amy. I really am looking forward to the wedding. Our wedding, that is."

"Good. Have you congratulated Amy and Tom?"

Derek admitted he had not. In fact, I noticed he had avoided going anywhere near Tom since the moment we arrived. "I'll congratulate the happy couple after the ceremony."

"That's my boy."

"But no way I will let them get away with moving Maeve to Nashville."

That was my boy, too.

It was time to change the subject.

"Who is that over there?" I pointed discreetly towards the elderly couple I had seen in conversation with Steve Sharpe. The woman was daubing her eyes with a white handkerchief.

"The parents."

"Whose?"

"Amy's. Needless to say, they hate me."

"That's their problem." I patted his firm thigh even as he began to rise. "Where are you going?"

Derek was looking red around the collar. "Little boy's room."

"The ceremony is going to start soon."

"I won't be long." Derek ducked his head and hurried away.

I sighed. "Poor Derek."

"Not to worry," offered Ben. "Derek will pull through fine. We need to get all this behind us and move on to some good news. Like your wedding."

"I know, Ben." Derek had had only court-supervised visits with Maeve and counseling up until a week ago. All of which had embarrassed and frustrated him immensely. Fortunately, the entire thing was behind us now.

"If only she hadn't blown the incident at the golf course out of proportion," Mom put in.

"If you ask me, it was Tom Visconti," said Derek's father, Ben. "When I tried to discuss the matter with him, he was quite intransigent. I get the feeling that man enjoys stirring up trouble."

"He's going to be Amy's trouble after today." For some wicked reason, that thought made me smile.

Derek reappeared, jostling my knee.

"What happened to your tie?"

"Huh?" Derek rubbed his throat with one hand. "I

was hot so I took it off. That's not the only thing bothering me. I think this shirt is too tight," he gave his collar a tug.

"What happened to your hand?" I lifted and inspected his right hand. It was covered with tiny scratch marks.

"I slipped on the path and brushed against some rose bushes." It had rained heavily the night before and certain areas of the grounds were muddy. I noticed thorn pricks in the sleeve of his jacket as well.

"Poor baby. We'll fix you up later."

Mom nudged us. "Quiet. I think the ceremony is about to begin."

"Where's the groom?" I swung my head around.

"I'm sure he'll be along any second."

The harpist had taken up her position on a small wooden stool beside her tall harp.

I stood.

"Where are you going?" whispered Derek. "You heard your mom, the ceremony is going to start any minute."

"I know," I whispered back. "This is your fault. Now I've got to go too." I figured I had at least five or ten minutes worth of harp music buffer before the ceremony proper.

I hurried down the grassy aisle towards the main buildings, which were a couple hundred yards away. To get there, guests had to navigate through one of two formal gardens. Although it was a bit more circuitous, I chose the one on the left because it seemed to be the higher ground.

If one was feeling lucky or plucky, one could take the shortcut through the maze garden. Of course, it was only a shortcut if you could navigate through it quickly.

I wasn't in the mood to test my navigational skills, neither was my bladder. I'd had too much tea with lunch.

Exiting the ladies room, I caught the sounds of the harp wafting through the warm air as if carried by gentle hands. The harpist was playing Bach's *Arioso*. It was a wonderful arrangement. But it meant that the time for the vows was probably getting close.

Too close.

I decided to cut through the maze garden to shave off some time. The last thing I needed was to be the last person sitting down for Amy Harlan's wedding vows. I would never hear the end of it from the woman. And I didn't want to give her any reason to make life more difficult for Derek.

Listening to the harp, I toyed with the idea of hiring the harpist to play a couple of tunes at our wedding next week.

I wondered if she knew any Broadway show tunes. In particular, my mother's favorite song: *Two Sleepy People* by Hoagy Carmichael and Frank Loesser. The song had been performed by the chanteuse and piano player hired to work Mom and Dad's wedding. Growing up, I'd sometimes catch them humming the sweet, soulful tune or whispering it in each other's ear.

Hitching up my skirt, I hurried into the maze garden. How hard could it be?

It didn't take me long to find out. One bush looked like another. One branch looked like another. Each path looked the same.

If only I were Ariadne and had a ball of string. Where was Esther when I needed her? She was bound to have a ball of yarn on her person somewhere. Sadly but predictably, Amy Harlan had not invited Esther to her wedding.

I struggled on. What choice did I have?

The hollies proved to be tougher than they looked. Prickly, too. After a minute or two of speed walking, I came to a dead end marked with a small stone bench.

Cursing, I turned around, moved left, right, then left. Then I backed up and moved right, left, right.

I was right back where I had started from. The stone bench seemed to be sneering at me. *I knew you'd be back,* it seemed to say.

I turned my back to it, darting my eyes to the left and right. I could definitely hear the music coming from somewhere to my right. Looking over the tall holly shrubs, the peaks of some pines became my inspiration. I remembered a stand of pines like that behind the gazebo.

Now all I had to do was keep my eyes on those treetops and my ears on the music. Unfortunately, the music came to an end about ninety seconds later, leaving me only the trees as my landmark.

At this point, I was contemplating forcing my way through the dense wall of shrubbery. Then again, I was also contemplating the damage such a brash charge might do to my flesh and the pretty new dress that Derek had bought me.

Of course, by now I could have been comfortably sitting beside my fiancé if I had simply gone the long way around.

Too late for that now. Fighting my mounting distress, I wiped the rising sweat from my brow and marched on, keeping my eyes on the tops of the pine trees in the distance. The good news was that they were getting closer.

That had to mean that the exit was close too.

Or so I thought.

I stopped, having reached another dead end. I backed out and made a sharp turn right and tripped. I threw out my hands to keep from hitting the ground face first. I bounced off the hollies, righted myself and looked to see what I had tripped over.

A pair of tuxedo trousers protruded from the wall of the maze. Two shiny black cowboy boots pointed towards the sky. The leathered bottoms revealed a hand-tooled ace of hearts on the left sole. The ace of diamonds featured on the sole of the right boot.

I frantically pulled back the hollies. A man's body lay tangled up amongst the branches, wedged between the V formed by two of the bushes.

The dead man's chin slumped forward on his chest. This man was no stranger. Amy Harlan was going to have to call off this wedding for good. Because the dead man was Tom Visconti.

10

"Help!" I jumped up and down, waving my arms in the hope that somebody would notice me. "Help!"

I heard a bustling in the hedgerow. Three house wrens flew off in a huff.

I ran up the next path and yelled so loud, my throat burned.

Moments later, Dan Sutton burst through the shrubbery, scattering leaves and twigs in his wake. Kim followed at his heels through the hole he had punched.

Kim's eyes were glaring and accusatory. Dan's were narrowed and alert.

More curious faces appeared on the other side of the hedge, peering anxiously through the shrubbery.

"What's wrong with you, Amy?" Kim huffed. "Look what you've done to my dress!" She tugged at the ragged tear running along the shoulder of her pink dress.

Dan grabbed my shoulders. "Are you all right?"

"What was it?" frowned Kim. "A fox? A bear?"

"It's Tom Visconti," I said.

"What about him?" complained Kim. "He should be on the gazebo. The ceremony is about to start."

"No, it's not," I said grimly. "Follow me."

"But everyone is waiting for the ceremony to start. Your shouting and disrupting the festivities has already got Amy-the-ex steaming mad."

"This is an emergency."

"It better be, for your sake," Kim replied.

"Come on," I urged.

Dan shrugged his shoulders helplessly in Kim's direction, saying "She's your friend," and followed me. Rounding the corner of the maze, Tom Visconti's legs blocked our path. Dan crouched beside the body and quickly checked for a pulse.

"Is he—" Kim couldn't bring herself to say the word.

Dan shook his head in the affirmative.

Kim dug her nails into my arm.

"What happened to him? Was it a stroke?"

Tom Visconti's blotchy face and sagging flesh made him look much older than his years. I pictured the now-dead groom nervously pacing alone in the maze garden awaiting the marriage ceremony. Had the stress gotten to him?

"Could he have keeled over and fallen into the bushes?"

"No." Dan patted his pockets and came out with his cell phone. "Did you touch anything, Amy?"

"Only the bushes."

"Not Visconti?"

"No."

"Let's move back. Watch where you step. There could be clues. Footprints."

"Footprints?" Kim scanned the soft ground.

Dan ignored her. "Hello, Chief? It's me. I'm out at Magnolia Manor and I think you'd better get out here."

Kim and I heard squawking coming out of Dan's phone. Jerry didn't sound happy.

"Yes, sir." Dan mindfully lowered his voice, frowning

at the nosy faces peeking through the hollies. "There's been a death." More squawking followed. "Yes, Chief. I think you should bring Larry and Al. You're going to be wanting an ambulance. Greeley too."

Andrew Greeley served as Ruby Lake's coroner. He also owned the local mortuary. Folks joked that he had a one-man monopoly on the dead in our little town.

Dan ended the phone call. He shooed us further back from the possible crime scene and took several cell phone shots of Tom Visconti and the surroundings.

"What's going on?"

I recognized Derek's voice and turned around. His ex-wife was clutching his arm. Under the circumstances, I resisted the urge to pry her loose.

"There's been an accident. I need everyone to keep back." Dan held out his arms authoritatively.

"Is that Tom?" Amy Harlan pushed free of Derek and surged forward.

Dan grabbed for her and missed. "Please, Ms. Harlan!"

"Tom!" Amy Harlan screamed like a hawk, high-pitched and blood chilling. She swung around. Dan reached for her again. She batted his hands away and leapt at me. "What did you do?" Her fingers wrapped around my throat.

The woman was throttling me. I was too surprised to move or scream.

My eyes bulged.

Fortunately, Dan and Derek had the sense to stop her before she did any real damage.

"Are you crazy?" I clutched my throat.

"You killed him!"

"I didn't kill him." I stopped, trying to rub away the pain ringing my neck. "I found him."

"Come on, Amy," Derek said softly, running his hand along his ex-wife's arm. "It's not Amy's fault."

"Sure," said Kim, coming to my side, "I'm sure Amy only tried to help."

"I did. The minute I saw Tom lying there, I shouted for help." Digging deep into my heart, reaching for sympathy rather than a club to beat the woman who'd just tried to strangle me, I added, "I am sorry, Amy. Really sorry."

Tears welled up in Amy Harlan's eyes, dark mascara cascaded down the sides of her cheeks. Derek laid a hand over her shoulder.

"Was it his heart?" asked the bride-never-to-be. "You'd never know it but Tom had a weak heart. Only about eighteen months ago, he told me he suffered a heart attack." She cried like a baby bird.

"This was no heart attack," Dan replied.

"What was it?" I asked the question that everybody was wanting to know the answer to.

"We'll have to wait for the medical examiner to say for sure but, in my opinion, Tom Visconti was strangled."

"Strangled?" My hands flew back to my throat.

"That means murdered." Kim paled.

"Are you sure Visconti didn't die of natural causes, Dan?" Derek asked. "You heard my ex."

"I'm no expert, Derek, but judging by the marks around Tom Visconti's neck, I'd say it is a good bet we are looking at murder."

That meant we were looking for a murderer.

Amy Harlan fainted. Derek caught her as she fell to the ground.

"There's a bench around the corner." I grabbed her

feet and helped carry her over. Derek settled her down on the bench. Kim ran to fetch her some water back at the main house. I feared she was going to need something much, much stronger.

After checking that his ex would be okay, Derek stood and pulled me aside. "I'd better go let Reverend Steve know what's transpired. Amy's parents, too," he added somberly.

"You are leaving me alone here? With her?"

"Come on, Amy. She's distraught. She needs a shoulder to cry on. A female shoulder."

"Does Tom Visconti have family here for the wedding? Like a sister or a daughter? Third cousin once removed?" I'd take anyone I could get.

"His folks are deceased. His son is attending today, according to Amy." He motioned towards his ex, seated stonily on the bench but for the tears dribbling down her chin. "I have no idea where his first wife is."

Derek planted a soft kiss on my jowl. "I'll be right back."

He disappeared around the corner. Amy Harlan's moans mingled with the blare of sirens as police cars roared into the parking lot. Not long after, the sound of Chief Jerry Kennedy and company thrashing through the gardens reached my ears.

Stealth was not his main suit. He'd never make it as a bird watcher.

"Where is she?" Chief Kennedy bellowed.

"It's a he and he's over here, Chief" came Officer Dan Sutton's reply from the other side of the wall of shrubbery.

Chief Kennedy, followed by Officers Larry Reynolds and Albert Pratt, scuttled past us. They were, in turn, shadowed by two grim EMTs laden down with gear.

I knew Andrew Greeley would be along later rather than sooner. Our coroner is over seventy years old. He is a sweet old thing but he's no Speedy Gonzalez.

I patted Amy Harlan's knee. "How are you holding up? I wonder what is taking Kim so long."

Amy Harlan sniffled. I handed her a paper tissue. Mud and grass stains covered the bottom hem of her wedding dress. "Poor Tom." She shredded the tissue in her fingers. The tatters fell to her lap. She brushed the damp bits to the ground.

Amy Harlan locked her blue eyes on me. "I told Tom we shouldn't get married here in Ruby Lake. Let's go someplace else, I said. Someplace romantic. Like Fiji. Maybe Maui."

Sobs racked her body, forcing her to stop. After regaining control, she continued. "But he insisted we hold the wedding here."

"Why not Nashville?"

"Nashville?"

"That is where you were planning on moving afterward."

"Nashville? Who told you that? Are you crazy? Cowboy hats and hootenannies?"

I've been to Nashville. It is so much more than that but I was not going to argue the point. Not now.

After a shake of her head, she muttered, "Look who I'm asking. Nashville. Please. I'd rather be dead." Her eyes widened in horror as she realized what she had said. "Oh!"

Once again, salty tears rolled down her eyes. She grabbed her lace veil from behind her head and swiped at them with the hem.

I had no words to console her with. What had happened today, I wouldn't have wished on my worst enemy. I took her hand. This was the first time that I had seen her engagement ring up close. I'd never realized what a big diamond Tom Visconti had given her.

"Simms!"

We both raised our eyes.

"What is it, Jerry?"

"Dan tells me you were the one who reported the dead guy."

I leapt up, grabbing Jerry by the shoulders. "The dead guy, as you say had a name, Jerry. It's Tom. And he is, was, Amy's fiancé."

Chief Kennedy appeared nonplussed. "What did I do?"

"Show a little compassion," I whispered harshly. "She has just lost her fiancé. This was supposed to be her wedding day."

Now it was turning out to be a funeral of sorts.

"Yeah, yeah." He pushed me away.

"You're still bent out of shape because she didn't invite you to the wedding, aren't you?"

"Don't be ridiculous. Go away and let me do my job."

"Fine. I've seen enough. I'm leaving." I turned to do just that.

"Wait." Chief Kennedy ordered. "Dan says you found him off the path?"

"That's right. Mostly in the bushes, except for his feet."

"In the bushes? What were you doing in the bushes? More of that stupid bird watching?"

"I got mixed up in this stupid maze. I was trying to get back. I tripped and when I looked down to see what

I had hit, I saw a pair of cowboy boots. Then I looked in the bushes and saw Tom Visconti lying there."

"What was he doing in the bushes?"

"I don't know. You figure it out, Jerry. That is your job." A job he could do better if he stopped ogling Amy Harlan's boobs.

Amy Harlan trembled and shook and blubbered.

"Now look what you've done," complained Chief Kennedy, hands on his hips, looking helplessly at the deeply troubled abandoned bride.

Although I wasn't exactly sure that having your soon-to-be husband drop dead or get murdered right before the vows were to be spoken could be considered abandonment, at least not deliberate.

Kim came running up the uneven path, bottle of champagne in hand. "I couldn't find any water bottles so I brought this." She slammed to a stop in front of Amy Harlan and, squeezing the bottle between her knees, popped the cork.

The cork blew sky high with a loud pop. A geyser of cold champagne shot out. Amy Harlan screamed. "My dress!"

"Sorry." Kim dabbed at Amy Harlan's gown with her hands. "So sorry."

Amy Harlan snatched the bottle from Kim's hands then pushed her off. "Get away from me."

"Sorry." Kim stepped as far back as the hedge would allow.

"Chief," Amy Harlan said regally, "I want that woman arrested." She had her fingers wrapped around the champagne bottle's neck. Not unlike how she had earlier had her fingers wrapped around my neck.

"It's only a little champagne," Kim retorted. "It will

come right out."

"Not you. Her."

Why was I not surprised she was pointing that accusatory finger at me?

"What did I do?"

"You say you found Tom. Maybe you did. Maybe," she suggested, "you found him and killed him."

Chief Kennedy looked at me. I could see he was considering her words.

"You are actually taking her accusation seriously, Jerry? Give me a break." I focused on Amy Harlan. "Why on earth would I kill your fiancé?"

"Because you were jealous. Jealous of me. Jealous of my position. You wanted Tom for yourself."

"That's ridiculous. I don't give a hoot about you. As for your position, why don't you bend over and I'll show you a new position."

I was trying desperately to maintain my cool under the circumstances but Amy Harlan wasn't making it easy for me.

"Liz told me she saw her leave right before the ceremony was to begin, Chief Kennedy," Amy Harlan continued. "Why? Is it a coincidence that she left and now Tom is dead? Strangled, according to your own officer?"

Jerry nodded. "It does look like somebody choked him with something. Greeley showed up a minute ago and that was the first thing he suggested. Maybe a rope. He isn't quite sure yet."

"Where were you?" I hollered back. Our truce hadn't lasted long. "We didn't see you until it was time for your vows. And where's Tom been all this time? How'd he end up here?"

"This is all your fault, Simms. You've ruined everything." She took a slug from the champagne bottle then tossed it to the ground.

"My fault? I'm the one who found the body." I was repeating myself.

"Yes, isn't it odd, Chief Kennedy, how it's always Amy Simms who finds the dead body?"

Jerry Kennedy was looking at me. And not in a good way.

11

"What's going on here?" demanded a man in a crisp charcoal pinstripe suit. That man was Robert "Bobby" Breen, Tom Visconti's best man.

I had met him an hour earlier during the cocktail hour. He was a tall, stocky man, the way a college football player gets when he has gone to seed. His thinning blond hair was held back with shiny gel. His voice was loud and deep like he was shouting up from the bottom of a stone-lined well.

"Bobby!" Amy Harlan threw herself into his arms.

Looking over her shoulder, Bobby Breen flashed his dark eyes at Chief Kennedy. "You in charge here?"

"That's right, I am. Who might you be?"

Hands planted on Amy's shoulders, he puffed out his chest. "Robert Breen. Tom's best man and business partner."

"I see," answered Chief Kennedy. "I'm gonna have questions for you, seeing as how you were friends with the deceased."

"So it's true?" Bobby Breen glanced at Amy Harlan, who nodded silently. "Tom's dead?"

"Strangled," said Chief Kennedy. Those callous words set Amy Harlan off on another crying jag.

I scolded him with my eyes.

"Strangled?" Bobby Breen raised a hand to his neck. Like Tom Visconti, he wore a bolo tie. His had a turquoise stone mounted in a silver setting. He wore the same brand black cowboy boots too. "Who did it?"

"It's a little early to say," Chief Kennedy admitted. "Unless you've got something to tell me?"

Bobby Breen held his tongue.

Turning to Deputy Reynolds, the chief said, "I want everybody here interviewed. Nobody leaves."

"What about the Magnolia Manor staff, Chief?" Larry Reynolds stands about six foot tall, with thinning blond hair and a pinkish complexion. He's a quiet man in his mid-forties and never been married. Somehow, his brown uniform always looked far more rumpled than those of his comrades.

"They're here, aren't they? When I say I want you to interview everybody, I mean everybody. Somebody must have seen something, heard something." He sucked in a breath. "And one of them must be guilty of murder."

"Does Mr. Greeley have any idea what time he was killed?" I asked.

"Within the hour. That's all he's saying." Chief Kennedy slapped his holster in frustration.

That fit. He'd been present during cocktail hour. When had he disappeared? And why?

"The murderer could be miles away from here by now, Chief Kennedy," countered Bobby Breen.

"Let's hope not for your friend's sake." Chief Kennedy turned and marched off. Over his shoulder, he ordered for Officers Reynolds and Sutton to see that everyone was gathered in the main building for interviews. "Pronto!"

"What about Amy? She's been through enough, Chief." Bobby Breen wrapped his arm around the bride' waist. "Why don't I take her home? You can interview her later."

Chief Kennedy spun round on his heels. He hated to appear like he was backing down but, under the circumstances, he reluctantly agreed. "Don't go leaving town."

"Don't leave town? The dear woman was supposed to be departing on her honeymoon tomorrow," Bobby Breen said derisively. "Do you seriously think she had anything to do with this, Chief?"

"If you're asking me if I think she killed the man, I—"

Amy's face was mottled red, swollen, and wet with tears. Her gown was filthy. Her husband-to-be was lying dead with his toes pointing skyward.

"I do!" said Vail Visconti, Tom's son, bursting in amongst us. "You're not going to get away with this!" he raged, waving his fist in Amy Harlan's direction. "Never. Do you hear?"

Vail was a snotty, twenty-one-year-old kid. At least, that was the impression he'd given me when I had met him earlier during cocktails. He'd shown up in a baggy brown suit, a loud chartreuse tie and canvas sneakers that looked like he'd drawn on them with colored markers. His hair hung over his ears. He was rail thin and pale as a pitcher of milk.

He had a mouth. And a temper.

"You're drunk," scolded Bobby Breen.

"And you're a crook and she's a slut." Vail lunged forward and took a swing at Bobby.

Bobby smashed his fist into Vail's face. Vail went down.

Chief Kennedy thumped Bobby in the chest. "That's

enough of that now."

Kim and I scooped Vail up. He was fuming and wiping the blood from his swelling lip.

"You'll pay for that," he vowed. I handed him a tissue and he dabbed the blood.

"We done here, Chief?"

"Yeah, you can git. But mind what I said."

With Amy Harlan's arm locked with his, Bobby Breen shouldered past Vail.

Vail's face flared red. "Are you just going to let them go, Sheriff?"

"That's, Chief. Ms. Harlan has had a terrible shock. She needs her rest. And you need to watch your mouth. Shouldn't talk about a lady like that, let alone your stepmom."

"She's not my stepmother and never will be."

"Yeah, that's true, isn't it?" Chief Kennedy eyed the young man with suspicion.

"She probably strangled Dad herself. And you're letting her get away."

"Who said anything about strangling?" Chief Kennedy asked.

"What?" Vail winced as he dabbed his lip with fresh tissue.

"You mentioned that your daddy was strangled."

"Did I? So what? I heard one of the guests mention it, that's all. What? You think I did it?" He threw his head back and laughed. "Is everybody in this hick town stupid?"

Chief Kennedy stared at the young man standing mere inches from him. "Son, I am going to let that go because you have had quite a shock yourself. Shock does things to people. Now, you are going to join the others up at the house. Me or one of my men will be along to interview you."

"I've got nothing to say," said Vail Visconti, tossing the blood-soaked tissue to the ground.

"You want to help us find the man who murdered your dad, don't you?"

Vail frowned. "Of course." In frustration, he grabbed a branch of holly and stripped it, letting the leaves fall to his feet. "I'll be inside."

As much as Chief Kennedy might have liked to sequester his herd of potential witnesses to keep them from talking too much amongst themselves and spoiling their stories, the only place large enough to accommodate the crowd was the indoor ballroom, which had been used for another event the day before.

The paper banner strung overhead read: *Congratulations On Your First 50 Years – Henny and Henry Smith.*

Black tablecloths draped the tables. Most still held soiled napkins and empty bread baskets.

"It was a lovely anniversary party," said Ben Harlan. He and my Mom had attended the Smiths' anniversary party. Ben squeezed Mom's hand. "How are you holding up? Shall I ask Chief Kennedy to allow you to go home?"

"No, I'll be fine. It's nice to sit down."

"This is ridiculous," Derek complained. He tugged at his watch. "It's taking the police forever to interview everybody. We'll be here all night at this rate. Chief Kennedy should let us all go home."

"Relax, son. There's nothing much we can do but wait. Care for another drink?" He lifted the champagne bottle near his elbow. Fortunately, the caterer had carried all the food and drinks indoors for us.

"I'll take some." I held up my glass. "At least we won't starve or go thirsty." I sipped thoughtfully. "Who would want to murder Tom Visconti?"

"And on his wedding day," said Mom. "What a shame."

"Wait," I said suddenly. "Where's Maeve?"

"With her mom. Chief Kennedy at least had the sense to let all the kids go home. Even he couldn't suspect them of murder. Larry shuttled them home in the school van."

"There's one I could suspect," I replied.

"Who?" Derek lifted his eyes from the salad bowl in front of him that he'd been stabbing aimlessly into.

"Vail Visconti." The young man was lying supine on the foot-high raised stage in the back of the tall-ceilinged room. His feet dangled off the edge, kicking lazily.

"The son?" Mom turned to look.

"Don't stare at him," I whispered.

"Why him?" asked Ben, who had also taken a peek in Vail's direction.

"Vail was really laying into Jerry earlier. And his dad's choice in brides. He accused Amy Harlan of murdering his father. And look at him."

Heads turned once more.

"Does he look broken up to you about the death of his dad?" I asked.

"Not really," agreed Mom.

"He looks more bored than anything," agreed Derek.

"Exactly." I slathered a cold sourdough roll with butter and chomped down. "Vail Visconti has the look of a killer."

"Patricide is a pretty heinous thing to consider," remarked Derek.

"I'm glad to hear you say that," chuckled his dad.

"How can you tell?" whispered Mom. "I mean, that a person looks like a killer?"

"I just can," I said.

"You know your daughter, Barbara." Derek grinned. "Amy can recognize a murderer as well as she can identify a bird. Maybe better."

"Ha-ha. I think I'll go give my condolences." I brushed a cloth napkin over my lips and stood.

"Too late," said Derek. "Vail's got company."

I frowned. "Isn't that Tom Visconti's assistant, Gloria?"

"Yep. That's her husband, Mark, with her."

"You know them?" I asked. Mark Bolan was a rather doughy figure, with short dark hair, a rounded face and shoulders. His brown suit was rumpled and ill-fitting.

"Vaguely. They live in Rivercrest. Mark is retired. I've seen him out on the driving range a couple of times. Never said more than hi."

"He's a little young to be retired, isn't he?" remarked Ben. Derek's dad was in his sixties and had no intention of retiring anytime soon.

"Health problems. I think he mentioned once that golf was suggested to him as physical therapy."

Mark and Gloria Bolan stood in front of the stage speaking with Vail Visconti. He had an icepack in his hand that he occasionally applied to his face. There was no way to hear what was being said.

Whatever it was, it wasn't making Tom Visconti's son happy. He jumped to his feet and said loud enough for everyone to hear, "Buzz off."

Tossing the icepack across the room, Vail bounded from the stage and exited through a door that led to the kitchen.

"I wonder what that was all about?" Ben remarked.

"I think I'll go find out." My curiosity was aroused. I hadn't liked Tom Visconti from what little I'd gotten to know him, but he had been savagely murdered and I had found his body. Had the killer been lurking nearby in the garden maze, mere steps from me?

That was a chilling thought.

Derek grabbed my hand. "No, you don't. Stay out of this one, Amy."

"But—"

"Please. We're getting married in a week. I don't want anything happening to you in the meantime."

"Does that mean you still want to get married?"

"What are you saying?" Derek looked shocked. "Of course, I do. Don't you?"

"Yes," I said quickly. "I only thought...I mean, under the circumstances, I thought maybe you would like to cancel it—"

"Cancel our wedding? Not on your life!"

"I didn't mean forever."

"Amy!" Mom looked aghast.

"And I didn't mean cancel exactly, Mom. Poor choice of words." I turned quickly to Derek. "I meant postpone it."

"Were you thinking of postponing the wedding, son?" Ben asked.

"No, Dad. And I don't want to." Derek appeared to hesitate but only for a moment. "Life is too short. Unless Amy wants to." He squeezed my hand.

I fought back the tears. "Not by even one minute." Derek was right. Life was too short and for Tom Visconti it had come to an early and abrupt end.

"Look what I found!"

All heads turned to see Kim awkwardly rolling a monstrous wedding cake on a four-wheeled cart between the tables.

"Where did you get that?" I gawked at the cake.

"I found it in the kitchen. Can you believe it?" Kim was all smile. "It was just sitting there."

"So you took it?" I pictured Amy Harlan's revenge and it was not a pretty sight.

I came to my feet and marveled. The delicate fondant-covered cake stood taller than me. It was sitting on a table but, still, even without the height advantage it would have come nearly to my chest.

Amy and Tom's seven-tiered masterpiece was done in all silvers and whites with gray pearl accents. The cake topper featured Eros posing with his bow and quiver. A heart-shaped arrow was locked and loaded.

"I think they were going to throw it away." Kim poked a hole in the fondant, stuck her thumb in the side of the cake and removed a chunk of frosting.

"No way."

"Yep." Kim quickly popped the creamy blob in her mouth and smacked her lips. "Who's going to miss it?"

"Where did they get a cake like this?" I wanted to know. I couldn't think of any place in Ruby Lake that could have produced this masterpiece.

"Liz told me Amy Harlan ordered from some chichi bakery in Charlotte."

"Wow." The three-level tower of cupcakes that Derek and I had ordered for our wedding from *C Is For Cupcakes* paled in comparison. Our wedding topper was going to feature a pair of plastic lovebirds that I had ordered from a bird lover's gift catalog, not some hand-carved cherub.

Kim grabbed an intricately carved, silver cake knife from the cart. "Who wants a slice?"

Every hand at the table went up. So did those at every table nearby. I reluctantly raised my hand too. What the heck, Amy Harlan couldn't kill us all.

"Did you see Vail?" I asked Kim, as she sliced up the cake and divvied up the pieces using the plates located on the cart's lower shelf.

"No, should I have?"

"I saw him go to the kitchen."

"I noticed a bunch of employees. That's all." Kim cut a big slab of cake and laid it on a china plate. "Have you seen Dan? I think I'll see if he's hungry?"

"Last I saw him, he was standing outside the event manager's office," Derek said. The event manager's office was located directly off the main hall. "Chief Kennedy is using the office as his makeshift headquarters."

"Thanks." Kim headed toward the entrance with a slab of cake for her and another for Dan.

MC and the Moonlighters appeared from the kitchen. The musicians lugged their instruments to the stage.

"Who's in the mood for a little music?" hollered MC, jumping up on the stage with a thump and a wide grin on his long, narrow face.

The band scurried around the stage, setting up a drum kit, an electric piano and speakers. The bass player had an upright bass and the guitarist a green and red electric guitar with a small amp. The conga-playing percussionist tapped out a bouncy rhythm to wake the crowd up from their I'm-supposed-to-be-at-a-wedding-but-now-I'm-sitting-around-waiting-to-be-interviewed-by-the-police-in-a-murder-investigation torpor.

"Music? At a time like this?" Mom scolded. "It seems in poor taste."

I offered to go talk to them. "Should you really be doing this?" I asked the leader, MC. "You must have heard about Tom Visconti's horrible death." They were musicians and I sometimes got the impression that such folk lived in a different version of reality from the rest of us, but still. "The wedding is off."

"Yeah. Tough break that. Good thing we got paid in advance. MC doesn't work for free."

"Right." I really couldn't think of anything better to say. "Have you seen Vail?"

"Tom's kid?" MC sneered. "Yeah, I saw the runt. He was sneaking out the kitchen door. He made a beeline for his car."

Up close, I could see the craters on MC's face. He was a gone-to-fat sixty-year old with a bad hairpiece and strong cologne. He had removed his tie somewhere along the way and unbuttoned his shirt far enough to show a tangle of hair that he no doubt considered a macho chick magnet.

Personally, I considered it gorilla-like. No offense to gorillas.

"He left? Without talking to Chief Kennedy?" Jerry was going to be mad as a hornet who's been kicked out of his nest.

"I wouldn't know, lady. Now," he rubbed his hands together, "what song of mine would you like to hear? How about *Magic In Your Eyes*? Went to number three in the charts back in seventy-nine."

"Know any funeral dirges?" I replied.

"Tsk-tsk. My job is to pick people up. Make them

dance." He turned to the Moonlighters. "Right, boys?"

A chorus of mumbled yeses came in reply.

"I've got a disco arrangement of Chopin's Funeral March." Without waiting to be asked, the keyboard player launched into his arrangement. The bass player thumped out a pulse.

The horn player's hand hovered briefly over his instruments, trombone, trumpet and sax. The musician had full lips and a wild shock of red hair that stuck a good six inches up in the air. Red selected his trumpet and screwed on the mouthpiece.

Quickly, as if responding to some primordial reflex, the guitarist, drummer and conga player joined in.

MC tapped his foot and clapped his hands. "I dig it, man. I dig it."

Steve Sharpe joined them on stage, clasping a battered acoustic guitar by the neck. "Thanks for letting me sit in, MC. This is a dream come true."

"No problem, man."

"Hi, Amy. Sticking around for the show?" asked the officiant.

Had the whole world gone mad?

"At least until Chief Kennedy tells us we can leave."

"That's what we like, don't we, boys?" quipped MC. "A captive audience."

"Yeah," said Steve, fingers fiddling with the tuning pegs of his guitar. "He just got done grilling me. Not that there was anything I could tell him."

Seeing the harpist seated alone in the back of the banquet hall, Steve waved her to the stage. "Do you mind, MC?"

"The more the merrier. I've never *had* a harp player. In the band, that is." MC gave Steve a nudge.

Ick.

This guy was the definition of sleazy.

I left in a hurry. It isn't all that easy to murder a dead man but MC and the Moonlighters were doing a bang up job of murdering long dead Frederic Chopin.

12

Instead of returning to our table, I motioned to Derek and the others that I was heading to the kitchen. There, I discovered several staffers in black Magnolia Manor polo shirts carrying boxes of supplies out to a waiting truck.

"Excuse me, I'm looking for a young man. Straggly dark hair, looks like a bleached out scarecrow?" with Vail's obvious short temper, it was a good thing he wasn't around to hear my less than flattering description of him.

"Yeah, son of the dead man," said one well-muscled young man. He tossed a three-foot square cardboard box to a coworker. "I saw him."

"Where did he go?"

"He left out the back door." The worker picked up another carton from the floor.

That information jibed with what MC had told me. I gazed through the open exit door leading to a parking lot with a half dozen cars scattered about. There was no sign of Vail Visconti in any of them.

I sidestepped the chair holding the door open. "Did he say anything before he left? Like where he was going?"

"Not to me, he didn't," answered the employee. "He

and Mickey had a few words for one another. Not friendly ones either." His coworkers, who had stopped to eavesdrop, snickered. "But that was maybe twenty minutes ago."

"Really? Who's Mickey?"

"Mickey Caswell." Noting the blank look on my face, he added, "You know, MC."

I gave myself a dope slap. "Of course. MC. They argued? About what?"

"What's going on here?" A dour-faced man in a stiff suit and squeaky brown shoes stepped into the kitchen clutching a clipboard. "These party supplies should have been loaded up an hour ago."

"Sorry, sir." The young man gave me an ugly look, like the scolding was all my fault, and quickly returned to his duties.

I left the kitchen and made a beeline back to the stage. MC was belting out another of his interminable disco hits. The band made quite a noise for having such a small, impromptu PA system. I cupped my palms over my ears until he finished.

"You're back," MC said, swaggering over and exhibiting a disquieting leer. "What would you like to hear?"

"I'd like to hear what you and Vail Visconti were arguing about earlier in the kitchen."

A small, dark cloud passed between MC's big black eyebrows. "Who said we were arguing?"

"A little birdie told me."

"Well, your little birdie should keep its big beak shut." MC stomped off.

"Wait!" I ran after him. "I'm sorry. I didn't mean to be sharp. It's this whole murder thing. It's got me upset."

MC hooked his thumb over his wide leather belt and

took a step back in my direction. As he bobbed his head, the skin under his chin rippled. "Sure, I get that. Nasty business."

"I'm Amy Simms." I extended my hand.

That elicited a smile. "I'd introduce myself but I'm sure you know who I am."

Oh, brother. That line sounded well-rehearsed. Like he had said it a thousand times before. I ponied up a smile.

"Of course, everyone knows who you are. Who wouldn't? You know, my mom, Barbara Simms—that's her sitting right over there." I pointed Mom out.

She looked startled but managed to smile and wave when MC wriggled his fingers at her. "She is your biggest fan, MC. We had all your records growing up."

I seemed to remember throwing two of them out my bedroom window. Firstly, to get them out of the house. Secondly, to see how far they'd fly.

MC seemed to inflate before my eyes. His blue eyes glittered with memories of faded glory. "Your mother is a discerning lady." He leaned closer, resting a finger lightly on the tip of my chin. "And she passed her beauty genes on to you."

"Thanks," I resisted the urge to shake wildly like a dog trying to shed a tick. "That's my fiancé over there. See him? The big strong guy in the dark blue suit."

"Fiancé, huh?" He withdrew his hand and grunted.

"We gonna play or what, MC?" hollered the drummer, giving the kick drum a tap with his foot.

"Yeah, yeah. In a minute," MC snarled over his shoulder. Turning his attention back to me, he said, "Sorry, duty calls."

"Right. Before I go, do you have any idea who would

want to murder Tom Visconti?"

"What are you, a cop?"

"No, I own a bird supply shop."

"A bird supply shop? What kinda supplies might a bird need?"

"It is a store for bird watching enthusiasts. You know, we sell birdseed, nesting boxes—"

"Yeah, yeah." He threw out his hands to stop me. "I get the picture. And no, I have no idea who would want to kill this Mr. Visconti. I barely knew the man. In fact, I never met him before today."

"Then how did you get the gig? Did you know Amy Harlan?"

"No. Visconti, or one of his people maybe, contacted my booking agent and set the gig up. I show up, do my thing, I get paid. End of story."

"Is that why you're performing now?"

"That's right. No play, no pay. The wedding might have ended earlier than expected but, like they say, the show must go on. Don't want anybody saying I didn't earn my fee."

I wasn't sure that adage about the show going on held true in the light of murder but I also saw nothing to gain in arguing the point with MC.

"About Vail..."

"I got nothing to say. The scrawny kid bumped into me and started running off his mouth, ranting about the murder."

"Like what?"

"Hell if I know. Kid made no sense. I couldn't wait to get away from him. We done here?"

"Sure, one last thing though."

"What?"

"Like I said, I am getting married next week. We have a local DJ spinning records."

"Good for you."

"Thanks, but a live band would be nice."

"Can't beat the live beat," MC quipped.

"Right." I cleared my throat. "So, just out of curiosity, how much do you charge for doing a wedding reception?"

MC scratched the top of his head. "I'd have to check with my agent to see what my schedule is like. You're giving me sort of short notice. The band might be otherwise engaged."

"Of course."

"But fifty should cover it."

I beamed. Even I could afford that. "Is that per person or for the whole band?"

"What you see," he said, jerking toward his Moonlighters, "is what you get. Hotel and food are gonna cost you extra. That means a suite for me and a couple of rooms for the guys to share."

"All for fifty dollars?" I wasn't one to tell a man how to run his business but even I knew that was crazy cheap.

MC withered me with a sour look. "Add a few zeros to that, bird lady."

I gulped. "How many zeros?"

MC laughed. "Hell if I know. I'm a musician, not a mathematician. Enough to add up to fifty thousand dollars."

"I'll let you know," I managed to blurt out in a daze before I quickly retreated to our table.

Two long hours later, we were allowed to leave. "It's

about time," I moaned to no one in particular.

We had watched jealously as person after person dribbled out the door, allowed to return to their homes after being interviewed by Chief Kennedy and his minions.

"He saved me for last on purpose," I complained. "All that boring waiting around and I had nothing new to tell him."

"Count yourself lucky," Derek said. "By the time he got around to us, his voice was shot and he was exhausted. He told me himself that all he wanted to do was go home and plop himself down in front of the boob tube with a cold beer. I wouldn't mind doing the same myself."

"I suppose you're right." I picked up my purse. "This day hasn't turned out the way I had planned." A nice meal, dancing with Derek under the stars.

"This day hasn't turned out the way anyone wanted," Derek said. "Except maybe whoever killed Tom Visconti."

"That would mean Tom Visconti's death was premeditated. That's a chilling thought."

"Yeah, who goes to a wedding planning to murder the groom?" Derek wondered aloud.

"I hope nobody gets a similar idea next week."

Derek's mouth fell open. "Don't even say that, Amy."

"Sorry." I kissed his cheek.

"I suggest we stop talking or even thinking about murder anymore today."

"Deal," I promised. "I didn't mean to spook you."

"Well, I don't mind admitting you did." Derek offered to bring the car around. Mom had come with Ben. He was giving her a lift back to our place.

Mark and Gloria Bolan were among the few guests left. They sat alone at a big round table in the corner. An empty bottle of champagne sat on the table between them.

Mark sat nursing a plastic cup of bubbly. We had been informed two hours earlier by the event manager that the food and drinks had officially stopped flowing and the servers, with Chief Kennedy's permission, sent home.

Gloria Bolan saw me standing alone. She turned to her husband and spoke a few words. He nodded and tossed back his drink.

I watched him stumble toward the front exit, tossing the plastic cup toward a gaping black trash bag. His aim was off. The plastic cup hit the side of the bag and rolled to the wood floor. He didn't bother stopping to pick it up.

Gloria Bolan approached me with a soggy, wadded up tissue in her hand.

"Ms. Simms?"

"That's right, Amy."

Gloria Bolan nodded, as if to indicate that I'd gotten my name right. "I'm Gloria Bolan."

"Yes, I heard you were Tom's assistant. I am so sorry. Now if you'll excuse me, my fiancé is bringing the car around." I muffled a yawn with the back of my hand. "It's been a long day. For all of us."

"Yes, it has."

Up close, something about Gloria Bolan's face struck me as being out of proportion. Her eyes were too small, her cheeks too pronounced. The warmth of her brown eyes, however, had not been diminished by her tears or the interminably long wait we had all endured.

Tom Visconti's assistant, now former assistant, wore a pale pink dress with a demure neckline decorated with a string of small butter-colored pearls, and low-heeled shoes. She exuded a hint of rose.

Gloria was not a beautiful woman by any means but she had a certain sex appeal and charm.

"Before you leave, I was hoping I might have a word with you, Amy." Gloria laid a hand on my forearm. Her polished fingernails were clipped short and painted a darker shade of pink.

"About what?" Over her shoulder, I noticed Derek idling behind the wheel of his silver Civic.

Mark Bolan was pacing back and forth out in the parking lot, puffing on a cigarette. Not the smartest move for a man who had had to retire early due to health problems. But who was I to judge?

Gloria sniffled and stuffed the soiled tissue into the maw of her black patent leather clutch bag. "I want you to find out who murdered Tom."

"You want me to—"

"Tom was a good man," she steamrolled over my words. "He didn't deserve to die like that."

Gripping her hands in mine, I said, "Believe me, Gloria, I know how you feel. Nobody deserves to be cut down in their prime. Were you and Mr. Visconti close?"

"I was employed by him for nearly four years now. I started working for Tom, Mr. Visconti, in the Nashville office. Then he transferred me here to help in getting the Rivercrest project off the ground."

Fresh tears spilled down her cheeks. "I suppose the project will die now that he's dead."

There was a lost look in Gloria Bolan's puffy brown eyes. I couldn't help wondering whether it was for loss of her boss or loss of her job.

"I'm sorry," I repeated. "I wish I could help but there's nothing I can do. I barely knew your boss. All I did was find him in the maze garden. Do you know what he was doing out there?"

"No." She dabbed the corners of her eyes with a fresh ball of tissue. "He did say he wanted to clear his head, collect his thoughts before the ceremony," she remembered. "He was into meditation. I suppose he went for a walk in the garden to get away from everything."

A walk straight to his death. This raised so many questions. Who had he met? Or had someone accompanied him? Did the police check for other footprints?

I'd have to check with Dan or Jerry. Though I'd only met him briefly, Tom Visconti did not strike me as the type of man into meditation.

"No, wait. I'm sorry, Gloria. I can't help you. I'm getting married in a week. In fact, like I said, my fiancé is waiting for me now." I began edging past her.

"Please." She grabbed my arm. "You've got to help. You've solved so many murders. I know you can help."

"As flattered as I am, why don't we leave it to the police to find your boss's killer? That is their job. It's what they do."

"Are you kidding me?" Gloria sneered derisively. "That dumb cop interviewed me for twenty minutes. Believe me, Amy, Chief Kennedy doesn't know what he's doing."

It was hard to argue with her there.

"I hear you're the real crime solver in this town."

Again, I couldn't argue with that. "But, I repeat, I am getting married. In one week. One week," I said again, holding my index finger in the air between us for emphasis.

"I'll pay you," Gloria offered. She reached into her clutch and pulled out a slender black leather wallet.

"I can't take your money." Could I take her money?

"No, no, I can't." She held up a pair of fifty dollar bills that looked like they had just jumped off the printing press.

"I'm getting married in a week." I blurted out the words once more like muttering a spell of protection and took a step back.

"How much will it take?" She riffled wildly through her purse. "I can get more money. Please."

"No, my wedding is more important to me than any amount of money."

"I'll give you two hundred dollars a day. Isn't that what the professionals charge?"

"I have no idea. I am not a professional. Like I said, Gloria, let's leave solving Tom Visconti's murder to the police. Better yet, if you really want to spend some money, hire a professional. Hire a private detective."

"A private detective? In this town? No way. You know what people are like in Ruby Lake. If I brought in a private detective from outside, they would stick out like a proverbial sore thumb. Nobody, I mean nobody would tell him or her anything."

"You do have a point." The woman could sure be persuasive.

"Please," beseeched Gloria. "All I am asking you to do is to look into Mr. Visconti's death. Talk to a few people. See what you can find out. And I'll pay you for your time."

"I'm not a licensed professional investigator, Gloria. Taking money from you to investigate the murder of your boss could get me in trouble. It could even be against the law."

"How can it be illegal?" retorted Gloria. "You're helping solve a murder."

"Well..."

"If you feel funny about taking my money, we'll donate it all to charity."

"The Seeds for Seniors program could use the funds," I admitted. The program provided bird seed and feeders to retirees. Bird watching gave the elderly something to do and Seeds for Seniors gave them the supplies and seed to do it with.

We had started the free program at Birds & Bees. We provided seed, feeders and accessories to assisted living and retirement facilities and even seniors living alone throughout the county now.

"Fine," I said in surrender. "I'll look into it. I can talk to some people, see what I can find out. But only for a few days. My wedding is my top priority."

"I understand. Thank you, Amy." Visconti's assistant rewarded me with a hug.

"Don't expect miracles," I said, pulling myself free.

"You're far too modest, Amy. Plus, you know Chief Kennedy. In fact, I hear you're friends."

"I wouldn't go that far." It was a sometimes fine line between friend and sparring partner.

"That will get you inside info on the case and a line as to what the police are doing."

With a final hug, Gloria Bolan made her getaway. "I'll check in with you in a couple of days to see how you're getting along."

"What was that all about?" came a voice I knew and loved.

I turned. "Derek. I didn't see you come back inside."

Derek grinned. "I got tired of waiting in the car. Muggy out there. What did Mrs. Bolan want? She was really talking your ear off. I didn't think you even knew her. Shall we?" He held open the door and I stepped through.

"I didn't before now. She wanted to hire me to find out who killed her boss."

"You're kidding, right?" Derek opened my car door for me. I smiled as I noticed his amorous eyes follow the line of my bare legs as I swung into my seat.

"Not a bit," I replied. "Wanna be my sidekick?"

13

The next morning, after talking my way past the stubborn guard on duty at the gatehouse protecting Rivercrest Country Club from the riff-raff—such as myself—I was standing nervously on the front porch outside Amy Harlan's house. Sunlight played among the leaves of a nearby elm spackling shadows on the manicured grounds. In keeping with my promise to Gloria Bolan, the first thing I was going to do was talk to the woman.

The postmodern design home had more angles than a politician. I hoped she didn't throw too many stones because practically every square inch of the exterior was covered in glass. Even the doors to the three-car garage.

Her home looked out of place in comparison to most of the other houses, which were of more traditional design.

While I waited for her imaginary manservant to deign to come to the massive eight foot walnut door, I rooted around in my purse for my compact. Cradling the basket of muffins and teas I'd brought as a condolence package in the crook of my left arm, I checked my makeup.

Studying my reflection, tired eyes and rumpled hair, I

dabbed a bit of blush over my cheeks. Sadly, that was as good as it was going to get.

Hearing the familiar sound of a lock being unbolted from the inside, I slammed the compact shut and shoved it back in my purse.

To my surprise, it was Bobby Breen, Tom Visconti's best man, who opened the door. He was dressed in a hip-length tan suede jacket, blue shirt, khakis and loafers. A stubby, unlit cigar was thrust tightly between the middle and index fingers of his left hand.

Without the cowboy hat, Bobby appeared so much shorter as he gazed out at me through a pair of blood-shot eyes. "Yes?" He peered past me, looking to right and left as if expecting even more riff-raff. "Can I help you?"

"It's me, Amy Simms. We met yesterday."

I could see his lips working. He wanted to say yes but his brain hadn't made the necessary connections.

"At the wedding," I said. "Or, what was supposed to be Amy's wedding."

"Right," he drawled. "You're that lady who found Tom."

"Sadly, yes." I felt the morning sun pressing its hot hand against the nape of my neck.

"You making some kind of delivery?" he asked, eyeing my bulging basket.

"This?" I lofted the gift basket. "I came to pay my condolences."

"Who is it, Bobby?" a listless voice called out from the recesses of the house.

"It's that woman who found Tom."

"Simms? What is *she* doing here?"

I smiled feebly.

Popping the damp cigar in the left side of his mouth,

he said, "You'd better come in."

Bobby waved me into the house. It was even more spectacular inside than it was outside. The spacious, bi-level living area was all leather, glass and plastic. The same stuff Amy Harlan was made of, no doubt.

And was that a genuine Andy Warhol hanging on the wall over the concrete and mosaic ceramic tile fireplace with the glass mantle in the shape of a moving wave? She must have sucked Derek dry in the divorce settlement.

"Amy's in the solarium. I'll get you some coffee. Cream and sugar okay?"

"Cream and sugar would be great," I replied.

Bobby Breen wandered toward the chef's dream of a kitchen, all stainless steel, Italian white-lacquered cabinetry and quartz countertops—and not an ounce of warmth.

Again, much like its owner.

The solarium overlooked an expanse of manicured green with a forest of trees beyond. Amy-the-ex sat stiffly at a glass dining table with a cup of coffee and an uneaten slice of plain, unbuttered white toast on the plate before her.

"What are you doing here?" She pushed the thin slice of toast around on her plate and gazed out the wall of windows.

"I wanted to tell you how sorry I am for your loss."

She nodded but remained silent.

I hadn't been asked to sit so I remained standing. "How is Maeve handling this?"

"She's a child. And she's tough, like me."

"Right."

"My folks have taken her to their condo in Boca Raton

for a few days. We thought it might be best."

"That's probably a good idea."

"I'm so happy you approve," Amy-the-ex said in a voice steeped in sarcasm.

Under the circumstances, I decided it was best not to bicker with my nemesis. "I brought you these." I set the gift basket on the table. It seemed ineffectual and meaningless now. "It's from all of us at the store. I know it's not much and can't begin to make up for your loss but —"

Amy Harlan's eyes rolled over the cellophane-wrapped contents. "Thank you," she said softly.

Wow. It almost sounded like she meant it.

I decided to sit and pulled out the wicker chair to her right. "If you don't mind my asking, can you think of anyone who might have wanted to harm Tom?"

"Can't you let me suffer my grief without coming into my home, uninvited, I might add, and playing detective?"

"I'm sorry," I said. "I only wanted to help."

"I do not need your help. I have my family and I have my friends."

"Speaking of family, how is Vail taking his father's death?"

Amy Harlan picked up her toast and hurled it at the window. It broke into several shards and fell to the slate floor. "Knowing Vail, he's probably dancing in the streets."

"Excuse me?"

Amy Harlan nailed me with her eyes. "Vail killed Tom."

"You think his son did it?" I paled at the thought.

"Why not? He hated his father. And he hated me for

marrying him."

"Did you tell Chief Kennedy this?"

"Of course."

"Does Vail have any violent tendencies that you are aware of? Has he ever been in any kind of trouble?"

Amy chuckled softly. "From what Tom's told me, and that hasn't been much, Vail has been nothing but trouble."

"Such as?"

"I've said too much."

"But this could be important."

"I'm very tired. There's so much to do." She wrapped her slender fingers around the cup for warmth. "I thought planning a wedding was a lot of work. You'd be surprised how much work planning a funeral is."

She raised her cup, sipped and frowned. "Lukewarm." She set it down quickly. "Thank goodness for Gloria."

"Tom's assistant?"

"She's helping with the funeral arrangements. Once everything is settled, Tom will be buried in Nashville."

"If there is anything at all I can do—"

"You should go."

"Of course." I scooted back my chair and slowly rose.

A man's voice boomed from down the hall. "Hello, Amy? Where are you?"

"That voice..." A chill rippled through me. I gazed toward the hallway leading to some bedrooms.

"Amy!" Derek said with surprise. He looked uncomfortably from one Amy, his ex, to the other.

Me.

"H-hello, Derek," I said, even as my mouth turned to dry paper. He was wearing pajamas. His feet were bare and his face unshaven. The air in the solarium suddenly felt twenty degrees colder.

Derek pulled up a smile. "What are you doing here?"

"I came to pay my condolences." I waved my hand at the gift basket. "What are you doing here? I didn't see your car when I pulled up."

"The same thing. My car's in the garage."

"You came calling in your pajamas?"

"Oh." Derek tugged at his PJ top. "Actually, let me explain. Amy asked me to stay the night. She didn't want to be alone."

"I see." My face was burning and my heart felt like someone had hit it with a sledgehammer. "I'd better go."

Derek came towards me. "Amy."

I brushed off his advance and headed for the door. "Goodbye." I hurried to the front of the house.

"Hey, where are you running off to?" Bobby Breen asked. He came toward me from the kitchen, balancing a cup and saucer in his hand. "I got your coffee."

"Give it to Derek," I said, throwing open the door. "Better yet, dump it over his head."

I slammed the door behind me.

14

Esther ogled me from the cash register as I barged noisily through the front door of Birds & Bees. The short drive had done nothing to calm me down. If anything, I was even more upset.

Why did AM Ruby have to be featuring a Hank Williams throwback day and be playing *Your Cheatin' Heart* as I drove with my eyes barely seeing the road as I returned to Birds & Bees in my anguish? Was the universe that cruel?

"Hi, Amy," Esther began. "Did you deliver our basket? How's the Harlan woman holding up?"

"Yeah," said Kim, wheeling a red dolly of five-pound bags of safflower seeds in from the storeroom. "Spill it."

"Amy Harlan is holding up just fine, thank you!" I found myself yelling, although I hadn't meant to. The blood was boiling in my ears.

I struggled out of my coat and shoved it down on an empty hook on the coatrack next to the front door. The rack tipped. The coat ripped. I grabbed for the rack and got tangled up in my coat. Coat and rack hit the floor, taking out a revolving display rack of bird notecards in its path.

I cursed under my breath, uplifted the card display, untangled my coat and set the wobbly coat rack back on its feet. "Stupid thing shouldn't be so close to the door.

Look at this mess." Notecards blanketed the entryway.

"I'll take care of it." Kim scurried over, bent down and began picking up cards and envelopes.

"Something wrong?" Esther asked, shooting Kim a look of concern.

"Nothing is wrong," I snapped, planting my hands on my hips. "Is anything wrong here?"

"No," drawled Esther. "Everything is jim dandy. Right, Kim?"

"Oh, sure," Kim replied. "Just jim peachy dandy." Her hands were filled with fallen cards which she was struggling to put back on the rack in some semblance of order.

"Great, then I'll leave the two of you to it." I stepped awkwardly over the dolly that Kim had left blocking the stairs. "Somebody is going to get hurt leaving this thing in the middle of the road. We don't need any lawsuits, do we?"

"No, of course not." Kim ran over and rolled the dolly up against the side wall for unloading.

"What's wrong with your face?" Esther asked. "You been crying?"

"I've got allergies," I said, grabbing the bannister. "Lots of allergies. Probably to imaginary cats." I aimed that statement straight at Esther.

"Here we go again," Esther replied.

"And here I go. Upstairs." My actions quickly followed my words.

"Wait, where are you going?" Kim demanded. "You're supposed to pull a shift." Kim had a dental appointment scheduled within the hour.

"To my apartment." I promptly stomped up the steps, bumping into Paul Anderson coming down from the second floor.

"Whoa, careful there, Amy. Watch where you're going." Paul scooted to one side and brushed off his black shirt like I'd just given him cooties. Princess, his black and tan hound dog, followed him.

"Sorry," I mumbled.

Princess licked my fingers as she passed.

"Say," Paul called up after me, "have you seen Derek? I want to go over some ideas for the bachelor party with him and—"

"Yes, I've seen him. You want him? Try his wife's house!"

"Wife's house? Paul scratched the top of his head.

I took the last flight of stairs two steps at a time and let myself in quickly, before I melted down in public any further.

I tossed my keys on the table next to the door. "Mom?"

No response.

Mom was out, thank goodness. I didn't want to see or speak to anyone considering the state I was in. Of course, she might have heard the fit I had thrown downstairs and be hiding in her bedroom closet but that didn't bear thinking about.

With the apartment to myself, I threw open the pantry. I grabbed bags of flour, baking powder, oats, cocoa, anything I could get my hands on, and started baking. At first, I was winging it and had no idea what I was making.

After fifteen minutes or so, it looked sort of like cupcake batter lying at the bottom of the deep glass bowl —deep as the pit in my heart—so I retrieved a couple of cupcake trays from the cabinet above the microwave and gave them a healthy spritzing with no-stick spray. While I was setting the oven to preheat, I didn't hear Kim enter the apartment. When I turned to the island, she was eyeing me curiously from the other side.

"Everything okay, Amy?"

"Fine. Just fine." I hefted the heavy bowl, grabbed a big spoon and sloppily filled the trays with wet brown batter. There were some weird lumps in the mix. Had I added nuts or raisins? I couldn't remember but I figured they would either be edible or melt away during the baking process.

"Making cupcakes?"

I frowned at her. "Lucky guess."

"Um, you might want to get some actual batter in the actual cups."

Kim wriggled her finger at the metal tray. There was as much chocolate batter along the top and sides of the tray, and the countertop, as there was in each individual metal depression.

I shot her my dirtiest look and considered, only for a moment, throwing the next spoonful of batter in my best friend's direction. "Now you're telling me how to bake?"

"No, no." Kim threw up her hands. "You're doing a great job. Great job."

"Thank you." I banged the metal spoon twice against the glass mixing bowl to remove some excess batter. A sharp crack followed. A long fissure appeared in the bowl—my mom's favorite. She'd had it for many years. I think it had been a wedding gift from one of her aunts. "Oops."

Amy grabbed a bag of store-bought mocha wafers from one of the open shelves. She popped one in her mouth and lined three more wafers up like little soldiers on the counter awaiting their imminent demise.

"You're eating cookies? Now? Can't you see I'm making dessert?"

Kim eyed me and my sort-of-cupcake concoction dubiously.

The batter was now gurgling. Actually gurgling. What batter does that?

Was it alive?

"I'm good." To prove her point, Kim bit another wafer in two and chewed with over-the-top relish.

The oven beeped to let me know it was ready, willing and waiting for whatever I wanted to shove inside it.

Instead, I shut the oven off, defeated.

"What's going on, Amy?" Kim slid the bag of cookies my way. "Wedding day jitters?"

I stared at the messy counter, the broken bowl, and the cupcake-batter-cum-alien-life-form that I had created. I was going to have to get all this cleaned up before Mom came home or it ate me.

A big fat tear rolled down my cheek, over my chin and plopped onto the countertop. I rubbed it with the palm of my hand.

"Amy? What's wrong?" I felt Kim's hand on my shoulder.

"There isn't going to be any wedding," I managed to say before the tears spilled out like the flood waters from a broken main water pipe.

15

"Amy, what are you saying?" Kim led me to the sofa. We sat shoulder to shoulder.

"C-can't talk about it." I hiccupped.

"Try." Kim patted my knee. "We're best friends. You know you can tell me anything."

Wiping the tears from my eyes with a tissue from the big box Kim handed me, I explained how I had delivered our basket to Amy-the-ex's house only to find Derek had beaten me to the punch.

"And he was wearing his pajamas?"

I could only nod and sniffle.

"There has to be a reasonable explanation for this," Kim insisted. "Derek loves you. That doesn't sound like him at all. He would never cheat on you. Especially with her."

"You're forgetting," I pouted. "He was with her before he was with me."

"True. But Derek *is* with you now. What did he say?"

"Nothing really. He looked surprised to see me there. I left as fast as I could."

"I know." Kim tapped a fingernail against her front teeth. "I'll get Dan to find out what happened."

"Oh, no. It's too embarrassing."

"For who? If Derek cheated, you need to know. If he

didn't, you need to know. Dan will get the truth out of Derek even if he has to threaten to shoot him. Which I just might tell him to do, if he finds out he really did cheat on you with his ex-wife."

Kim went to the phone in the kitchen and lifted the receiver. "You leave this to me."

"Thanks," I sniffed.

"Please, that's what friends are for." Kim dialed. "Hello, Dan? Have you talked to Derek today? No? Well, you need to talk to him. And when you do, you ask him what he was doing spending the night at Amy Harlot's house. What? Harlan, Harlot, what's the difference?

"I want to know what the man thought he was doing spending the night with her when his bride-to-be is sitting right here bawling her eyes out. That's right. Bawling her eyes out." Kim rolled her eyes for my benefit and mouthed, "Men can be so dense."

To Dan, she said, "I don't care. Put out an APB or something. And tell him," Kim said with a sudden smile, "tell him that if he doesn't make this right, and fast, Amy is going to cancel the wedding."

I heard loud squawking coming over the line. Dan sounded like a frightened hen. He had bought a new suit for his best man duty and put down a nonrefundable deposit on a hotel suite in Asheville for the bachelor party.

"That's right. I said cancel." More affectionately, she said, "You're a sweetie. Goodbye, Dan." Kim hung up and wiped her palms with satisfaction. "That ought to do it."

Esther barged into my apartment. She took in the sight of us, one smirking, the other crying. "What's with you two?"

"Making cupcakes," Kim replied. She held up the sloppy cupcake tray, dripping with batter.

Was it my imagination or was the batter actually eating away at the metal pan like some sort of strong corrosive acid?

"Well," said Esther, hands in the pouch of her store apron, "I hate to interrupt such important matters but you," she pointed to me, "need to get your butt downstairs. Somebody wants to see you."

"Who is it?" I unfolded my legs from under me and ran my fingers through my hair. "Is it Derek? Tell him I do not want to see or talk to him."

Esther looked at me curiously as if I were a new specimen she had stumbled upon while peering through a microscope. "It's not Derek."

I slumped, dejected. "Who is it then?"

Ignoring my question, Esther asked one herself. "Why don't you want to talk to Derek? He's your fiancé."

"Now is not the time, Esther," cautioned Kim.

"Time for what?" Esther was exasperated.

"Just tell me who wants to see me, Esther." I arranged the pillow on the sofa and straightened my slacks. "And shouldn't you be watching the store? Some thief could be robbing us blind as we speak."

Esther waved away my concerns like she was swatting away a mildly annoying horsefly. "Some fella named Miles Sheffield. You coming or what?"

I crossed to the kitchen sink, splashed some cold water over my face and dried myself off with the towel. "I don't know any Miles Sheffield. Who is he? A salesman?"

Being a store owner, sales people of one sort or another were always popping in unannounced. Sometimes selling office supplies, other times, cleaning products, some bird-related items and once even some middle-aged woman trying to sell me llama-grooming supplies. I had politely accepted her card and told her I would definitely keep her in mind the first time I had a request for llama toe nail clippers or a matted hair splitter—whatever that was.

"Maybe," Esther said in reply to my question. "But if he is a salesman, he's the funniest looking one I've ever seen."

Kim poured herself a glass of soda from the jug in the fridge. Next, she attacked the wafer cookies again. "Why do you say that?"

"Hey, how about sharing?" Esther snatched the bag of wafers from Kim's hand and thrust her fingers inside. "Thanks." She poured some cookies in her apron pouch for later.

"Tall, red-headed guy," Esther explained. "Wearing shiny black pants, a fringed leather coat and pink high-top sneakers. He's got eyeglasses with thick lime-green frames. Not bad looking, if you're into tall, skinny and oddball."

"Maybe he's selling tickets to the circus," joked Kim. "Is the circus coming to town?"

Crazy as Esther sounded, the description seemed to remind me of someone. "I think that's the lead guitar player."

"What lead guitar player?" both wanted to know.

"He's with MC and the Moonlighters. I wonder what he wants with me."

"There's only one way to find out," Kim said.

I cleaned myself up and went downstairs. I found the tall redhead with his nose plastered to a nesting box, his eyeball pressed to the hole.

"See anything interesting in there?" I asked.

Startled, his head banged against the wooden box. The birdhouse tumbled from the ledge. He caught it before it hit the ground and set it back on the upper shelf.

"Nice reflexes."

"Sorry." His face turned red as a robin's red breast.

"It was my fault. Can I help you? Mr. Sheffield, is it?"

He showed me a smile. "Miles."

"Amy." Esther was right. He was cute. Rather adorable even, in an odd bird sort of way. Very colorful, like male birds usually are, in fact. "Was there something I can help you with? Are you interested in birds?"

"Actually," Miles Sheffield glanced furtively around the store, like a wren on the lookout for a circling red-shouldered hawk, itself in search of a midday snack, "I was hoping I could have a word with you."

"Sure, what's up?"

"Um, in private?" He bobbed his head toward the sales counter where Esther and Kim were pretending to be studying an inventory form but were clearly intent on eavesdropping on us.

"Let's go over here," I suggested. I started towards the nook in the corner of the store then thought better of it. Esther and Kim had a habit of sneaking up and listening in from the other side of the shelves.

I stopped midway. "On second thought, why don't we go to the diner? It's right across the street."

"Suits me."

I grabbed my coat.

Miles held the door open for me. Inside Ruby's Diner, Tiffany led us to a table at the window. Esther and Kim would probably be spying from across the street, but let them. They could see but they couldn't hear.

Ruby's Diner had started life as a gasoline service station. The diner owner, Moire Leora Breeder, had purchased the building and the lot it stood on from the retiring grandson of the original owner.

Loving the funky charm of the gas station, Moire had been loath to change anything more than absolutely necessary. The place still looked pretty much like a gas station and the occasional tourist sometimes mistook it for one. The sign with the big green dinosaur at the top still stands proudly in the parking lot at the edge of the street. As an homage to the original corporate apatosaurus, Moire Leora serves up her own take on a bronto burger.

It was commonplace for the occasional tourist to pull in looking to fill up their gas tank.

"Hi, Amy." Tiffany slapped a couple of menus down on the table. "I hear you found another one."

There was no need to clarify. We both knew what she meant.

Another dead body.

"Yes. Did Robert tell you about it?"

"My ex? Please, you know we don't talk any more than necessary." Most of their conversations revolved around their son, Jimmy. "Besides, Robert didn't have to. The whole town is buzzing about it."

"I don't suppose they're buzzing about who killed him?"

"Most folks are figuring, or at the very least hoping, that Amy Harlan did it." Tiffany smiled at the stranger accompanying me. "Folks around here aren't exactly fond of our other Amy."

"So I've heard," replied Miles.

"Who's your friend?" Tiffany asked me.

"This is Miles Sheffield. He's with MC and the Moonlighters."

"Oh, sure. I didn't recognize you without the rest of the band in tow." MC and the Moonlighters had been frequenting the diner day and night. "MC is a big tipper."

"Yeah," said Miles. "He can afford to be. He gets the big bucks while the rest of us work for peanuts."

"Have you heard anything else of interest?"

Tiffany chewed on the tip of her pencil for a second. "Not really. You know how it is around here. Anytime something interesting happens, the rumors begin to swirl.

"Besides blaming Amy Harlan, some blame Reverend Steve—"

"Reverend Steve? He's harmless."

"You asked. I'm telling. Others think it was some random nut job from out of the area. Always a fan favorite," Tiffany said, throwing Miles a wink. "Then there's Riley."

"What does my cousin think?"

"He thinks the killing was the work of one of those green guerillas."

"Green gorillas?" Miles asked, mimicking an ape with his hands. "What kind of wildlife do you have around these parts?"

Tiffany chuckled. "Not the apes, the eco-terrorists."

"Why would some environmentalist want to strangle Tom Visconti?" I asked.

"Think about it," said Tiffany. "Mr. Visconti was going to develop all that land. I hear he's big on chemicals too. Didn't care what it took, so long as his properties looked perfect and remained bug free. According to

Riley, strangling Mr. Visconti was symbolic."

"I get it," Miles said. "This Visconti character was strangling good old Mother Nature—"

"So our mysterious guerilla strangles him." I had to admit that made sense. Not often the case with Cousin Riley. I made a mental note to talk to him. Maybe he had seen someone suspicious around the golf course or Magnolia Manor while he was mowing the lawns.

Tiffany glanced over her shoulder and back again. Perched on her stool at the cash register, Moire Leora had her watchful eyes on us. The diner owner is a short blond, who doesn't bother to hide the gray creeping in, with a round face and blue eyes. The young widow carries a few extra pounds wherever she goes—one of the perks and/or curses of owning a diner and being around tasty diner food all day.

"I'd better get hustling," Tiffany said. "Moire doesn't like it when we gossip with the customers." She chuckled to herself. "It makes her feel left out. You two ready to order?"

"Let me buy you lunch, Amy," offered Miles.

"You don't have to do that. Coming here was my idea."

"But I'm the one who wanted to speak to you. Besides, I want to."

I shrugged and ordered a Portobello melt on toasted pita bread, sliced tomatoes and a sugar-free tea with fresh lime. Miles ordered the open-face roast beef sandwich with mashed potatoes and gravy and a caramel malt with whipping cream.

Sure, he could order all those calories and carbs. He wasn't getting married.

Then again, was I?

Miles watched Tiffany walk our meal ticket to the kitchen.

I couldn't blame him. All the men watch Tiff when she leaves. She's a buxom, green-eyed blonde. Moire Leora has all her staff dress in cuffed khaki pants and Kelly green shirts with white name patches, stylistically reminiscent of the uniforms worn by old-school gas station attendants.

Tiffany simply happens to look better in her uniform than most women look in a string bikini.

I didn't hate her for it. But there were times I got a little envious.

Glancing out the window and across the street, I spotted Esther and Kim in the window looking back at us in our booth. "Good grief."

"What?" Miles leaned forward and glanced out the window.

"Laverne and Shirley are spying on us."

"Who?"

"Two of my employees." I dug my phone out of my purse and started texting.

"Oh, yeah. I see them now." Miles, bless his heart, laughed. "Are those binoculars they're holding up?"

"Yep." My fingers typed faster.

"What are you doing?"

"Reminding Kim that she's late for her dentist appointment." My phone pinged. I read the message: *rescheduled*.

I shook my fist at the two of them through the window.

"I think they're cute."

"You do?"

"Sure."

"You don't mind that they're spying on us?"

"Nah. I'm a musician. I'm used to people watching me on stage." He waved to Esther and Kim. They waved back.

I felt like hiding under the table.

"Coming through." Tiffany dropped our hot food on the table along with some condiments.

"Let's eat," suggested Miles. "Before our food gets cold. Then I'll tell you what I wanted to talk to you about."

I ate quickly. Not that I'm a glutton, I just couldn't wait to hear what this odd musician could possibly have to talk to me about.

Miles pushed back his empty plate after licking up every speck of gravy with his finger. "You remember when you asked MC what he was arguing about with the dead man's kid?"

"Of course. How could I forget?"

"Right. Well, it got me wondering."

"About what?"

"I want to know whether or not MC is up to no good."

"No good? You mean, like murder?"

"I mean like a crook or a drug dealer or something."

"Is there some reason for your suspicions or is this based solely on the fact that he underpays you?"

Miles took my remark with good humor. "You wouldn't know this, but we, MC and the Moonlighters, often do gigs for free for Tom Visconti."

"Why would MC do that? MC doesn't strike me as the work-for-free sort. Besides, MC told me he didn't even know Tom Visconti."

"That's a laugh. He knows him and knows him well. As for why he came whenever Visconti snapped his fingers, I have no idea. MC is definitely not the work-for-free sort."

Miles sucked on his milkshake. "So why does he travel across the country to perform a free concert for Visconti and his pals whenever Visconti snaps, or snapped, his fingers?"

"Blackmail?" I suggested, earning a nod from the guitar player. "You think Visconti had some kind of hold over your boss."

Miles leaned closer and said softly, "I've heard rumors that MC is dealing."

"You mean drugs?"

Miles tapped his finger to his nose. "Mind you, I've never seen anything but I would like to know if the guy is on the up and up. If he is supplying drugs, I want out of the band. I'm not getting messed up in anything like that."

"I understand."

"No, you don't. You see," Miles hesitated. "The same thing happened to my kid brother, Mark. He OD'd on the stuff."

"I'm sorry."

"Thanks." Miles ran his hand across his forward. "So you can see why I feel strongly about this."

"Yes, but what can I do?"

"Easy, you know all the players. You're local. Nose around. Maybe play up to MC. Act like you want to score some weed off him or something."

"Oh, no. I don't even want to pretend such a thing. Besides, won't you and the band be leaving Ruby Lake soon? In fact, I'm surprised you're still here."

"That police chief of yours is making us stay in town. MC doesn't mind so much because he says that we're probably going to get another gig out of this."

"Oh?"

"Yeah, your wedding."

I snorted. "Fat chance. I can't begin to afford him."

"Hmm, that's not the impression he says he got from you."

"I'm going to have to set him straight. And fast. I am not about to mortgage my house to pay for MC and the Moonlighters to perform a few songs at my wedding. No offense," I added quickly.

"None taken."

"You seem a little young to be one of the Moonlighters."

"Yeah. Twenty-seven. MC only hired me a few years ago. Most of the guys are double that or more. Old pals of MC's who've been with him since the beginning."

"What do they think about your suspicions?"

"Are you kidding? I wouldn't dare broach the subject. Those guys are loyal. MC is a god to them. He's their bread and butter. They wouldn't hesitate to go running straight to MC and rat me out. I'd be on the next bus back to Miami."

Glancing out the diner window, my eyes grew wide. "What's *he* doing there?"

16

"Who?" Miles followed my gaze.

"Nothing. It's not important." My hands shook and my heart doubled its pace. Derek extracted himself from his Civic and marched up the steps to Birds & Bees, his coat draped over one shoulder.

"Look," I said quickly, "if I learn anything that I think might interest you about MC, I'll let you know. No promises."

"None expected."

"You know where to reach me. How can I reach you?"

"We're staying at the Ruby Lake Motor Inn. I'm in room 107."

"Got it." The historic Ruby Lake Motor Inn was located only a mile or so up Lake Shore Drive. "I'd better get back to work." I picked up my coat from the benchseat. "Thanks for lunch."

Moire Leora stopped me before I could get out the door. I should have known I wouldn't get past her without sharing whatever I knew or was conjecturing about the wedding-that-wasn't and the murder of Tom Visconti.

Moire Leora was like that troll under the bridge or Charon on the banks of the River Styx, only in her case the coinage was gossip, not food or money.

By the time I had escaped Moire's well-intended but sticky clutches, Derek had gone.

There was also no sign of Kim. I considered her absence immaterial. And commonplace.

"Where'd he go?" I wiped my feet on the mat like a nervous hen.

Esther, half-asleep at her stool behind the counter, opened one rheumy eye. "Who?"

"Derek. I saw his car parked out front from the diner." I glanced madly around the store, knowing it was futile. Derek's car was no longer at the curb.

"You just missed him."

I sagged against the counter. "What did he want? Did he say anything? What did he say?"

"What do you mean did he say anything?" Esther stood, bent to touch her knees with her fingertips. I heard snapping sounds at knees, fingers and spine. "You think the man would come all the way here and not say anything?"

"Tell me what he said, Esther."

"He wanted to talk to you."

"I know that, Esther." I was losing patience fast. "About what?"

"He said you're an idiot."

"What?" My hand flew to my heart.

"Wait." Esther shook the cobwebs of her mind. "No, no. That was me. I said you were an idiot after he told me how you ran out of Amy Harlan's house without giving him a chance to explain himself."

"I believe I know what I saw, Esther. I was there. You were not. A picture, as they say, is worth a thousand words. I know I saw and what I saw—"

"Even one of those goofy Cubist things?"

"Excuse me?"

"Or one of them hallucinogenic, melty Dali paintings? Are those pictures worth a thousand words?"

"I see your point." I thumped my elbows down on the counter and rested my head in my hands. Sometimes my take on reality could be a mite skewed. "Did Derek say when he would be back?"

"He said to call him. He wants to have dinner with you."

"Fine then. Maybe I will. Wait," I said, following after Esther as she retreated to the storeroom and grabbed her capacious purse from the hook near the backdoor. "Why didn't you tell him I was across the street at the diner?"

"I did. I even showed him in the binoculars. He took one look and decided you were busy and that he didn't want to bother you." A car horn sounded and Esther threw open the door. "See ya."

"Where are you off to?"

"Floyd's taking me to the matinee." Esther waved to Floyd. I waved to Floyd seated behind the wheel of his lovingly-restored 1956 Chrysler. It was red with tan leather interior. I watched the aged pair bounce down the alley.

When I turned around, I discovered Violet Wilcox and Lance Jennings glaring at me.

"Holding out on us, Amy?" Violet was the first to speak. "And I thought we were friends."

"Yeah, same here." Lance thumped a pencil against his ever-present notepad. "You know it is too late to cancel your wedding announcement."

"What's that supposed to mean?"

"And what about the dead body? You found Tom Visconti and didn't phone me? After all I've done for you?"

"What have you ever done for me?"

"Do you hear her?" Violet asked Lance. She was rocking a tight-fitting, plum-colored sweater and snug white slacks.

"I hear her." Lance looked angry, which wasn't easily managed considering how harmless he normally looked.

The reporter is about forty years old and forty pounds overweight, which the rumpled suits he wears do little to hide. He has dark, wavy hair with a receding hairline, same as his father, William Jennings. Daddy owns the paper Lance writes for, the Ruby Lake Weekender. As far as I was aware, working for Daddy's paper was Lance's first and only job.

Violet Wilcox, by contrast, is an over-the-top beauty whose hair is the same fake color of one of those phony platinum albums I've seen lining the reception area out at her radio station, AM Ruby.

Her complexion is what the poets like to call milky. Whether this is due to her long hours spent indoors DJ'ing behind a microphone or catching forty winks in a secret silver-encrusted coffin, I couldn't decide. Probably fifty-fifty.

Violet can be brassy and pushy. Two things that Lance Jennings was not. The two reporters were media rivals and it seemed the only thing that united them at the moment was their desire to beat the truth, as they saw it, out of me.

I hurried to the front of Birds & Bees, hoping the presence of customers would throw the pair off. Sadly, we were alone in the store.

Violet's stilettos click-clacked noisily across the floor

as she scurried after me like a baby bird chasing its first bug. Lance's gait was more of a stomp-shuffle. Something I would have expected to see and hear from a tired hippopotamus after a long day pounding the beat.

"So it is true you found the body?" Violet asked sharply. "What was it like? Paint us a picture."

"Did you notice anything suspicious?" Lance held his pencil at the ready. "Did you hear anything unusual?"

"I—"

"Speaking of pictures," Lance interrupted. "Did you think to take any photos?"

"I was there for a wedding, not to take crime scene photos, Lance." I flexed and straightened my fingers, praying for a customer to walk through the door or a lightning bolt to strike the roof and burn the place down to cinders.

I hadn't even properly answered the first of their stupid questions when Violet hit me with the next. "What about the wedding, Amy?"

"There was no wedding," I snapped. "The groom was dead, remember?"

"*Your* wedding, silly." Violet rolled her eyes.

"Yeah, Amy." Lance bumped up against me in an effort to block Violet. "Is it true that the wedding is off?"

"Off?" I glanced at one then the other. "Where did you hear that? I mean, I don't—"

"Rumor has it you caught Derek in bed with the other Amy, Amy," Violet was practically purring with delight at the salacious image. "Is it true?"

"Is that what the big cat fight was all about?" demanded Lance.

"What cat fight?" I blurted. "And where did you hear that I caught the two of them in bed?"

"So it is true." Violet gushed. "Sweet!" She checked the portable recorder she had been cramming in my face to be certain the red light was blinking and that the device was recording.

"You and Tom Visconti," Lance explained. "You two fought—"

"No," gasped Violet, clutching the reporter's arm. "I get it now. Amy and Derek fought."

"Huh?" Lance was confused.

I couldn't blame him. She'd lost me too.

"Don't you get it?" Violet continued. "Amy and Derek killed Tom Visconti so they could be together."

"Oh, brother. Do you hear yourself?" I was practically shouting now in a vain attempt to get through to the ditz. "Why would they kill Tom Visconti? If they wanted to be together, all they have to do is be together."

Ugh, that was so true.

"Besides," I continued valiantly, "Derek was with me and Amy Harlan was on the gazebo when—"

"The bride would not have been standing at the altar first, Amy. You should know that," countered Violet Wilcox. "It's simply not done."

"True that," Lance said.

"I suppose that's correct," I admitted. I didn't know exactly where anyone had been at the time of Tom Visconti's death. Amy Harlan would have been waiting in back somewhere, probably inside the mansion, in anticipation of making her grand entrance.

"And Tom Visconti was nowhere to be seen for a solid twenty minutes before the ceremony. Maybe longer, according to eyewitness accounts," Lance said, studying his notes. "Not even the best man saw him."

"Well?" demanded Violet Wilcox.

"Well, what?"

"What do you think, Amy? Who killed Tom Visconti?"

"And is Derek shacking up with his ex-wife?" added Lance. His pencil hovered over the lined paper as if he actually expected me to dignify that question with an answer.

"Do you really expect me to answer that?" I snapped. "Besides, if Derek was shacking up with his ex-wife, why would he have asked me to dinner tonight?"

Violet Wilcox shot a sad smile. It had been intended for Lance but I caught it. "Yep. The classic breakup dinner."

"I know what that's like," Lance muttered sadly.

"I'm sure you do," I couldn't resist saying. Okay, that was mean. My frustration was making me lash out. "Besides, if anybody is breaking up with anybody, it's going to be me."

Violet laid her icy fingers on my shoulder. "You should come down to the station. You know I do a show for the lovelorn late night Fridays."

I tossed her hand away. "I am not lovelorn. Even if I was, I wouldn't go on some silly radio show and blab about it to the world. Now," I said, throwing open the front door, "why don't you two go find someone else to question, like Tom Visconti's son, Vail, or MC for that matter—" I slapped my hand over my mouth and froze, horror in my eyes.

Violet and Lance stared at me.

"You think Visconti's son offed him?" Lance asked. He scribbled furiously. "That is news."

'No, no, I—" I stammered. "You cannot print that!"

"Or Mickey Caswell, leader of MC and the Moonlighters, holder of six gold and three platinum albums?" Violet said.

Like a shark sensing blood in the water, the two hungry newspersons circled around me.

"No comment!" I bolted out the door, leaving Birds & Bees unattended and scattering the nibbling wrens and chickadees that had been perched on a tube feeder on the front porch and the foraging brown thrashers in the flowerbed below.

If any customers came, Lance and Violet could deal with them.

17

After an awkward telephone call, Derek and I agreed to meet for dinner at Lake House. Practically across the street from me in the Ruby Lake Marina, and boasting a picture postcard view of Ruby Lake, Lake House is the town's most upscale restaurant. Arguably the most romantic spot in the whole town.

Red velvet draperies hug the floor-to-ceiling windows. Each piece of furniture from the tables and chairs to the art on the wall was a valuable bit of Americana.

The hostess led us to a cozy table for two near the massive fireplace, hand-built with Carolina river rock. A wood fire blazed brightly in the deep hearth.

"Thanks for giving me a chance to explain." Derek squeezed my hand.

"I'm listening," I said, cautiously. Violet Wilcox's words stuck in my ear like a stubborn gnat that refused to leave. "Damn her."

"What?"

"Nothing," I colored. "You were saying?"

Over cocktails and starters, Derek explained that after he got back to his apartment the night of the wedding turned murder, his ex had called him. "She wanted me to come over to her house.

"Maeve was off to see her grandparents. The house

was big and empty. Her fiancé had been murdered and her wedding ruined. She needed some comforting."

"I'll bet. I'm sorry," I said immediate. I took a quick sip of my merlot. Amy Harlan had had her fiancé violently snatched from her. Understanding. I needed to be understanding. "Go on."

"What was I supposed to do? Say no? And, for the record, Bobby was there too."

"Bobby Breen is staying with her?"

"No, he's bunking at Visconti's place. He was there when I arrived. He stayed for a drink then left."

"I didn't realize Tom Visconti owned a home in Rivercrest." It made sense though seeing as how the businessman was adding the property to his fiefdom.

"He doesn't. Didn't. He'd been renting from a pro golfer buddy of his who only uses the house in his off-season. Neither Amy nor I wanted him living in her house prior to their marriage. Not with Maeve living there."

"Of course." The Lake House pianist, a dapper older gentleman in a black suit and tie, skillfully played a ragtime Scott Joplin piece. "So you and Amy were alone in the house."

"Yes, in separate bedrooms, I might add. I wish you would trust me, Amy. We're going to be married. We have to learn to trust one another. In fact, until this whole ugly mess, I thought we already did."

Derek looked so handsome sitting there in the glow of the soft firelight. Wearing his best suit, clean-shaven. Smelling of manhood.

Like a knight in shining armor.

"Oh, dear," My lower lip quivered. My emotions were crumbling. Tears tumbled down my face like warm summer rain.

"Amy? What's wrong?" Derek said in alarm.

"Nothing," I sobbed, dabbing my face with my dinner napkin. "Be right back." I jumped from my chair and hurried to the ladies' room.

I splashed cold water on my face, reapplied my makeup and headed to our table. Before I could get back to Derek, something caught my eye that demanded my immediate attention.

I hurried over to the nook in the corner near the baby grand piano, which now sat empty. A pile of green bills floated in a large glass snifter at the corner of the ebony piano.

Violet Wilcox and Lance Jennings stood shoulder to shoulder, hiding behind a six foot fiddle-leaf fig tree.

"What are you two doing here?" I whispered harshly.

"Amy, this is a surprise." Violet fluffed her hair. She wore a flirty black dress and matching heels. But I could see she wasn't here for the food. It was the mini-cam in her hand that gave her away.

"I'll bet."

"We came for the fireworks," Lance admitted. He looked the same as he had earlier that day. For all I knew, he slept in that suit.

It would explain the ever-present wrinkles.

"Fireworks?" It took me a minute to decode his sentence but I did. I planted my hands on my hips. "You mean you came to see Derek break up with me? That's awful!"

The volume of my voice crept dangerously upward. "I'm having you two thrown out."

"Good luck with that," Lance quipped. "Violet tipped the manager fifty bucks to let us hang out here."

Now I was practically spitting fire. "Can't a girl get a little privacy anywhere in this town? All I want is a quiet, romantic meal with my boyfriend. No, make that fiancé."

"The wedding is still on?"

Was that disappointment I heard in Violet's question?

"Yes, very much so."

"And if you two want to keep your wedding invitations, I suggest you leave now." I pointed to the exit. I noticed Derek watching us. I flashed him a smile then redirected my anger to Lance and Violet. "Well?"

"Fine," pouted Violet. "We're going. Let's go, Lance." The station owner grabbed Lance's arm. "I guess Amy's busy. Too busy for us. Say hello to Derek for me."

"But what about—" Lance blustered.

"No, no," Violet said in a voice so sickly sweet I felt two new cavities open up in my molars. "Amy is not interested in hearing what we found out about Vail Visconti and Mickey Caswell. Let's go, Lance."

She gave her bumbling accomplice a shove toward the exit. Lance grabbed a butter roll from the basket of a deserted table as he stumbled along.

I gritted my teeth, raised a finger to Derek with an accompanying smile to let him know I'd be right back, then darted after the pair.

Once again, my curiosity had gotten the best of me.

"What about MC and Vail Visconti?" I demanded, grabbing hold of Lance by the back of his sweaty collar.

Lance's eyes bulged and I loosened my grip. "Geez, Amy. What's gotten into you?" He straightened his shirt and tie.

"Not dinner, I can tell you that." I could see my juicy

steak sitting on a fine china plate growing colder by the minute. "So talk. One of you, please, so I can eat."

"Well," Violet smirked, "we did some poking around and—"

"I dug into the newspaper files and online data bases," Lance boasted.

"Which he wouldn't have done if I hadn't told him what to look for." Violet Wilcox gave the print reporter a look that would have withered a fat, healthy rose bush.

"The point," I insisted. "Get to the point."

Violet raised a hand to stifle Lance who was about to reply. "We found out that there appears to be a connection between Vail Visconti and MC."

I sighed. "I already know that. MC performs a bunch of free concerts for Visconti and Vail's his kid. No news there."

"Okay, maybe not," admitted Violet. "But did you know that one Mickey Caswell once bailed one Vail Visconti out of a Taos, New Mexico jail cell?"

That was news. And a connection. But what did it mean, if anything?

My mind raced. My heart raced too and my heart won out. I wanted to get back to my dinner with Derek. He mattered more than anything else right now. We mattered more than anything else. I had to focus on us, if I wanted there to be an us.

"Thanks," I said, grudgingly. "If you find out anything else, let me know."

"Only if you'll do the same," Lance replied, nibbling contentedly on his leftover dinner roll.

"Meaning what? I'm busy enough with my wedding right around the corner."

"Please, it's all over town that Gloria Bolan has asked

you to look into Tom Visconti's murder," Violet argued. "How much is Visconti's company paying you for your services? Why wouldn't they hire a professional investigator?"

"Yeah," chuckled Lance. "Instead they hire a bird watcher."

"Watch this," I snarled, rising up on my tiptoes and waving my fist in his face.

"Come along, Lance." Violet took Lance by the elbow. "And put that down." She slapped the remains of the roll from his hand. The roll fell to the carpet, much to the chagrin of a passing waiter who quickly bent to retrieve it.

18

"What was that all about?" Derek wanted to know the minute I returned to my seat. He set down the wine list he'd been reading to pass the time.

"Nothing. Lance and Violet were hoping for some candid pre-wedding shots."

"Uh-huh," Derek muttered in disbelief.

"Fine. They thought we were going to break up and wanted ringside seats to the event."

"Break up? Why on earth would we do that? And who gave them that idea?"

"I don't know. I mean, we wouldn't." I wondered if Amy-the-ex was spreading rumors, already setting her evil and lascivious sights on Derek once again now that Tom Visconti was dead.

"That's better." Derek refilled our wine glasses. "Let's eat, dinner is getting cold. Shall I ask them to reheat it?"

"No, it's fine." To prove my point, I took a bite. "Thank you for not thinking I'm completely crazy and for not giving up on me," I replied. "I don't know what came over me."

"Wedding jitters," Derek answered.

"That's what Kim, Esther and Mom said. I guess they're right. As if there hasn't been enough to deal with," I said, "with our upcoming wedding, you ex's fiancé getting murdered has sent me over the edge."

"How about coming back to earth," Derek said. "At least until after the wedding. Then I'll take you to the moon and back."

His fingers traced a path up my arm and I shivered, even as my legs turned into warm puddles of flesh, blood and bone.

"Tell me about the moon," I whispered.

"Later. First," Derek said, raising his glass, "how about if I tell you what my ex-wife told me about the day of the murder? I'm guessing you're dying to hear. No pun intended."

He took a long, slow sip of wine. "Unless you'd rather talk about birds. We could talk about birds. You could tell me what new and unique species you found to add to your life list or maybe how when blue herons nest they—"

I folded my arms across my chest and glared. "Spill it, mister. Before I spill the contents of that wine glass over your head."

Derek chuckled. "Amy said that Bobby told her Tom left his dressing room about forty minutes early. One of the staff delivered a note to him. A few minutes later, he told Bobby and his mates that he wanted some fresh air and would be back in time for the ceremony."

"What did the note say?"

Derek could only shrug. "I have no idea. Amy didn't know. She said that Bobby said Tom read the note then stuck it in his pants pocket. A little after that, he made his excuses and left."

"Then Jerry will have the note." I twirled my fork around in circles on my empty plate. "That means it probably meant nothing."

"I suppose," agreed Derek. "Unless he ended up tossing it in the trash somewhere along the way."

"Even then, the police should have found it. What about your ex? Where was she?"

Derek smiled. "Hoping she's a murderer?"

"No, of course not," I protested. "It's important to know where all the players were at the time of the murder, that's all."

"According to my ex, she was in her dressing room with a half-dozen bridesmaids up until the time they heard all the commotion."

"So that lets her off the hook."

"I'm afraid so. Besides, I can't really picture my ex-wife strangling anyone. Sucking the life force out of a man, now that I can see." Derek's brow twitched nervously. "Do not tell her I said that."

"I promise. What else did she have to say?"

Derek leaned back in his chair and considered the question. "Nothing that comes to mind. What about you? Making any progress looking for answers for Gloria?"

"No. Talking to people has raised a lot more questions than it has answered. Did your ex say anything about Mickey Caswell or Tom's son, Vail?"

"Who is Mickey Caswell?"

"MC. From MC and the Moonlighters. Miles Sheffield, his guitarist, hinted that MC might be supplementing his income."

"How?"

"Selling illicit drugs," I replied. "And Vail might just be a customer."

I further told Derek how Tom Visconti pretty much snapped his fingers and MC performed free concerts for him whenever the businessman requested.

"To top it off, Lance Jennings and Violet Wilcox just told me that Mickey Caswell once bailed Vail Visconti out of a New Mexico jail."

"That is interesting," admitted Derek. "It is not, however, evidence of either of them being a killer."

"You sound just like a lawyer."

"But I am right."

"I know."

"How do you know this Miles Sheffield?"

"I don't. At least, I didn't. We saw him at Magnolia Manor, remember?"

"Not particularly."

"Anyway, he came by the store. He said he wanted to talk to me. That's who you saw me talking to at the diner this afternoon."

Derek's face turned pink with embarrassment. "I didn't mean to spy on you. Esther insisted I look. I had no idea what she wanted me to look at. When I saw it was you and some redheaded guy, I gave her back the binoculars."

"You could have crossed the street and come said hello."

"I didn't want to interrupt. Besides, I wasn't sure if you were even talking to me after the way you ran out on me."

I apologized once again.

Our waiter appeared, waving the dessert menu and began, unbidden, to describe the heavenly delights of today's homemade cherry cheesecake. "Please, go away," I pleaded. "Before I say yes."

Derek ordered a brandy from the bar.

"Maybe I'll pay a visit on Vail tomorrow," I said.

"Go easy on him. The boy has been through a lot, Amy."

"According to your former wife, Vail hated Tom."

"Maybe. Still, the man was his father."

"True." I helped myself to a sip of Derek's brandy. "I only want to pay my respects."

"And pry some answers out of him."

"Yeah, that too," I admitted. "I suppose he's staying at Tom's house?"

"No. Amy says Vail is sleeping in his van here at the campground."

"In the town park?"

"Yep."

That would be the public campground adjacent to the marina and the restaurant we were sitting in at that very moment.

"Interesting. What about you, Derek? Did you notice anyone or anything unusual when you left to go to the restroom before the ceremony?"

"No. But then I don't have the keen eye for birds and killers that you do."

"Very funny."

"Seriously, there were dozens of people milling around, coming and going. Many of them drinking and boisterous. Not to mention the staff. Face it, Amy, this might be one case that even you can't solve."

"Maybe. But I can promise you one thing."

"What's that?"

"If the killer isn't apprehended by the weekend, I don't care. Nothing is going to spoil our special day."

"Or our honeymoon," Derek added, clasping his warm hands over mine. "I hope."

"Speaking of our honeymoon, when is Corey arriving? I'm looking forward to meeting him." With Derek's apartment being so tiny, Corey had taken a vacation rental condo at the Ruby Lake Marina for his stay in town.

Derek's friend Corey was going to be visiting up from Saint John in the U.S. Virgin Islands. He owned a boutique resort there. He was giving us a great deal on our honeymoon.

Derek and Corey were college friends, former roommates, in fact. They had gone through the ordeal of law school together. While Derek had made a career for himself as a lawyer, Corey, after three years at a major Boston legal firm, had chucked it all in.

Following his heart, Corey Lingstrom sold his Beacon Hill brick row house and his Jag, and donated his pricey wardrobe to charity. With the proceeds, and a small inheritance, he had impulsively purchased the twenty-four room Rumrunners Hotel on the shores of Cinnamon Bay Beach, renamed it Second Chance Inn, as in second chance in life.

"I'm picking him up at Charlotte International tomorrow afternoon. From there, we'll come back here to pick up Paul and Dan. Then we're off to Biltmore."

"To do your guy things." The men had a couple night stay booked at the Inn on Biltmore Estate, located on the sprawling grounds that were home to the Biltmore House, commissioned by George Vanderbilt near the end of the nineteenth century. The country house boasted a mere two hundred and fifty rooms and an indoor swimming pool.

While the French Renaissance-inspired chateau contained about forty acres of floor space, that was nothing compared to the eight thousand or so acres of property surrounding it.

"This was your idea, remember?"

"Actually, it was Kim's dumb idea." Kim felt, and talked me into going along with the idea, that Derek and I being apart for several days leading up to the wedding would increase our desire and anticipation for each other.

I was already regretting that I'd brought the idea up with Derek and missing him already. As far as desire and anticipation, I was beginning to desire and anticipate getting a new best friend. One who did not come up with dumb ideas which she then poisoned my brain with.

Derek grinned like a little boy skipping school. He rubbed his hands with glee. "Target shooting, golf, fly fishing...I mean, I'm going to miss you but—"

"Yeah, yeah. I know." My bridal shower was going to be low key by comparison, exactly the way I wanted it. A few family and friends, some laughs and some tears, all ending with a movie double feature: *Runaway Bride* with Richard Gere and Julia Roberts, followed by *Father of the Bride*, the original version with Spencer Tracy, Joan Bennett and Elizabeth Taylor.

"Just promise me you won't have so much fun that you forget to come home in time for the wedding."

"That's a vow I can keep," promised Derek.

19

The following morning, I bundled up in preparation for a three-mile bird watching hike sponsored by Birds & Bees and led by me.

The day was humid and cool. Gray clouds barely scratched the surface of the sky that was turning bluer by the minute. As we walked, we spotted dozens of species, most typical for the area and time of year, thrashers, woodpeckers, robins and Carolina wrens. We even got a look at a couple of Eastern Phoebes perched on an old fencepost, wagging their tails up and down.

There were six of us on the hike, including Esther and her sister, Gertie. Esther's special friend, Floyd Withers, Karl Vogel, our curmudgeonly ex-police chief and, very much to my surprise, Mark Bolan, made up the remainder of our motley crew.

"Look, everyone," I whispered, drawing my binoculars slowly up to my eyes.

I pointed out a green heron nesting in a tree along the margin of the lake. The green heron is a beautiful wading bird with iridescent green feathers on their backs and crests, chestnut-colored chests and backs, and yellow-orange legs and feet.

"Is that a bird?" Karl blinked and rubbed his eyes. His binoculars were almost as ancient as him and his vision was on the poor side.

"Of course it's a bird, you dummy," grumbled his best friend, Floyd.

"Shush," I admonished them.

"He is beautiful," remarked Mark. There was a high-pitched quality to his voice. "It is a he, isn't it? Didn't I hear the male is always the prettier of the two?"

"Same as people," chuckled Karl.

Floyd elbowed him. He didn't want Esther to take Karl's comment the wrong way.

"Yes, that's right, Mark. Generally, the female is the smaller and duller of the sexes."

That drew additional snickers from Karl.

"What are you, five years old, Karl?" snapped Esther.

I ignored the bickering, hoping to refocus their attention on birds. "Green herons are one of the smarter birds. Like crows. They use tools."

"Like claw hammers and chisels?" Karl asked. "Or power tools?"

I shuttered my eyes. Karl was on a roll. "Like debris or a scrap of food. They'll play with it on the surface of the water to attract fish."

"The unsuspecting yet curious fish comes to check it out and gets gobbled up, is that it, Amy?" Mark asked.

"Right you are, Mark. It's nice to see someone taking birding seriously."

"Suck up," I heard Karl mutter under his breath.

"Did you get a picture of the heron's nest, Gertie?" I asked, as I urged my group to move on up the trail. We'd already been walking for close to two hours. That was a long time for some of them to be on their feet.

"Of course, I did," lied Gertie. She turned around as quickly as a woman her age could and snapped off a couple of parting shots.

Gertie Hammer is a small woman, shrunken by time, with age-defying brilliant blue eyes, gray-black hair and crooked teeth. Her personality has a certain crooked bent to it as well.

Gertie's ancient body was buried somewhere inside a floppy black turtleneck sweater and a pair of droopy black wool slacks. Her boots looked like genuine US Army issue. I had a hunch that pair of boots weighed about as much as she did in the buff.

Not that I ever wanted to see proof.

I rolled my eyes. I would have liked to have included a photo of the nest in our next newsletter. I could see that wasn't going to happen.

Gertie was taking her role of official wedding photographer way too seriously. Throughout the hike, she had snapped more pictures of me than she did of the birds.

"Seriously, Gertie," I admonished her yet again as we stopped at a small outhouse to accommodate those in the group over sixty-five, which meant everyone but myself and Mark Bolan. "How many pictures do we need of the bride-to-be with a pair of binoculars glued to her face?"

"I'm keeping my options open," Gertie replied, quickly snapping off yet another unflattering shot of me. This one of me admonishing her for taking pictures of me.

I closed my eyes and counted to ten as one member of our group stumbled out of the outhouse while another of our group tumbled in.

Most new brides love to show off their wedding albums. Not me, mine was going to be the wedding album from hell.

I turned my back on Gertie and gazed across the finger of lake to the campground on the other side. Tents, vans and RVs dotted the landscape. One of those temporary abodes held the specimen I was seeking, the elusive Vail Visconti, a tall, skinny, two-legged critter who may or may not have predatory tendencies.

And a drug habit.

Had he sent his father a pre-ceremony note? Had he lured him into the maze garden only to strangle him to prevent his marrying Amy Harlan?

I turned to my little group of bird lovers and made a show of checking my watch. "That about wraps it up for this morning, everyone. Esther, would you mind escorting everyone back to Birds and Bees? I have something I need to do."

"Fine." Esther hitched up her sweat pants. "Don't forget to use you ten percent off coupons when we get back to my store, people."

Her store?

As an incentive to keep the bird walks going, we offered ten percent off coupons good any purchase the day of the walk only.

"Can't we go a little further?" Floyd asked.

"Sorry, Floyd. Next time, okay?" I planted a kiss on his cheek. "And don't forget, we've got coffee and powdered sugar mini-donuts in the store for you all."

"Thanks for the use of the binoculars, Amy." Mark Bolan handed me the loaners. I always keep a few spares around for the newbies.

"Would you mind dropping them off at the store? It's on your way, yes?"

"Sure." Mark took back the binoculars. "Is that coupon Esther mentioned good on optical gear?"

"Anything in the store."

"Nice. Maybe I'll purchase a pair." Mark had come dressed in loose-fitting jeans, white sneakers and a long sleeve brown polo shirt. He had brought a small digital point-and-shoot camera for the bird walk, which he had used to shoot practically everything in sight.

"Come on, Floyd. I don't want to miss out on the donuts." Karl began marching faster than he had all morning. Knowing Karl, he'd be the first person in the door and the first to pour himself some free coffee. Mark Bolan was dogging him at a distance.

"Mark," I called.

"Yes?"

"Wait. Got a minute?"

"Sure." Mark walked slowly back. "What is it?"

"I wanted to thank you for coming this morning. It's always great having a new birder in our group."

"I enjoyed myself."

"I could tell. And your bird call imitations were spot on."

"Thank you." Mark lowered his eyes sheepishly and kicked the ground with his toe. "It's something I've always had a good ear for."

"Maybe you can help me work on mine. If you plan on joining us again, that is?"

"I'd like that." Mark smiled. "To tell the truth, I wasn't so sure about this bird walking stuff at first. This was Gloria's idea that I come. She said a hobby, and a little outdoor exercise, would do me good. Do me good to get out of the house too, she says."

"Yes, I heard about your...stroke, was it?"

"Heart attack. I was a public accountant. Gave it up. Couldn't handle the stress anymore. The doctor said it could kill me."

"I'm sorry to hear that."

"It's okay. I mean, I was pretty depressed about it for a while but I'm over it now. Keep myself busy. Gloria even got Mr. Visconti to give me some part-time work around his place."

"That's wonderful." Of course, his work and Gloria's might end now with Visconti's death. I wished there was some way I could help them, if their jobs did end but Birds & Bees was already stretched to its financial limits.

Still, I could ask around town if things got rough for them.

I suddenly realized Mark was still talking. "We love each other. I would do anything for her and she would do anything for me. I've been keeping an eye on Mr. Visconti's rental property for him while he's out of town. Do a little gardening. Pick up the mail. Stuff like that. Keeps me out of trouble."

I smiled. "How is Gloria holding up? Will she be able to keep her job?"

"She's okay. Busying herself with her work and the funeral and all."

"Keeping busy is the best way to handle the tragedy."

"That's what they say. As for her job, my wife says she's hopeful that Mr. Breen will go ahead with the Rivercrest project. Visconti's group had a lot of money invested in it already."

"That's nice." For Gloria and Mark, at least. As for Ruby Lake's environs, I wasn't looking forward to more development.

"Speaking of the tragedy, I know it's early days, but have you learned anything that might help the police,

Amy?"

"If you mean do I know who murdered Tom Visconti, I'm afraid not. But you tell your wife not to worry, I've got a few clues that I'm following up on."

"What sort of clues?"

I glanced at the crowded campground. I wasn't sure but I thought I might have seen Vail Visconti walking towards the public restrooms and bathing facilities on the far side of the beach volleyball court. "I can't say yet. Tell Gloria that if I learn anything that might be useful, I'll let her know, okay?"

Mark promised he would and we parted.

I followed the fork in the trail leading to the camping area. Campers lingered around stone-lined fire pits. Others sat inside their humongous air-conditioned RVs, engines idling, watching the outdoor world from the inside. I didn't get that at all but to each his or her own.

Wandering between the multicolored tents, RVs, pickups and vans, inhaling the smell of fresh brewing coffee, frying bacon and burning charcoal briquets, I found Vail Visconti seated at a folding table with a paint-speckled plastic top and bent metal legs poking into the grass.

The table sat a couple feet from the van's gaping side panel doors. A couple of backpacks hung from hooks. A thin mattress held a tangle of blankets. The cargo hold's bare metal floor was layered with bits of dirt and pine straw, and littered with empty plastic water bottles, a couple of takeout pizza boxes, beer cans, a crushed box of cereal and more.

Two equally scruffy folding chairs were positioned at the table. Vail occupied the chair in the shade cast by his Ford van. Dressed in wrinkly green cargo shorts, a white

T-shirt with a hoodie overtop, and leather sandals, he was eating a late breakfast, eggs, sausage and toast.

"What are you doing here?" Vail banged his fork down on a melamine plate. "Get lost in the woods?" he asked, taking in my outfit, from my wide-brimmed hat to my hiking boots.

"I was in the area. Bird watching. I heard you were camping here and was hoping we could have a chat. I'm very sorry about your father."

"Go away." He snatched a tall can of energy drink and gulped it down furiously.

"You can talk to me or you can talk to the police."

"Ooh, like I'm scared. Really scared." He rolled his eyes and tossed the empty drink carelessly to the ground. "What do you want from me, lady? Dad's dead. Life goes on for the rest of us. You're the one that found his body. Take some sick pleasure in murder, do you?"

"Do you know Gloria Bolan?"

"Of course. She's an idiot who worked for my dad."

"Idiot?"

"If you work for my dad, you must be an idiot."

"That's not a very charitable way to talk about your deceased father."

"You didn't know my dad, did you?"

I admitted I hadn't. The few interactions I had had with Tom Visconti had not left me with a good impression of the man. That did not, however, mean that he deserved to die. "Mrs. Bolan asked me to see if I could help find out what happened."

"You mean who killed dear old Dad?" Vail Visconti stuffed some runny eggs in his mouth. "That's easy. She killed him." He wiped his lips with the back of his arm.

"Gloria Bolan?"

"No, that gold digger he was marrying."

"Amy Harlan?"

"That's the one."

"Why do you call her a gold digger? And why should she strangle him *before* they were married?"

"Wow, you're as dense as the rest of the yokels around here. She was a gold digger because Dad had millions. She wasn't wealthy, was she?"

"I suppose not. But it's not like she was exactly hard up. And that still doesn't explain why she would murder your father before they were even married."

"Wouldn't she wait until they had been married a few years before bumping him off? If that was even her plan. Certainly, there are more subtle ways to murder than strangulation."

"Greed does funny things to people." Vail stood and scraped the remainder of his breakfast into a metal bucket. "The fact is, she and Dad already were married."

"What?"

"Think about it, lady. Dad and her had gotten married already. They had a civil ceremony beforehand. The fancy to-do at Magnolia Manor was all for show. Throw a big party. Show off to their friends."

That was food for thought. Amy Harlan was now Amy Visconti. But would the marriage hold up in a court of law? I would have to ask Derek about that.

Not that I agreed with Vail Visconti's theory about Amy wanting his father dead. She had seemed genuinely happy to be marrying.

"Are you saying that she inherits everything?"

Vail spat. "Not if I have anything to say about it. It wouldn't surprise me if she wasn't in on it with Breen."

"Bobby Breen? You think your Dad's partner and Amy

Harlan conspired together to kill him?"

"Why not?"

"I can think of a million reasons why not. Maybe not for Bobby Breen, I barely know the man, but Amy Harlan would never do such a thing." Holy heavens, I was defending Derek's ex-wife! What was my world coming to?

"Says you."

I tried another tack—a much more blunt one. "Why did MC bail you out of a New Mexico jail cell?"

Shock exploded over the young man's face. "I don't know what you're talking about."

"I'm talking about Mickey Caswell doing your dad all kinds of favors, like performing free concerts whenever the man asked. I'm talking about MC being your drug dealer. Was your father a user too?"

Before he could answer, I asked another question. "And why did MC lie to me about knowing your father?"

Vail pulled open the passenger side door of the van and popped open the glovebox. He turned around to face me, clutching a long, sharp hunting knife in his right hand. "Take a hike, lady."

He jabbed the knife at my stomach.

I flinched and jumped backward.

The tumbled blankets on the thin mattress in the back of the van sprang to life. A scrawny pink face showed itself. Two long-fingered hands yanked the sheets away.

A young man about Vail's age, wearing nothing but a pair of baggy striped boxer shorts, extracted himself from the van. He yawned and rubbed his puffy, whiskered cheeks. "What's up?"

"I caught this woman snooping around," Vail said,

his voice low and hard as nails.

The other young man rooted around the floor of the van and came up with an unopened can of energy drink. "Isn't it legal out here in the boonies," he said, casually popping the lid, "to kill intruders? A man's home is his castle and all that?" he added lazily before taking a swig.

"Yeah, I think it is." Vail took a step towards me.

I yelped and fled.

It wasn't my greatest moment but it was far from my worst.

20

Deciding a trip to Ruby Lake Motor Inn was in order, I walked quickly to Birds & Bees. I grabbed my keys off the hook inside the back door and set out in my van. I hadn't gotten a mile down Lake Shore Drive when a police car came roaring up behind me, lights flashing, siren squawking.

"Now what?" I grumbled, checking the rearview mirror. "Are you kidding me?"

It was Chief Jerry Kennedy in all his splendor.

I pulling over to the side of the road, threw open the door of the van and jumped down. I waited beside my vehicle, fuming, as Jerry eased in behind me so close our bumpers were nearly kissing.

The howling siren came to a sudden stop.

The car door opened and Chief Kennedy slowly extracted himself from his squad car.

"Can't you turn off that stupid light?" I hollered. We were attracting more attention than another widow of the lake sighting.

Every town has its ghost story our two. Ours included the widow Mary McKutcheon. The story goes that she'd drowned herself after her husband was murdered by marauders around the time of the Civil War. Before her death, she laid a curse on the men and they had died one by one, each death more hideous than the previous.

After the last man died, she walked into the lake and disappeared. Some say she still rises from the center of the lake once a year, on the anniversary of her husband's death.

Being a reasonable, modern woman, I do not believe in spirits. It is merely a coincidence that I sleep with one eye open around that time each year.

Jerry reached inside his squad car and flipped off the light bar.

"What do you want, Jerry?" I planted my hands on my hips. "I was definitely not speeding."

Jerry smirked. "Actually, Simms, you were going a couple of miles over the posted limit but I'm feeling generous and I'm gonna let that pass."

"Gee, thanks so much. What's this all about then?"

"I hear you are investigating the death of Tom Visconti." Jerry cupped his hands over his eyes and peered through the back windows of my van.

"If you're looking for contraband, or the loot from my last heist, it's in my other getaway vehicle. And how did you hear that I was investigating Tom Visconti's death?" Would Gloria Bolan have told him? That seemed unlikely.

"You just get off the bus, Simms?" Jerry shook his head side to side, some of his ever-expanding belly moved with it. "Everybody in town knows."

"Okay, so what if I am? You've got coffee on your tie."

"Here's so what." He wiped his damp tie against his chest, only making matters worse. "You, Amy Simms are no private investigator. You've got no training and you've got no license."

He was right but there was no sense pointing that out. "That doesn't make it a crime for me to help out a friend." At least, I didn't think it did.

"You and Gloria Bolan are friends? That's news to me." His eyes scoured my face, trying to read me.

"She wants to know what happened to her boss. Again, no crime, Jerry."

Townspeople were staring at us from the sidewalk and passing cars. I felt like a criminal. I wanted to wave my hands and say, "Hey, folks, nothing to see here."

"No, but what happened to Visconti is a crime. An actively being investigated crime. By me." He stabbed his finger into his shiny badge. "Got it? That means you stay out of this and let me do my job."

"If only you would," I mumbled.

"What's that?"

"I said, have you found out anything? Any leads as to who the killer is?"

"That's for me to know and you *not* to find out. Understand? And," he added, "if you should happen to stumble on anything that does concern my investigation, I expect you to tell me about it. Pronto." He snapped his fingers.

"Did you find a note on Tom Visconti's body?"

"What sort of note?"

"I don't know. Maybe a note from somebody asking to meet him out in the maze."

"What makes you think there's such a note?"

"According to Amy Harlan, her fiancé received a note about forty minutes before the ceremony. It wasn't long after that that he decided to take a stroll in the maze garden."

"That doesn't necessarily mean it was a message

from the killer, Simms. What's he gonna say, 'Please meet me in the garden so I can strangle you?'" Jerry snorted. "Besides, we didn't find any note."

"Maybe you should look harder. He might have trashed it."

The police chief mulled over my words. "I'll send Reynolds over to Magnolia Manor to poke through the trash. But I doubt we'll find anything."

"That's the spirit," I wisecracked. "Have you interviewed MC?"

"Sure," Jerry said. "Got his autograph. I'm gonna have it framed and hang it up on the wall behind my desk."

"You may want to hold off on that."

Jerry's eyes narrowed to slits. "Why?"

"Because there's something fishy about that guy."

"You think there's something fishy about nearly everybody."

"I'm only saying you might want to check him out. Vail Visconti, too."

"The victim's kid?" The chief looked dubious. "What for?"

"He could be dangerous."

Jerry outright laughed. "I've seen more dangerous looking slices of white bread."

"Oh, yeah? He threatened me with a knife, Jerry."

"What's that?"

I explained how I happened to be conducting a bird watching hike in the vicinity of the campground when I ran into Vail Visconti. "It was less than an hour ago, Jerry. We had words."

"You do have a way of riling folks up, Amy." Like him.

I ignored the jibe. "Then he took a poke at me with a nasty looking knife."

"Took a poke at you?" Jerry could not have sounded any more dubious.

"Okay, so he sort of jabbed it in my general direction. You should have a word with him. An official word. In fact, I'd like to file charges."

"Charges? What charges?"

"Criminal charges."

Jerry laughed. "I ought to be charging you with interfering in an official police investigation."

"This is serious, Jerry. That kid is dangerous. I demand you arrest him."

"I've got no grounds."

"No? How about attempted murder? Scaring an innocent woman half to death? I don't know." I shook my head in frustration. "You're the police chief. Come up with something."

"Do you have any witnesses to this purported altercation?"

"No." The only potential witness was Vail's camping companion. Even if he had seen Vail threaten me, he'd never take my side.

"In other words, you ain't got spit for proof. Knowing you, you probably provoked the boy. He just lost his daddy, for crying out loud."

"Are you saying I deserved it?" I asked, incredulously. "Because, if you are—"

"No, don't go climbing on your high horse. All I'm saying is, again, knowing you, you probably stuck your nose where it wasn't wanted and nearly got it bit off— sliced off in this case. All the more reason for you to stay out of my investigation. If Vail Visconti did threaten you, that's all the more reason to do so." Chief Kennedy ran his tongue over his upper lip with relish, like he'd just polished off a hot dog with all the trimmings.

"I'm out of here." I stomped back to my van and yanked open the door.

"You're getting married in a few days, Simms," Jerry hollered. "How about you concentrate on that? I'll concentrate on catching the criminals!"

I slammed the door shut and my foot down. Jerry wasn't wrong. All the more reason the man infuriated me so. Leaving Jerry to eat my dust, I hightailed it to the Ruby Lake Motor Inn.

Yes, I was getting married in a few short days. But a little bit of a sidetrack to ask Mickey Caswell a few questions couldn't hurt.

Could it?

21

Constructed in the forties, the L-shaped Ruby Lake Motor Inn skirted Lake Shore Drive. A fenced in, thirty-foot in-ground swimming pool was the perfect place to catch a few rays while listening to the hum of the cars passing by and maybe watch the sun set over Ruby Lake.

Behind the motor inn itself, small, rustic cabins with kitchenettes had been added to the property in the nineteen fifties. The inn had its own attached diner. The food wasn't bad.

Rust-scarred thirty-foot-tall steel posts held aloft the giant ruby-red neon sign. A smaller, amber neon sign braced high up between the posts proclaimed that all rooms had satellite TV and AC.

Business was good. There were no vacancies.

I pulled into a slot near the office, intending to pry Mickey Caswell's room number out of the inn manager. Miles Sheffield had told me his own room number but I had no idea which room or cabin MC was occupying.

I stepped into the office and discovered Dick Feller on duty.

"Amy," greeted Dick. "What brings you here?" The front-office manager perched on a wooden stool behind the counter, perusing a recent copy of Rabbit Fanciers Magazine. His thumb was pressed down on a picture-filled page featuring an article titled Hooked On Bunnies.

"Hi, Dick. I'm looking for MC, Mickey Caswell. What room is he in?" The enticing aroma of cinnamon apple streusel wafted through the lobby from the attached diner.

"Tsk-tsk. You know I can't tell you that, Amy. Against inn policy." The manager tugged fastidiously at the sharp cuffs of his button-down shirt.

Dick Feller is a thin, fortyish fellow with receding dirty brown hair, pasty white skin and a thick Southern drawl. He blinked his espresso-brown eyes at me. I'd never noticed before how rabbit-like his own features and mannerisms were.

"Come on, Dick. It's not like I'm some hormone-driven teenybopper looking to get the guy's autograph. I met him at Amy Harlan's wedding. We hit it off. He even offered to have the Moonlighters play at my wedding."

Sure, for fifty grand.

"Ah," Dick splayed his fingers across the counter. "Your wedding. Your wedding to which I did not get an invitation."

Oops.

"Gee, you mean it got lost in the mail?" I slapped my forehead. "How did that happen? I mean, you should have told me."

My grin couldn't have gotten any bigger. Or faker. But Dick did not have to know that.

"Of course, you're invited. It wouldn't be a wedding without you now, would it?" I gave him a friendly slug to the shoulder.

"Ouch." He winced and rubbed his shoulder.

"Sorry. Chicken or steak?"

"What?" He looked confused.

"What do you want for dinner? Are you bringing a plus one?"

Dick perked up. "Do you know someone?"

My brain went into overdrive. "Um, sure. Moire is coming. Alone. You two should come together."

"Moire Leora?" Dick Feller smoothed his necktie. "From Ruby's Diner?"

"That's right."

"She's cute. You think she would? I mean, go with me to the wedding?"

"Absolutely, positootly. In fact…" I leaned over the counter and waved him closer. "Do not tell her I said this but…"

"Yes?" whispered Dick. I could practically hear his heart thumping with anticipation.

"She asks about you all the time."

Dick gasped. "She does?"

"She does." Okay, so it was a small white lie. My Aunt Betty says that white lies are the grease that make the world go round.

I'd talk to Moire later. I was sure she'd agree to go as Dick's date. Her husband was long deceased and her last boyfriend had turned out to be no good.

"Mr. Caswell is in cabin number six." The front-office manager gave a heartfelt sigh. "I wonder if Moire likes rabbits?"

I was pretty sure she did but from the perspective of a chef. Still, there was no sense bursting Dick's romantic bubble.

"Thanks, Dick. See you Saturday."

"Wait."

I swung back around. "Yes?"

"Mr. Caswell is not in his cabin."

"Oh?"

"MC is out there." Dick pointed out the big plate glass window. "Sunbathing."

"Right-o."

"Please, do not tell him I told you where he was. The man is a big star. He likes his privacy, Amy."

Big star? MC's star had been fading since the seventies disco craze.

"Don't you worry, Dick, I am the very soul of discretion."

I opened the safety gate and sauntered down to where MC lay stretched out on a webbed chaise lounge.

The ultimate cold-blooded lizard basking in the life-giving rays of the sun.

The pool was empty of swimmers and the deck deserted of sun seekers but for Mickey Caswell. Was it a coincidence that there was no one around or had the guests been scared off by the sight of what appeared to be a beached, oiled-down whale in a too-tight red Speedo?

"MC?" I could not see his eyes through the mirrored sunglasses. Was he snoozing? Two empty beer bottles and a butt-filled tin ashtray rested at the side of the chair. Very much against the posted swimming pool rules which forbade glass bottles and smoking.

I tried again, kicking the foot of his lounger ever so slightly with my toe. "Hello, Mr. Caswell?"

He stirred. "Hey, I remember you." The singer lazily ran his fingers through the thatch of wiry black hair on his bronzed chest. "Pull up a seat. Amy, right?" He waved to the empty lounger beside him.

I sat. The hot rubbery straps seared my thighs.

"Did you bring my check?" he asked.

"Check?"

"For the gig, babe."

"Oh, my wedding. No." I squeezed my knees together, sensing his eyes roaming over me. As for my own eyes, with his state of undress, I was keeping them well north of the equator. "I'm afraid there's been a bit of a misunderstanding about that."

"Yeah?" He pulled his sunglasses lower and looked down his nose at me.

"Yes. You see, I'm afraid my budget is completely maxed out."

"Bummer. It would have made sticking around this second-rate hole of a town almost worthwhile."

"Ruby Lake is a lovely town, thank you very much." I snapped in defence of my home.

"Could have fooled me." He picked up a beer bottle and shook it. Held it up to the rays of the sun. "Out of beer."

"Tough break."

"Not to worry. I'll get one of the boys to hit the market for me."

He pulled a black cell phone from under his pool towel and began texting. "So you can't afford to hire the band and I'm stuck cooling my heels in this lovely little burg where people go around strangling grooms on the day of their wedding."

"Why did you tell me that you didn't know Tom Visconti prior to coming to town?"

"Did I?"

"I happen to know that you've performed for him many times."

"You must have misunderstood me," MC said casually. He picked up a tube of sunscreen and squirted a generous amount over his belly and arms.

He proceeded to rub the coconut-scented cream into his skin, moaning with pleasure as he did so. "What do you people do for fun around here?"

"You could try bird watching."

MC laughed loudly. "You are a hoot. No owl pun intended," he said with a big stupid grin on his face. "Say, I'm burnin' up here. How's about you join me in a swim?"

"I'm not much of a swimmer, thanks."

MC slid off his lounger and stretched his arms overhead. "Come on, Amy. Let's take a dip." He offered me his hand.

"Sorry. Even if I wanted to, I didn't bring a swimsuit."

"No problem. We can skinny dip."

"No, thanks."

"Why not? There's nobody around. Besides, I won't tell, if you won't."

"No, really, I couldn't. I'm afraid of the water. That's why I never learned to swim." I was lying.

"Bummer." He looked longingly at the blue water of the pool. "I could teach you."

"Another time, maybe." I clutched my purse and gazed at the motel sign. Anything was better than looking at the nearly naked crooner standing an arm's length from me. "What I really came to talk to you about was Tom Visconti and his son, Vail."

MC grunted and jumped into the swimming pool, sending a spray of cold water over me.

I gasped and waited impatiently while he swam clumsily from one end of the pool to the other. Finally, he emerged dripping wet and coughing. He climbed the metal ladder and shook himself like a wet dog.

Wrapping his towel around his waist, he reclaimed his lounger. "Ah, better." He twisted his neck one way then the other. "Where the hell is that beer?"

"About Tom Visconti?"

"What about him? The police already asked me and everybody in the band. We're musicians, not stranglers."

I decided to be blunt. "Why did you bail Vail Visconti out of jail in Taos, New Mexico?"

MC slid his sunglasses over his eyes and stared into the sun, his arms at his sides. "Who says I did?"

His left hand shot up. "Wait, don't tell. It's that little birdie of yours again. Well, your little birdie is wrong. I never bailed anybody out of jail. Well, except maybe a musician or three. The boys do have a way of getting themselves into trouble now and then.

"But it's all good, clean, harmless fun. You know, drinking, carousing, a bar fight with a jealous boyfriend or husband. I slip the local gendarmes a few bucks for the next policemen's ball, maybe offer to play a benefit, if absolutely necessary, and we're good to go."

"Drug dealing?" I suggested.

"My guys are clean."

"What about you?"

"What about me?" demanded MC, suddenly angry.

Had I struck a nerve?

"I had a very interesting conversation with Vail this morning. He not only told me you bailed him out of jail, he practically accused you of being his dealer."

I was lying on all counts but MC didn't know that. Vail had told me nothing. Miles Sheffield had suggested MC might be dealing drugs. I couldn't expose him. He could lose his job for telling tales on his boss.

"That scum?" MC grabbed a cigarette from a soggy pack at his feet and lit up with a gold lighter carrying his initials. "What a punk. Look, I had a fling with the kid. It was fun while it lasted but I dumped him."

"A fling? With Vail?"

"Yeah. I'd appreciate if you'd keep that between us. I've got a reputation to uphold."

"Did Vail's father know about this fling?"

"Yeah, he found out. Why do you think I perform for him like a puppet on a string?" The performer chuckled. "Did." His fat lips sucked hard on his cigarette.

"How long have you known the Viscontis?"

"Sorry," MC tossed his smoldering cigarette through the fence. "Show's over."

I climbed to my feet and rubbed the backs of my fried thighs. "Mrs. Bolan would really like some closure. She asked me to look into the matter because I'm local."

"Gloria is the reason you're nosing around?" He shook his head. "Sweet lady. Good for a tumble."

"A tumble? Are you trying to say that you and she..."

"That's right."

"Did Tom know?" Not that I necessarily believed him.

"Sure. I knew Gloria before he did. I'm the one who introduced them. Got her the gig with him."

"Gloria is married to Mark."

"This was long before she was married. She was working for a promoter part-time years ago. That's how we hooked up. She's good in bed but not all that bright."

"Why do you say that?"

"Because Tom's killer is no local. She's wasting her time and money, if she's paying you to nose around."

"What makes you so sure?"

"Because it's got to be the kid, Vail. He hated his dad. To the core. Blames him for his sainted mother's death."

"I didn't know that."

"Now you do. Trust me. Family aren't all they are cracked up to be. Sometimes blood relations can lead to blood. Period." MC took my elbow. "Shall we?"

He gave me a nudge.

I took a step and found my foot hovering over open air. I yelped. An instant later, I was plunging into six feet of cold water.

My feet hit bottom and I shot up. "Help me out!" I spluttered, spitting heavily chlorinated swimming pool water—water that MC had recently been swimming in —from my nostrils and mouth.

MC extended a hand and pulled me out. He passed me my purse, which had mercifully fallen to the concrete deck and not ended up in the pool with me. "Better be careful."

I silently vowed that from then on I would be.

22

"He pushed you into the swimming pool?" Kim grabbed my shoulders.

Esther threw a damp bath towel over my head.

"I don't know. I'm not sure." I grunted as Esther began rubbing my face with the towel. She had run upstairs and snatched the bath towel from her apartment. It smelled like a wet cat. "Seriously, Esther, are you trying to completely erase my face?" I pushed the towel away. "I don't know. I've thought about it and thought about it."

Did I fall or was I pushed?

"One thing I do know for sure is that Vail got mad when I asked him a few relatively harmless questions and pointed a knife at me. MC seemed to get just as riled. And maybe tried to drown me."

"In a six foot deep swimming pool? Really, Amy, that's ridiculous. Don't you think you're letting your imagination get the best of you?"

"Is it ridiculous? I told MC I didn't know how to swim." I sneezed hard and rubbed my nose with the side of my index finger. "I know one thing. I'm done with this murder business."

"Good." Kim handed me a tissue. "The whole idea of playing detective is dumb. And dangerous."

"I agree," offered Esther. "You're definitely not cut out for the work."

I was in no mood to argue. "I'm going to go see Gloria Bolan and tell her what I've learned. Maybe she can get the police to take her seriously. When I told Jerry about my run in with Vail, he didn't take me seriously at all."

"No surprise there," quipped Kim "From class clown to chief of police. Who could have predicted that?"

"And that's it. After that, I'm done." I waved my hands. "Time to focus on me."

"And your wedding," Kim added.

"Right."

"Yeah," quipped Esther. "It might be a good idea to try to stay alive until Saturday."

"I have every intention of doing so."

"Speaking of which," began Kim, after studying her watch. "You'd better go upstairs and shower. Better yet, take a hot bubble bath," she suggested. "The guys will be by shortly to pick up Paul and head off to the Biltmore."

"Yeah," cackled Esther. "You don't want lover boy to see you looking like this, do you?"

"No. You're right." I ran up the three flights of steps and ran a hot bath.

I fell asleep in the tub with my head resting on a folded towel and my feet dangling over the side. The radio played softly in the background.

The banging on the apartment door roused me. I picked my cell phone off the tile floor and checked the time. "Yikes." It was late. Derek was waiting for me at the door to say goodbye.

I wrapped a bath towel around me and flew to the door. "Derek!"

"Hi, Amy." Strong arms folded around me and lifted

me off the ground.

"Alex?"

Alexander Bean kissed me solidly on the cheek. "Surprised to see me?"

"Yes. Very." My face heated up and my heart skipped a beat.

Alex lowered me slowly to the ground. My towel slipped dangerously, if not lewdly. I hastily refastened it up under my armpits.

"Am I interrupting something?"

I gasped. Derek stood on the top step of the staircase gazing curiously at me and Alex.

"Derek!" There I was standing almost naked on the landing with my old high school sweetheart. Nothing between us but a thin bath towel. I turned pink in places that had never seen the sun.

"Hello, Amy," Derek called, his voice steady. "Did I come at a bad time?" He bounced his eyes off Alex. "I only came to say goodbye."

"Goodbye?" My heart sank.

"The guys and I are driving to Asheville for a couple of days, remember?"

"Yes. Of course." I cleared my throat and clutched my towel. I was torn between running back inside my apartment or simply squeezing my eyes shut and disappearing from the face of the earth forever. "I've been expecting you."

"Have you?" Derek asked.

From his tone of voice, I couldn't decide if he was angry, suspicious or merely surprised. Lawyers could be enigmatic when it suited them. "Um, Derek, this is Alexander Bean."

"Pleased to meet you, Derek." Alex extended his hand

in greeting.

Derek's face wore a stiff mask of disapproval as they shook. "Same here." He gave me a cold peck on the cheek. "I'd better be going. Paul and the guys are already in the car. I don't want to keep them waiting."

"Wait, Derek," I hurried after him to the stairs, struggling to hold up my bath towel.

"Yes?"

"Can't you stay? I can explain." Actually, I couldn't. I had no idea what Alex Bean was doing at my doorstep.

Derek hesitated. I didn't know what to say. As I tried to form thoughts and turn them into sentences, he smiled sadly and walked away.

"Was that the groom?" Alex inquired.

"You'd better come inside," I said. I went to get dressed in my bedroom. "And tell me what you are doing here."

After changing into a pair of conservatively cut blue jeans and a warm over-sized sweater, I offered my old high school boyfriend a soda. I placed myself in my dad's chair while he planted himself on the sofa.

"How long are you visiting?" I pulled my legs up under me.

"I'm not. Haven't you heard? I'm reopening the bookstore."

"No, I haven't heard a thing. I've been so busy with the wedding."

"Right." Alex grinned.

It was the smile of youth that I remembered. He was as handsome as ever, in a more grown up sort of way in his dark jeans and cable knit sweater the color of fresh-cut straw.

"Thanks again for the wedding invitation."

"The what?"

"Invitation. You sent it to my DC address. It's a lucky thing the post office is still forwarding my mail."

"Lucky, yes." I could only half-listen, my mind was on Derek and the look on his face before he had gone.

Had he gone for good?

Was I being overdramatic?

Alex was still talking. "I've got to admit, I was surprised you thought of me, Amy. How long has it been anyway?"

My mind did some mental math. Not my strong suit, especially after what had occurred on the landing with Derek. "A long time," I said finally.

Alex was my first love, my high school boyfriend. We both went off to separate colleges, me to the University of North Carolina at Chapel Hill, him to the University of Virginia in Charlottesville.

Then I fell head over heels for the king of all heels, Craig Bigelow. Sometime later, I finally came to my senses and left Craig and Chapel Hill, returning to my roots in Ruby Lake.

Now Alex had come back too and he was going to stay and reopen the bookstore. Ruby Lake had one bookstore and that had closed due to unfortunate circumstances.

"How long have you been back?"

"A couple of weeks. I'm staying at my mom's place. The painters, plumbers and carpenters won't be finished up at the store for another week or so."

Alex drained the last couple ounces of his orange soda. "I guess I'd better be going. I just wanted to stop in and say hello."

"I'm glad you did." I walked him to the door.

"Next time, I'll call first."

"Good idea." I opened the door.

"I hope your fiancé, Derek, didn't get the wrong idea. I didn't mean to make any trouble."

"Don't worry. I'm sure you didn't," I said. But I was not so sure at all. I felt a pang in my heart. Derek.

The guys had gone on the trip with a firm no-cell-phone rule, except for Dan, in case of emergency, because he was a police officer. Would my wanting to call Derek and explain how what he had seen wasn't what it had seemed be considered an emergency?

I walked Alex out.

He climbed into a small red convertible and drove off. I turned the Open sign to Closed.

Kim appeared magically at my side. "Well, were you surprised to see Alex?"

"And then some." I turned off the overhead lights.

"Wait, you knew he was coming?"

"Not to the store, I didn't. I mean, I knew he was coming to the wedding..."

"You did? Why didn't I know? And who invited him?"

"I did." Kim looked two shades paler.

"Why would you do that?"

"He was on the list."

"List?"

"You told me to invite everybody in your address book whose name you put a little star next to." Kim marched to the sales counter, pulled my purse from underneath and dragged out my address book. She began furiously flipping pages.

"See?" She jammed her index finger down on the page. "Alex Bean." She dragged her finger to the right. A little star."

She slammed the address book shut.

I snatched it from her grasp and threw it open. "That's not a little star, it's a skull and crossbones."

"It is?" Kim squinted at the page. "Wow, you're a terrible artist. I didn't get that at all. Anyway, why would you draw a skull and crossbones next to Alex's name? You two were sweethearts."

"Because I dumped him the day before senior prom, remember? I was angry because he took that big-boobed Judy Jenkins instead."

"Oh, yeah. I kind of remember that." She scratched behind her ear. "Only, I thought Alex dumped you."

"Shut up." I tossed my address book in the trash can.

"What are you so mad about, Amy?"

"Because Derek came upstairs, saw me dangling half-naked in Alex's arms and left."

Kim gaped. "Define half-naked."

I explained what had happened.

"You were hugging and kissing?"

"No! Alex grabbed me, I didn't grab him. He kissed me. I did not kiss him," I insisted. "And it was nothing, really. Alex is only a friend, at best. We lost touch over the years. I had no idea he was in town. There is absolutely no spark."

"Oh, dear. You need to tell Derek all that you just told me."

"No cell phone rule, remember? Unless you'd be willing to call Dan for me?"

"Oh, no." Kim waved her hands back and forth in the air. "Dan made me promise not to call. Only Chief Kennedy is allowed to call him in case of emergency."

"This is an emergency."

"Nope." Kim grabbed her coat and car keys. "I'm sure

this will all blow over. You and Derek will be laughing about the whole incident on your honeymoon."

Kim pecked me on the cheek and said goodbye. "See you at eight."

"What's at eight?"

"Bridal shower at my house, dummy. Don't be late."

The minute she left, I dialled Derek's number. The call went straight to voice mail. I left a message telling him I loved him and couldn't wait until he got back.

23

The bridal shower went great, all things considered. At least, what I could remember of it. Mom drove us there and back, tucking me into bed at about two in the morning. That was a long night for me and I slept fitfully. It was a night filled with bad dreams and strange, unidentifiable noises in the night.

All fueled by angst, alcohol and enough sugar to keep the town of Hershey running for a day.

Morning finally showed its jeering yellow face. I crawled from bed with a nagging headache, checked the bird feeders, bathed and found a pot of coffee and some leftover bridal shower cake waiting for me in the kitchen.

There was no sign of my mom.

With my headache grinding away inside my skull, I got ready for work and headed downstairs to Birds & Bees. Esther stood at the counter poring over the weekly sales figures.

There was no sign of my maid of honor.

The way Kim had been partying the night before, I had a feeling she would be sleeping in. If she showed up for her shift at all, it would be very, very much later than scheduled.

"Hi, Esther." The old woman looked fit and well-rested. How was that possible? She had chugged rum after rum like Blackbeard the Pirate the night before.

Esther was the only one of us who had not dozed off during our movie double feature. She had even insisted on watching a Charlie's Angels rerun afterward.

During the episode, she had made some absurd claim as to having been a consultant on the show.

"Where's Mom?"

"Barbara's out front. She wants to get things picked up before we open."

"What things?"

Esther wiped the counter with her apron. "See for yourself."

I stepped outside.

Mom had a dustpan in one hand and a broom in the other.

All of my bird feeders were broken, smashed to pieces. The flowers lay trampled and broken.

"Good morning, Amy."

"Hi, Mom." I walked to the edge of the covered porch. "What the heck happened here?"

"I have no idea." Mom briskly swept up shards of plastic and wood from the sidewalk. Not a single feeder had been spared, not even the hummingbird feeders that had been hanging high up in the branches of the oaks.

I surveyed the ground. Nothing but a little morning dew. "There couldn't have been a storm. There's no sign of rain."

"No. There are a few footprints in the flower bed there." Mom pointed with the dustpan before dumping its contents into a plastic trash barrel.

Sure enough a half-dozen prints were visible in the topsoil but I couldn't identify anything distinguishing about them. They were too smudged.

I stared at a cluster of roses and torn vines in the shape of a skull and crossbones. "Is that what I think it is?"

"Strange, isn't it," replied Mom.

"There is no way that is natural. Who would do such a thing? And why?"

"I don't know," Mom remarked. "But it's sick, if you ask me."

"Speaking of sick..." I bobbed my head toward the street.

Chief Kennedy screeched to a halt at the curb and hauled himself out. He tipped his cap to my mother. "Morning, ma'am. I got your call."

He stepped around a busted pine nesting box. "What's the trouble?"

"What's the trouble?" I said, angrily. "We've been vandalized. Can't you see?"

"I see, I see. Don't go getting your dander up. What I'm asking is if you know who did this." Jerry bent to the lawn and scooped up a handful of mixed bird seed.

He wasn't really thinking of eating that, was he?"

"If I knew who had done this, I would—" I stopped myself. I didn't know what I would do.

"Did either of you hear anything?"

"Not me," said my mother. "I'm afraid I slept like the proverbial log."

I rubbed the back of my neck, hoping to lure my headache down from my frontal lobes. "I thought I heard something a couple of times but I can't be certain." I showed him the skull and crossbones on the lawn.

"Probably some kids pulling a prank." Jerry let the bird seed fall through his fingers and rain on his shoes.

"I'll check with the neighbors to see if anybody saw or heard anything."

"Kids? A prank?" Being around Jerry Kennedy was like being locked inside a pressure cooker. "This was a nasty, malicious act, Jerry. Not the result of some kids having some harmless fun."

"Okay," Jerry sat himself down in one of the porch's rocking chairs and settled his hat on his knee. "That being the case, who have you annoyed enough to want to do this?"

"Shame on you, Jerry Kennedy," snapped my mother. She swatted his feet to sweep up the broken birdhouse beneath his chair.

"Amy is a wonderful young woman. She wouldn't hurt a fly and you know that. Whoever did this," she said, tossing the shattered remains of the wren house into the trash barrel, "must be some maniac."

"Sorry, Mrs. Simms." The chief of police had a healthy fear of my mother, his former school teacher. "All I'm saying is that Amy here has been poking her nose into my murder investigation, hiring herself out as a private detective and—"

Mom came to a halt. "Excuse me?"

"Playing detective," Jerry Kennedy said.

Uh-oh.

I forced a chuckle as Mom eyeballed me. "Did I forget to tell you that Gloria Bolan asked me to see what I might be able to learn about her boss's death, Mom?"

"Yes, you did, young lady."

"And did you forget to tell her that Vail Visconti pulled a knife on you?" Jerry was enjoying himself.

I vowed to get even with him someday, somehow.

"What?" shrieked Mom. "All this and a week before

your wedding?"

"It's not a big deal, Mom."

Jerry snorted.

"Not a big deal, Amy? What if your snooping got somebody mad enough or scared enough to do all this?" Mom indicated our wreck of a front yard.

"You're right, Mrs. Simms. This could have been a warning," Chief Kennedy said, eyes glued to me.

Mom looked close to tears. "Amy, what if this wasn't a prank? What if some madman isn't happy with you trying to find him? This time it was your property but what if he comes after you next?"

"Or your mother," Jerry offered.

"Jerry," I snapped. "Don't even say that."

I grabbed a handful of broken petunias and piled them near the side of the house. I'd add all those ruined plants to the compost bin later. "Anyway, it doesn't matter. Because I'm done poking around."

"Glad to hear it," snapped Jerry at the same time that Mom said, "Good."

"In fact," I announced, wiping damp soil from my hands, "I'm on my way now to tell Gloria Bolan just that. From now on, my focus is going to be on getting married and my future with Derek."

Assuming he wasn't furious with me over last night and that we still had that future.

Gloria Bolan had left my name at the entry gate. Following the security guard's directions, I had no trouble finding the Bolans' home, a quaint, attached villa with a white roof located near the clubhouse.

Mark Bolan stood in his front yard in khakis and a thin flannel shirt with the sleeves rolled up to his elbows. He held a green garden hose and was spraying a fine mist of water over rows of white rose bushes.

I crossed the lawn and joined him.

"Good morning, Ms. Simms." He twisted the nozzle, shutting off the stream of water. "What brings you by?"

"I was hoping to have a quick chat with your wife. Is she around?"

"She is at Mr. Visconti's house, taking care of a few things."

Perfect. Despite my assurances to my mother and Jerry Kennedy, I was curious to get a peek at Tom Visconti's last residence. "Do you think she'd mind if I pop in?"

"Nah. Follow me." He motioned for me to follow him. We passed between a narrow grass gap between his villa and his neighbor's.

"That's it over there." Mark pointed across the pond, which was ringed on this side with villas. On the opposite side, there were larger, detached homes with backyards facing the pond, some with swimming pools. "The one with the blue shutters," he added. "And the putting green."

"Thanks." I started to leave then had a second thought. "Have you heard anything more about the murder?"

"Not a peep." Mark slowly coiled up the garden hose and set it at the edge of the porch near the spigot. "The police searched Visconti's house but Gloria said they didn't find anything. What about you?"

"Not much," I admitted. "I have my suspicions about a couple of people but no proof."

"Like who?"

I shrugged. "Vail Visconti for one. Mickey Caswell, for

another."

Mark stroked the tip of his chin. "Could be. I don't know about MC but the kid's got a temper. I've seen him and the old man going at it a time or two."

"You mean they argued?"

"Only when they were in the same room," he said with a little chuckle. "Sort of makes me glad that Gloria and I never had kids of our own. You have any, Ms. Simms?"

"No. Not yet, that is." Derek and I had not had that talk yet.

Mark turned his head toward the house as we heard the sound of a phone ringing inside.

"I'll let you get that," I said.

"You know what I think?" Mark called out as I pulled open the door to my van.

"What's that?"

"I think it was Bobby."

I held the door open. "Bobby Breen? Tom's partner?"

"Yep." He approached me. "Of course, Gloria thinks I'm wrong but, if you ask me, he's the guy."

I chewed on that a moment. "What makes you think so?"

"Bobby's ambitious and avaricious."

"Wasn't Tom the same?"

"Exactly," agreed Mark. "Two sharks swimming in the same pond."

"And the pond wasn't big enough for the two of them."

"Precisely. Gloria told me that Tom learned that Bobby had gone behind his back and bought up a whole bunch of land around here under a phony corporation's name."

"So?"

"So then he resold that property to Visconti at an inflated price."

"Did Tom find out?"

"Oh, yeah. I don't know how but he found out, all right. And when he did, he and Bobby practically came to blows. Gloria said she had to just about peel them off one another."

Ouch. "But they were partners. Why would Bobby Breen do that?"

"You ever watch Formula One racing?"

"No."

"Well, each team has got two drivers and two cars. While those two drivers may be teammates on paper, they're actually more like fierce rivals. Neither really wants the other to succeed."

"I had no idea."

Mark nodded. "And there's nobody a driver wants to beat more than his own teammate."

Mark Bolan's words stayed with me as I drove to Tom Visconti's rented house.

Was Tom's best man also his worst enemy?

24

Tom Visconti's rental property was a sprawling two-story home with a circular drive. A pink florist van sat near the front door. A tree trimmer's pickup truck and attached trailer was parked near the three-car garage. A crew of three was busily pruning various trees on the grounds.

An older dark blue Mercedes sat on the street. I pulled in behind it.

Bobby Breen opened the door dressed in black trousers. His button-down striped shirt gaped, showing all the world that he had lots of tan and absolutely no chest hair. His right eyebrow went up when he saw me on the front porch. "Amy Simms. Don't tell me, you've come to pay your respects again? It seems to me the last time you tried to do that you quite upset the bride."

"I'm not here to pay my respects, Bobby, I'm here to have a word with Gloria. Do you have a problem with that?"

"No," he seemed to find my anger humorous, which only served to make me angrier. "Come on in. She's working in the office. I'll let her know you're here."

"Thank you," I said stiffly. The home's AC must have an Arctic Circle setting. It was freezing inside.

The interior had been furnished extensively with

golf memorabilia, from framed photographs of famous golfers to monstrous trophies. Golf clubs, some contemporary, some definitely antique with their faded leather grips and tiny wooden heads, hung on the walls.

As he retreated along the marble-tiled floor, I said, "With Tom out of the way, shall we say, I suppose you will be taking over the business completely."

Bobby Breen stiffened. His hands turned to fists as he turned to face me. "What are you implying, Ms. Simms?"

"Nothing. I'm only saying that it will probably make some things easier for you with your partner permanently removed."

His eyes narrowed. "Are you implying that I killed him? I was his best friend. His best man."

"Best man or worst enemy? Where were you before the wedding ceremony? I don't believe you told me."

Bobby Breen chuckled mirthlessly. "And I don't intend to. You aren't a cop and you sure as hell aren't a detective, in spite of what Gloria might think."

I reddened. So he knew about Gloria asking me to look into the death of his former business partner. "I hear you and Tom frequently butted heads."

"Yeah, so? We're both pretty pig-headed when it comes to business." He folded his arms over his chest. "That was what made us great business partners."

"Really? I hear you went around his back and purchased a lot of land in these parts, hoping to make yourself a healthy profit selling it back to your partner at inflated prices."

"Nonsense."

"I'll bet when Visconti found out, he went ballistic. Maybe you thought murdering him was your only option."

"That's slander."

"Not without witnesses. I wonder what the police would make of your underhanded business dealings, if they knew about them. Chief Kennedy might consider them a motive for murder."

Bobby Breen stared at an abstract painting on the wall for a minute, a crisscross of reds and green slashes. "You're way off base, Ms. Simms. It was nothing but a small misunderstanding. Stop trying to make something out of nothing. I explained everything to Tom and he understood. Do you really think I'd stand as his best man if things weren't good between us? We were business partners to the end."

"What happens to that business now?"

"Life simply goes on," Bobby Breen said. "Tom would have wanted it that way."

"What about Tom's share of the business?"

Bobby Breen ran a manicured nail along the side of his cheek. "That depends on the new Mrs. Visconti and Vail. And the courts, I'd bet."

"Did Tom leave anything for you?"

"Oh, yeah. He left me plenty." There was a mischievous twinkle in Bobby Breen's eyes.

"Like what?"

"Like a load of bull to take care of, including a thousand annoying business details, millions in loan debt, a snotty kid who thinks the world owes him everything and then some. Oh, and I almost forgot, a grieving widow who's trying to tell me how to run my business."

"What's going on out here?" Gloria Bolan poked her head from around the corner. She held a pencil in her hand. "Oh, Amy, it's you. I'm with the florist. We are having a small memorial service for Tom tomorrow. Did you want to see me?"

"Yes, if you have a minute? Mr. Breen and I were having a chat first."

"Yes, Amy Simms is quite the detective," Bobby Breen said derisively. He turned and stomped off.

Gloria said a few words to the waiting florist, then approached. She wore open sandals and a dark blue peasant dress. "What is it, Amy?" She rubbed a trail of scratch marks on her arm. "Roses. I told the florist no roses. I never cared for the scent or the barbs."

"I wanted to tell you that I've decided that I need to focus on my wedding."

"I'm sorry to hear that. I mean, I do understand but I was hoping that you might be able to come up with something, some reason that Tom might have been killed."

I told her the few things I had learned about Vail, MC and even Bobby. "Not that any of it means that one of them is a murderer."

"No." Gloria Bolan sighed. "We may never know who the culprit is." She rubbed her hand up and down her arm.

"I'm afraid there is always that possibility." Especially with Jerry Kennedy in charge.

"Let me pay you for your time."

"That really isn't necessary."

"No, a deal's a deal. I'll get my purse." Gloria Bolan wrote me a check for a donation to the Seeds for Seniors program.

The florist slid by us, silently carrying a dozen roses out with him.

I thanked her for the check and dropped it in my bag.

"How is Mrs. Visconti holding up?"

Gloria Bolan looked at me blankly. "Oh, Amy. She's doing well. I haven't seen much of her."

"Bobby seems to think you'll be seeing a lot more of her."

"You mean at the funeral."

"No, Bobby said that Amy intends to get involved in the day-to-day operations of the business."

Gloria smiled. "Really? That's nice. We could use a little more woman power around here. And a little less testosterone, if you know what I mean."

"I do."

I thanked her once again for her generous check and moved to the door, passing the florist on his way back.

"Carnations." Gloria Bolan gently ran her fingers over a blossom. "Yes, much better."

"I don't suppose you spoke with MC's nephew, did you Amy?"

"Nephew?" I paused on the porch. "No. I didn't even know he had a nephew."

"Sure, Miles. He's with the band."

"Miles Sheffield? The guitarist?"

"That's right."

"I didn't know the two of them were related." I felt my headache, which had mercifully disappeared, return for its encore performance. "Why? What about Miles Sheffield? You think he had something to do with Tom Visconti's murder?"

"Oh, I'm sure it's nothing. Mark says I have a vivid imagination. Too vivid." She gave a self-deprecating little laugh.

She said goodbye and shut the door. Bobby was peering at me from behind a wispy curtain from a front bedroom. He looked angry.

Angry enough to strangle someone? Like me or his now ex-partner?

Without a doubt, if looks could kill, I would have been a dead patch on the lawn.

And what was all that about Miles Sheffield?

Safely behind the wheel of the van, I shook my head from side to side like my skull was an Etch-A-Sketch, trying to erase Gloria Bolan's provocative words from my brain.

I had bigger fish to fry.

Derek would be home soon.

The wedding countdown had begun.

25

A cool, gentle breeze wafted across the glen. The day was picture postcard perfect. Magnolia Manor shone like a jewel in a sea of green. The sky was sunny, blue and perfect.

My wedding was going to be perfect.

Moire, from the diner, had even allowed Dick, from the motor inn, to escort her to the wedding. It had taken some arm-twisting and pleading on my part, but, in the end, she had acquiesced.

She didn't look completely thrilled with her date or me, sitting there in row four in a lovely peach-colored dress. How was I supposed to know Dick would wear a yellow hounds-tooth jacket complete with vest and matching driver's cap to my wedding?

It could have been worse. He could have brought his pet rabbit, Ralph, along.

Derek stood erect on the petal-strewn steps of the flower-covered gazebo, its columns decorated with climbing, sweet-scented amethyst wisteria vines. My heart beat madly. I marched slowly up the grassy aisle towards him.

He beamed seeing me for the first time wearing my Mom's newly-altered wedding gown. It was perfect and I felt his love wash over me like a calming wave.

This was it. It was really happening. I was getting married. And to the most wonderful man on earth.

Maeve, wearing a fresh Florida tan from her days in Boca Raton looked radiant in a lovely pink dress and flowers in her hair. She stood to one side of the altar, along with Dan Sutton who wore his new suit and looked quite handsome himself. I hoped that Kim would be as lucky as me one day soon.

Then I winced and sucked in a breath.

Was it my imagination or had there been an almost imperceptible twitch of Derek's left eyelid as he spied Alex Bean seated in the third row? But what could I do? I couldn't have uninvited him.

Besides, Derek and I had talked on the telephone the night he returned from Asheville. I had explained everything all over again, even though he told me that it wasn't necessary.

He loved me and had faith in me.

His words, not mine.

On the plus side, Craig Bigelow had not shown up for the wedding. He emailed his congratulations and said he was in the middle of some big business deal.

Good. I did not need another ex-boyfriend at my wedding. One was already too many.

And there must have been seventy-five to one hundred people out there—some I didn't think had even been on the invitation list but that was life in a small town. I could barely see anyone else in attendance because of the tears of joy in my eyes.

I sniffled.

Kim whispered and dabbed my nose with a handkerchief, "This is it, Amy."

Behind me, Reverend Steve cleared his throat.

The wedding music came from a portable sound system that Violet Wilcox had provided for the occasion. Gertie crouched in front of the front row, Civil War-era camera at the ready. I hoped she had remembered to load it with film or stone tablets, or whatever it used.

Jerry Kennedy's wife and daughter were present but there was no sign of the man himself. That figured. All his fussing about an invitation and he was probably home watching football or baseball or whatever it is that men do on weekends when they should be outside attending weddings and garden parties.

The music stopped.

My heart lurched.

Derek smiled at me.

Reverend Steve spoke but with the ocean crashing in my ears, I could barely understand a word he was saying.

Derek took my hand and I offered my trembling finger.

My mouth was dry and my tongue was a sheet of eighty-grit sandpaper.

Reverend Steve's words came into focus. "Do you, Amy Simms, take this man—"

"I'll take that man," boomed a voice from far back.

A voice I knew far too well.

"Jerry!" I screamed. "What are you doing?"

His mortified wife leapt to her feet, knocking over the chair in front of her and sending its occupant flying.

A roar of voices followed.

Gertie was snapping photographs left and right like there was no tomorrow.

Jerry had shown up in a navy suit that I swear was the same suit he had worn to our junior high prom. It hadn't fit him well then either. It was too long in the legs and too short in the arms. And now it wouldn't button shut.

Jerry tromped up to the wedding platform in his police regulation boots. Didn't he own a pair of shoes with big boy laces?

"What are you doing, Jerry?" My voice shook. Rage rose in my throat. "Do not spoil my wedding."

"Sit down, Jerry," yelled his wife, Sandra. Her face was the color of a boiled lobster. I couldn't blame her. This little scene of her husband's would be the talk of the town for years to come.

His impending death by my hands would be right up there in the top ten, too.

Jerry Kennedy looked up at my fiancé, who had remained oddly silent, although his mouth hung open. Jerry waved a wet necktie in his right fist. I noticed he wore a pair of nitrile gloves. "Derek Harlan, I am arresting you for the murder of Tom Visconti."

"What?" My mouth fell open and tears sprang like leaks at the corners of my eyes.

"Are you out of your cotton-picking mind?" Kim slugged the chief of police in the upper arm.

Jerry cursed her.

Dan jumped across the aisle and pinned Kim's arms to her sides as she was winding up to punch him a second time. Someplace more sensitive. "Easy, honey," he implored.

Dan was stuck in a no-win situation. What do you do when your girlfriend is beating up your boss?

Mom and Aunt Betty clutched one another. Masks of horror took over their faces.

Reverend Steve looked befuddled.

Lance Jennings lumbered forward. He whipped out a pen and notebook. "What's going on here, Chief Kennedy?"

"Yes," cried Violet Wilcox, pushing the reporter aside with a well-practiced hip thrust. "What are these new developments, Chief?"

Esther took my elbow. "Let's get you out of here."

"Yes," agreed her date, Floyd, looking dapper in his best suit, the one he wore every Thursday to the bank prior to his retirement.

"No, I want to hear what's going on!" I pulled myself free of Esther's grasp.

"Derek," I pleaded. "Say something! What is happening? Tell me I'm dreaming and that this is some horrible nightmare. Tell me the bedside alarm is going to go off, I'm going to wake up in my bed and that we are getting married today."

"I don't know what's going on," Derek stuttered. "What is this, Chief?"

"Yeah, come on, Chief," Dan Sutton said, still struggling mightily to hold Kim back from renewing her attack on the lawman. It was taking both Dan and Paul to subdue her.

I spotted Officer Larry Reynolds standing near the back row. He looked unhappy.

That made at least two of us.

"One of the employees here noticed a toilet wasn't working right. She pulled off the lid and found this tie wrapped around the doohickey inside," barked Jerry Kennedy.

"She said she didn't think much of it at first then remembered about the murder last week and the guy getting strangled. She told her manager who called me over to have a look."

Jerry got all up in my fiancé's face. "Does this look familiar to you, counselor?" He waved the pale blue tie in Derek's face.

Uh-oh. The necktie was embellished with a small hand-embroidered brown thrasher in the center. I had given Derek a tie just like that for his birthday.

Derek peered at the soggy tie. "Is that my tie?"

I felt my blood rushing to my toes and swooned. Hands caught me and kept me from cracking my skull against the marble steps of the gazebo. I wasn't sure if that was a good thing or a bad thing.

The arms that caught me belonged to Alex Bean. "You okay, Amy?"

"Yes, thanks. Let me go." I shrugged free and rushed to Derek's side as Chief Kennedy was pulling him down the aisle in a pair of disposable plastic handcuffs.

"Derek!" I leapt in front of the men. "You're making a mistake, Jerry. Don't do this. This is my wedding," I pleaded as tears soaked my bridal gown.

"This is the man's tie. I've got proof. One minute he was wearing it, the next he wasn't. I'm guessing that's because he used it to strangle Visconti. And I'm guessing analysis of this and the contents of that toilet tank are gonna find maybe blood and skin that *ties* our man to the victim."

"But Jerry—"

"Face it, Amy, the only mistake being made, or about to be, is you marrying a murderer," concluded the chief. "I'm doing you a favor. You'll thank me later."

"A murderer?" I snapped. "Derek wouldn't harm a fly and you know it."

From the corner of my eye, I spotted Derek's daughter, Maeve, crying wildly in my mother's arms.

The poor girl. What must she be thinking?

One week her mom's future husband is murdered and the next week her father is accused of the murder.

"Out of my way, Simms," Chief Kennedy snarled and jerked his fat thumb at my almost husband. "If you want to do something, I suggest you get this lawyer a good lawyer."

Chest heaving, racked with tears, I watched as Jerry led Derek away.

"This is not the way it was supposed to go," I cried in Kim's arms. "Not the way it was supposed to go at all..."

Derek was leaving. But not for his honeymoon with me.

"I know," Kim said, smoothing my hair with the soft touch of her hand. "Can't you do something, Dan?" she said, turning to her boyfriend.

Dan threw his hands in the air. "What can I do?"

"You can talk some sense into Jerry's fat head, that's what you can do," Kim snapped.

Dan sighed. There was no sense arguing with Kim. "I'll see what I can do. Are you going to be okay, Amy?"

I felt the weight of hundreds of eyes on me as the crowd hovered uneasily, unsure of what to do and where to go. "Talk to Derek. Ask him how his tie got in that toilet tank."

Dan nodded and turned to go to the police station.

"And Dan," I said softly.

"Yeah?"

"Tell Derek I love him."

26

Night fell hard and heavy.

What was supposed to be a thrilling, love-filled wedding had practically turned into a sad and gloomy wake.

I pictured Derek sitting all alone in a dreary jail cell. Although I was surrounded by dear friends and family, I felt like I was in a jail cell myself.

My chest felt so tight I could barely breathe. Someone or something seemed to have sucked all the oxygen out of my apartment.

I liked to think that someone or something was Jerry Kennedy, but I knew there was someone or something bigger and more dangerous involved.

So as much as I wanted to throw myself down on my bed, bury my face in my pillow and cry, I couldn't let myself fall to pieces.

I had some serious thinking to do.

I opened the kitchen window to let some air inside.

Mom, Kim, Esther and Ben kept me company. I'd swapped my wedding dress for my softest, comfiest gray sweats and a pair of thick wool socks. Not exactly the sexy little silk number I had packed for my honeymoon. My gown lay across the bed like the husk of the woman I was meant to be.

Paul Anderson and Corey Lingstrom, Derek's friend

from Saint John, had stopped by earlier. Corey had retired to his rented condo out at the lake and Paul had a
restaurant to run. Both had urged me to remain upbeat.

Easy for them to say.

We huddled together in my small apartment and
stuffed ourselves on warm champagne, cold chicken
and wedding cake.

At the moment, Ben Harlan stood in the far corner,
having a muffled conversation with a lawyer friend in
Atlanta, with whom he was discussing Derek's situation. He looked miserable. What was that like? Having
your son locked up on suspicion of murder?

I had to do something.

"Forget what I told Jerry, forget what I told Gloria
Bolan." I pushed an uneaten ice cold chicken wing
across my dessert plate. I had no appetite left. "I am
going to figure out who killed Tom Visconti."

"Please," begged my mom, "leave it to the police, Amy.
Hasn't there been enough trouble?" She knew about Vail
threatening me with a knife and MC trying to drown me
in the swimming pool at the Ruby Lake Motor Inn.

On top of that, someone had busted up all our bird
feeders and trampled all our flowers.

I couldn't blame her for worrying about her only
daughter. Somebody out there just might want to tram-
ple on me.

The truth was, I was a little worried about me myself.
But I was more worried about Derek.

I shoved everything to one side of the kitchen table
and slapped a scratchpad down on the tablecloth. Using
the sparkly gold-ink Sharpie I'd bought to write thank
you notes, I drew up a list of suspects.

Bobby Breen

Mickey Caswell
Vail Visconti
Miles Sheffield
Amy Visconti née Harlan

"Amy?" Kim gaped. "You think she could've murdered Tom?"

"I don't know." I yawned. "I just don't know. Could she have had time to go to the maze garden without any of her bridesmaids noticing?"

"Not likely."

"Yeah." Frankly, I wasn't putting her at the top of my suspect list for another reason. That reason being that as much as I disliked and had a history with the woman, I couldn't see her murdering the groom, let alone framing her ex-husband, the father of her only child, for the dastardly deed.

Mom handed me and Kim each a cup of warm jasmine tea.

I took a small sip. "She does have a motive. She's Mrs. Visconti now and inherits everything or so it seems. Bobby Breen implied there might be a legal battle over Tom's estate."

"I'll bet." Kim took my marker. She drew a witch's face and a pair of dollar symbols next to Amy Harlan's name.

"What about this Miles Sheffield?" asked my mother, reading the list over my shoulder.

"He's the guitar player with MC and the Moonlighters. Remember? He was the one who told me his suspicions about MC."

"Then why would he strangle Tom Visconti?" Kim wanted to know.

"I have no idea," I said, my words riding on a sigh.

"But Gloria Bolan intimated that he might be involved. I'd like to ask her why."

"Now is your chance," Esther said, pulling back the curtain at the front window as someone rang the bell and banged on the door below.

"What?"

"That's Gloria Bolan," said Esther. "She just stepped off the porch and is looking up here." Esther, balancing a glass of bourbon and soda, waved to the woman. "You want me to let her in?"

"You stay here," said Ben Harlan. "I'll go downstairs and let her up. If that's okay with you, Amy?" I nodded and he pecked Mom on the cheek. "I'll talk to you all tomorrow."

He kissed me next. "Don't worry, Amy, Marcus Vargas is a dear friend and an excellent defense attorney. He's promised he'll fly up here, if necessary. I told him to hold off for a day or two and see if things sort themselves out." He tossed his coat over his arm. "Let's hope this all blows over before then."

"If it doesn't blow up first," I grumbled.

Ben was a dear but I was afraid he viewed the world far more benignly than I did at the moment. Derek was in trouble and it was going to take far more than wishful thinking to get him out of it.

Ben Harlan disappeared. A few minutes later, Gloria Bolan came up the stairs in pale green slacks and a turtle neck sweater the reddish-brown hue of a wood thrush.

"Hello, Amy." She paused, halfway up the flight of steps, hands gripping each side of the railing. "I heard what happened and wanted to talk to you. This is awful. I mean, how awful for you."

Had she come to vent her rage at me because she

had heard my fiancé had murdered her ex-boss? "Derek didn't strangle Tom."

"I know that, Amy. Believe me." She tugged at a dangling silver earring. "I called the police station the moment Mark told me the news. I told Chief Kennedy he was making a big mistake but he wouldn't listen. He is so sure he has Mr. Visconti's killer that he refuses to consider anything or anyone else."

I invited Gloria inside the apartment. "Where's Mom, Esther?"

"Off to bed." Esther offered Gloria a beverage. She declined. Esther poured herself another and retired to my dad's old cozy chair for a lie down.

"Sorry to drop by so late. I was driving back from Charlotte. I dropped a few of Tom's friends off at the airport. They had come for the wedding and stayed for the wake. I saw your light on and took a chance."

"No problem."

"I suppose you think it's silly of me for wanting to get to the bottom of Tom's murder. You see, he was like a big brother to me. After my Mark got sick and couldn't work any longer, things got really rough for us. For a spell, we didn't know how we were going to make ends meet. The medical expenses were mounting. There was no money coming in."

"What about insurance?"

"It only covers so much. We were on the verge of being evicted from our home. I was looking for work everywhere. Tom offering me the job with his firm really saved our skins."

"I understand. Sometimes we can all use an angel here on earth."

"That's a sweet way of putting it." Gloria Bolan

peered at my list of suspects on the kitchen table. "What's this?"

"The names of the people I think might be responsible for the murder."

"So you haven't given up, after all?"

"With Derek in jail for Visconti's murder, you might say my enthusiasm for solving the crime has been reignited."

Kim's cell phone rang and she answered quickly. "Hi, honey."

After an excruciating three minutes of nodding, grunting and sundry noises she ended the call.

"What's up?" I asked.

"That was Dan. He's off-duty. Just got home."

"What did he say about Derek?"

"Only that Jerry is still holding him on suspicion of murder and is sending his tie off to the state lab tomorrow for DNA analysis. If they find traces of Tom Visconti's skin and blood on it, Derek could be in serious trouble."

"How did Derek's necktie end up in a toilet tank at Magnolia Manor?" asked Gloria Bolan.

"I don't know," I was forced to admit. I hadn't had the chance to ask Derek. Yet.

"Are the police even sure it's his? I mean, one necktie looks pretty much like another, right?" Gloria remarked.

"True but this one had a small hand-embroidered brown thrasher on it. I gave it to him for his birthday." I had ordered it from a small company in Minneapolis that sold them online through Etsy.

"Yes, I remember mentioning it to Mark. That's when we started talking about birds and him taking up bird watching as a hobby."

"Tell me, Gloria, you mentioned Miles Sheffield earlier."

"Yes?"

"You seemed to be suggesting that you thought he might have strangled your boss. Why?"

A snort reverberated out Esther's nose. Her nose tilted toward the ceiling. Her head pressed into the cushion. She had fallen into a deep slumber.

Kim delicately removed the liquor glass from Esther's hand and draped a throw over her chest and legs. "I'm going to get out of this," she said tugging at the bodice of her yellow bridesmaid dress. "And take a shower."

It looked like I'd be having another house guest. Kim had already insisted on spending the night despite my protests. Now I'd have Esther for company.

"May I?" I nodded and Gloria Bolan pulled out a kitchen chair and sat on the edge of it, like a wary sparrow about to take flight at the first sign of trouble. From her small leather purse, she extracted a tube of lip gloss and traced her lips. "If you will remember, I told you that Miles is MC's nephew."

"And?" I still hadn't figured out why the guitar player had failed to mention that he was related to the band leader.

"Miles has always felt that MC, Mickey, cheated his father out of his fair share of the songwriting royalties."

"I don't understand."

"Jim Sheffield, Mickey's cousin, wrote the lyrics to a number of MC and the Moonlighters biggest hits. Mickey took all the credit."

"Let me guess," I interrupted. "He also took all the money?"

Gloria Bolan smiled. "That's right. At least, the lion's share of it. Miles' father earned a living as an auto mechanic until he was forced to retire due to health issues."

"While MC lived the extravagant life of a pop star," I said. "Okay. I can see why Miles and MC might not be best friends."

I clamped my hands over my knees. "But what does their strained relationship have to do with Tom's murder? If anything, Miles would want to murder his uncle Mickey, not Tom."

"MC sold Mr. Visconti the publishing rights to a number of songs in his catalog."

"Why would he do that?"

Gloria Bolan shrugged. "He was low on funds, I suppose. I hear he pocketed quite a bundle."

I drummed my hands on the table. "And he shared none of it with Miles' dad."

"That's right. Of course, Mr. Visconti was an astute businessman. He turned right around and sold those publishing rights to another Nashville-based music publisher.

Leaving Miles high and dry.

Silence reigned as Gloria and I were wrapped up in our own thoughts. An owl hooted in the distance, sounding like an aural symbol of loneliness and solitude. An omen of things to come?

Gloria cleared her throat as the hands on the clock on the wall above the stove turned to midnight. The witching hour. "There is one thing."

"Yes?" I eyed my suspect list gloomily. I was no detective. Derek was doomed. I hoped Ben's lawyer was as sharp as he claimed he was. Maybe I should look for a private detective myself.

"You'll think it's silly."

"No, I promise. My fiancé is in jail. I'll take anything I can get." I wriggled my fingers in come-hither fashion. "Tell me. What is it?"

"What if Mickey is next?"

"What do you mean? Next what?"

Esther snored loudly and turned on her side. I had a clutch of clothespins in the utensil drawer—they were cheaper than bag clips. Maybe I should try clipping one to Esther's nostrils.

"Victim."

"Victim? As in murder?"

"I told you you would think it's stupid." She dropped her eyes, embarrassed.

"No, not at all. But I admit, I don't understand."

"Well, what if Miles, I don't know, sort of flipped finally and decided to murder the men that he held responsible for cheating his father out of his fair share of the royalties," Gloria Bolan said quickly.

"So first he strangles Tom Visconti—"

"And next, he intends to strangle Mickey."

I fell back in my chair. It wasn't implausible. All that stuff Miles had told me about Mickey, it could all have been nothing more than a con. Words meant to lead me astray. Lead me away from the real killer. Him.

"Have you shared this theory of yours with MC?"

"He told me I was crazy." She chuckled. "Then he tried to get in my pants, can you believe it?"

I could.

"But that's just MC being MC."

"Yeah, what a guy." Mickey Caswell was a slug, no offense to slugs everywhere, but that didn't mean he deserved getting strangled. Slapped, yes.

"How did the memorial service go yesterday?" I had heard through the Ruby Lake grapevine that the memoriam for Tom Visconti had been held at the chapel in town with a meal served afterward at the Rivercrest Country Club clubhouse.

"Bobby got drunk, Amy cried and Vail picked a fight with just about everybody present."

"I'm almost sorry I missed it." I'd had plenty on my plate with my impending wedding. Not to mention, I had not been invited. Only close friends and family.

"Sorry." I clutched Gloria's hands. "I didn't mean any disrespect."

"I understand." Gloria stood. "I'll let you get some rest. If there is anything I can do to help, please let me know. In the meantime, I'll put my thinking cap on. Seeing your list of suspects has inspired me. I might have some ideas of my own."

"Anything you feel like sharing?"

"Not yet. Give me time to think. Dig into things."

"Okay." I walked her downstairs and unbolted the front door. "If you can find out who really strangled your boss and help me get Derek out of jail—"

I peered off the end of the porch, eyes narrowed.

"What's wrong, Amy?"

"I thought I saw somebody moving around over there by the side of the yard," I said softly.

"Are you sure?"

"No. Let me walk you to your car." Gloria Bolan's car sat at the curb. "We had some vandalism the other night. Someone or someones wrecked all my bird feeders and trampled my flowerbeds."

"That's terrible." Gloria moved around to the driver's side and opened the car door. "Sometimes I don't know what this world is coming to."

"Me, either. Esther suggested we get some night-sight security cameras for outside but I refuse to live that way."

As Gloria Bolan drove away, my lonely owl hooted a goodnight from a shadowy tree somewhere in the distance. The waters of Ruby Lake shone dully under the light of a cloud-obscured moon. The neon sign for the diner flickered off. The diner closed at midnight.

Through the glass, I saw one of the line cooks lazily mopping the dining room floor.

A rustle in the holly bush behind me made me jump. I ran inside the house and locked the door behind me.

I'd rather face the night with a snoring Esther than a possible unknown menace with murder in his heart.

And that's saying a lot.

27

I washed up, dressed and followed the scent of eggs, toast and coffee to the kitchen.

Kim and Esther were scarfing down scrambled eggs at the kitchen table when I showed up. Mom was at the stove doing the scrambling, spatula in hand. White smoke wafted from the toaster.

"Eggs, dear?" she asked.

"Not now, Mom." The weather was chilly this morning. I had thrown on a pair of loose hiking slacks and a flannel shirt.

"You've got to eat something, Amy," scolded my mother.

"Really, Mom, if I tried to eat anything, I think I'd vomit." My head felt fuzzy and my tongue seemed to have doubled in size overnight.

All I could think about was Derek behind bars and our Cinnamon Bay beachside honeymoon suite lying empty.

Esther shoved her plate to the center of the table. "And thank you very much for that lovely vision." Esther was in the same clothes she had had on the night before but now wore my best plush robe overtop. She sipped strong black coffee from my favorite mug.

I get no respect, not even in my own home.

I grabbed my purse from the hook by the door. "I'll be back later."

"Where are you going?" asked Kim.

"To see Derek." I missed him so much already. But what I could do to set him free and feel him in my arms again, I had no idea.

At least I didn't have to worry about running Birds & Bees. I had scheduled a ten-day honeymoon. The ladies could take care of bird business while I took care of getting-my-man-out-of-jail business.

If anything, under Esther's command, the store would probably see a bump in sales.

"Let us know what you find out." Kim grabbed the remainder of Esther's scrambled eggs with scallions and dumped it on her plate. "I haven't been able to learn anything new. Dan has gone into cop mode. He isn't telling me a thing."

"Don't worry," I said grimly. "I'll squeeze it out of him and the entire police force—with my bare hands, if need be. Starting with Jerry."

Speaking of whom, I stopped downstairs at the self-service bins and filled a paper sack with sunflower seeds and another with shelled peanuts. Two of Jerry Kennedy's favorites.

Contrary to what they say in the books and movies, I found that a little bribery could work wonders.

Unfortunately, it was Officer Albert Pratt who was manning the station when I arrived.

"Where is everybody?" I demanded, clutching my bags of nuts and seeds.

"Police business," said Officer Pratt, seated at his desk near the center of the squad room. He is a large black man from New Orleans with curly black hair. Rumor had it that he was already considering a new job in Detroit. Jerry Kennedy has that effect on people. "What have you got in the bags?"

I dumped the paper sacks on his desk. "Some nuts for the nut," I quipped, nodding toward Jerry's desk. "A fat lot of good they're gonna do me now."

"Any more vandalism out at your place?" He poked his nose in the bag of peanuts and sniffed. "I prefer cashews."

"No, nothing. Did anyone else report any vandalism that night?"

"Nope, only you." Officer Pratt tried the sunflower seeds. He spat. "Tastes like bird food."

Which it was. "So, you say Jerry isn't here?" I glanced towards the cell.

"That's right." Officer Pratt grinned. "But if you are thinking that I am going to let you see the prisoner, you can forget it. Chief says nobody is allowed back there without his direct permission."

"It's a good thing I'm not nobody." I raced past his desk to the cell.

"Hey!" Officer Pratt leapt from his chair and followed me.

"Derek!"

Derek lay on his cot with his shoes off and his feet crossed. He shot up when he saw me. "Amy!" We held hands through the bars and managed a soft kiss with the hard bars pressed against our cheeks.

"Are you okay?" I asked, pushing away the tears that had sprung from my eyes.

"I'm fine. Really." His face was pale and puffy, unshaven. His wedding suit was rumpled.

"They haven't tortured you, have they?"

Derek laughed. "No cudgels or billy clubs yet. Just a lot of Jerry hounding me with questions."

"I have a few questions for you myself." I squeezed the cold jail cell bars with my hands, wishing I could pull them apart. Get closer to him.

"Okay, now you've seen him," barked Officer Pratt, although he didn't sound angry. He sounded nervous. "Now you gotta get out of here. Chief's on his way."

"And if I refuse?"

"No, you'd better go," Derek cut in. "Dad said he's retaining a lawyer. I told him it wasn't necessary. I didn't kill anybody."

"I know that," I sobbed and stroked his cheeks. "What I don't understand is how your necktie could've been used to strangle Visconti."

Derek turned his eyes to Officer Pratt. I got the message. We were not alone. "I don't know, Amy. I took it off before the wedding last week. I thought I put it in my pocket. I must have dropped it."

"It could have fallen out of your pocket," offered Officer Pratt. He snapped his fingers. "Or maybe somebody picked your pocket."

"Either way, that somebody got a hold of your tie and used it to strangle Tom Visconti and frame you." I said this more for Officer Pratt's benefit that Derek's. "But who?"

"Believe me, Amy. I've spent all night thinking about just that." Derek rubbed the back of his neck.

"Is there anything you need? Anything I can get you?"

"A fresh change of clothes and some toiletries would be nice."

I promised I'd stop by his apartment and pick up

everything he might need. "Even a sharp saw and a chisel," I whispered in his ear.

He chuckled.

We kissed a reluctant goodbye. I fled out the front door as I heard Officer Pratt welcoming Chief Kennedy as he was coming in through the rear entrance.

My next stop was the law offices of Harlan and Harlan, located at the opposite side of town near the farmer's market. Ben Harlan lived in a small brownstone within walking distance of the office.

Derek and I had swapped house keys months before. I planned to grab a few things for him then go to Ben's house to discuss the situation before returning to the police station with Derek's care package.

Ignoring the No Parking signs along the curb, I pulled up to the door and glanced through the window.

Although it was a Sunday and the offices were normally closed on the weekend, Ben was seated behind his desk. Standing across from him was Mrs. Edmunds in an eggplant-colored skirt suit with gold-thread edging. Her brown hair was pulled up in a loose bun. A single white carnation in her perfect hair served as her crown.

If she had a first name, she wasn't sharing it, at least not with me. Derek had told me what it was once but I had forgotten. It might have been Battle Axe or something close to it.

Ice Box, maybe? No, that wasn't it either.

My gut told me that she harbored a secret crush of her own on Derek. Not that I minded. He was decidedly worth crushing on.

Ben saw me through the window and smiled. Mrs. Edmunds noticed me and made a face like she'd just been forced to drink a glass of sour milk.

"I'm surprised to see you working on a Sunday," I said, stepping into the unlocked office. Mrs. Edmunds frowned at me and said something about making coffee and cleaning up.

Ben merely nodded.

"Everything okay?" I asked.

Instead of one of the usual conservative business suits I was used to seeing him in, Ben wore a pair of faded gray trousers and a charcoal sweater. A pair of thick, black-framed glasses rode the tip of his nose.

"The police left only minutes ago. Chief Kennedy and Officer Sutton."

"What did they want?"

"To search Derek's office and apartment."

"What? They can't do that. I mean, can they?" He was the lawyer, not me.

Ben Harlan pointed to a document on his desk. "They can when they come armed with this."

"What is it?"

"A warrant."

Mrs. Edmunds came bearing coffee. "Two sugars and a drop of half and half."

She hadn't brought me a cup.

"I'll get started cleaning up now," she said grimly.

"Maybe we should call a service," offered Ben Harlan. Turning to me, he explained. "Chief Kennedy was a bit heavy-handed in his search."

Mrs. Edmunds surprised us both with a rather un-ladylike snort. "Apes at the zoo treat their cages with more respect. But not to worry, I can handle it, Ben. Enjoy your coffee. Will you be staying long, Ms. Simms?"

"Let's find out together, shall we?" I threw myself

down in one of Ben's guest chairs. "That was snappy of me but I wasn't in the mood for her attitude," I told Ben.

Ben chuckled. "Mrs. Edmunds means well."

"You could have fooled me."

"I heard that," came Mrs. Edmunds angry voice from Derek's office on the opposite side of the wall.

I sank in my chair. "Oops." Ben offered me his coffee and I accepted a small sip. "So what did Jerry want, Ben?" The senior partner had suggested that I call him Dad. I was still rolling that idea around in my head. I had discussed it with Mom and she saw no harm in it and told me that my own father wouldn't have minded in the least. "What was he looking for? Did he say?"

Ben slid open the top left drawer of his desk and pulled out a fat cigar. "Do you mind?"

"Not at all. It's your office." Derek's dad liked to puff on the occasional cigar. I didn't know what kind they were but they had a pleasant enough spicy vanilla scent.

"Thanks. They help me think." He held a platinum lighter to the tip and lit up. "And steady my nerves."

Ben Harlan did seem rather shaken up. From the whiskers and sallow complexion of his cheeks to the bags holding court under his eyes, I could see he hadn't gotten much sleep last night either.

Finally, he spoke. "I'm not certain if they were seeking anything in particular. It was what we lawyers like to call a fishing expedition."

"And did he catch anything?"

Silence followed as Ben Harlan sucked on his cigar.

"They took some papers and his laptop."

"Nothing incriminating, I'm sure."

Ben Harlan mashed the end of his cigar into a glass ashtray on the credenza beneath the front window.

"There was one thing."

I felt a frisson of alarm. Suddenly, there seemed to be a crack in the wall of the dyke that kept me safe and dry. "What?" I asked, despite my trepidation.

"Derek had a file on Tom Visconti."

I took a moment to let that information sink in. "What sort of file?"

"He was worried about Amy, his ex, that is. So he paid one of those online services to run a background check on the guy."

"And? What did he find out?"

Ben Harlan rubbed his jaw. "He said the man came up clean as a whistle."

"I don't know. This was no random act of violence and it wasn't a robbery. People who are clean as proverbial whistles don't go getting strangled in gardens, in my opinion."

"I agree with you. But what can we do? Derek's necktie is a strong piece of evidence. And he did have a fight with him."

"A fight? Oh, right. I almost forgot. At the golf course." I muffled a yawn with the back of my hand. Lack of sleep and food was catching up with me. "Mind if I go upstairs? Derek asked me to bring him a few things."

"Of course, not. Help yourself, Amy. How is Derek doing?"

"Well enough under the circumstances."

"Good. I was planning to go to the police station first thing this morning, then Chief Kennedy showed up with this search warrant. If you talk to him, tell him I'll be by later."

"I will."

I made my way along the long narrow hallway to the backstairs which led to Derek's second-floor bachelor pad. The door was unlocked so I hadn't needed my key at all.

Ben Harlan had been right. The police had made a mess of things. Not that Derek was neat. I knew few men who were, but Derek was neater than most.

Magazine and work papers were scattered over the sofa and chairs. A few had tumbled or been dropped to the floor. A half-eaten peanut butter and jelly sandwich sat next to a bag of chips on the kitchen table.

The bird feeder I had given to Derek was nearly empty. I kept a small bag of seed in the hall closet. I refilled the feeder then continued my search. The problem was I didn't know what I was looking for.

Plus, the police had come and gone. Who knew what they had found? I sometimes got the feeling Chief Kennedy couldn't find his own pants to get dressed in the morning, let alone find a clue. Dan, on the other hand, was sharp as they come.

Derek's bedroom wasn't looking much better than the rest of the apartment. I pulled the dark curtains aside to let in some sunshine. The bedcovers had been thrown back and the mattress was tilted to one side.

Opening his tall dresser, I removed a couple of pairs of jeans, some casual shirts, socks and underwear. In the bathroom, I grabbed his travel toiletry kit and stuffed it with everything I could think of that he might need.

An open suitcase rested on the only chair in the room. A mid-century modern piece with buffed hardwood legs and a sculpted orange seat.

Derek had packed for a Caribbean honeymoon, flip-flops, shorts, colorful T-shirts, and a couple pairs of flowery bathing trunks that he had purchased for the occasion.

Our airline tickets for our flight to Saint John leaned like forgotten soldiers against the tableside lamp.

"You about done in here?"

I jumped out of my pants. "Mrs. Edmunds." I put my hand to my heart in a vain attempt to quiet it. "You scared me."

Mrs. Edmunds rolled her eyes. "I'd like to straighten up." She plucked a pair of boxers from the floor then grabbed the tangle of comforter and cotton sheets and deftly unwound them. "If you don't mind." She waved them briskly in the air, nearly snapping my nose off.

"Go for it," I said, slipping past her. As much as I wasn't thrilled with her handling Derek's skivvies, I knew that was as close as she'd ever get to what was inside them.

Shoving Derek's toiletry kit and clothes into his black backpack, which I found on the floor of the closet, I let myself out.

"Ms. Simms!"

I glanced back through the open door. What had I done to annoy Mrs. Edmunds now?

"Something does not smell right." She gave me a stern look from beside Derek's bed. She had already shoved the mattress back into place.

An efficient woman, our Mrs. Edmunds.

I uneasily turned my nose towards my armpits. Was she talking about me?

"I'm talking about this." She spread her arms to indicate the mess.

"Trust me, I don't like it either. Maybe you should

take Ben's advice and hire a cleaner. Send Chief Kennedy the bill."

"No." She shook her head. "You don't understand. When Ben called to alert me that the police were coming, I hurried right over. We arrived together. Ben and I."

My hands parted. I didn't know what to say or where this monolog was leading.

While her hands folded dress slacks that had been unceremoniously dumped in a pile on the floor, she continued. "We came in through the back door."

"And?"

"And I got the impression that someone had been here before us."

I moved back into the living room, breathing in the scent of Derek. Longing tugged at my heart. I pursed my brows. A titmouse pecked at the feeder in the window. Outside the world went on as if everything was normal.

While my life was anything but normal.

"You mean before the police arrived?"

"That's right. You see, I was certain I had left the hall light off. It was on when we arrived."

I blew out a breath. "Maybe Derek left it on?"

"I don't think so. You see, I was the last one in the office yesterday." Mrs. Edmunds explained that she had come in Saturday to catch up on some photocopying. "I went out through the back door. It's shorter."

Her house was two streets back. If she chose to go out the front, she would have had to circle the block.

"And Derek was already gone?"

"That's right. He left with Paul and Dan. I stayed another hour or so, went home then arrived at Magnolia Manor a little before the wedding."

Derek had insisted on inviting her. He said it would

be awkward for him if we did not.

"And the hall light was off?"

"The light was off. I'm sure of it."

"And the light was on when you arrived this morning?"

Mrs. Edmunds nodded once.

"Did you ask Ben about it?"

"Ben never came in."

"Did you tell this to Chief Kennedy?"

"Of course. He told me to stay out of their way and went about his business."

I frowned.

Either the woman was messing with me or something strange was going on. Derek had not left the light switched on before the wedding and he had been arrested and couldn't have come back and turned it on any time since then.

So who did?

I wished a lightbulb would go on inside my head—like a cartoon revelation or spark of brilliant intuition—but it didn't. I had no idea what was going on or why.

No idea at all.

28

I returned to the police station and confronted Jerry.

"I see you found the snacks I left for you," I said, hovering over him at his cluttered desk. "You don't keep your desk any neater than you left Derek's apartment."

Jerry chuckled. "Heard about that, did you?" Scraps of sunflower seed shells decorated his uniform. "These peanuts are darn good," he remarked, yanking a handful from the bag on his desk. "But, if you don't mind my saying so, those sunflower seeds were a mite stale."

"Why don't you let Derek go, Jerry?" I leaned my butt on the corner of his desk. He hated when I did that but I wasn't in a mood to care. "You know he's innocent. I know he's innocent. The entire town knows he's innocent."

Officers Reynolds and Pratt were pretending not to listen from their desks but we both knew they heard everything.

There was no sign of Dan.

"Do we now, Simms? Do we all know that your boyfriend—"

"Fiancé."

"*Fiancé* is innocent?" His boots thumped the floor. "I, for one, don't."

"But Jerry—"

"Uh-uh." He held up a hand. Using his other hand, he rummaged around his desk and lifted a printed map that was sealed in a plastic bag. "See this?"

"What is it? You finally get your diploma from an on-line police academy?"

"Very funny. A real hoot. Let's hear how hard you laugh when I tell you that this is a map of the maze garden over at Magnolia Manor. It seems they print them out for folks who don't want to get lost."

"Great." I crossed my arms over my chest. Here I was wasting time talking to the chief of police when Derek was mere feet away. "Be sure to carry that with you the next time you—"

Jerry's brow wrinkled with an amusement that I was not sharing. He interrupted me to say, "Know where I got it?"

"Magnolia Manor?"

"Nope. I mean, of course you can get these maps there. Some of the tourist shops around town, too." Jerry Kennedy shook his head slowly side to side. He laid the baggy carefully on the desktop. "I found this particular copy under your *fiancé's* mattress."

I didn't know what to say. My eyes glued themselves to the map. This was strange. Very strange.

"That's crazy," I said finally. "In fact, it is impossible."

"You trying to say I planted it?" The chief's face blew up like an angry red balloon. "Sutton and I found it together."

In fact, Dan had found it himself but the police chief rarely saw any reason to give one of his officers sole credit when he could share the glory with them.

"That is not what I meant at all. I helped Derek flip his mattress earlier this week. There was no map there then, Jerry."

"Maybe he moved it from one place to another."

I shoved my sweaty palms into my eyes. "This can't be happening."

"I'm guessing that our number one suspect used this map to familiarize himself with that maze garden. That way he wouldn't get lost on his way to strangling Tom Visconti. Nor have to worry about getting lost on his way out once he had done the deed."

"That's ridiculous. In fact, that is the most ridiculous thing I ever heard. Somebody must have planted it."

"Under his mattress?" Jerry planted his hands on his desk. "Who Simms? And why?"

"I don't know. But somebody did. Mrs. Edmunds said she told you about the hall light being on."

"She did."

"Did you dust the light switch for fingerprints?"

"As a matter of fact, Dan did," Jerry Kennedy said smugly. "And there were no prints. Only a smudge."

"That doesn't prove anything."

"Bah." Jerry tossed a hand in the air. "She probably imagined it. That woman is daft."

That wasn't a subject I felt like pursuing.

"What did Derek say about the map?"

"He denied all knowledge of it."

"He's telling the truth, Jerry. That map was not there before—"

A phone rang and Officer Reynolds answered it quickly. "Chief, it's a call for you."

"Who is it?" Chief Kennedy bellowed.

"Some lawyer calling from out of town. He says he's got Judge Arbuckle on conference call."

"Judge Arbuckle?"

"That's right, Chief."

"Crap."

Everyone in the county knew Judge Arbuckle. He has been doling out justice in western North Carolina for over thirty years and he showed no sign of letting up or retiring.

Jerry sighed and pulled himself to his feet. Why did he always make it seem so hard? Turning to me, he barked, "Remember what I said a minute ago about getting lost?"

"Yes. What about it?"

Jerry steadied his eyes on mine. "We're done here. Get lost."

I dashed towards the jail cells. Jerry cupped a hand over the phone and ordered Officer Pratt to cut me off.

"Sorry, Amy," he said, extending his arms to block me.

I told Albert it wasn't his fault and left.

I headed next toward the edge of town and the Ruby Lake Motor Inn. MC's shiny black tour bus sat in the parking lot, taking up more than its fair share of spaces. Several of the underbelly luggage compartments hung open and were half-filled with luggage and stage equipment.

MC, the eternal lounge lizard, was sunning himself at the swimming pool. Two of his bandmates were with him but not the one I was looking for.

I leaned over the pool fence. "Can you tell me where I can find Miles?"

"In his room, I suppose," drawled MC. He grabbed a can of beer from the cooler at his side. "Come on in and take a load off. The beer's cold. And *you* are hot."

He winked and I cringed.

"Another time," I said. When he was sober and not slathered in oil. As much as I was coming to loathe the man, I did have some questions for him too.

"We may not get the chance," he drawled. "The memorial is over and Tom's killer is in jail. Me and the boys will be hitting the road soon."

"That is good news," I said. And I meant it but not for the reasons he was probably thinking. And, if Gloria Bolan was right, it might just save MC's neck if he was our murderer's next intended target. Under the circumstances, I felt safe not bothering to share her concerns with him.

I knocked on the door to Miles Sheffield's room and he shouted for me to come in.

"Oh, it's you. I figured you were the maid." Miles was packing a battered red suitcase. "I can't wait to get out of this dump. What's up?"

He moved to the closet and pulled down the hangers holding his stage clothes. He draped them carefully on the unmade bed nearest the window.

The old rooms of the motor inn were small by today's standards. Two double beds all but filled the space with barely enough room for a nightstand between them. An anachronistic modern flat-screen TV sat on an original 1940s walnut dresser.

The room reeked of alcohol and pot.

"I want to know why you lied to me."

"Lied to you?" Miles grabbed a red electric guitar attached to a leather guitar strap from the chair near the window. "About what?" He picked up a hard shell guitar case, laid it on the bed and carefully placed the guitar inside after removing the strap and rolling it up.

"About you and Mickey." When he didn't start spilling his guts, I pressed on. "About how you and MC are related and how he cheated your father out of his share of some lucrative songwriter's royalties on some of his biggest hits."

Miles placed the strap in a hollow beside the guitar, snapped the lid shut, then sagged against the double bed. "You found out about that, huh?"

"Yes, I did. What I want to know is why you didn't tell me all this in the first place."

"Because I didn't think it was relevant."

"Tom Visconti was strangled. Everything about him and his life is relevant." I was practically shouting.

"You think *I* killed Visconti?" Miles Sheffield moved to the mini-fridge and extracted a beer. "Want one?"

"No, thank you. Tom Visconti purchased your father's share of those songs then sold them to another publisher. How much money did your father lose?"

"Fine." He opened the can angrily and sipped. "Hundreds of thousands, is my guess."

I whistled out a breath. "That is a lot of money. Enough to murder for."

The guitar player ran his fingers over the fretboard of the second guitar lying in the open guitar case on the other bed. "Murdering Tom Visconti wouldn't get my dad's money back."

"No, but it might have given you a sense of justice." I remembered Gloria's warning. "What about MC? Why work for the man? You must hate him, hate how he cheated your father. Is he next on your hit list?"

"Yeah." Miles Sheffield squeezed the empty beer can in his hand and tossed it in the trashcan. "I hate him. And he knows it. He's also badmouthed me with every other act out there. I gotta earn a living. Treats me like a dog, too. Even makes me drive the lousy tour bus."

"The way Mickey spread the word around about me being a druggie—all false, by the way—I'd be lucky to get a free gig at an open mic night in a local pizzeria."

He slammed the tweed guitar case shut. "But kill him? I need him. I need this job. Plus, he's promised me that if I can come up with any tunes half as good as my dad's, he'll record them and I'll get my share of the proceeds."

I didn't know about that. Mickey Caswell did not seem like the kind of man to keep any bargain, not unless it was decidedly in his favor.

"Besides," continued the guitarist, "it was your fiancé who murdered Visconti."

"Nonsense."

Miles Sheffield shrugged. "If you say so, but I heard the police have some solid evidence."

"Evidence that somebody planted," I insisted. "Come to think of it, where were you Saturday night?"

"Here. Hanging out with the guys. Why?"

"Because somebody smashed all my bird feeders and stomped on my flower beds."

"Sorry. Wasn't me."

"Can you prove it?"

"I don't have to prove it." The guitarist's face flamed red. "Can you prove otherwise?"

He reached the door in two steps and threw it open, startling a passing housekeeper pushing her cleaning cart. "We're done here." He hollered at the woman that she could have the room in an hour.

I had no choice but to follow him out to the breezeway. "Tell me, all that stuff you told me about Vail and

MC, was that all a pack of lies too?"

"For the record, I was not trying to mislead you and I wasn't lying. I was trying to help you. Now, I wish I'd never met you." The guitar player stormed off towards the tour bus and climbed inside, slamming the accordion door behind him.

The housekeeper fiddled with a stack of towels on her rolling cart, enjoying the show.

"I'll be right back." I smiled at her. "I left my purse inside." I flew in the door before it could register with her that my purse was hanging off my shoulder.

I eased the motel room door shut behind me and held my breath. After a moment, I heard the squeak of the cleaning cart moving along. Good. This was my chance to search Miles' room.

I riffled through the guitar player's suitcase first and came up empty. Nothing but the usual tattered jeans and T-shirts. I opened the first guitar case and gently lifted the guitar enough to check the accessory compartment.

Again, nothing that didn't belong. Ditto, the second case on the bed opposite.

I spotted a brown, soft-sided gig bag leaning against the wall near the bathroom. I laid the gig bag on the bed and unzipped it. A battered black bass guitar with an American flag decal rested inside along with a red, white and blue guitar strap. The bass player was obviously Miles' roommate.

I put the bass guitar back where I had found it and checked the bathroom. Wet towels hung from the door and drooped from the sink. Others were bunched up all over the floor. These musicians, at least, were pigs. I felt a twinge of pity for the maid who was going to have to clean up this mess.

An open bottle of Kentucky bourbon sat beside the sink. Empty plastic cups filled the trash bin under the sink to overflowing.

A drip from the tub faucet pounded away the seconds. What if Miles returned and found me in his room? How would he react? If he was a killer, I could be in serious trouble.

I was about to leave when I spotted something shiny under the bed furthest from the door. I bent down for a closer look. Amongst the dust bunnies, lay a silver baseball bat with a red grip.

There was a knock at the door and I jumped to my feet.

"Anybody here?"

It was a man's voice but one I didn't recognize.

I dropped to the ground as the man came into view in the hotel room's window. I recognized him as one of Miles' bandmates, the drummer.

"Hey, Miles, you in there?"

I spat dust and rubbed my eyes. The carpet was filthy and my nose was only an inch from inhaling it.

"That snoopy woman was here asking about you. Miles?"

He rapped on the glass. A moment later, he banged again on the door, louder, then cursed. "Screw it."

I waited for his footsteps to fade away before rising and scurrying out the door myself, but not before peeping out to be sure the coast was clear.

The maid poked her head out from the room next door as I exited.

"Got it." I smiled once again, and tugged at the strap of my purse. "Have a nice day."

I turned on my heels and slammed into MC.

He threw his arm against the wall, blocking me. His smile was anything but pleasant. "Find what you were looking for?"

"Yes, yes, I did. Miles and I were having a very nice conversation, in fact. About baseball."

"Baseball?" MC appeared skeptical. "You a fan? 'Cuz, if you are, I could teach you a thing or two."

He leaned in like a vulture smelling fresh road kill. He sniffed my hair, his lips hovering near my ear. "Like how to round the bases, *all* the bases." He fingered a lock of my hair. "If you know what I mean."

"I know exactly what you mean," I replied, fighting to keep my voice steady.

I grabbed his fingers and bent them back far enough for him to feel the pain before I let go.

"Ouch!" MC cursed. "What did you do that for?" He shook out his hand.

"Let's call it positive reinforcement." I heard the maid snicker next door.

MC looked angry and embarrassed.

"You are aware of the fact that Miles hates you?" I said.

This elicited a deep laugh. "Oh, yeah. I'm aware. So what?"

"So you might want to watch your back."

MC laughed once more. "You think that boy would try to harm me? Not on your life. I treat him good. Just like I did his dad."

"That's not the way he tells it. He says you cheated his father out of hundreds of thousands of dollars that were due him."

"Miles talks out the side of his butt. He knows I did

everything I could for Jimmy. I paid him plenty good for those songs. Without the money I gave him, he couldn't have even afforded to get Miles guitar lessons.

"If anything," he said adamantly, poking his bare, oily chest with thumb, "they owe me."

"Can you think of a reason why Miles or his roommate—"

"Vince?"

"Right, Vince, would have a baseball bat in their room?"

MC wrinkled up his face. "What sort of question is that? Why do you care about a bat?"

"Why are you avoiding answering the question?"

MC blew out a breath. "Me and the boys like to play a little softball in our down time. Nothing serious. Only some pick-up games wherever we go. Helps to have some fun on the road. Let off a little steam. This is a stressful business. Know what I mean?"

Was there no end to this slimeball's innuendo?

And stress? He seemed to spend most of his time lounging poolside and drinking. This guy didn't know what real stress was. He had probably never had a real job in his entire life.

MC was still talking. "We carry around bats, gloves, balls, even some rubber bases on the bus."

"Somebody smashed all my bird feeders to pieces. A baseball bat would have been the perfect weapon."

"You know what your problem is?" MC put one arm on either side of my head and pressed his hands against the wall, essentially surrounding me.

"What?"

"You don't know how to have any fun."

"Do you know what your problem is?" I cooed, locking my eyes with his.

He grinned. "What's that?"

"You're going to have to relearn to sing your songs as a soprano if you don't move your hands. Now."

29

Kim and I agreed to meet at her place for dinner. We planned to cry some, laugh some and plot some. I did my part by picking up the red wine and garlic bread at Lakeside Market. Kim was in the kitchen when I arrived.

"Here." I set the wine and bread on the kitchen table. "Brain food."

"You won't get any argument from me," Kim said over her shoulder. She was cooking up the pasta, standing barefoot on the cool tile floor in a pair of stretch jeans and a long-sleeved red turtle neck shirt.

Our agreed upon menu consisted of spaghetti with vodka marinara, garlic bread and a green salad with pickled beets and walnuts.

Her frilly white apron was splattered with tomato sauce and her hair was a wreck. The red shirt had been a good choice. Kim and kitchens don't play well together but I had to give her credit for trying.

"Where's Paula?"

"Not back from Arizona."

"I thought she'd be back by now."

"She was supposed to be. Things are taking longer than expected. As far as I'm concerned, there's no hurry." Kim had mixed feelings about the woman. On the one hand, Paula was very nice—you couldn't help but like her. On the other hand, she worried frequently that Dan would someday choose Paula over her.

I ran a fingernail along my forehead. "Give her a chance. Dan loves you, you know."

"He'd better," Kim grumbled, stirring the bubbling sauce vigorously with a wooden spoon.

After urging me to open the wine, Kim told me to go check the coffee table by the TV. "I've laid out a bunch of movies. Take your pick. Dinner will be ready soon."

"And," she said, waving her wooden spoon and splashing tomato sauce across her toes, "before you ask, I don't know anything new about Derek."

"Rats. What good is a friend in the police force if you can't pump him for information once in a while?" I dipped a finger in the sauce in the pan on the stovetop and licked. "More vodka."

"Dan has been annoyingly tight-lipped. He says Jerry has ordered them all to say nothing to anyone unless they want to lose their job. Which is fine, except that I tried to explain to Dan that such blackouts do not apply to me."

"I'll reach out to Violet and Lance. They might have some news." Jerry may want to keep me in the dark but he had a habit of shooting off his mouth and boasting to the press.

"Good luck with that."

"What are you saying? I know Violet can be a tough nut to crack but Lance is like putty in my hands."

"Yeah," quipped Kim. "Silly putty."

She wasn't wrong.

With a frown on my face and a glass of wine in my hand, I dutifully walked through to the front room. Kim lives on the opposite side of town in a charming Craftsman-style bungalow with a spacious front porch and a detached garage in back.

Three beds, one and a half baths. Now that she was sharing that house and the only full bathroom with a tub and shower with Paula D'Abbo, the house seemed half as big to Kim as it used to.

Kim sometimes threatened to sell the house from under Paula and move into one of those new one-bedroom condos down by the lake.

Only Kim desperately wanting to stay in Dan's good graces kept her from kicking Paula out. Kim's last relationship, a poorly judged one seeing as how she had been dating a man who kept promising to get a divorce then didn't, had left her determined to make her relationship with the adorable police officer work.

Paula, on the other hand, thought she was doing Kim a favor by rooming with her. Kim, being Kim, had overreacted when Paula first arrived in Ruby Lake, went a little nuts and preferred that Dan think her a bit to the left on the crazy vs. sane scale rather than admit to her intense jealousy.

A jealousy that, in my opinion, seemed unfounded. Dan, to all appearances, seemed to treat Paula more as a sister than a potential mate and rival to Kim.

On the other hand, Paula was, as they say, smoking hot.

I pretended to sift through the pile of movies, although I already knew what I wanted to view. "Actually," I called, riffling disinterestedly through her selections, "I was hoping to watch a documentary tonight."

"A documentary?" Kim replied, skeptically.

"There is a new BBC documentary on the birds of North America airing tonight on the public station."

There was no missing Kim's ensuing groan.

"A *bird* documentary? How about a nice rom-com instead?"

After some discussion and me playing the pity card —I was the one whose wedding had recently blown up in her face, after all—Kim reluctantly agreed to the bird documentary.

In return, I agreed to watch *Heartburn* with Meryl Streep and Jack Nicholson afterward.

We ate first because spaghetti and sofas do not mix either. Kim and I had learned that the hard way. Her sofa still bore the stains to prove it.

Skipping dessert, we microwaved a six-quart bowl's worth of popcorn, drenched it in enough salt and butter to satisfy a small army and made it to the sofa in time for my documentary.

It wasn't long before half the popcorn, and a surprisingly tasty box of wine that we found in the pantry, was gone and Kim was out like a proverbial light on the sofa beside me.

Night fell. The wind blew. Clouds rolled silently across the sky like threatening ghosts. The dark shadows were spooking me. I rose quietly and pulled the curtains closed.

Kim's snores mingled with the bird calls coming from the built-in TV speaker. The soft glow of Kim's thirty-six inch TV in the corner provided the only light. I hugged my throw pillow more tightly in my lap.

Halfway through the ninety-minute program, a segment on a fascinating bird named the killdeer appeared. The killdeer is brown on the top, white on the bottom and orange on the butt. They also have distinctive double-banded brown-and-white throats.

But that is not the most unique thing about the birds. Killdeer are famous, at least in the birding world, for what I like to call their broken wing routine.

"Misdirection!" I shouted as I watched the killdeer in action. The bowl of popcorn in my hands had gone flying. Buttery kernels scattered like fat lumpy hail on me, Kim, the furniture and rug.

The green ceramic bowl hit a spot of bare hardwood floor on my side of the sofa and cracked from one side of the rim to the other.

Oops.

"Huh?" Kim squirmed and rubbed her puffy eyes. "What are you talking about?"

"I'm talking about Gloria Bolan." I leaned closer, pointing to the TV screen. "And that killdeer."

"What's a killdeer?" Kim squinted at the screen. "All I see are birds."

"That bird is the killdeer. Didn't you hear the narrator? Oh, right. You were asleep," I said. "Killdeer are very clever plovers. Devious, practically."

"Devious?" Kim sounded askance. "A bird?"

"Killdeer make shallow nests on the ground."

"So?"

"So that makes their nests vulnerable to predators, like possums and skunks and even other birds. When one of those predators comes too close, the parent killdeer will distract them by bobbing its head, calling loudly and running away from the nest, often while feigning a broken wing."

"That's weird." Kim's eyes were glued to the screen where a mother killdeer was doing just that—running through the tall prairie grass to distract a prairie dog.

"But effective. A hungry predator will give chase to

the apparently injured bird, hoping to make an easy meal out of them."

"That doesn't sound like it is going to end well for the bird. I mean, if a prairie dog eats them, who is going to protect the babies?"

I chuckled. "When Mr. Prairie Dog or Mr. Fox, or whatever beastie, gets too close for comfort, the killdeer flies away."

Kim massaged the bridge of her nose. She felt an incipient headache coming on. Was it the booze, the best friend or both? "Okay, but I don't see what this has to do with Gloria Bolan. Is she the bird or the beastie?"

A look of horror spread across Kim's face.

"My rug!" Kim fell to her knees and began plucking buttery kernels of popcorn off her rug. "Why don't we watch TV at your place next time," she mumbled.

"Don't you see? Gloria Bolan doesn't want me to find out who murdered her boss."

"She doesn't?" Kim diligently scooped up the dirty popcorn from the floor and furniture and dumped it on the coffee table. "Where's my popcorn bowl?"

I ignored the question I did not want to answer and replied to the more important one. "No. She doesn't. Gloria wasn't trying to lead me *to* a killer, she was trying to lure me *away* from one."

"You've lost me, Amy." Kim squeezed her head between her hands. "I think I've got some aspirin in the medicine chest." She climbed to her feet.

"Don't you move," I ordered. "Think," I said. "Let's think." I pounded my own head with my fist.

"Let's? I'm too tired to think," complained Kim. "Why don't we go to bed and think tomorrow?"

"No. This is too important. Do I have to remind you

that my fiancé is in jail? How would you feel if you were in my place and Dan was locked up?"

"Fine." Kim pouted and switched off the television. "I suppose the rom-com is out now."

She sank into the sofa, crossed her arms over her chest like a mopey ten-year-old and propped her feet on the coffee table. "Your phone is ringing."

We both turned our ears in the direction of the kitchen.

I rose and grabbed my cell phone from my purse, which I'd draped over a kitchen chair.

"What do you know?" I said, looking at the number showing on the screen. "It's the queen of misdirection herself."

"Gloria Bolan?"

"Shh." I held my hand over my cell phone and twitched my brow meaningfully at Kim.

She rolled her eyes and reluctantly zipped her lips shut.

"Hello, Gloria," I said. "What's up?"

"Well?" whispered Kim.

I turned my back on her and was rewarded with a throw pillow to the head. I retreated to the far side of the kitchen, putting a wall between me and any incoming missiles, and listened with great interest to what Gloria had to say.

After several minutes, we ended our conversation. Conflicting thoughts bounced around inside my skull as I set my phone down on the kitchen table.

"Well?" demanded Kim. "What did she want?"

"It's funny. Interesting, really. She said that she was looking through her boss's things and wants to talk to me. She said she thinks she knows who the killer is."

"Sounds a bit mysterious to me," answered Kim. She scooped as many of the popcorn kernels as she could from the coffee table to the top of a bridal magazine and started to the kitchen with her load.

"My bowl!" Kim exclaimed as she rounded the corner of the sofa and her eyes spotted the broken popcorn bowl. The magazine drooped from her hand. The popcorn atop it hit the floor.

Frowning, she picked up the two halves of the ceramic bowl. "This was my favorite bowl." She vainly tried to line up the two jagged pieces but it was hopeless. Too many little bitsies lay scattered on the hardwood. There would be no putting that bowl back together again.

"Sorry. But, if you'll remember, that is actually one of *my* bowls."

Kim blushed but only a tad. She has absolutely no sense of right from wrong when it comes to "borrowing" from her best friend.

"Still, it was my favorite." Kim dumped the two halves of the bowl unceremoniously in the trash and returned with a broom and dustpan. "It sounds to me like you were wrong about Gloria."

"How is that?"

"I mean, why would she be calling you up to talk about the case if she was trying to string you along? And now she thinks she knows who the killer is and wants to share that information with you?" Kim dropped a load of popcorn in the trash can. "Maybe I should call Dan. Maybe Gloria should call Jerry. Tell him what she's found. I mean, no offense, but why you?"

"Maybe," I said, "Gloria wants to talk to me first." The truth was, I was a tad offended. "She might not really be completely sure. She might want to run her theory by me in case she's wrong and doesn't want to make a fool of herself."

"Maybe." Kim washed her greasy hands in the kitchen sink.

"One way or the other, I'll know soon enough," I vowed. "I'm going to go see her right now."

"Be careful, Amy. You said it yourself, Gloria could be the killer. Instead of running a theory past you, she may be intending to run over you."

Not a lovely thought but I shook it off. "Gloria is not going to try anything," I said with far more assurance than I was feeling. "When she telephoned, I told her that I was with you at your house. She wouldn't dare."

"I hope you're right, girlfriend."

"That makes two of us."

30

It was pushing eleven o'clock at night as I arrived at Rivercrest Country Club. I didn't see a star in sight but I heard the distinctive deep, soft hoot of a great horned owl calling from somewhere over on the deserted golf course that wound like an emerald necklace through the community.

I pulled up in front of Tom Visconti's rented house, an uneasy feeling bouncing around in my gut. A small sedan sat parked in the shadows on the opposite side of the driveway. The lights of the nearby homes eased my worries.

Having a killer loose in our town was never a pleasant thing to think about.

Gloria had asked me to meet her here at the rental rather than her own home. When I questioned why, she said she hadn't wanted to disturb Mark. Besides, this was where the evidence lay, according to her.

I recognized her Mercedes at the top of the circular drive. Further along the street, located near a small park skirting one of the fairways, two dark figures moved, a person walking a dog on a leash. The beam of a small, bright flashlight danced over the ground.

The figure holding the leash and flashlight paused for a moment and appeared to look at me before moving along.

My head was clear even if my thoughts were not. It was a good thing Kim had done most of the drinking. I cut off the van's engine and slid my purse over my shoulder.

What had Gloria found out? The identity of the person who had murdered her boss?

A single porchlight glowed at the front door. As I approached, I saw that the door was several inches ajar.

I sucked in a breath and peeked through the door. It was too dark to see anything clearly. "Gloria? Bobby?"

I frowned. "Where is everybody?" Neither the door nor the mosquitos and moths buzzing the porchlight bothered to answer me.

The door opened silently as I pushed against it with the quivering knuckles of my left hand. "Hello," I called. "Anybody home? Gloria? It's me, Amy."

Down the dimly lit hallway, a dark head poked out of the room that I remembered being Gloria Bolan's office.

The voice that spoke did not belong to Tom Visconti's assistant. "Amy?"

This was a deep man's voice.

I shrieked and clutched my chest. My heart caught in my throat. I ran for the open door and the safety of the outdoors.

"Amy! Stop!" Running footsteps chased me.

My left sandal flew from my foot. I tripped over the rug in the entry and slammed into the wall. Pain exploded in my shoulder. Stars clouded my view.

"Amy, it's okay. It's me." Strong hands gripped my shoulders. "It's me," he repeated more softly.

"Ohmygod!" Tears tumbled down my cheeks. "Derek!" I slugged him in the arm. "You scared me to death!"

He helped me to my feet. "Are you all right?"

"Am I all right? You just about gave me a heart attack." I squeezed him nonetheless. The stars dancing madly before my eyes disappeared one by one. "What's going on? Where is everybody? What are you doing here?"

Derek blew out a troubled breath. "It's a long story."

My eyes narrowed. "You didn't break out of jail, did you?"

Derek managed to chuckle despite the circumstances. "No."

"Last time I saw you, you were behind bars." I fumbled around on the floor, found my sandal and slipped it back on my foot, leaning on him for support.

We hugged again. Tears filled my eyes. "I'm never letting you go again."

"Chief Kennedy had to let me go. Dad's lawyer pal and Judge Arbuckle let him have it with both barrels."

"I'm so relieved."

"Don't be too relieved. It's not over yet. I'm out but I am still a person of interest in Visconti's death," he explained with accompanying air quotes. "I am not exonerated. Not by a long shot. And now this."

"What?" A chill raced up my arms.

"Come on," he said grimly. "I'll show you."

Our footsteps echoed down the dimly lit hall. "Shouldn't we turn a light on?"

"No." Derek turned on me. "And don't touch anything, Amy."

"What is it, Derek?" I clutched his arm. "You're making me nervous."

He led me into Gloria Bolan's office. The yellow shade

of a desk lamp lit the scene. Gloria Bolan was slumped in her high-backed black leather chair. Her face pressed against the blotter on the desktop. A small pool of liquid trailed from her gaping mouth.

A galaxy of stars raced across an inky background on the screen of her open laptop.

A half-full cup of water in a tall, clear glass and an open bottle of pills rested near her hand. A blue-and-yellow strip of cloth was knotted tightly around her neck. The flesh around it was a dull purplish-red in hue.

I squeezed Derek's arm more tightly. "What happened?" I whispered.

"I wish I knew."

"That thing around her neck..." My right hand flew of its own accord to my neck.

"A necktie."

"Don't tell me—" I gasped.

"Yes," Derek confessed. "That's one of my ties."

"This is a nightmare! Are you certain?"

"As certain as I can be without examining it up close. That's my fraternity tie."

"How did it get here? Surely you weren't wearing it." Derek wore denim jeans and a white polo shirt with a pair of leather moccasins. Not at all the sort of attire to wear a dressy tie with.

"No. I've had that tie since my undergraduate days. I can't remember the last time I actually wore it. It might have been years. It was on my rack in the closet with the rest of my ties. I must have a dozen of them, maybe more."

I pictured the tie rack in his bedroom closet. It was mounted to the wall on the right side and slid out for ease of use. I figured there were at least twenty ties on it at any given moment.

"Someone is setting you up."

"Yeah. Again."

I stared gloomily at the eldritch scene for a sign, any sign of who might be behind these murders and the attempt to set Derek up as the killer.

"Where is Bobby Breen?" I asked.

"I haven't seen him. I haven't seen or heard anyone since the moment I arrived. Until you showed up."

"Why would anyone want to murder Gloria? She was harmless."

"Was she? Think about it, Amy. She said she found out something about Tom Visconti's murder. Maybe the killer knew that she found out, overheard her telling me."

"And decided she had to die." I squeezed Derek's hand. "She called me too."

"So the killer had to strike again. And wants to point the finger of blame on me."

"But where did they get your tie?"

Derek shrugged. "I have no idea."

"I do. I just realized. Whoever planted that map of the maze garden in your apartment could have stolen one of your ties just as easily while they were there. Who would notice?"

Derek nodded. "Good point. If it hadn't shown up here, I might not have missed it for months. Years, maybe."

"Derek, you don't think the person responsible for these murders holds some sort of grudge against you, do you? I mean, think about it. First, Tom Visconti is murdered with the tie you had worn to your ex-wife's wedding. Now another of your ties is used to murder again."

"I don't know. Nothing about this makes any sense. If the killer took my tie from my apartment, that makes this murder premeditated. Not a crime of passion at all."

I agreed.

"One thing I know," stated Derek, "is that the minute Chief Kennedy sees this crime scene, he is going to have me in his sights for two murders."

We both studied Gloria Bolan's corpse. I had been fearing just that, which was why I was postponing the inevitable.

"Have you phoned the police?" I finally asked.

"Not yet. I had just arrived when I heard somebody outside. You." He looked out the open front door. "I was about to check the house to see if anyone else was here."

"You think someone could be hiding somewhere inside?"

"You never know."

"Are you certain she's dead?" I took a half-step closer. Gloria Bolan hadn't moved a muscle. If there was anything we could do to save her, there was no time to waste.

"She's cold, Amy. Besides, I checked her pulse. Feel free to confirm, if you like."

"I'll take your word for it," I replied, clutching myself. I dug my phone out of my pocket. "I'll call the station."

I dialed 911 and explained the situation to the dispatcher. "Anita said she'd send help right away."

Derek moved idly to pick up a fist-sized rock near the center rear of Gloria Bolan's desk. It was a polished smooth brown stone with the word TRY carved into its face.

"Careful," I said. "Fingerprints."

"Right." Derek looked embarrassed. "I should know better." He stuffed his hands in his pants pockets.

"Why don't we wait in the hall?"

"Good idea," agreed Derek.

From the hall, we could see the master bedroom. The drapes were pulled back. Across the pond, the outdoor corner lights of Gloria and Mark Bolan's villa twinkled. "Poor Mark."

"Yeah," Derek said softly.

"While we're waiting for the police to get here, tell me about this background check you had run on Tom Visconti."

"You know about that?"

"Ben told me. By now, the whole town probably knows." Even the police in Ruby Lake had a hard time keeping secrets.

"It was nothing, really. I had a funny feeling about Visconti."

"Such as?"

"Nothing I could put my finger on. Something about him just didn't ring true. Know what I mean?"

"Yes, I get that. I take it the background check didn't turn up anything that might give a clue as to why someone wanted to murder him?"

"Not that I could see. He was hardly a saint but no one thing stuck out as a reason for someone wanting him dead."

"To be honest, I can't imagine what your ex-wife saw in the guy."

"Are you trying to say she has poor taste in men?" Derek followed me to the front of the eerily quiet house. We hadn't seen or heard anyone else in the time we had been there. Then again, I didn't feel like confronting a desperate murderer, so that was fine by me.

"Oh, no." I wagged my finger at Derek. "I am not step-ping into that trap. Let's just say I thought she could do better this time around."

"Anyway, I paid for the detective agency to run a background check. I wanted to make sure everything about Tom Visconti was on the up and up. I've got my ex-wife and daughter to think about," he argued in his own defense. "They were going to be living with that guy."

"You don't have to explain yourself. That was per-fectly understandable." A cool wind swept through the open door. I thought I saw someone moving in the shadows near a cluster of trees between the houses. It was a good thing the police were on their way. "What did you find out? Anything useful at all?"

"Nothing much. Good credit rating despite one bank-ruptcy action, a chapter seven. A divorce, former wife now deceased."

"And the map to the Magnolia Manor maze garden that Jerry says he found under your mattress?" I asked, changing gears.

"My fingerprints were not on it, Amy. It wasn't mine."

"And you have no idea how it got there?"

Derek kicked the wall in frustration, leaving a black scuff mark. He cursed when he realized what he had done. "Your guess is as good as mine."

"Jerry's going to have a field day with this."

"After I left the police station, I went home, fixed a sandwich and a tall glass of beer. Then Gloria called. She said she was anxious to talk to me. I asked her if it could wait until tomorrow—the last thing I wanted to do was leave the apartment—but she was very insistent."

Derek looked troubled and tired. "She said she had discovered some things about Tom Visconti's murder and that she thought I'd like to hear what they were. She said she was sure that she could exonerate me."

"She told me more or less the same thing."

"Is that why you're here?"

"Yes."

"I don't mind admitting, she got my attention. I'd do about anything to get out of this mess."

"And you drove here and found her. Why didn't you call me, Derek? Why didn't you tell me you were out of jail?"

"I'd only just been released. Corey dropped me off. He offered to keep me company but I told him I would be okay alone. I was going to phone you. I needed a little time to myself first. To think. You understand."

I wasn't sure that I did but I said yes anyway.

"The next thing I know, Gloria is calling me and wants me to meet her straight away." His hand ran again and again through his hair. "Imagine my shock, finding her. Like that. At her desk. Dead." He sighed. "Now, I'll never know what she found out."

"I was at Kim's when Gloria telephoned me and, like I said, she told me pretty much the same thing she told you. That she had been looking through her boss's things and wanted to talk to me. She said she knew who the killer was."

"Did she give you a name?"

"No."

"Me either."

"I wonder why she didn't tell me she had called you, too?"

"Who knows? All I know is that when I arrived, the

front door was unlocked. I called several times and got no answer. I came inside and found her."

"You want to know what the funny part is? I mean, not funny ha-ha, but funny weird?"

"What?"

"Minutes before Gloria called me, I was telling Kim how I thought *she* had murdered her boss."

"Gloria? Why?"

"I wasn't sure why," I admitted with a frown. I explained about the killdeer and the misdirection that I thought Gloria Bolan had used to lead me in circles.

"Only you could find clues to a murder while watching a documentary about birds."

"Hey, I could have been right."

"Nothing about these murders makes any sense except that Gloria was murdered before she could share what she knew. Somebody didn't want her talking."

"It would appear that way."

While Derek talked, I did some thinking. Being here was not going to do his chances of staying out of jail any good. "Go, Derek." I touched his arm. "Before the police get here."

"What?"

"Go." I pushed him towards the door but he planted his feet and held his ground. "Come on. I'll say I found Gloria's body."

"No, I can't do that. It wouldn't be right." He ran his finger under my chin. "We both know that."

I sniffled.

Derek glanced out the front window. "Here they come."

The headlights of a fast-moving vehicle roared towards the house, splashing up gravel as it barreled up the driveway and slammed to a stop in front of the porch.

31

Violet Wilcox, wrapped in a navy windbreaker and slinky gray yoga pants, jumped out of the driver's seat of the AM Ruby station van.

Lance Jennings, following in his compact sedan, wasn't far behind. He slid to a stop inches from her rear bumper and flew towards the house, notebook in hand. Not quite the clothes horse, he had thrown a blue sport jacket over a pair of baggy brown and red-striped pajama bottoms.

Violet snarled at him. "This is my story, Lance. Go away."

"Not a chance, Wilcox. Our readers are going to want the scoop."

She gave him a two-handed shove that sent him reeling. "So will my listeners." She shoved a microphone attached to a small recorder in my face. "You called the police and reported a death. Who is it? How did it happen?"

"Sorry," Derek said, laying his hand over the mike. "We have no comment."

"What? You can't do that."

"I'm afraid this is a police matter," asserted Derek.

"How did you two get here anyway?"

"We heard it on the police scanner," they said as one.

"Isn't that illegal?" I asked. Truly, I had no idea.

Neither reporter thought the question worth noting, let alone answering.

"Give me a name," urged Lance. He licked the tip of his pencil and stabbed at an open page of his spiral notebook.

"I'll give you a name," I said. "Chief Kennedy."

"Huh?" Lance scratched his ear with his pencil.

Violet Wilcox was practically rubbing her leg along Derek's in an effort to get him to open up.

She and Lance turned as I pointed up the street.

The unnatural flashing red, blue and white lights of two police cruisers lit up the houses and street, coming to a stop at the top of the driveway.

I turned to Derek. "Last chance to make a break for it," I said. "We could keep you out of this."

"Are you kidding? I'm in this thing up to my neck whether I like it or not. No," Derek said grimly. "Let's let them in and take it from there. The sooner these two murders are solved, the sooner life can get back to normal."

Jerry Kennedy stomped across the pea gravel. "What's this all about, Simms?" He glared suspiciously at Derek as the EMT unit pulled in behind him.

"It's Gloria Bolan. She's inside. She's been strangled."

"Strangled? Cuff him," the chief ordered Officer Larry Reynolds.

Larry looked unsure. "Chief?"

"You heard me."

"Shouldn't you check things out inside first?" I suggested.

Jerry reluctantly agreed and everyone got suited up. Except for Lance and Violet who were told to retreat to the street or face charges of obstructing the duties of the police.

Inside the office, Chief Kennedy watched as an EMT examined Gloria Bolan. He pronounced her dead.

Jerry tugged at his watch. "Did somebody call Greeley?"

"Coroner is on his way, Chief," replied Officer Albert Pratt. He was photographing the office from all angles.

Jerry turned to me. "You found her?"

"Actually," Derek explained. "I found her. I was here first. Then Amy arrived."

"But Gloria was already dead when we arrived," I added quickly.

Jerry harrumphed. "You mean, she was already dead when *you* got here. Who's to say," the chief said, eyes on Derek, "that she was alive or dead when Harlan got here?"

"She was," Derek said, meeting the police chief's gaze. "I found her right here. Amy and I haven't touched a thing."

"How is it that the two of you are here in the first place?"

We each explained how Gloria Bolan had telephoned us separately.

"She said she had something important to tell us," I said. "Something about who murdered Tom Visconti."

Jerry ordered me and Derek out of the office.

"Before we go," Derek began. "There is something you should know, Chief."

"What's that?"

"Derek, are you sure this is a good idea?" I knew Derek. I knew exactly what he was going to say. But I was praying I was wrong. *Do not say it, do not say it,* I fired the words telepathically at his skull.

"That's one of my neckties around her neck."

Jerry's brow shot up. "You mean to say—"

I cringed and squeezed my eyes shut. The big dummy had said it.

"Yes, Chief. I want to make it clear that I did not strangle Gloria Bolan but that it is my tie around her neck."

"Derek, please." Tears of frustration and fear cascaded down my cheeks.

"It's okay, Amy." Derek took my hands in his. "Don't you see? It's better this way. Chief Kennedy is smart. He was going to find out sooner or later." Releasing my hands, he turned to the chief. "I have nothing to hide."

Officers Reynolds and Pratt exchanged startled looks.

I felt myself slipping into some sort of weird otherworldly dimension or bizarre dissociative fugue state.

An ugly smear of satisfaction sprung up on Chief Kennedy's face as he pictured the headlines announcing his solving two gruesome murders. Lucky for him, two upstanding members of the press were waiting right outside on the street, ready to print and/or announce any dumb thing he claimed.

"I don't care what Judge Arbuckle says," growled Jerry. "You're spending the night with me, counselor. Come on."

Derek hugged me briefly then complied.

Jerry ordered me to go down to the station in the morning and file an official statement.

I raced out the front door behind them. Lance and Violet were shouting questions from the curb and snapping pictures.

"Derek is helping the police with their inquiries," I

snarled. "If either of you dares to imply otherwise, we will sue the pants, or pajamas in your case, Lance, off of you!"

"You can be a real buzz kill," whined Lance. He slid his slender little digital camera inside his coat. "I'm only trying to do my job."

"Do a real job and find out who is committing these murders."

"What can you tell me about Corey Lingstrom?" demanded Violet Wilcox, brushing against me.

"Derek's friend from Saint John?" The woman came up with the most unlikely questions but this one really had me thrown. "What's he got to do with this?" Did she think he was our potential necktie strangler?

"Nothing." The reporter's long lashes flickered. "He asked me out to dinner. He's really quite charming. Handsome too, in a beach bum sort of way. What's his story?"

"Ask him yourself." I muscled her out of my way and marched toward Derek's car. I had seen a man lingering there. A man with a dog.

"Excuse me." I waved to him. "I was wondering if you might have seen—"

The lurker stepped away from the tree's massive trunk.

"Alex? Is that you?"

"Hey. Evening, Amy. What's going on? All these police and emergency vehicles." He was dressed in a black fleece jacket, track shoes and blue jeans.

As he spoke, Andrew Greeley's black hearse lumbered up the street. The stretch vehicle was almost as much a dinosaur as was the man himself.

"Somebody die?" Alex asked. The dog tugged at its

leash.

"That's Mr. Greeley, the coroner."

"Greeley?" Alex shoved the slender flashlight into the pocket of his jacket and scratched the chocolate lab behind the ear. "Wow. He's still alive?"

"Alive and ticking. Who's your friend?"

"This is Lucille."

I bent to one knee and petted the friendly dog. "She's a beauty." Lucille slobbered all over my hands to show her appreciation for my compliment.

"Yeah. She belongs to Mom."

"Your mother lives here in Rivercrest?"

"That's her house up there. I told you I was staying with her, right?"

I nodded. "Small world."

"Isn't it?" Alex smiled. "Other side of the park, across from the thirteenth tee." He laced the loop of the leash around his wrist. "Isn't that Derek Harlan over there talking to the police chief?"

I glanced over my shoulder. Derek stood stiffly next to the squad car, flanked by Officers Pratt and Reynolds. Jerry Kennedy, chest puffed like a proud rooster, was bragging to the reporters. "Yes, I'm afraid so. The police want to question him."

"Poor Amy." Before I knew what was happening, Alex had wrapped his arms around me and planted a kiss on my forehead. "I'm here for you."

I pulled myself from his grasp. "I'm fine, Alex. Really." Oh, no. Derek had seen everything. Not that there had been anything to see. What was with Alex? I didn't remember him being all hands—and lips—before.

I took a step backward.

Derek settled into the rear seat of the chief's squad

car and disappeared from sight.

"So who got offed?" asked Alex.

"Gloria Bolan."

Andrew Greeley, with the help of a young EMT was struggling into a Tyvek suit, booties and gloves. Our coroner was finally getting with the times.

"The assistant to the guy that was killed at his own wedding? Wow. That is something."

"It's something, all right. A nightmare."

"Yeah, I'll bet. What were you and Derek doing here at this time of night?"

I explained how we had each received mysterious phone calls from the newly deceased asking us to drive over. "Other than that, I'm afraid I can't say, Alex. A woman has been murdered and Jerry will throw a fit if I reveal anything he might not want spread around."

I wasn't sure that was even remotely true. There was as good a chance that Jerry would be the one doing the spreading himself, whether it was the truth or wild conjecture. I just didn't feel like sharing with Alex.

"What about you, Alex? Did you notice anyone around? Particularly, any strangers?"

Alex played with Lucille's wagging tail for a minute and appeared to give my question some thought. "No, I can't say I did. Lucille keeps me pretty occupied."

"Right." To prove her point, Lucille threaded her way between our legs, tangling the leash around us. Alex worked us free. "Was that you I saw across the street walking Lucille when I arrived?"

"Yeah. I was curious about what was going on over here. I didn't realize that was you. I knew Tom Visconti was dead and I saw that other man that was living here go out."

"Bobby Breen?" I asked.

"I guess so. What's he look like?"

"Tall, dark and sleazy." To Alex's addled expression, I elaborated. It wasn't a flattering description that I spun but I was confident that it was reasonably accurate.

"Yeah, must've been him. He was with the widow."

"Amy Harlan, I mean, Visconti?" I wasn't sure which name she was using these days.

Alex nodded. "Then there was that kid in the van."

"Kid in a van?"

"Well, not so much a kid, really. Early to mid-twenties, maybe. Had a buddy with him."

"Can you describe him?"

Alex did. His description matched Vail and his traveling companion.

"Did you see anybody else?"

"Only your boyfriend. By the way, you two still together?" Alex asked.

"We're getting married, Alex."

"Right." Lucille tugged at the leash as a woman's voice called from up the street. "That's Mom. Probably wondering where we've gotten to. Want to come say hi? I'm sure she'd love to see you."

"Another time."

"Okay. Say, I can ask her if she's seen any strangers around. She's home all day. Me, I'm out at the bookstore, fixing up to open. Lots to do."

His mother called once more and Alex waved to her. "Over here!" he shouted. Turning to me, he said, "Stop by the bookstore sometime. I'd love to show you what I've done to the place."

I promised I would but I had my fingers crossed behind my back. I had lots of reasons for not wanting to return to that bookstore, even after it had been re-painted, remodeled, renamed and reinvented.

Some things, like the sight of a dead body, there is simply no erasing.

32

I spent the night on my hot mattress, tossing like a toy ship on a roiling sea. In the morning, my bedcovers were bundled on the floor and I was a bundle of raw nerves.

Images of Derek dressed in drab gray prison garb, shackled and breaking jagged granite rocks with a heavy sledgehammer in the hot sun boring down on him in the prison yard at Alcatraz, with vultures circling round hungrily above, stayed with me like a bad smell.

There were times when my imagination was my worst enemy.

Two cups of black coffee and a thick slice of stale, leftover wedding cake did little to calm my nerves or my brain. I dressed quickly and winged it to the police station.

The visit had been short and anything but sweet. Back at Birds & Bees, I vented my emotions on my best friend.

"And that's when things turned sour," I explained.

"So I heard," Kim said, remaining calm. Dan had already telephoned her and given her the heads-up on what had gone down inside the police station between the chief and Amy.

"I told Jerry Kennedy everything I knew about Gloria Bolan's murder. Absolutely nothing."

"Right." Kim was busy unboxing a shipment of suet cake cages that had arrived that morning. I was helping by sagging against the sales counter looking glum.

"Then I gave him a piece of my mind."

Kim suppressed a grin. Dan had described Amy's behavior as epic lunacy. Kim thought the term had a nice ring to it and had decided to tuck it away in the corner of her brain for further use.

"How dare you keep Derek locked up, I shouted. He's no more a murderer than you are, Jerry. How do we know you didn't snatch that necktie from Derek's apartment when you were searching it? How do we know you didn't then use said necktie to strangle her."

"You really said all that?" Kim laid a handful of suet cages on the display shelf.

"Yep. That was when Chief Kennedy had me thrown out of his office. I never even got the chance to see Derek, let alone speak with him." A yawn exploded from my mouth. "I can't say I blame Jerry. I might have gotten a little carried away with that accusing him of murder thing."

"Gee, you think?" giggled Kim.

"Shut up," I said. "I'm tired, hungry and mad as a bull in the ring."

"Then get something to eat and take a nap. But, before you do, go see Corey Lingstrom."

I rested my chin on my elbows. "What for? Why would Derek's old school chum want to see me?"

"I don't know. It's you he wants to see."

"Is he at the marina?" It had to be a half-mile walk. I wasn't up to it.

"Nope. He's next door, in Brewer's. At least, he should be. He left here not twenty minutes ago and said he was going to eat lunch. You can grab a bite at the same time."

I yawned again, stretched the kinks out of my back and grabbed my purse. "Give me a push towards the front door."

She did.

A little harder than was actually necessary, too.

Inside Brewer's, sixties rock music played softly from the old-fashioned jukebox in the far corner near the blue-felted billiard table.

Corey Lingstrom stood near the center of the bar, feet apart, feathered dart in hand. He flashed me a bright smile, revealing the cute little gap between his front teeth. He winked then tossed the dart expertly at the board some eight feet distant.

The dart sailed quickly in a shallow arc, landing in the lower portion of the small green circle just outside of the bull's eye.

"Nice shot," I said.

"Thanks." Corey ran a firm hand through sun-streaked blond hair sweeping to one side of his ruggedly tan and handsome face. The man stands a little over six feet and has the build and color of a seasoned surfer. Befitting the role, he wore a baggy red T-shirt, equally baggy board shorts and brown leather sandals.

He pecked me on the cheek. "Glad you could make it, Amy. How's our boy holding up?"

"So-so, I guess. I didn't actually get the chance to see him this morning."

"Oh?"

I explained about my little to-do with Jerry Kennedy. Corey chuckled breathily. His accent is an odd blend of Bostonian and Caribbean. "Everything will work out. You'll see."

"I hope so."

Corey invited me to sit. He had already ordered a roast beef sandwich and fries along with a pitcher of beer. He called for a second mug and filled it for me. While the waitress was hovering, I ordered a smoky cheese and tomato crostini.

"Thanks." I took a sip of the dark ale. "What did you want to see me about? Anything special?"

Corey folded his hands in front of his beer mug, nodding to the waitress as she set his plate in front of him. "You tell me. I was hanging out on the balcony of my condo over at the marina when what do I see?" He didn't wait for an answer. "I see Mark and Gloria Bolan talking to Vail Visconti over by one of the boat docks."

"Are you sure it was them?"

"Yep." He popped a handful of salty fries in his mouth and chewed while talking. "I may be new around here but I remember those two. Derek pointed them out to me one time. Same for the kid."

"Did you hear what they were talking about?"

"Not a word. Too far away. Gloria seemed to be doing most of the talking. Her hubby shook his head up and down a lot and puffed on a cigarette like it was giving him the breath of life."

"More like death," I quipped. I smiled at the waitress as she slid the warm crostini under my nose.

I nibbled at my lunch while Corey polished off his burger in four bites. "There is one other thing."

"What's that?" I asked.

"They handed Vail a small green shoulder-strap bag, like a carry-on luggage bag. What do you think that was all about?"

"I have no idea. I think I'll go pay Vail a visit after lunch."

"What some company? I can be your muscle." He raised his right arm and flexed his biceps.

"Impressive, but I don't think that will be necessary," I said on a small wave of laughter. "In the middle of the day, in the middle of a campground, he won't try anything."

"Okay." Corey rose, extracted his wallet and dropped enough cash to cover both our tabs and then some. "I've got to split."

He turned serious. "Look after Derek, Amy. My boy may look like he has a hard exterior, but he's got a soft underbelly. I worry about him. I don't want to see him get hurt or end up in prison for a crime he didn't commit."

"We're all worried, Corey, and doing our best. How long are you staying in town?"

"Until this is settled. The couple that own the condo hardly ever use it. They told me it was mine for as long as I need it."

Corey made his way out. I waved the owner, Paul Anderson, over to my table.

Dressed in his usual jeans and tight black T-shirt bearing the Brewer's Biergarten logo and showing off the fact that he worked out daily at the gym, Paul sauntered over. He twisted around the chair Corey had recently vacated and threw his legs over. "What's up, Amy? How's Derek?"

Grabbing the fork beside me, he cut off a chunk of my crostini and popped it in his mouth. "Hmm, not bad." He licked his upper lip.

"Derek is still at the station, waiting for Jerry to interrogate him and for his attorney to drive up from Atlanta."

"That's tough." He leaned forward, shoved the polished-nickel napkin dispenser out of his way and draped his arms over the table. "What do you say we break him out?"

I chuckled. "I wish." I did like the sound of that, as preposterous as it was. "I suppose you heard about the second murder last night."

"Tom Visconti's assistant, Gloria Bolan. The whole town's talking about it. That's the good thing about owning a place like this. People talk."

"Do any of these people admit to murdering Tom Visconti or Gloria Bolan?"

It was Paul's turn to laugh but not in a happy way. "Sorry, Amy. Not even a whisper. What about her husband?"

"Mark? If he and Gloria ever fought, my money would have been on her. He's not much in the muscles department, at least not since he took sick. I heard Gloria was an avid jogger and did Pilates. Besides, Jerry said Mark had been sleeping when they notified him of his wife's murder. He'd taken a couple of sleeping pills and they had a hard time rousing him."

"I feel sorry for the man. Maybe I can find him some work to do around here." He swiveled his eyes round the busy restaurant.

"I'm sure he'd appreciate that. He could use something to keep him busy and build his confidence up. Jerry made the ugly remark that Mark couldn't tie his own shoelaces without a roadmap. He said Gloria wasn't just Mark's wife, she was his mama, his babysitter, everything."

"Between you and me, Chief Kennedy is—"

"Is what?" a hard-edged voice demanded.

We swirled our heads around.

Jerry stood in full uniform not a foot from our table. His boots were highly polished and his gun smelled freshly oiled.

"Shouldn't you be out looking for more innocent people to put behind bars?" I asked.

Paul gave me the funniest of looks.

"Hello, Chief Kennedy." Paul stood quickly and extended his hand in greeting. "Good to see you, sir. What a coincidence, I was just telling Amy what a top notch investigator you are."

"Were you now?" Jerry squeezed his brows tight and glared at me.

I couldn't blame Paul for caving. As a business owner, it was important to stay in the good graces of the local authorities.

Unfortunately, I had not mastered the art.

"What does bring you here, Jerry?" I asked. "If you're looking for some new instruments of torture, you've come to the wrong place. Try the hardware store up the street. They've got all manner of hard, sharp, pointy things."

"Very funny. I ordered some takeout," he barked at Paul. "Is it ready?"

"I'll go check." Paul gladly retreated.

"You may as well face it, Amy," drawled Jerry Kennedy, sinking back on his heels. "This time, there is nothing you can do. Your fiancé is going down. He's committed two murders. Two." He held up two fingers.

It was all I could do not to swat them down. "If you'd

stop assuming Derek is guilty, maybe you'd find the real killer."

The chief shifted his heavily-laden, black-leather belt and pressed a hand against the table. Did he really need a gun, a Taser and a truncheon to pick up his takeout lunch? "Such as?"

"Such as—"

"Here you go, Chief." Paul Anderson had reappeared with two large paper bags, which he handed over to Jerry. "There're extra napkins in there. I threw in an order of our homemade cinnamon and sugar pretzels, too."

"That's mighty kind of you, Anderson." Jerry opened one of the two bags and took a big whiff. "It's nice to see some townspeople appreciate the job we professionals are doing."

I resisted the urge to stick my tongue out at him, opting instead to say, "I hope you've got enough food there for Derek."

"As a matter of fact, I do." He scrunched the top of the sack shut and headed for the exit. "Even a jailbird has got to eat," he added with an unkind chuckle.

I fought down the urge to slug him. Too many witnesses. "When can I see Derek, Jerry?" I hollered at his retreating backside.

"Anytime you like," Jerry answered without breaking stride.

I half-rose from my seat. "Really, you mean that?" That was so un-Jerry-like.

"Sure." The hostess held the door for him on his approach. "You've got a photo of him, don't you? Help yourself. Look all you want. I won't try to stop you."

Ooh, that was so Jerry-like.

33

Chief Kennedy slid out the door of Brewer's Biergarten like the snake he was.

I gritted my teeth. "I wish there was something I could do to get Derek out of jail *and* wipe that fatuous smile off Jerry's face."

"I wish I could help you, Amy. Derek's my friend too. But whoever is setting him up is doing a good job of it."

"It has to be either Amy Harlan, Bobby Breen, Vail Visconti, Mickey Caswell or Miles Sheffield. Then again, it might be any of the Moonlighters."

"Or none of the above. I hate to say it, but the killer might not be anyone that is even on your radar. Everybody you just mentioned was here last night."

"Everybody?"

Paul nodded. "Every last one of them. Except for Derek's ex, that is. You don't really suspect her, do you?"

"No." The woman was guilty of a lot of things but murder wasn't one of them. I was sure of that. "Don't you think it a little odd that they were all here?"

"Nothing odd about it at all." Paul sounded a bit put out. "Brewer's is a popular place."

I apologized. "I didn't mean anything. I just thought it quite the coincidence."

"Peculiar or not, they were all here at the beer garden," insisted Paul. "And they were pretty much thick as thieves."

"Do tell."

"Well, first MC and the Moonlighters showed up. The whole band. It was awesome. A lot of the diners recognized MC. After a bit of cajoling on my part and the part of the diners, they put on a free concert for everybody."

While Gloria Bolan was getting strangled.

"And that everybody included Bobby Breen and Tom's son, Vail?"

"Yep."

"What about Vail's friend?"

"Who's that?"

"I don't know his name. About the same age." I gave a general description.

"Sorry, couldn't say." Paul waved to a regular then continued. "I do remember one thing. Bobby Breen and Tom's kid were sitting right there at that table." He pointed.

"Friendly?"

"Who's to say? They sat there alone, just the two of them for a bit. Seemed to me it was a pretty intense conversation. Ordered a couple pitchers of beer. Either Bobby was trying to get Vail drunk or vice versa. To what end, again, I couldn't say."

"Could someone have snuck out during the time that everyone was here?" I asked. "I mean, you were busy, right? And then MC and the Moonlighters were performing."

"I suppose," Paul said slowly. "I don't see why not. The place was packed once word got out about MC and the Moonlighters playing for free. News spreads fast around here, you know."

I knew.

"The band even played a few instrumental numbers, now that you mention it, while MC took his breaks. So any one of them might have snuck out, even MC himself. It wasn't like I was trying to keep tabs on them. I've got a business to run and this place can get chaotic at times."

"Of course." I scooted my seat back as a busser cleared away our things from the little table.

"When did Bobby Breen and the others arrive?"

"Let me think. Vail was here first, as I remember." Paul scratched his head. "Maybe around seven o'clock. Then the band, then Bobby. Yeah, I think that was the order."

"How long did they stay?"

"More or less till closing. One a.m."

"Still, it's a short drive from here to Rivercrest Country Club. Any of them could have made it over there in time to murder Gloria and get back again."

"If you say so," agreed Paul.

I had a sudden, and troubling, thought. "Paul, you said that Amy Harlan wasn't here?"

"I didn't see her. What are you thinking?"

The hostess approached and asked if the table was free. Paul urged me to follow him outdoors to the sidewalk.

Picking up where we had left off, I explained. "I'm thinking that Amy lives in Rivercrest. She easily could have gone to Gloria's house, I mean Tom Visconti's house, and strangled her."

"But why on earth would she do that?" demanded Paul. The sidewalk traffic was heavy and we kept our voices low.

That was an interesting question. A question to which I had no answer. I might need to interview her again. "I wonder if the police asked her for an alibi?"

""Beats me. Good luck to Chief Kennedy if he tries."

I agreed.

"Listen, Amy. Have you considered the idea that maybe these murders are part of a larger plot?"

"A larger plot? You mean like a conspiracy? You aren't one of those nuts who think there is an ultra-secret society or an advanced alien civilization behind everything, are you?"

"Very funny." Paul dug his fingers into his pockets. "I'm wondering if maybe somebody was out for revenge. Somebody who Visconti's company screwed over, for instance."

I pursed my lips. That wasn't a bad theory at all and I wished I had thought of it myself. "You may be right. But that opens up the list of potential suspects exponentially."

"Have you tried talking to Amy? She was closest to Tom, after all. Maybe she has some insights."

"No but it's a good idea."

"Come see me anytime. I'm full of good ideas." Paul said with a grin. "Gotta get back inside the beer garden."

Standing at the curb, waiting for the traffic to clear so I could cross Lake Shore Drive, I mulled over what I had learned from Paul.

Why was everybody at the beer garden on the night Gloria Bolan was murdered? Had it been nothing more than a coincidence?

Even more perplexing was that it appeared that, with Tom Visconti dead, his frenemies were suddenly all friends. Period. What was that all about?

I skipped across the street and wound my way down to the campgrounds.

There was no sign of Vail or his friend at the camper van. An older couple sat reading outside a silver Airstream nearby, while some burgers sizzled on a portable grill. I waved and acted like I belonged. They didn't seem to be paying me much attention.

I peeked through the windows of the sliding door on the side of the van. Deserted.

I tried the handle, giving it a squeeze. The door popped open with nothing more than a grunt and I hopped inside. Fluttering my hand in front of my nose, I reached between the front seats and cranked the window open on the driver's side.

The inside of the van reeked to high heaven. That delightful little scent you get when you mix beer, pot, sweat and skunk.

Trying hard not to breathe any more than necessary, I did a little poking around. A number of decent-looking fresh paintings, one I recognized as our own beloved Ruby Lake, filled the back corner of the camper van. A big plastic bucket held an assortment of paints and brushes. A small pottery wheel, caked with dried mud, was tilted against one of the wheel wells.

I peeked under the lightweight mattress that was stained with all manner of things I would rather not know the origins of.

I looked through the bedding and toiletries, and under the car seats. What wasn't icky or sticky, was gooey and damp. I wished I had worn my gardening gloves. My decrepit old water heater in the basement didn't hold enough hot water for the shower I was going to need when I was done here.

I found what I was looking for tucked away inside a stiff-framed backpack. This had to be the bag Corey Lingstrom described seeing Gloria and Mark handing over to Vail at the marina.

I pulled it out and unzipped the top pocket. The interior was stuffed with personal belongings. A brown calfskin trifold wallet sat atop the heap. I flipped it open. There was Tom Visconti looking back at me, somber, stern and maybe—was it my imagination?—a little accusing.

The van rocked suddenly. Before I knew what was happening—earthquake?—a rough hand with sharp fingernails snatched the wallet from me. I gasped as another hand ripped the bag from my hand.

"I guess you must really want to spend the rest of your life in jail along with that murdering boyfriend of yours," Vail Visconti, crouching in the van, said in a low, threatening manner.

"Vail. I didn't hear you coming."

"No kidding." He reached for me. I shoved him against the side of the van and dodged to the open sliding door.

His companion blocked my way. He sneered, revealing yellow teeth. An ugly scar down the side of his cheek turned white as he did so. "The ranger warned us we might see a bear or two. Didn't tell us we'd have to be on the lookout for crooks."

"I am not a crook." I lashed out at him with my right foot, smacking him hard in the hip. He cursed but I got what I wanted. He moved out of my way.

I jumped down from the van.

The two young men had me boxed in. There was no sign of the couple overnighting in the Airstream.

"Why were you in the van? What do you want with my dad's stuff?" demanded Vail.

"If you must know—"

"Oh, we must," said Vail. "Right, Jake?"

So that was his name.

"Right, Vail. Unless she really does want to go to jail."

I blew out a breath of defeat. The last thing I, or Derek, needed was for these buffoons to sic Chief Kennedy on me. "Somebody mentioned that you had received a bag from the Bolans. I was curious to see what it contained."

"Who?" Vail asked.

"It's not important."

"You want to see what's in the bag?" Vail hurled the pack at me. "Take a look."

Trembling, one wary eye on them, I riffled through the bag. Mostly, clothes, a tie pin, a watch and a few other personal items.

"Nothing but a few of Dad's things. They said that was all they had. Everything else, either that black widow wife of his took or had already been shipped home to Nashville."

He snatched the bag back, nearly ripping my hand off in the process. "Satisfied?"

"I won't be satisfied until my fiancé is out of jail and cleared of a murder he didn't commit."

"Says you," snarled Jake, in a dirty-white sleeveless tank that hung off his scrawny, pimpled frame. His black chino shorts looked custom-made for a Sumo wrestler. Either one strong belt or a dose of magic must have been required to keep them up.

And I hoped they stayed up.

Jake's grimy feet were bare. Paint streaks mottled his

hands, arms and legs.

Deciding that the I-am-woman-hear-me-roar approach was not achieving optimal effect on these two louts, I decided to throw a little sweetness their way.

"You mentioned your father's black widow wife. You mean Amy Harlan?"

"Harlan, Visconti, whatever she calls herself. Yes, of course, I do. What else would you call her? She got everything she wanted. My dad's name, his money."

"And, don't forget," said the ever helpful Jake, "she got your father out of the way so she could enjoy it all for herself."

"What about Bobby Breen? Could he be involved?"

"Wouldn't surprise me." Spittle flew off Vail's lips as he railed. "Look, I loved my father. Sure, we butted heads. That's what fathers and sons do. Even in spite of all the insults."

"Insults? Like what?" I couldn't help but ask. Besides, if I kept him talking long enough, maybe I would learn something useful. For all I knew, he might even finally admit to both murders himself.

"Like insults about Mom and my name, Vail. He loved to make fun of it. Especially in front of those boozing friends of his." Jake threw a loving arm over Vail's shoulder as the young man bawled.

Seeing my confusion, Vail rubbed his puffy red eyes and continued. "You know how I got that name?"

I shook my head no.

"For two reasons. First, Vail, Colorado was my mother's favorite ski resort. At least until guys like my dad started overdeveloping the place. Trying to turn it into nothing but another overcrowded tourist attraction."

"Mom was different. She loved nature, the outdoors. She adored the White River National Forest. Second, Mom told me it was because when she had me, it was like a *veil* had been lifted. And she finally knew what her life was meant to be all about. To raise me. And she did. The very best she could."

"Where is she now?" Hadn't someone told me she was dead?

"Mom died several years ago." Vail hung his head. "Alone. I blame myself for that. And him."

"Why?" Might she have been murdered? By Tom?

"Never mind."

"Okay, but I still don't understand what you mean when you say your father insulted you because of your name."

Vail stiffened before plunging ahead. "My dad told everybody my mom insisted on the name Vail. He wanted nothing to do with the name. Like he wanted nothing to do with me.

"Dad claimed that she named me Vail as a dig at him. He said Mom had cheated on him with some ski bum from Vail. He said he didn't think I was even his kid."

Vail's face turned purple with anger. "But it was a lie. A dirty, lousy lie."

He laid his head against Jake's welcoming chest.

"I'm sorry." If what Vail said was true, Tom Visconti had been a crummy husband and an even crummier father. Amy Harlan and Maeve might just have dodged a bullet.

That had been a horrible thing to do to Vail. Had the son enough pent-up rage and resentment inside him to kill his own father?

Vail slumped off to a nearby picnic table and poured

a glass of water from a jug into a plastic cup from which he drank quickly.

"How do you fit in all this, Jake?"

"Vail and I are friends. We look out for one another."

"I saw some quite nice paintings inside. Acrylics and watercolors. Let me guess, the two of you are painters?" I rubbed my finger over blotches of dried paint on the sill of the van.

"Wrong. We're artists. I prefer to paint. Vail's medium is pottery." He held out his hands for inspection. "I've always wanted to do pottery but my fingers and arms aren't that strong. Vail keeps trying to teach me," he said with a glance at his companion seated at the picnic table. "But it's hopeless. I'll stick to paintbrushes."

"Yes, I suppose it must take strong hands to be a potter." Strong enough to strangle somebody without any trouble.

Were those real tears Tom's son had been shedding or crocodile tears?

"Between you and me, that was always one of the problems between Vail and his dad."

"What do you mean?"

"Mr. Visconti liked to play the bigshot businessman. Vail is an artist. His father didn't understand that. He couldn't understand why money didn't mean anything to him.

"Mr. Visconti wanted him in the family biz. That guy thought everything, the whole world, was dollars and cents."

I walked slowly over to the picnic table. Jake followed closely by my side. He was limping. My kick to the hip must have been a good one. "You were both at Brewer's Biergarten across the street last night, correct?"

"That's right." Vail sniffled and wiped his nose with his shirt. "What about it?"

"What were you and Bobby Breen talking about? I hear you two were locked in conversation."

"None of your business," snorted Vail. "Maybe he was interested in buying some art. Yeah, that's it. We were dickering over the price of pots." He found himself very amusing and laughed loudly.

Don't let him goad you, I commanded myself. "Did you notice anything strange?"

Vail kept me on tenterhooks while he stared into space a minute. "Strange? How about a sixty-year-old man jumping around on a tiny stage in a purple leotard making a fool of himself?"

I couldn't help giggling. I almost wished I had seen that.

"Let me put it this way, did you notice anyone who was *not* there?"

"What kind of stupid question is that?" Vail's ire was rising again like the second tide of the day. "Show her the door."

Jake grabbed my elbow and squeezed. "Let's go, lady."

"One more thing," I said, over my shoulder as Jake pushed me along towards the path out, "other than the black widow, who do you think would have wanted to strangle Gloria Bolan?"

"The way you go poking around bothering every-body, I'm surprised more people aren't out trying to strangle you," Vail shouted.

With that most unkind, yet profound, remark, Jake released me. Wiping his hands, he said, "Come back again at your own risk."

Jake may have been bluffing but I took his words to

heart.

34

I hightailed it straight to Amy Harlan's house. Bobby Breen answered the door.

"This is getting to be a habit," I quipped. "Are you the new valet?"

A frown creased Bobby's high forehead. "The police have requested that I no longer occupy Tom's house. It's a crime scene now." He looked past me to the street as if expecting something or someone. "What do you want?"

His face appeared ashen and drawn. His checked blue shirt was rumpled and hung loose. His designer jeans were in need of some serious redesigning. The only thing shiny about him was the pair of shiny black cowboy boots he squeezed his feet into.

Too much booze or too many murders weighing down on his conscience? Or was it too much of both?

"Would you believe I came by to borrow a cup of sugar?" I improvised, giving him my best grin.

"Would you believe I am about to slam this door in your face?" He gripped the edge of the door and pulled.

Hmm, apparently my best grin wasn't good enough.

I grabbed the door to keep it from shutting. "I was hoping for a word with Amy."

"Regarding?"

"It's about Derek."

He sighed but he still wasn't budging. "She's not here."

I peeked around the corner of the door. "She's not? Are you sure?"

"Very sure." He stepped to block my view. "I took her to Charlotte myself."

"Maeve too?"

"Maeve too."

Thinking that he meant the airport, I asked, "Where did they go? Florida?"

"Not that it is any of your business," began Bobby Breen, puffing out his chest. "But mother and daughter are staying with friends in Concord." Concord was one of the suburb towns surrounding Charlotte. There was a huge mall there. Amy Harlan could drown all her sorrows in a brand new Coach handbag.

"I can't say that I blame them," Bobby Breen went on. "This town is all a bit too much, don't you agree? I mean, what time do they roll up the streets around here?"

"No, I don't agree." Nobody disses my town. "And if you think that way, why were you and Tom Visconti so intent on investing here?"

"Business is business." He folded his hands neatly over his chest. "Tom saw an opportunity, discussed it with the team, and we took it."

"If you say so. When was the last time you saw Ms. Bolan alive?"

"Right before I left to pick Amy and Maeve."

"What time was that?"

"Around five thirty. And yes, Gloria was very much alive. She came to Tom's house, saying that she had a few things to take care of."

"On a Saturday night? Isn't that unusual?"

Bobby smirked. "She was Tom's assistant. It was not my place to question her hours or her duties."

The sun burned the nape of my neck. I stepped into a spot of shade on the corner of the small front stoop. This guy was never going to invite me inside. Not even if my hair caught fire.

"Did she say anything particular, like what kind of things she had to take care of?"

"Nope." Somewhere inside the house, a telephone softly rang. He ignored it.

"Gloria told me, and Derek, that she thought she knew who strangled Tom."

He shrugged. "If she did, and I say if, she didn't share those thoughts with me. And, if you ask me, the woman was delusional. Just like that feeble husband of hers."

"Why do you say that?"

"It's not important now."

"Two people are dead. I think any and everything could be important. I'll bet the police feel the same way. Shall we call them?" I stuck my cell phone in his face.

He glared at me, I stared at him.

He caved first.

"Fine. Gloria fancied herself more than an assistant. She thought she was indispensable and irreplaceable. Trust me," said Bobby Breen, "nobody is. As for Mark, I've only met him on a few occasions, like when he was doing some work over in Tom's yard times when I was in town. The man used to be a professional. Now he mows grass and plucks weeds from flower beds. And he's always talking to himself."

"Have some sympathy. He had major health issues and was forced to retire young."

Bobby Breen snorted. "If I'm ever that frail of body

and feeble of mind, I hope they put me out of my misery."

"Believe me, I'll do everything in my power to make that happen." This guy was a Major Jerk. No, a Four-Star General Jerk.

The telephone started ringing again.

"Are we done here?" Bobby Breen asked.

I was about to say no when he slammed the door in my face without waiting for my answer.

35

While I was in the neighborhood, I decided to go see how Mark Bolan was holding up and pay my respects.

It was a short drive over to the villa and would have made a nice walk. Gloria had mentioned she often walked to work. I parked across the street and studied the house. The curtains were pulled shut. The garage door was down tight. Not a sign of life.

I went to the front door and rang the bell, wishing I had brought some small token rather than arriving empty-handed. The chime echoed hollowly inside. No one came to the door. Was Mark out? Making arrangements for his wife's funeral, perhaps?

I wondered for the first time if he and Gloria had any family local. Because this was the time when he would need them the most.

I turned away from the front door and walked along the well-kept flower beds lining the driveway. Mark did a nice job of keeping everything manicured and attractive.

The sound of a muffled cough broke the silence, then ceased. I stopped and waited. After a moment, I heard it again. The coughing came from the backyard.

I cut across the lawn between his villa and the next. The units weren't more than a dozen feet apart. The grassy backyard was no more than twenty feet deep and sloped gently towards the water. The pond itself lay still, like a drop of mercury in a surrounding sea of green.

Mark was seated in a white Adirondack chair facing the pond. His legs stretched out in front of him. He wore baggy blue jeans and a dark green sweatshirt, sleeves rolled up to the elbows.

"Hello, Mark."

Mark flinched and swung his head around. "Oh, it's you."

"How are you holding up?" I asked, moving closer. The smell of alcohol and tobacco filled the air.

Spotting a tray birdfeeder on a faded aluminum pole near the screened-in porch, I smiled.

Mark took a slow drag on the cigarette he'd been gripping between his middle and index fingers. He held his breath a moment, then released a languid trail of gray smoke.

"You're out," I said.

"Huh?"

"Of birdseed. You're out of birdseed." I jerked my thumb toward the feeder. "I can bring you a bag of seed next time I come, if you like. No charge."

"Oh, that," he said wearily and with a profound disinterest. "That thing was here when we moved in. Gloria never did care for it. We never put any food in it. She said it would only attract squirrels."

The new widower squashed his cigarette against the armrest of the chair, leaving a dark smudge on the paint. The stub fell to the ground where it joined several others piled around him. Mark must have been sitting there for a long time.

"Not sure why she cared. What did it matter if we had a few squirrels? Squirrels gotta eat too, right?"

"Right. Of course, if you put a baffle around the pole, that would keep the squirrels from reaching the seed."

"Sure."

I got the impression that he neither knew nor cared what I was talking about. I couldn't blame him. His wife had just been murdered. Now was not the time to be talking about birds and squirrels and the benefits of baffles.

Still, I'd bring him a baffle from Birds & Bees as well as some seed. Feeding the birds would give him a little something to help occupy his mind at such a difficult time.

"Do you mind?" I inquired, indicating the empty Adirondack chair abutting his.

"Help yourself." Mark leaned to the ground and picked up his pack of cigarettes. He pulled out a fresh stick and lit up. He sniffed the air as if it were a balm. "I hear you found her."

"Me and Derek, yes." I laid a gentle hand over his. "I am so sorry, Mark. Please, let me know if there is anything at all that I can do for you."

"There's nothing." He tugged at the plastic thingie noosing a six-pack of beer from which two cans had already been disposed of before my arrival. The empties lay crumpled beneath his feet. "Beer?" He dangled the remaining cans in the air, balanced on the strip of plastic atop his finger.

"No, thanks."

He popped a fresh can open, tipped his head and drank.

"Are you sure there's nothing I can do to help? Times

like these, we need to help one another. Do you have any family here in town?"

What I really wanted to do was to tell the man to stop drinking and smoking, especially in his physical condition.

Then again, after losing his wife, how much harm could a little nicotine and alcohol do? It might even help make the hours and days more bearable for him for the moment.

"Nah. No family around here. Me or her. Mine's in Oklahoma. Gloria's family is mostly in Tennessee." He pulled at his cigarette, his unshaven cheeks moving in and out. "My brother called and offered to come. I told him don't bother."

"I know that Chief Kennedy is holding Derek on suspicion because one of his neckties seemed to have been the murder weapon, but I want you to know that Derek had nothing to do with your wife's murder."

"I never said he did." Mark slumped forward, resting his elbows on his knees. His hands took turns, one feeding him the hot cigarette, the other his cold beer.

Portrait of a man whom life has defeated.

Cigarette smoke formed a poison cloud around us, tickling my nose and tearing up my eyes. I rubbed my nose, resisting the urge to wave my hand wildly in an effort to disperse the stench.

"Thanks. I'm glad you don't think he was involved."

He merely nodded.

After a moment, I felt it safe to ask, "Do you have any idea who might have wanted to hurt Gloria?"

Fresh tears swam in Mark's eyes.

"Oh, dear," I exclaimed. "Now you're making me cry, too." I swatted away my tears while Mark let his fall to his lap.

"Don't you see, Amy? The police asked me the same question. Who would want to harm Gloria? I don't know. Sure as hell not Derek. I mean, why would he?"

"He wouldn't," I said, still struggling to control my sobs.

"Gloria would do just about anything for anybody." He flicked the remainder of his cigarette into the pond.

I watched the stub drift slowly along the grassy edge of the bank. A green-headed mallard nudged it with its beak, then swam past in search of better grub. I didn't have the heart to scold him.

"I can just about picture her over there," Mark said, wistfully, his eyes drifting over the water to the home Tom Visconti had been renting. "Sometimes, I'd see her across the pond, working in her office. I felt bad, you know?"

"Why is that?"

"Me being unable to work." The broken man threw his beer can into a bed of petunias against the porch. Spilled beer drizzled into the soil. I couldn't help wondering whether that would help or hurt the flowers.

"You're working. Maintaining the house, the yard."

Mark scoffed. "I used to earn a real living." He angrily snatched another cigarette out of the quickly-dwindling pack and lit up. He puffed furiously.

"You're doing the best you can." I patted him on the shoulder.

He shrugged.

The tears had subsided. I dabbed my face with a tissue from a pouch inside my purse.

"Do you remember anything special about that evening?" I asked softly. "Anything that might help?"

"No. Like I told the police chief, Gloria had to go to work. She left some dinner for me. So I watched a nature show."

"The one about birds?" I asked.

"Yeah. I thought I'd try to learn a little." He managed a small smile.

"I watched that special too. Wasn't it good?"

"I'm afraid I took a sleeping pill with supper. I probably slept through a chunk of it. I woke up on the sofa and went to bed," he said sheepishly. "I did make some notes about some birds I wanted to ask you about. I was curious if we get them around here."

I smiled. It was nice to see I had had a hand in Mark taking up birding. It was a great hobby and any hobby at this point would only help him get through these difficult days ahead. "I'll be happy to take a look at those notes for you."

"Thanks. Maybe later," he answered hollowly. A breath hitched in his throat as he turned his sad eyes on me. "That was the last time I saw her, you know. She said goodbye at the door."

"Would you mind if I take a look inside the house?"

He drew his brows together. "What for?"

I explained how Gloria had telephoned both Derek and me to say that she wanted to see us because she had found out some things which she thought pointed to the killer's identity.

"Yeah." Mark blew out a puff of smoke. "I heard all that. The police told me."

"And Gloria never told you anything?"

"Nothing. Not a hint. I had no idea she was nosing around. I knew she had asked you."

Mark turned his eyes on me. "But she never told me

she was looking into the murder herself. She sure never told me she knew who murdered Visconti."

He pressed the nicotine-stained fingers of his left hand into his eyes. "She probably figured I couldn't handle the pressure. She was always worried about me."

"That's understandable. So, can I look inside? You see, I'm wondering if she may have left some evidence somewhere here."

"The police have already looked through the house, Amy. They didn't find anything worth mentioning."

"They might have missed something." If Jerry had led the search, there was a good chance they had.

"I'm sorry, Amy. Later, okay? Now is not a good time." Mark rose unsteadily to his feet, using the back of the Adirondack chair for support. "I just want to be alone."

My heart went out to Mark as, muttering to himself, he shuffled to the screen porch and retreated into the dark villa.

36

I spent the afternoon taking care of business. Bird business, that is. With the rest of my staff having come up with one excuse or another, it had remained for me to run the store until the end of the day.

Gertie Hammer came by around six and slammed a shiny blue photo album down on the counter. "Thought you might want these."

She unwound a peach-colored woolen scarf from her neck and rubbed her hands together like she had just come in from a blizzard, yet it was sixty degrees outside.

"Thanks." I flipped to the first page mostly out of politeness. The last thing on earth I felt like looking at at that moment were pictures of my failed wedding. "I guess I owe you."

"Yes, you do. A deal's a deal."

"I know." I turned the pages slowly. It was like watching a movie in slow motion, a movie in which the hero and heroine die at the end.

"Of course, if you'd like to change that deal…"

I slowly closed the photo album and peered warily at Gertie. The two of us had had our differences and been at odds more than once. "What did you have in mind?"

She laid her hands and her cards on the table. "You could sell me back my house."

I sighed. "We've been over and over this, Gertie. This is my house now. And my business." Gertie had been trying to get the property back almost from day one that she had sold it to me. Some of those attempts had been downright underhanded. Always with the idea of making a better profit on the deal. I wonder who or what she had in mind this time. But whatever scheme she was planning, she was going to have to forget about it.

The corner of her lips turned down, creasing her face up like a stretched paper sack. "Is that a no?"

"It's a no, Gertie."

"You're hopeless, Simms. This business of yours is going nowhere. If you're smart, you'll take the money and run. Better still, let Derek Harlan take care of you once you're married."

"In the first place, business is fine. More than fine." Okay, actually it was less than fine. Maybe far less—I didn't dare look at the books. But that was really none of her business.

"In the second place, I don't need Derek or any man to take care of me. Derek and I will take care of each other."

Gertie snorted. "You're almost as batty as my sister, you know that?" The old woman didn't wait for an answer. She turned on her heels and started to the door.

I folded my arms. Now she was comparing me to Esther? I wasn't sure if I was feeling offended or complimented.

And that was a scary thought.

"Thanks again for the photo album," I shouted but I don't know why I bothered. Gertie was out the door and shambling towards her Olds Delta 88 hunkered down at the curb like a waiting minion, this particular one being a Paleolithic beast.

I closed the store as the sun went down and the last customer of the day shuffled out with a selection of mixed bird seed from the bins lined up along the front wall and a welcome mat insert featuring a pair of nesting bluebirds.

Gertie's photo album felt like a fifty-pound weight as I lugged it and myself up to the third floor. I had called the police station twice in vain. Each time to be told that I could not speak with Derek because he was unavailable.

What did that mean?

Unlocking the door to my apartment, I called out, "Mom? You home?"

My keys clattered in the glass dish next to the door as I let them slide from my fingers. "I guess it's just me," I said to the walls.

I dropped the thick photo album on the kitchen table, fixed myself a cold cheese and avocado sandwich on whole wheat with mayo and grabbed a cold orange soda from the fridge to wash it down. Leftover wedding cake rested on a plastic plate on the middle shelf of the refrigerator. I could swear that I heard it whispering my name. Maybe I'd throw myself a pity party later and finish it off.

That way I would never have to see it again. It brought back nothing but bad memories.

Speaking of which, for some masochistic reason, as I chewed my sandwich, I found myself looking at the photographs that Gertie Hammer had taken at my almost wedding.

I had to admit, she was pretty good with a camera. Derek looked heartbreakingly handsome. I wiped a tear from the corner of my eye.

But seeing those pictures set off something in the back of my brain. Something that I couldn't quite reach.

Still struggling to push my thoughts forward, I licked up the crumbs from my plate and set it in the sink. I needed somebody to talk to. Somebody to bounce ideas off.

Mom was out. Kim was on a date with Dan, dinner at Jessamine's before Dan's shift later. I had begged her to pump her boyfriend for information on the murders. Kim promised she would telephone me after her date ended. Paul would be working at the beer garden. The man rarely took a day off.

I frowned.

That left Esther.

Then again, Esther sometimes saw things I didn't.

I ran down to the second floor and banged on her apartment door. "Esther? Are you in there?"

My fist was poised to strike again when I heard the sound of a chain sliding from its channel. The door cracked open.

"What do you want?" asked Esther.

I peeked through the narrow opening. The aroma of canned tuna and dollar store perfume swam up my nose. "Open up. I need to talk to you." I pushed the door but the weight of Esther's body prevented it from opening.

"Go away," said Esther, whose hair was in bright pink plastic curlers. A blue chiffon dress peeked out from her plush white bathrobe. "I'm trying to get ready for my date."

"Who with?" I teased, knowing full well the answer. "Floyd?"

"No, with Jimmy Carter." Esther gave me her patented eye roll. "Of course, with Floyd. Now go away." She went to close the door in my face.

"But this is important!"

The door stopping moving.

"How important?"

"I need to talk to you about the murders. Must I remind you that Derek is still locked up under suspicion of having killed two people?"

"Sounds like your problem, not mine."

Esther wasn't going to make this easy. Still, she hadn't shut the door in my face. We were making progress. "Come on, Esther, you like Derek."

"Yeah, I suppose so," she agreed. "Not so sure about his taste in women..."

Ha-ha, very funny. I decided to let the barb slide. "So can we talk? This really is important. It doesn't have to take long. I don't want you to be late for your date."

"Important enough to give me the day off tomorrow?" Esther's twisted fingers squeezed the doorknob.

"Fine."

"With pay?" Her conniving eyes dared me to refuse.

"With pay," I agreed.

Esther twisted her lips into a smile, fingers tugging on a tight curl on the side of her head. "Okay, I'll give you five minutes."

"Thank you." I pushed on her front door. "*Now* can I come in?"

Esther glanced over her shoulder. "We'd better use your place."

"What's wrong with your apartment?"

"I just had it fumigated for termites." She squeezed into the hall.

"Fumigated? Termites? I'm the landlord. If we have termites, you really should have reported it and—"

Esther pressed her fingers to her pink and wrinkly cheeks. "Did I say fumigated? I meant painted. *Freshly* painted."

"You had your apartment repainted?" Esther was already halfway up the steps and I quickened my pace to catch up. "I think you're supposed to ask me before you do that."

"I know, I know." She tossed her hand in a careless over-the-shoulder gesture. "You're the landlord. Next time, I'll file a formal request. In triplicate."

Esther threw open my apartment door like she owned the place. "Now," she stopped in the entrance, folded her arms over her chest, and confronted me. "You want to spend the rest of your five minutes blathering or do you want to talk about these murders?"

"Have a seat," I said, indicating her favorite chair, which had been my father's favorite too. "And let's discuss the case."

Esther grabbed her work-in-progress from under the seat cushion and knitted quietly while, seated on the sofa, I explained my doubts, fears and theories.

When I finally ran out of steam, Esther peered across at me, her knitting needles clacking softly in rhythm.

"Is that it?" she asked.

"Pretty much," I sighed. "I mean, I thought Gloria herself was the murderer and now she's dead, too. Chief Kennedy is sure that Derek's the culprit and, to be honest, I can hardly blame the man. The only hard evidence found so far leads to him.

"Everyone else that might have had a reason to murder Tom Visconti, let alone Gloria Bolan, either has a rock-solid alibi or could have slipped away unnoticed. Both at the wedding when people were milling all around the grounds—"

"And again during the time of Gloria Bolan's death. Either our killer is very lucky or very clever. Maybe both," concluded Esther.

"Any idea who that killer might be?"

Esther carefully set her knitting on the side table beside the lamp. "Let me see that photo album." She motioned with her fingers.

The photo album Gertie had prepared lay beside me on the sofa. I grabbed the album, rose, handed it to Esther and returned to my spot. "What are you looking for?"

"Shush."

I waited impatiently as Esther slowly turned the pages, one by one by one. "Esther, would you please tell me—"

"Uh-uh." She wagged a gnarly finger of caution.

I bit my lip and held my temper although my brain was like a pressure cooker about to explode. What was the woman doing looking at my disastrous wedding photos now for?

"Ah-ha." Esther clicked her tongue.

"Ah-ha, what?" I dared asked.

"Just as I thought." She pressed her index finger against the page open on her lap. "Take a look."

I crossed to her side and stared at the page. It was a photograph of Derek flanked by Paul and Dan. My fiancé looked adorable, excited and handsome.

The sky behind him was a perfect Carolina blue with just the right amount of white fluffy clouds for contrast.

"Judging by the angle of the sun, that picture must

have been taken maybe an hour before the ceremony." I caught a sob in my throat. "What's so special about this photograph?" I gently pulled the photo album from her hands to see it close up.

"That tie Derek is wearing."

"Yes?"

"You remember that tie he was wearing last week? At Amy Harlan's wedding? The one with the thrasher on it?"

"Of course, I remember. That was the tie I gave him. I'm not senile, I'll have you know."

"If you say so. But look at the way Derek is dressed in that picture. Notice anything?"

I looked. Hard. "No," I confessed. "What do you see?"

"Do you remember when Gloria was in the store after Amy Harlan's wedding? I was there too and you were talking about her boss's murder."

"I remember, Esther." I was beginning to lose my patience and starting to doubt the wisdom of having invited her to discuss the murders.

Esther massaged her arthritic knees. "Then you'll remember that when you told her how the police knew the tie belonged to Derek because of that particular detail that Gloria herself said she remembered seeing it."

I slammed the photo album shut and dropped it on the coffee table. "I still don't see what any of that has to do with catching a killer." This had been a waste of my time and Esther's.

"Take another look," said Esther. "This time, pay particular attention to Derek's necktie."

Indulging the old woman, I flipped through the photos a second time. Once I was done, I settled back on the sofa with the album in my lap. "Done. And I still don't see—"

Esther literally cackled. "That's just it. It's what you don't see."

I pushed my fists into my temples. "What don't I see?"

"You don't see a brown thrasher," Esther said smugly. "That is, you wouldn't see a thrasher."

"I wouldn't see a—" There was no doubt that the old woman had lost me. The question was had she lost her marbles?

"You wouldn't and couldn't see a little brown thrasher, if there had been one on Derek's tie that day. His buttoned up suit jacket would hide it completely."

I thought back to the day of Amy and Tom's wedding. Derek had kept his coat buttoned. No one knew the thrasher was there but us.

I gasped and widened my eyes. "So how did Gloria Bolan see it?"

"Bingo." She cleared her throat. "I could use a glass of water."

"I don't know, Esther. It sounds like a slim lead at best," I said, fetching us each a cold cup of water from the jug in the fridge. "Not to mention, Gloria Bolan is dead now, too. Besides which, what if you're wrong?"

"I'm not," she assured me. "In fact, that young woman Paul has been dating was in the bar the other afternoon when I was having lunch with Karl and Floyd."

"Liz?" I set my empty cup on the coffee table.

"That's the one. She had her cell phone out and was showing Paul and us a bunch of pictures from the wedding day. You and Derek were in a couple of them. What wasn't in the photos was a brown thrasher."

"If you say so." I wasn't sure I believed her. I wanted to believe her. I just wasn't sure that I could. This was a woman who sometimes left the water in her kitchen sink running for hours on end and had, on countless occasions, forgotten to lock up the store at the end of the working day.

"Assuming you are right, what does it mean?"

"It means I'm late for my date." Esther thrust her cup at me and leapt from her seat. She grabbed at her curlers. "Help me get these things out."

I quickly helped her remove the plastic curlers that had covered her skull like a wobbly helmet. Her hair had stayed in too long and she now looked like Shirley Temple on a bad hair day.

"How do I look?" Esther asked anxiously, gently patting her hair.

"Adorable," I lied. "Cute as a button." What good would it do to shake her confidence? She was going on a date.

"Good. Good." She crossed to the front door, stopping to rub her knees once more. "Since I'm late and it's all your fault, I'm gonna need you to pick up my prescription at Lakeside Pharmacy."

"What prescription?" I called as she took the stairs down.

"My arthritis meds."

"Are you sure they'll give them to me? Isn't that against the rules?"

"Ask for Pat. He knows me and he doesn't care too much for rules."

I heard the sound of her door squeaking open.

"You can leave them outside my door, if I'm not home."

The door slammed shut. A moment later, it opened again and she peered up the stairs at me, face pinched, curls bouncing like rubber balls. "Outside my door, not inside."

She disappeared from view and I heard her door close once more. I flopped down on the sofa. The photo album lay open on the coffee table. I leaned forward and studied the photo album once again.

Darn, Esther was right.

But what did it mean?

37

It was nearly eight o'clock. The pharmacy would be closing in an hour. I'd get Esther's prescriptions before deciding what to do next. If I didn't, I'd be hearing about it for days.

Locking up the apartment, I drove to Lakeside Pharmacy, which occupies a space adjoining Lakeside Market towards midtown.

I pulled into an empty slot in the small lot on the side of the building and tugged at the sleeves of my sweater. With the sun disappearing behind the mountains, a chill had swooped into our valley like a silent snowy owl.

I stepped into the warm store to be greeted by a sterile medicinal smell that always reminded me of hospitals. A teenaged girl chewing a wad of green spearmint gum manned the cash register near the automated door. I asked for Pat and she directed me to the prescription counter. "Ring the bell, if you don't see him. He could be in back."

"Thanks." I sauntered down the aisle between shelves laden with deodorants on one side and contraceptives on the other. An odd combination but who was I to judge their sales tactics? I was hardly the business guru of Ruby Lake.

The clerk had been correct. There was no sign of Pat behind the tall counter fronted with vitamin pills and travel-sized shampoos, soaps and conditioners.

I pressed the button on the counter next to the register and waited, like the sign taped to the counter read: Press once, then wait.

And wait I did. I drifted down the aisle over and picked up a tube of Mom's favorite toothpaste—it was on sale—and I was about to check out the candy aisle—candy is never a wrong choice—when a man called out. "Hello, can I help you?"

I poked my head up over the shelf. "Pat?"

"Yes?" He was a pleasant looking man with chubby cheeks and a thinning head of hair atop a very round skull. Thick brown-rimmed eyeglasses ringed his eyes. He wore a pharmacist's *de rigueur* white jacket, indicating that he was a man of the pill *and* a good guy. The pinned-on nametag read: P. Johnson.

"I'm here to pick up a couple of prescriptions for Esther Pilaster."

"Ah, Esther." His face brightened considerably. "Such a dear. How is she?"

Were we talking about the same woman?

"She's fine. Although I guess her joints are acting up a bit."

"Right." He snapped his fingers twice. "I've got her prescriptions right here. Give me a second." He turned his back on me and riffled through a bank of alphabetically-arranged prescription sacks on the wall behind.

He handed them across the counter. "You tell Esther to give me a call if she has any questions."

"Thanks, I will." I set my purse on the counter. "How much do we owe you?"

Pat waved his hands at me. "It's all covered."

"Great." That was a relief. Getting Esther to give money back was not the easiest of tasks.

Pat leaned forward putting his hands on the counter. "Is Esther still dating Floyd Withers?"

"Yes, she is. In fact, they have a date this evening." Did I detect a note of disappointment? Interesting. The pharmacist looked a good ten years younger than Esther, not that that meant anything. Was he interested in Esther romantically too?

"Shall I tell her you said hello?"

"Please do," he said, his words shaped by a smile. "And tell her to take her medications, pharmacist's orders."

"I will."

"And to watch her blood pressure."

"Is her blood pressure a problem?"

"Not particularly, given her age. But I hear running that store of hers—oh, what's it called?" He snapped his fingers and narrowed his brows. "Birds and Beasties?"

"Birds and *Bees*," I corrected.

"Right, anyway, the way she talks, managing the business can get quite stressful at times."

"You don't say." My ears grew hot.

"I do say." He leaned even closer and said softly, "Confidentially, I hear some of her employees don't seem to be pulling their weight."

Sure, I could guess where he'd heard it too. Straight from the horse's, or in this case, Pester's mouth.

"I see." My own blood pressure had gone up about thirty points but I held my tongue in check.

"Life is too short as it is. Just look at that man that was killed last week. And then Gloria Bolan." He shook his head mournfully side to side. "What is the world coming to?"

"I wish I knew. I suppose you know Gloria's husband, Mark."

"Yes, it has been a while since I've seen him, however."

"Oh? I got the impression that he was on a number of medications—for his heart condition. And then those sleeping pills he's taking."

Pat knitted his brow and ran a fingernail along the crease in his forehead. "I don't know about that. Gloria and Mark each had a couple of scrips, I do recall that much. More than that, I couldn't say. As a professional, it wouldn't be ethical."

"I understand."

"If you ask me personally though," said the pharmacist in a conspiratorial tone, "Mark's ailments are more of the soft tissue variety." He tapped a finger against the side of his skull. "If you know what I mean?"

I did. I thanked him once again and left.

Between Esther's observations and what I had just learned from the pharmacist, the questions were boiling over in my brain.

I really wanted to examine those photographs from Amy-the-ex's wedding. Unfortunately, Bobby Breen told me she was out of town. I could contact her and ask her to text some to me. But she wasn't likely to agree. There was a good chance she wouldn't even take my call.

Then it hit me. Derek might have a key to her house and there may be some printed photographs lying around. If not, maybe some digital copies on a computer or a tablet.

Leaving Esther's meds on the passenger seat of my

van, I drove straight to the police station.

There was no sign of Chief Kennedy's personal vehicle on the street or in the back parking lot. Good. He'd probably refuse to let me even see Derek, let alone have a private word with him. Not that I was going to tell Jerry what I was thinking regarding the murders. He'd laugh in my face and/or yell at me that I didn't know what I was yammering on about.

And, frankly, I wasn't so sure yet about anything myself. I needed proof. I needed cold, hard facts. Without them, Derek would remain in jail and I would remain nothing more than a mosquito buzzing around Jerry's barbecue.

Jerry Kennedy. Beneath that hard exterior...lies a heart of stone.

Maybe I could suggest that for his tombstone.

Imagine my surprise when I entered the main door of the police station to find the squad room empty. Closing the door slowly behind me, I called out, "Hello? Where is everybody?"

The strong smell of stale coffee wafted from the pot near the rear. A telephone rang then immediately ceased. Anita Brown, the dispatcher, was probably working from home and had picked up the call.

"Help, police!" I half-shouted. This was followed by a muttered, "Okay, this is weird."

"Amy?"

My brow shot up.

"Derek, is that you?"

"You expecting to find somebody else locked up here tonight?"

Following the sound of my fiancé's voice, I discovered him clutching the dark steel bars of his cell with a big grin on his weary face.

We kissed through the bars.

"Where is everybody?" I inquired.

"Dan's on duty tonight. He had to step out for a couple of minutes. Mrs. Hermann called about her schnauzer getting loose."

"Again?" Mrs. Hermann has never been able to keep Mimi, her miniature schnauzer, in her yard. Everybody in town was familiar with the friendly, bearded pooch who was often seen wandering the fair streets of Ruby Lake. Mrs. Hermann claimed Mimi had wanderlust and the woman didn't appear to do much to discourage her behavior.

"So what brings you?" asked Derek. We held hands through the cell bars.

In a rush of words, I told Derek everything new that I had learned so far about the murders. I also explained Esther's theory about the ill-fated, custom brown thrasher necktie and threw in what the pharmacist had told me about Mark Bolan.

Derek scratched under his chin. "That's a lot of info. You've been busy. I'm not sure what any of it means though. If anything."

"Neither am I. You don't think Mark could have been involved in Tom Visconti's murder, do you?"

"No. Even if he had a motive, and I can't see a good one because the dead man was responsible for his wife's paycheck, I saw him seated in the aisle before the ceremony. I don't believe he would have had time to strangle anybody. I'm not even sure he's strong enough."

"Me either. Besides, he's really distraught over all this. So where does that leave us?"

"I have no idea. There is one bit of news," announced

Derek. "The coroner has completed his initial autopsy. Greeley figures Gloria Bolan was probably dead for an hour or so when she called me. Once my lawyer gets here and hears that, I'll be out in no time."

"Huh? That makes no sense. You're saying that Gloria was dead before she called us?"

"So I hear."

"Okay, now I am truly and totally stumped." I chewed on that bombshell for a long moment but it got me nowhere.

"Dead people don't make telephone calls. How does Jerry explain that?"

"He doesn't. He's arguing that Greeley is wrong. But I don't think so. At least, I hope not. I don't think Chief Kennedy thinks so either. He just can't come up with another reasonable explanation for what's going on."

"And knowing Jerry, he doesn't like that one little bit."

"Right. So until he can find somebody else to pin these murders on—"

"He's going to pin them on you." I frowned and cocked an ear.

"What is it?"

I pressed a finger to my lips. "I thought I heard something," I whispered. "Be right back."

38

I tiptoed down the narrow corridor and peeked into the squad room. Empty.

"I guess it was the wind or something. Anyway, you can see why I really want to get a look at those wedding photos. If Esther is wrong, that's that. But if she's right..."

"It opens up a whole other can of worms." Derek sighed. "I wish I could help you but I don't have a single photo. My ex never sent me any."

"No," I answered with a grin. "But you do have a key to her house, don't you?"

Derek lowered his eyes at me. "Yes. You are not suggesting breaking in, are you? What if she catches you?"

"It's not breaking in if I have the key. Besides, she won't have to know. Bobby told me she and Maeve are staying with friends in Concorde."

"Okay, then what if Breen catches you?"

"Simple. If I see he's at the house, I won't go in."

"Even simpler, why not ask him if you can look for any photos she might have in the house?"

"Because," I countered, "he could be the murderer. I don't want to tip my hand."

Derek chuckled. "No, you just want to risk your neck."

"Please, Derek. I'd risk anything to see you free and the real culprit caught." Tears puddles in the corners of my eyes. "Besides which, like I said, if Bobby is there, I'll simply wait for another time."

I could see him mentally fighting with himself. "Please?" I asked again, with big ole pussy cat eyes.

Finally, he caved. "Okay. You win. You'll find a spare key in the drawer in my kitchen. The one where I keep a few household tools. Unless the police have confiscated it. But I can't imagine why they would."

"I know the drawer you mean."

"However, I don't think you should be going over there on your own. Like you said yourself, Bobby Breen could be the killer. I'm beginning to wonder if he and Gloria Bolan might not have been in it together."

"You mean Tom's murder?"

"Yep. Her boss and his partner. Think about it."

I did. "That might make sense, except that Gloria is dead now too."

"So? A falling out amongst thieves, isn't that what they say?"

"You're right."

"Thank you. But wait, there's more," Derek said. "Mark might have seen something. He was obviously intimate with Gloria. Who knows what she might have confided in him."

"Or might have figured out for himself."

"And Visconti's house is just across the pond."

"You're right. He told me himself he could see plenty from the villa. What if he saw the wrong thing?" I thought back to my last conversation with Mark. He had seemed broken. "He seemed deeply troubled, maybe even scared. And it's more than just losing his wife."

"Maybe because he saw something he shouldn't have. In fact, he may not even realize what it is he saw."

"And what if Bobby is afraid that Mark might figure out what's going on? What if Bobby decides to eliminate him next?"

"All the more reason for you to back off and not try anything yourself. Let the police handle it."

"The police? What good have they done so far? All Jerry's done is lock you up. Twice."

"I am getting a little homesick. My little bachelor pad is beginning to seem like a mansion compared to the accommodations here." His eyes swept over the hard cot and the stainless toilet standing exposed in the corner.

Yuck.

"I have an idea," I said. "Be right back."

"Now where are you going?"

I glanced across the still deserted police station. So far, so good. I remembered that Jerry kept the key to the cell in his bottom left-hand drawer. I'd seen him pull it out a time or two.

Mostly when threatening to lock me up on one trumped up charge or another—simply because he was annoyed with me at the time. Sure enough, there it sat under an open carton of Hostess Twinkies.

I snatched up the key on its official brass Town of Ruby Lake keyring and rejoined Derek who had been squeezing his head through the bars trying to see what I was up to.

I smiled my broadest and held up the key.

Derek blanched. "Is that what I think it is?"

I inserted the key in the lock and gave it a twist. "Bingo!"

"No bingo, Amy. No bingo." He backed away as I

yanked open the cell door.

"Don't be a ninny, come on, Derek."

"Amy, I know you mean well and I appreciate it. I really do. But we cannot, I repeat, cannot break out of jail."

"You could hardly consider this a breakout," I insisted. "We're using the key."

"*You* are using the key."

"Besides," I said as I gathered up Derek's personal belongings, "I'm not really breaking you out. I'm only borrowing you."

"Borrowing me?" Derek nervously looked down the corridor towards the door of the police station as I grabbed his coat.

"Borrowing you. Come on, let's go." I pushed him out of the cell. "I'll have you back before anybody even begins to notice you're missing."

"You think so?" I detected a quiver in his voice.

"I'm positive. Mrs. Hermann's problems never get solved in under ninety minutes."

"What if someone calls the station?"

"Anita will pick up from home and take care of it. If necessary, she'll request a squad car. But what are the chances of that?" I pushed him down the hall to the rear exit. There was no point going out the front and making a spectacle of ourselves.

"By the way, what was Alex doing out in Visconti's neighborhood?" Derek asked, trailing so closely behind I could feel his warm breath on the back of my neck.

"He's staying with his mom until his apartment above the bookstore is remodelled. Her house is up the street from Visconti's."

"Quite a coincidence."

"You're not accusing Alex of murder?"

"No, I guess not. But why is it every time I see him, he's got his hands on you? Is there something I should know about?"

I paused at the door. "No, Derek. I admit Alex is a bit... overly demonstrative but he's history, pre-Colombian period." I clutched the steel door handle. "Now, can we go, please?"

Derek sighed. "This is wrong on so many levels." He grabbed his coat from me.

I opened the door slowly. "Come on," I said, looking back over my shoulder. "All I want is for this to be over with and us to be together. You've got to believe me."

"That's what I want, too," whispered Derek. We hugged briefly and made our escape.

39

Derek took the lead. "Uh, Amy."

He froze suddenly. I slammed into his backside.

"Careful there, big guy." I dropped my purse and turned around to retrieve it off the floor. "Not that I haven't missed you and the things we might be doing together on our aborted honeymoon, but this isn't the kind of conjugal visit I had in mind."

I wiped my hands over the side of the purse to rid it of grit. "Don't they ever clean this place?"

"Not now, Amy." Derek gently grabbed my elbow and pulled me up. "We've got company."

I felt a chill.

"Company?" I squeaked.

"Hello, Amy, Derek. Going somewhere?"

Under the glow of the porchlight, Dan stood on the back stoop, feet planted firmly on the concrete pad, hands planted just as firmly on his hips. The yellow bulb from the fixture above the rear door gave his stern face the look of a disappointed spectre.

The good news was that he hadn't drawn and was not brandishing his police issue weapon.

"This isn't what you think," I blurted out.

Dan pointed and said, jaw barely moving, "Inside, you two."

Derek, on the other hand, swore. Quite colorfully, I might add, then recovered to say, "Evening, Dan. How'd things go with Mrs. Hermann? Find her schnauzer?"

Dan waved his arm as if to sweep us back into the police station. Derek and I clutched each other and shared a troubled look as we reentered the station.

Dan moved to the coffee pot and poured himself a cup of stale coffee. I noticed miniature schnauzer hairs sprinkled all over his uniform. His tattered left pant cuff led me to believe that Mimi had either been very hungry or very angry.

Dan sipped silently, eyeing us over his steamy mug. After a minute, during which I could practically picture the gears in his head turning at near light speed, he gestured towards the cell and we complied.

"What on earth were you thinking, Derek? Where did you think you were going?"

Derek spread his arms helplessly as we shuffled closer to the cell.

"Bathroom break," I said quickly. "You know it is inhumane to lock a man up without allowing hourly bathroom breaks."

"There's a toilet in the cell," Dan replied flatly.

He pointed. I looked.

"That thing?" A shiny steel bowl glistened in the corner next to the cot.

Yuck.

"That's not a proper toilet. It's a public humiliation. How could anybody be expected to go to the bathroom on that thing? There's no door, no privacy. It's inhumane, Dan." I gave my head a sad side-to-side shake to express the inhumanity of it all.

"Give me a break, Amy." Dan Sutton was having none

of it. He unzipped his leather jacket. "I've seen this guy pee in the woods."

"Well, that's gross."

"Look," Derek said stepping away from my side and grabbing back his personal things. "We're sorry, Dan. It was a dumb idea. Maybe we could forget this ever happened?"

"Derek, I can't simply ignore—"

"Besides," Derek interjected before the proverbial axe could fall, "I'm not even sure I ever was under arrest. Not this time, at least. Chief Kennedy kept saying things like protective custody and person of interest."

"And you didn't press the matter?" I demanded, in shock. "I'd have been screaming my head off at the injustice. Demanding my freedom. Alerting the newspapers. I ought to call Violet and Lance right now!"

"No, Amy. I figured it was easier to go along than to argue," Derek said with a shrug. "I knew I was innocent and that this would all get straightened out soon enough."

"So," I huffed at Dan. "You see? You can't break out of jail, if you aren't really in it, can you?"

"Amy," said Dan, scratching the back of his head. "That doesn't make any sense but—"

"Nothing about these murders makes any sense, Dan. Don't you see that?"

Derek slumped down on the cot in the cell. "Go home and get some sleep, Amy. We'll talk about this in the morning." He gave me a meaningful look.

"But what about...you know what?"

Dan cocked his head. "What is you know what?"

"Nothing," Derek answered. "Please, Amy, go home and lock all the doors. You need to be careful," warned

Derek. "Somebody killed Gloria because she was nosing around in Visconti's murder. You could be next."

"But Derek," I said in frustration. "I still think that—"

Dan was frowning at us. He crossed his arms over his chest. "What are you two trying not to say?"

I opened my mouth but Derek shot me a warning look. I caved. "Fine. Tomorrow. I'll be by first thing in the morning. Don't worry, we'll get this whole thing sorted out."

I blew Derek a kiss and turned to go. Dan clamped his hand on my right shoulder.

"Umm, I am free to go, right?"

Dan gave me his scariest cop look. He worked his jaw back and forth for a minute. "Lucky for the both of you that the chief is down in Charlotte at a Hornets game."

"Amen to that," Derek said, rubbing his tired eyes.

Dan may look, and sometimes act, all tough and by the book, but inside he's soft as the center of a jelly donut.

Speaking of which, I made a mental note to myself to bring him some first thing in the morning—raspberry jelly, his favorite. A little something to brighten his day and dull his anger.

"This never happened." Dan slammed the door to the cell shut. "Go home, Amy."

No, I realized in frustration, but it had *almost* happened.

Time for Plan B, whatever that was.

40

I tried to go home, I really did. And I knew that I had promised Derek that I *would* go home, lock all the doors and stay safe.

And I did that, too. I climbed out of my clothes, into my nightgown and under the covers.

For all of about five minutes. But how could I sleep with Derek locked up in that awful cell and the killer of two people running around loose in Ruby Lake?

I couldn't.

So I climbed back out of bed, out of my nightgown and into my street clothes.

And then into my Kia.

I was on my way to Rivercrest Country Club and Amy-the-ex's house. Hopefully, Amy-the-ex's deserted house.

Derek would understand. Not that I looked forward to confessing.

I had left him a very nice—if I do say so myself—note of apology on his kitchen counter, propped right up there on the stovetop where he couldn't miss it, signed with lots of hugs and kisses, when I stopped in to pick up his ex-wife's spare house key.

Yep, Derek would understand...once he calmed down. I simply had to take a peek inside Amy Harlan's home to see if she had any photographs from her own ill-fated wedding. Photographs that would point to a killer. I wouldn't be able to sleep until I did.

The sleepy guard watching a movie on a tiny TV in the sentry shack at Rivercrest Country Club waved me in. I cruised up the dark, empty streets to Amy Harlan's home. The tires hissed over the pavement, damp from a recent rainfall. I pulled up to the curb and killed the engine. The house appeared deserted.

I approached the front and peeked into the garage through one of the tiny window panes running along the top. There was no sign of a vehicle inside.

Perfect.

I slipped the house key from my pocket and inserted it in the lock. It fit and the door opened soundlessly.

I paused on the stoop, staring into the gloom. Seeing nothing. Hearing nothing.

It was black as pitch inside and scarier than the middle of the Cherokee National Forest at midnight.

"Hello?" My voice quavered. My arms and legs tingled like high-tension wires racing with electricity.

I took a step into the entry hall. "Anybody here?"

There was a blur of movement. I felt the air of something moving nearby. Before I could even think, let alone react, a thick muscled arm hooked around my bare neck and contracted.

I gasped, a scream caught in my throat.

A hard body pressed against my back and another arm wrapped itself tightly around my waist.

I felt myself growing dizzy. With my last ounce of energy, fueled mostly by fear, I drove the heel of my foot down on my attacker's toes and jammed my elbow into his ribcage.

The man howled and his grip loosened. I surged forward, turning as I did, arms extended and fingers taut. I clawed at the face that was nothing more than a dark shadow coming towards me.

I crouched, every fiber of my being bristling. The sound of both of our heavy breathing filled the air.

Was I about to meet my end just the same way that Tom Visconti and Gloria Bolan had? Strangled by a madman?

The entry light came to life illuminating Bobby Breen's ruddy face and bloodshot eyes. A fresh scratch ran from the outside corner of his left eye to his lip.

"Bobby?" I tugged at my collar. Even though his hands were no longer wrapped murderously around my neck, I still couldn't breathe. My skin burned where his heavy wristwatch had scraped my flesh.

"What are you doing here?" Bobby demanded. His hair was rumpled and he was dressed for bed in satin navy bengal-striped pajamas with waist patch pockets.

He traced his wound with a finger.

"What's wrong with you? You tried to kill me."

"I thought you were the strangler, coming for me next." He wiped a bead of sweat from his brow. "You didn't answer my question, Ms. Simms. What are you doing breaking into Amy's house?"

"I didn't break in. I have a key." I held up the shiny brass key for his inspection. "See?"

"Oh." He slumped against the door.

I sagged to the floor.

Finally, he moved, saying, "I need a drink."

I picked myself up and followed him to the sleek bar in the corner of the living room.

He picked through the bottles, settling on a bourbon,

straight. "You want one?" He offered the bottle.

"No, thanks." I could have used one but I needed to keep my wits about me. This could all be some sort of trick. He could still be a vicious killer.

"Suit yourself." He set the bottle down on the shelf. He studied his reflection in the silver-framed mirror behind the bar and swore. He splashed some cold water on a towel at the edge of the wet bar and dabbed at the fresh scrape. "Did you have to scratch me?" He threw the wet towel in the sink.

"I could use a glass of water."

"There are bottles in the refrigerator in the kitchen. Help yourself."

"Thanks." I walked to the open kitchen and flicked on the crystal chandelier suspended from the ceiling. Of course, Amy Harlan would have a chandelier in the kitchen. She probably had one hanging over her king-sized bed too, and probably one over her toilet and bidet.

I picked a bottle of imported Italian water out of the door shelf and twisted off the cap, drinking quickly.

"You still haven't explained what you're doing here."

I jumped and whirled about, spilling ice cold water down my chest. "Don't sneak up on a person like that!"

Bobby Breen cursed and set his crystal tumbler of bourbon on the marble countertop. "You're making a hell of a mess. Amy doesn't like messes."

He ripped off several sheets of paper towel from a roll on the counter and mopped up the water. He waved his hand over a stainless steel trash can at the end of the counter. The lid magically popped up and he tossed the damp paper towels inside.

Wiping his damp fingers on his pajama bottoms, Bobby said, "Talk." He picked up his drink.

I gulped what was left of my water, giving myself time, still trying to get my wits about me.

How much should I tell him?

What did he know?

Was he the strangler?

Was he toying with me, pumping me to see what I knew before he strangled me next?

Was he playing with me like a cat plays with a bird, knowing that in the end I'd never talk?

"I'm waiting," Bobby Breen said, sipping cooly.

I decided I didn't have much to lose. "I'm looking for wedding photos."

"Wedding photos? At this hour?" He downed his drink and went back to pour another. "What wedding photos?"

This was my chance to run to the door and make my escape. Except I didn't. I followed him to the living room but maintained a healthy, out of arms' reach distance. "The ones the photographer took the day of Amy and Tom's wedding."

"What do you want to see those for?"

"I'm looking for evidence."

"Of?"

I wasn't sure I was ready to tell him yet. "Did you strangle Tom Visconti? Were you and Gloria Bolan in on it together?"

Bobby chuckled. "You are amusing. And stupid."

I glared at him.

"If I did murder him and admitted so to you, wouldn't I have to strangle you next to prevent you telling anyone? That is what they do in the movies."

"I prefer to think of myself as gutsy. Besides, the police know I'm here. So does the security guard at the gate. I had to tell him who I was visiting. He wrote down my name." At least, I hoped he had. He seemed far more interested in the movie he was engrossed in than in me.

Bobby frowned. "Despite what you may think, I didn't strangle anybody."

"You almost strangled me."

"I told you," he said with sudden anger. "I thought you might be the killer. I heard someone prowling around. Saw a shadowy figure. What else could I think? This neighborhood isn't so safe anymore. I'm glad I don't live here permanently. And I sure as hell don't want to die here."

Bobby slammed his empty tumbler down on the bar. "As for your accusation, I was never alone that day. Not for a minute. From the time we got to Magnolia Manor up to the time poor Tom's body was found. I was never alone."

"Says you."

"Say the dozens of people who saw me. Whether you want to believe it or not, I don't give a damn. The police seem satisfied. I'm leaving tomorrow."

It didn't take much to satisfy Jerry Kennedy as far as I was concerned but I kept that opinion to myself.

"I didn't see your car in the garage when I arrived."

"It was a rental. I returned it. The shuttle is picking me up at seven-thirty tomorrow morning." He glanced at a thick gold wristwatch. "In fact, I'd like to get some sleep, if you don't mind." That wasn't a question.

Bobby Breen led me to the door and opened it. A pale brown moth flew past us and headed for the kitchen. Obviously a connoisseur of chandeliers.

I hesitated in the doorway. "About those photographs —"

"I'll tell Amy you inquired."

"But—"

He held up his hand to stop me. "If it's any consolation, I haven't seen any photographs lying around here pertaining to the wedding. And I doubt very much Amy has any. I'd rather think she would like to forget, at least as much as possible, that the day and the event ever happened."

I stepped onto the porch and looked up at the stars. But I wasn't done with Bobby yet. "Let's say I believe you. Let's say you didn't murder your partner or Gloria Bolan."

"How very kind of you," he said, his voice thick with sarcasm. His hand gripped the edge of the door.

"So who did?"

Bobby sighed. The strong smell of bourbon hit me in the face. "If you want to know the truth, I thought it was your boyfriend."

"Derek? He's no killer."

"No, no, no." Bobby shook his head. "The other one, Alex something."

"Alex Bean?" I took a step back and fell off the porch. I recovered my balance but not my senses enough to ask, "Why would Alex strangle Tom Visconti and then Gloria Bolan?"

"Tom had this thing about dogs. Hated 'em, in fact."

"And?"

"A couple of times, Tom complained that Alex's mutt had pooped on his lawn and the kid wouldn't pick up after it. They exchanged some heated words."

"That's it? It sounds like a typical suburban spat, nothing to strangle anybody over."

"Well, Tom did take a shot at him."

"At Alex?" I gasped in horror. "With a gun?"

"No, the dog. He was merely letting off steam. Making his point, you might say. He didn't actually hit him. Never intended to. It was only a .22, for chrissakes."

"Was there a police report?"

"No, the whole thing got swept under the rug. Tom talked the kid's mom into letting the incident go." He cracked a grin. "Tom was a sly old dog himself. There wasn't a woman he couldn't charm the pants off of. And very often did, if you get my drift."

That was a vivid, if disgusting, bit of imagery I could have lived without.

I chewed on Bobby's parting words as I walked down to my van at the street. I could feel his eyes on the back of my head the entire time.

He shut the front door as I pulled away from the curb. There wasn't a single light visible at the front of the Bean house and I didn't dare disturb Mrs. Bean. I'd check with Alex as soon as possible and get his side of the story.

41

Pondering my next move and still wired and wide awake, I cruised past the Bolan villa and parked across the street. I simply had to get a look in Gloria's house to see if any evidence of what she claimed to have found concerning her boss's murder was inside.

Light leaked from under the bottom rubber lip of the garage door and spilled over the driveway. A lamp glowed in the living room.

I turned off the motor and rolled down my window. I could hear soft music coming from the direction of the garage. I climbed out and started up the driveway. As I approached the garage, I heard voices. Two of them. A man and a woman.

Mark had company. That was a good thing. This was no time to be alone.

Maybe now he would let me take a look through his wife's personal possessions, especially any computer or notebooks she might have left behind.

I turned the corner to the side door leading into the garage. I lifted my hand to knock on the glass pane in the upper half of the door. "What the—"

I dropped my hand and pressed my ear to the door. I heard the voices again, louder yet still muffled. The man I recognized as Mark.

But the woman...she sounded eerily like Gloria.

A sister maybe or her mother, come to visit and help out Mark?

I rapped my knuckles on the door. "Mark? It's me, Amy Simms." I swatted a mosquito who seemed to think my nose was its dinner.

The door squeaked open and Mark slowly poked his head out. A tiny bead of sweat followed the edge of his hairline. "Amy, what are you doing here?" He peered left and right.

"I was in the neighborhood and saw your lights were on. Can I come in?"

"Sure, I guess." Mark stepped away from the door. "I was working on the truck. Keeps me busy." He wiped a greasy red shop rag over his dirty hands.

An old Ford pickup from the sixties sat on cement blocks in the center of the single-car garage. The hood was open. The cab doors had been removed and leaning against a garage wall amid myriad other car parts. Rows of wooden shelves littered with all manner of things, half of them covered in cobwebs, climbed to the ceiling.

One of those big rolling tool boxes, this one chest high, sat next to the truck's engine compartment. The smell of gasoline, oil and sweat was overpowering. An empty can of tuna fish on the floor beside the water heater was filled with cigarette butts.

"Nice truck," I said because I couldn't think of anything else to say. Never insult a man's truck. I knew that. Especially when he's recently been widowed.

Mark shrugged. His hair was tucked under a blue ball cap. He wore a pair of loose-fitted denim overalls with a black T-shirt. "She's a work in progress."

I moved slowly around the disabled and half-crumbling vehicle, brow furrowed.

"What are you looking for?"

"I thought I heard voices. Two." I held up my fingers, making eye contact with Mark over the bed of the truck.

"You and a woman."

"A woman?"

"You'll think this is crazy but she sounded to me a lot like your wife. Who is she? A relative of Gloria's?" I pointed with my chin to the white raised-panel door connecting the garage to the interior of the house. "Where is she? Did she step inside the house? Maybe I could say hello?"

"Really, Amy, I don't know what you are talking about. It's only me. Alone. Working on my truck, like I said." Mark lifted his ball cap, scratched the top of his head and replaced his hat. "Oh, I know," he said with a grin. "You must mean the radio. I had it blasting a minute ago. That Violet Wilcox woman is on the air. I love the oldies."

"I could have sworn I heard you and a woman talking."

Mark crossed to the ancient gray cassette AM/FM radio player on the shelf and switched it off. "You all right? You look exhausted. Can I get you anything?"

I leaned against a six-foot plastic shop cabinet along the inside wall. "I am exhausted. It's been a long day. A long week, actually."

"I bet."

"Of course, nothing I've been through can compare to what you've had to deal with."

"No, I suppose not. Funeral is the day after tomorrow, by the way."

"I'll be there," I promised.

Mark nodded.

"Would it be okay for me to take a look through Gloria's things now? As I explained, I'm looking for any evidence that she might have had—"

"Gloria didn't have any evidence, Amy."

"Are you certain? She might have. On her computer, maybe?"

I crossed to the door connecting the garage with the house and laid my hand on the doorknob. "Let me take a quick look." I turned the handle. "I won't be long and I won't disturb you at all."

I smiled my friendliest. "You keep on working on your truck."

"I said no, Amy." A flash of anger crossed his face. "I mean, I'd rather you didn't, that's all." He stuffed the red rag in his rear pocket.

"Really, I'll only be a minute." I cracked open the door. "Please? We could help find something that leads to the person responsible for both Tom and Gloria's deaths." Not to mention, clear Derek once and for all. "It might help ease the pain."

Mark's eyes turned red and his nostrils flared. "Just let me take a look. I'll only be a minute. Nothing for you to worry about. You work on your damn truck," he whined.

Mark swung around and kicked the Ford's rear bumper. "No, dear, it's not what you think." Bang! He slammed his foot against the bumper once again. "Why can't you leave me alone?" Bang!

I watched in horror. Mark was falling completely apart.

Worse yet and scary, the more he spoke, the more he sounded like Gloria.

Dead Gloria.

And then I remembered how well he had mimicked the birds when he had gone bird watching with my group the other day. Mark had boasted that morning, saying he had an ear for mimicry. The woman's voice I had heard as I approached the garage had been Mark imitating his dead wife.

Mark Bolan was truly and deeply insane.

Then I thought about the telephone calls that Derek and I had received from Gloria asking us to come to Tom's house. Calls that she could not possibly have made because she was already dead by that time.

"Oh!" I gasped. My heart thumped in my chest. "It was you. It was you, wasn't it?" My throat was so dry the words caught in my mouth as I struggled to spit them out.

"It was you, wasn't it," aped Mark, lips curled. His hands balled into tight purple fists. "Yes! Yes, it was me, Amy. It was me!"

"You strangled Tom? And your wife?"

Mark sneered. "I didn't strangle Tom. Don't you get it? That was Gloria."

"Gloria? No, I don't believe it."

"Believe it or not," Mark said, in his own voice. "She did. Strangled him." He chuckled madly. "She thought I was weak but I guess I showed her. I'm not so weak now, am I?"

I forced my breath to slow and asked softly. "Why would Gloria murder her boss, Mark?"

"Because he was getting married to Amy Harlan. Gloria hated him for that. She wanted him all for herself."

He wiped the spittle on his chin with the back of his

arm. "Tom said the marriage didn't mean anything. He promised the two of them could keep the affair going. That only made Gloria all the madder."

Mark reached for a pack of cigarettes in the pocket of his overalls. He slid out a cigarette, grabbed a book of matches lying on the open bed of the truck and lit up. "You don't ever want to make Gloria mad, Amy. Trust me. My wife decided that if she couldn't have Tom all for herself, then no woman was going to have him."

"She and Tom Visconti were lovers?"

"Oh, yeah. That's what they were, all right. But Tom didn't think she was the marrying type, not for him, anyway," raged Mark.

"She didn't think I knew about them. She tried to hide it at first. But I saw them. I saw them, all right. Across the pond. In his bedroom." Mark picked up a big adjustable wrench and hurled it at the wall. It punctured the drywall and clattered to the floor.

My heart speeded up again. I had to get out of there. And fast. Get help.

I leaned my shoulder ever so slightly against the connecting door. If I could get inside the house and lock the door behind me, I'd gain some time.

"I figured if Gloria wanted to be with Tom so badly, I figured I'd make that happen." Mark smiled a crazy, ugly smile. "And I did. They can rot in hell together."

"That was you pretending to be Gloria on the telephone. Why did you call me and Derek?"

"To frame Derek for the murder, of course. Having you arrive and find him was a nice touch, I thought. Muddied the waters, too."

Yep, the man was bonkers.

Worse yet, he was dangerous. Deadly dangerous.

42

Mark sucked furiously on his cigarette, the tip glowed orange-red like the tip of a blacksmith's hot tongs. He sniffed and tossed the cigarette to the cement floor, mashing it under the sole of his boot.

"You killed her in cold blood," I said. "Why not simply divorce her?"

"You can't prove I did anything," said Mark. "Nobody can."

"I wouldn't be so sure about that. Forensics can practically work miracles these days." I wasn't sure if that was true but I was betting he wasn't either. "Besides, the coroner believes Gloria died hours before she called me and Derek. How are you going to explain that?"

Mark glared at me in silence. His hands reached for a long, yellow-handled screwdriver lying in the truck's flatbed. He gripped it tightly in his right hand and turned towards me.

I edged backward. "I don't think you can explain it. In fact, do you want to know what I think?" I didn't wait for a reply. "I think you need help Mark. We can get you help," I said softly.

Mark rolled the pink tip of his tongue along his upper lip.

I gulped. "What do you say, let me help you?"

"I'm sick of people trying to help me!" Mark roared. He lunged at me with the screwdriver.

I tugged my purse from my shoulder and swung it at the blade as it stabbed towards me. The purse deflected the blow.

Mark bellowed and snatched my purse from my fingers.

I lashed out wildly with my right foot, kicking him solidly in the thigh. He teetered backwards. I ran into the house and slammed the door behind me.

Police. I needed the police. But my cell phone was in my purse and my purse was in the clutches of this madman. A madman banging furiously to get inside. The blade of the screwdriver crashed through the door, splintering the wood.

That could have been my chest.

I screamed and looked wildly around the kitchen for an escape route. The sliding door to the patio was the nearest exit.

I took it.

All I had to do was get to the Bean house across the pond. Alex and his mother were bound to be there. I could get help.

As I anxiously jiggled the fiddly sliding door lock, the door connecting the garage to the kitchen burst open. Mark had smashed through with a short-handled sledge hammer. "This won't work, Amy. Don't make this any harder than it has to be."

I screamed again as Mark hurled the sledge hammer at me. I ducked to one side and felt the whoosh of the heavy hammer's passing.

There was the sound of an explosion as the hammer struck the sliding glass door. The glass shattered into a million jagged pieces. I jumped through the opening to the screened-in porch.

Cicadas sang and danced in the dark, humid air. I threw open the screen door, took my bearings and started running along the soggy edge of the pond towards the Bean house.

Huffing and puffing, I sprinted through the muck and weeds.

I didn't dare look over my shoulder but, from the sound of it, Mark Bolan wasn't far behind.

My lungs burned and I felt my energy failing. I vowed that if I got out of this alive, I'd take up running in earnest, maybe join a cross-country track team.

Lost in my head when I should have had one eye on the ground below my feet, I slipped in a damp patch of grass and fell clumsily on my butt. My ankles sank in the mud.

Mark, not much more than a dark, deadly blob, wasn't more than twenty yards behind.

I yelped and twisted my leg. My sneaker popped free of my foot. With a sob, I scrambled to my feet and took off running once more.

Mark Bolan was slowly but surely closing the distance. His hands were bare but I wasn't going to underestimate his ability to kill me. I tried to scream, hoping to get somebody's attention or at least wake someone, but my throat burned with the exertion of running and it was all I could do to keep breathing and moving.

I swung around the side of the pond, careful to avoid getting too close to the treacherous ground once more. Mark came ever nearer. I ran up the sloping drive to Mrs. Bean's enclosed front porch. I banged my fists against the hard blue door. "Alex! Mrs. Bean! It's me, Amy!"

Mark bellowed as he came around the side of the house. Knowing I'd be trapped if I stayed where I was, I ran back along the drive and down the road towards the clubhouse.

A car passed in the distance, its headlights weak. I waved my arms in frustration but the driver rounded the corner without noticing me. I forced myself on, running awkwardly and painfully, my bare foot slapping the hard, wet pavement.

Mark was huffing up the street behind me. Fortunately, the out-of-shape brute was slowing down too.

Two rows of empty electric golf carts sat near the starter's station, damp with rain and awaiting the morning's golfers. I raced over the empty parking lot and cut across the practice putting green.

I hopped in the first cart in the front row. The key was in the ignition slot near the steering wheel. I gave the key a twist and the motor cranked into life.

I screamed as Mark threw himself at the golf cart. The tiny vehicle shook. Mark was breathing fast and hard, I felt the heat of his breath on my face. He gripped the top of the golf cart with one hand. With his right hand, he reached for my neck.

I stabbed my foot on the gas pedal and the little cart lurched forward. Mark lifted his legs and pushed them through the opening. Keeping one hand on the wheel, I used my free hand to grab his foot. I gave his ankle a savage twist. Mark howled and jerked his leg back.

I swung the steering wheel hard to the left, then hard again to the right. Mark tumbled off the golf cart and rolled into a nearby sand trap.

The rear wheels of my golf cart slid sideways as the weight shifted dramatically on the sloped ground. The right side of the golf cart lifted for a moment and my wet butt slid to the left across the slick black vinyl cushion. I struggled to hold on but gravity and inertia seemed to be fighting me.

The cart fell on its side. For a moment I was seeing stars, but not the real ones hanging in the night sky, these floated before my eyes.

Then my vision cleared and I saw Mark coming for me. He had a sharp, long-handled rake in his hand, the kind they use to keep the bunkers and sand traps pristine.

I cowered inside the upturned golf cart as he drew the rake over his head and brought it down savagely on the fallen golf cart.

The sharp tines only missed me by inches but the rake had gotten tangled up in the steering wheel. While Mark struggled to free the rake, I squeezed out the back of the golf cart.

I had no choice but to run. I bolted as fast as I could. Mark grabbed my ankles and I fell face forward into a bunker. My mouth filled with sand. I spat and turned over, kicking Mark in the chest as I did.

I heard a loud wail and saw a flash of bright lights but I had no idea what it meant until a running figure leapt on Mark's back, wrestling the howling man to the ground and straddling him.

It was Derek.

I sat up, still spitting up sand and struggling for breath as another man came up beside us. "Derek? Dan? Thank goodness, you're here."

Dan laid a hand on Derek's shoulder. "I've got him. You can get up now."

"Are you sure?" Derek asked as Mark writhed in anger

beneath him.

Dan nodded and pulled a pair of handcuffs from his belt. Derek released his hands from Mark's chest and climbed to his feet as Dan deftly cuffed him.

I threw myself into Derek's open arms and sobbed. "I'm so glad you're here."

Derek squeezed me. "I was worried that you would break your word with me to go home and lock the doors. You have a certain stubborn streak."

"Yeah, a stubborn streak that might have gotten you killed," grunted Dan as he swung his prisoner around. Mark appeared cowed now and breathed heavily, his chin hanging on his chest, sweat oozing from every pore. "Lucky for you, Derek convinced me to come check it out."

Lucky indeed.

I looked at those handcuffed hands that, if Derek and Dan had not shown up when they had, might have been locked around my throat.

"Are you okay," Derek brushed the hair from my face. "Did he hurt you?"

"No, I'm just a little shaken up is all." A light rain had begun to fall once more and the clouds had shuttered the stars. A barred owl hooted in the trees. *Who cooks for you? Who cooks for you?* the bird seemed to ask.

"Are you sure you don't need to see a doctor, Amy? It's no trouble taking you to the medical center," Dan said kindly.

"No, really. I'll be okay. Once my heartbeat gets back to normal," I said, placing my fingers over my thrumming heart.

"Good. If anything happened to you..." Derek planted a gentle kiss on the bridge of my nose.

I blinked back tears and walked side by side with Derek as Dan escorted his prisoner to the squad car.

"We drove by my ex's house first. Mr. Breen said you had come and gone," explained Derek.

As Dan slid his prisoner into the rear seat, Derek continued. "We decided to swing past Visconti's house."

"Lucky we did," said Dan, slamming the door on his prisoner. "That's how we saw you and Mark out here on the fairway."

"I went to Mark's house after talking to Bobby Breen. Did you know he can imitate his wife's voice exactly?"

"Can he now?" Derek's brow went up.

"Uh-huh. It's eerie. The first time I heard him, I'd have sworn it really was her. Back from the dead."

"That explains a lot," Derek remarked.

"It was Mark who murdered Gloria," I blurted. "But he told me that it was her who strangled Tom Visconti."

"Why?" demanded Dan.

I explained how Gloria had been having an affair with Tom and, crazy with jealousy, decided that if she couldn't have him, nobody could. "Right, Mark?"

Mark refused to answer and glared at me with murder in his eyes.

"So why strangle his wife afterward?" Derek wanted to know.

"He said...he said so she could be with her lover." The words hung in the air. Nobody knew what to say to that.

The thud of running steps broke the spell. We all turned to see who was approaching.

"What's going on?" demanded Alex, breathing heavily. He wore baggy striped pajama bottoms and was shirtless. "Mom heard all kinds of commotion. She woke me and I told her to call the cops. The dispatcher told us they'd be on their way."

He was looking at Officer Dan Sutton. "You're fast. I'll give you that."

"We were already here," Dan said stiffly. "Everything is under control. You can go home, Mister—"

Alex extended his hand. "Alex Bean. Amy's friend." To prove it, he wrapped his arms around me in an embrace. "You okay?"

I blushed and freed myself.

Derek remained mum beside the squad car. His hands in his pockets.

Dan spoke to Officer Reynolds via his radio. "Larry phoned the chief and filled him in. He was already driving up from Charlotte. So he should be back soon. In the meantime, I need to get this one locked up."

"Where's your car, Amy?" Derek asked.

"I parked outside of Mark's house."

"Okay, I'll walk you over and see you get home okay."

"Oh, no," said Dan. He pointed at Derek. "You're coming with me, Derek. You are supposed to be in my custody, remember? I don't want to get in anymore trouble with the chief than I have to. We can drop Amy off at her van. But first thing tomorrow, you'll need to come down to the station and file a report."

I nodded.

"Right," Derek caved. "Sorry, Amy." He gave me a kiss on the lips.

"Hey, I can walk Amy back to her van for you," Alex said. "You guys go on ahead."

"Are you sure?" Derek looked at me for clarification.

I knew that the best thing for him was to be back at the police station before Jerry showed up. "There's no point upsetting Jerry any more than necessary. You go on. I'll be fine."

"I'll see to it," Alex said.

Not helping, I thought.

On the short walk back to my van, I said, "You know, Bobby Breen thought you might have had something to do with all these murders."

"Me? Why?" Alex stopped dead in the middle of the street.

I explained about the incident with the dog.

"That's crazy. One time, one time I didn't have a baggy with me. I left the poop on his lawn and went home to fetch a bag. That's when he took a potshot at me and Lucille. Mom was furious. She threatened to call the cops. To appease her, Visconti donated a thousand dollars to the local animal shelter in her name."

"I can't imagine what Amy Harlan saw in the man."

"Yeah, the man was a lunatic. No wonder Mark strangled him."

"Mark didn't, at least, he says he didn't."

"Oh?" He was waiting for explanations but I was too worn out to give him any.

43

The next morning was a blur of activity. I don't think I'd had more than two hours' sleep the night before. I was running on buttered toast and coffee fumes.

In between customers in Birds & Bees, I gave Mom and Esther an abridged version of the night's events. Esther found some humor in the tale. Mom, on the other hand, blanched and alternately admonished me and thanked the lucky stars that I had lived to tell my tale.

Kim smiled knowingly. Dan had already filled her in.

Chief Kennedy had telephoned me as I was opening the store for business and insisted on my immediate presence. I went down to the station where the big man took my statement himself, which meant he probably got half of it wrong.

But that didn't matter. Derek was free to go and Mark Bolan would be on his way to a state facility by the end of the afternoon. A pair of troopers was scheduled to arrive for the official transfer.

Mark had already confessed that, while Gloria was distracting me the night she had unexpectedly come to the store, Mark, at her bidding, was planting evidence in Derek's apartment. That evidence being the map of the maze out at Magnolia Manor. And—I'll bet Gloria never expected this of him—stealing that tie off Derek's tie rack that he later used to strangle her with.

Mark claimed that Gloria had found the brown thrasher necktie I had given Derek lying beside the Magnolia Manor restroom facilities. She was ready to kill and Derek's tie gave her the perfect weapon, one that couldn't be traced to her.

According to Mark's statement, she had sent Tom the note asking him to meet her in the maze garden. She followed her lover into the maze, ostensibly so they could talk away from prying eyes and ears. Little did Tom Visconti know that what Gloria really had in mind was murder.

Despite what he had done, part of me felt a little sorry for Mark Bolan. It must have been hard on him knowing that his wife was cheating on him with her boss on top of all his personal physical and mental health issues.

The police had interviewed the neighbors after Mark's arrest. Mark's next-door neighbor claimed that he often heard Mark having "conversations" with Gloria, sometimes angry conversations with her when she wasn't there.

In Derek's legal opinion, there was every chance that Mark Bolan would end up institutionalized rather than put in prison.

I barely had a minute alone with Derek. His Atlanta lawyer, Marcus Vargas, and father had arrived and whisked him away. Vargas was talking lawsuits against the police and the town itself, which had Jerry shivering in his size ten boots.

I couldn't blame him. If he lost his job as chief of police, he'd be lucky to get a part-time crossing guard gig down at the elementary school.

I didn't bother to tell him that I knew Derek well enough to be certain that there was no way he was going to sue anybody. He was too nice a man.

Jerry could suffer just a little. It couldn't hurt. In fact, it might make him think twice about being so quick to judge next time.

If there was a next time, which I would just as soon there was not.

Derek and I agreed to meet up at Brewer's Biergarten for an early dinner. I was really looking forward to it. We'd celebrate and begin planning our future anew.

After finishing work for the day, I showered and slipped into a cute, ankle-length floral dress I had purchased the month before but hadn't had the right opportunity to wear yet.

It was a short walk up the street to the biergarten and the sun was shining and reasonably warm so I carried a blue cotton sweater in my hand, swinging my arm.

Paul greeted me at the door.

"Is Derek here?"

"Haven't seen him yet," Paul said. "But I've reserved you guys a quiet table on the patio. "Have a seat at the bar. I'll buy you a drink."

I thanked Paul, slid onto an empty barstool, and ordered a light beer from the bartender.

"Hi, Amy."

I glanced at the woman beside me. "Paula, this is a surprise. I thought you were still in Phoenix."

"I got back this afternoon," Paula D'Abbo explained.

Like always, she looked like a million bucks, even dressed casually in skintight jeans, a white cotton shirt and denim jacket. The beautiful young brunette with eyes the delicate golden brown of a kestrel's wing feathers and curly, long lashes looked like anything but a police officer, which she was. At least, before she had taken leave of absence from the Scottsdale PD.

"Does Kim know you're back?" If so, my best friend had said nothing to me, which was a shocker.

"I haven't seen her yet. I haven't been out to the house. I did stop in the police station to say hi to Dan. You've been busy."

"That's one way of putting it." I could think of a million other ways to describe the past week or so, none of them flattering.

She raised her glass. "All's well that ends well, right? And to think, I felt bad that I had to go out of town and miss your wedding. It turns out I didn't miss it at all. I missed a boatload of excitement though."

She took a healthy drink of the red wine bouncing around in her glass. "Have you rescheduled?"

"Not yet."

"Well, when you do, this time I promise to come. Mom, too. If that's okay?"

"Of course, if you think she would be up to making the trip. We'd love to have her." My beer arrived and I drank quickly.

"Didn't I mention? Mom is with me."

"Oh, how wonderful. I can't wait to meet her."

"I'll bring her by Birds and Bees. She's into all that bird watching stuff. Maybe you can give her a deal on a feeder?"

"Okay." I dipped my hand in the pretzel bowl and nibbled. "Is she intending to stay long?"

Paula had flown to Scottsdale to help her mother who'd been living alone in her house after her husband's death. The idea was for her to sell the house and move into one of those retirement places.

"She settled into one of those Sun City retirement communities, right?"

"That was the plan. But the good news is that Mom decided to move here."

"Here?"

"Yep. To Ruby Lake. With me. Isn't that great?"

"Yes, great." I wondered what Kim would think. Was Paula planning on having her mother move in with her and Kim? That would go over like the proverbial lead balloon.

There were only the two small bedrooms.

And one very fragile ego—Kim's.

"Dan found a house for us right across the street from his. Isn't he a dear?"

"He's a dear, all right." And dense as a brick when it came to women, leastwise the one he was in a relationship with.

On the one hand, Kim would be thrilled that Paula would be moving out of her house. The girl liked her privacy.

On the other hand, Paula and her mother would be living across the street from Dan.

I could see only trouble brewing on this horizon. Kim still considered Paula something of a threat for Dan's affections.

"It was great seeing you, Amy." Paula leapt lightly from her stool and gave me a squeeze. "We'll have to get together and catch up real soon." She looked at a slender silver watch on her wrist. "I have to run pick Mom up at the market. She's doing some shopping."

"Great seeing you, too. Say hi to your mom."

"I will. Oh, and guess what." Paula was beaming.

"There's more?" Despite the cold brew, my throat was parched.

"I'm up for a job with the Ruby Lake PD."

"Really? I didn't know there was an opening."

"Yeah. Dan says I'm a shoo-in. He says Jerry really likes me." She winked at me and left.

Wait until Kim heard that bit of news. Paula and Dan working together. Day in, day out. Side by side.

What could possibly go wrong?

I turned to the bartender and ordered a refill.

As I contemplated married life with Derek, I felt a pair of big, strong hands settle on my shoulders and begin massaging my upper back. I felt my aches and knots and worries melting away.

"Umm, that feels good," I groaned with delight.

"Feels good to me, too."

I lurched and spun my head around at warp speed. "Alex? I thought you were Derek!"

"Hey, Amy." Alex leaned in, his hands still on my shoulders. "Buy you another drink?"

"No, I'm waiting for Derek. And I wish you would stop touching me like this." I removed his hands from my shoulders. "It's inappropriate, Alex."

Alex's face turned a muddy red. "If you say so."

"I say so."

"Everything all right here?" demanded Paul, popping up beside us. He must have seen the look of agitation on my face.

"Yes, Alex was just leaving. Right, Alex?"

"That's right," Alex forced a smile. "I only wanted to tell Amy how happy I am that everything worked out for her and Derek."

"See you around." Alex gave a hip-high wave, turned

and walked out.

"What was that all about?" asked Paul.

"I think Alex had been hoping to pick things up where we left off in high school. Hopefully, I've cured him of that delusion."

"Doesn't that clown realize you're engaged?" Paul shook his head in disgust. "If he gives you anymore trouble, you let me know." He ground his fist into his palm.

"Thanks, Paul." I patted his arm. "Speaking of engaged, have you seen Derek?"

Paul looked around the restaurant. "That's funny. I was talking to the chef when I saw Derek come in."

"He's here?"

"No, that's the thing. He walked in, stopped, got this funny look on his face, then turned and walked right out again."

I shuttered my eyes and groaned. He must have seen me. He must have seen Alex.

He must have seen Alex giving me a massage.

"What's wrong, Amy?"

"Tell you later." I slid off my barstool. "Thanks for the drink. I'll have to owe you for the second one." I grabbed my sweater and purse from the bar.

"No problem, but what—"

"No time to explain," I called on my way to the door.

I hurried out and looked quickly up and down the sidewalk. There was no sign of Derek or his Honda Civic.

I hurried to my van parked behind Birds & Bees and climbed inside, scouring the streets as I headed towards Derek's apartment.

I didn't spot his car on the road or parked anywhere along the route. I arrived at the law offices and found no sign of him or his vehicle there either.

I reluctantly went back to Brewer's where Paul told me Derek had not returned.

Dejected, I went back home and waited to hear from him. I called Derek's number over and over but there was no answer. I left a half dozen messages hoping he would hear them and give me a call.

Mom came in and asked what was wrong. I told her nothing. She had enough on her plate because her illness was acting up again and more troubles she didn't need.

After a fitful, sleepless night, I checked my phone, which I had kept on the bedside table all night in the hope that Derek would telephone. He hadn't.

No calls. No texts.

I shook the cell phone to see if it would jar a message loose from inside. It didn't.

Anxious and blue, I showered quickly, slipped on a pair of jeans and a striped Fair Isle sweater, skipped breakfast and drove to the offices of Harlan and Harlan. It was a workday. Surely Derek would be back behind his desk.

We could get this silly misunderstanding behind us and move one.

Ben was sitting behind his desk looking dapper in his brown suit with the pencil-thin black stripes. Mrs. Edmunds was looking immaculate as ever in a lilac skirt and jacket with a frilly white blouse. She was peering over his shoulder, notepad in one hand and pen in the other.

As I entered the office, Ben and his secretary exchanged uneasy glances. I noticed that Derek's office door was firmly shut.

"Good morning, Ben, Mrs. Edmunds. Is Derek locked up in his office with a client?"

Mrs. Edmunds's brow rose ever so slightly, just enough for me to see that it was indeed possible for her brow to wrinkle. Not much, but enough to show she was human.

She made some excuse about needing to type up some notes and departed.

Ben laid his hands on the edge of his desk. "No. I'm afraid my son is not in this morning, Amy."

"Do you know where he is? I was hoping to speak with him."

Ben cleared his throat. "Actually…"

"Yes?" Why was my heart thumping so madly?

"Have a seat, dear." Ben waved to one of the comfy chairs facing his desk.

I sat on the edge of the seat, holding my breath.

Ben fiddled with his fountain pen a moment before speaking. "Derek left for St. John this morning. With his friend, Corey Lingstrom."

"He what?" I felt my pupils dilating, my blood turn to ice and my heart fall from my chest and shatter on the rug.

"He's going to stay with Corey there for a bit."

I struggled to speak. "How long a bit?"

"Sorry, I couldn't say."

I could barely believe it. I bit my lower lip to muffle the swelling pain in my heart. "Did he say why?"

Ben refused to meet my eyes. "He said he went to Brewer's to meet you last night and saw you canoodling, shall we say, with some old boyfriend of yours by the name of—"

"Alex. Alex Bean," I interrupted. "It was nothing. It

isn't what you think, Ben. It wasn't what Derek thought. I was at Brewer's to meet Derek. Alex came up behind me. I thought it was Derek. It meant nothing, Ben. Alex means nothing to me. It's all a big misunderstanding."

Ben lifted his eyes. "You don't owe me an explanation, dear."

He was going to get one anyway. "I told Alex to leave me alone. That we were friends in high school and that's all." I slapped my hand on Ben's desktop. "Why didn't Derek let me explain?"

"I guess he was hurt, Amy. Everybody gets hurt now and again."

"But I didn't mean to hurt him. I love him. You know that."

"I know that. Deep down, I think my son knows it too. And I know he's mad in love with you."

"What should I do?"

"Give him a little time. Maybe a few days in the sun will have him seeing straight."

"You think?" I was thinking of hopping on the nearest jet to St. John's and knocking some sense into the man.

"Yes. Don't worry. Give him some time. He will come around."

"Maybe I should call him. What time does he land?"

"Later this afternoon. But he left his cell phone with me. He didn't even take his laptop."

"Your ten o'clock call is ready, Ben," came Mrs. Edmunds' voice from the doorway.

I rose to leave. Ben stood and gave me a fatherly hug and told me once more not to worry. "Everything will be okay," he said softly.

But would it? I walked out in a daze. The birds were

singing but I didn't hear them. The sun was shining but I couldn't see it. The man of my dreams was somewhere over the Atlantic on his way to a distant island.

He had left behind his phone...and me. I had no sure way of getting in touch with him until he came back.

If he came back.

The End